Th

It was a thing of bea...
The runes along the blade glittered with a furious grace.

"My sword?" I said, unable to believe him.

He nodded. "It searches. But not for me."

He thrust it toward me. But even as my fingers touched the cold, gleaming metal, it fell through my hands like water. The blade flashed once in the darkness, then disappeared. I didn't hear it hit the ground.

I went to my knees, groping blindly. But it was gone. When I looked up, so were the two men and the campfire.

I was all alone on the mountainside.

"Tolkien fans take note! [Ann Marston] has the spirit and heart of Tolkien."
—*Bookends*

CLOUDBEARER'S SHADOW

Here Begins the Saga of Sword in Exile

Books by Ann Marston

The Rune Blade Trilogy

Kingmaker's Sword
Western King
Broken Blade

Cloudbearer's Shadow
King of Shadows
Sword and Shadow

First book in the Sword in Exile Trilogy

CLOUDBEARER'S
SHADOW

Ann Marston

An Imprint of HarperCollins Publishers

This is a work of fiction. Names, characters, places, and incidents are products of the author's imagination or are used fictitiously and are not to be construed as real. Any resemblance to actual events, locales, organizations, or persons, living or dead, is entirely coincidental.

EOS
An Imprint of HarperCollins*Publishers*
10 East 53rd Street
New York, New York 10022-5299

Copyright © 1999 by Ann Marston Gyoba
Cover illustration © 1999 by Yvonne Gilbert
Map by Barbara Galler-Smith
ISBN: 0-06-105977-3
www.eosbooks.com

First Eos paperback printing: September 2000
First HarperPrism paperback printing: February 1999

Eos Trademark Reg. U.S. Pat. Off. and in Other Countries, Marca Registrada, Hecho en U.S.A.
HarperCollins® is a trademark of HarperCollins Publishers Inc.

Printed in the U.S.A.

OPM 10 9 8 7 6 5 4 3 2

For David and Susan Bollinger,
who taught me the real meaning
of gallantry and courage

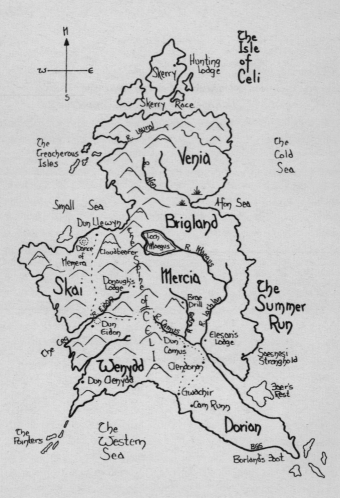

Prologue

All I know of that time before the yrSkai fled to the northern island of Skerry I learned from Fyld, who was my father's Captain of the Company. My father never spoke of it, and pain clouded his eyes when he heard others tell of the days before coming to Skerry. The story of how my father, Brennen, exiled Prince of Skai, and his sister Brynda spirited away Sheryn, widow of Prince Tiegan of Celi, and brought her safe to a Tyadda steading deep within the mountains of Skai has been made into myriad tales and ballads. These are told and sung by bards around fires in all places free Celae gather. But no bard ever heard the tale from my father. Fyld it was who spread the hope-giving story.

And Fyld it was who told me of my father's painful journey from the mountain steading of the Tyadda through Skai and on to Skerry.

Brennen ap Keylan ap Kian, Prince of the Royal House of Skai, did not leave Skai easily. He had fought beside his king in the battle against the invading Maedun, and had wept when King Tiernyn and his son, Prince Tiegan, fell on the field at Cam Runn. He had fled the field only when it became obvious that the men of Celi could not stand against the overwhelming blood sorcery wielded by the black sorcerer, Hakkar of Maedun. But he did not immediately go home to his wife and family in Dun Eidon. He did not go until he had discharged his final duty to his king and his prince. Before he saw to his own family, he and his sister Brynda escorted Sheryn, widow of Prince Tiegan, safely to the hidden steading of her people in the mountains of Skai, where she might safely bear the son who would be King of all Celi.

Shortly after he left the high-country meadow and the mountain lodge where Sheryn was now safe with her parents, Brennen found the remnants of his army of yrSkai. Of the three hundred men of Skai he had led into battle, only ninety-three followed him back to Dun Eidon. They fought their way home knowing that all the eastern provinces had fallen to the Maedun behind them. Celi lay dying, as both the land and the people succumbed to Hakkar's strangling sorcery.

All the news they heard was bad. Dorian and the Summer Run had fallen to the Somber Riders of Maedun. Dorian's prince was thought to be dead and his family with him. The Saesnesi under their Celwalda Aellegh had fought valiantly, but were overrun and vanquished. Aellegh and his family might have survived, but no word came as to where they might be. It was the same throughout all Celi. The Duke of Mercia was dead, his family slaughtered with him, as was the Duke of Brigland. There was no word of Connor, Duke of Wenydd, or his wife Torey and their three sons.

None could stand up to the blood magic of the black sorcerer of Maedun. Brennen himself had seen what happened when the men of Celi tried to join battle against the dark armies of Hakkar. He had seen the black sorcerer on a hill above his advancing army, and he had watched the smothering black mist of sorcery engulf the army of Celi so that the men of Celi fell stunned and helpless under the spell. Because he knew what would happen, he refused to lead his men into skirmishes with patrols of Maedun they encountered on their trek back to Dun Eidon.

"But, my lord Prince, we can't just turn and run," Fyld, his captain, cried in despair. "We are men of Celi. Of Skai. We do not flee—"

Brennen turned on him fiercely. "You're right," he said, his voice deadly calm. "We don't merely flee danger. But neither do we throw our lives away for nothing. You've seen it, Fyld. You've seen what that cursed sorcery can do . . ." His voice trailed off, and he shuddered. Then he shook his head. "No, we do not merely flee from danger. But we cannot fight again if we are dead—uselessly dead with no enemy accounted for as well."

Fyld turned away from the expression of haunted grief and horror in his prince's eyes. Helplessly, he agreed. Brennen bent forward and clasped Fyld's arm.

"We must go home, my friend," Brennen said softly. "We must go home to Dun Eidon. We can do more good there than here."

All of Celi lay beneath a pall of smoke. The men of Skai rode past destroyed farms and burned villages. Whenever they encountered a company of Somber Riders accompanied by a warlock, they hid themselves, biting back their shame, until it was safe to continue. A warlock could not spread the same deadening miasma that Hakkar could, but he had the ability to turn arrows, swords, and spears back against the men who tried to use them. No Celae wished to die by his own weapon.

They found great destruction in Skai. Never thickly populated to begin with, the green glens and gentle lower slopes were now deserted. The few villages they passed were burned and abandoned. The Somber Riders of Maedun had passed like a pestilence through the countryside, where there were few to oppose them.

Just before they reached the deep, blue coastal inlet called the Ceg, at the head of which sat the palace of Dun Eidon, they were surprised by a column of Somber Riders and had no choice but to fight. Even unaccompanied by a warlock, the Riders were arrogant and careless, thinking themselves unopposed in these mountains. The short, violent encounter left none of them alive to spread the word that they were not quite so unopposed as they had thought.

Gifted—or cursed—with a glimmering of the Sight, Brennen knew what lay ahead of them long before they found the ruins of a small shrine to Adriel of the Waters at the ford at the foot of the road that led to the palace. Nothing remained of the little wooden building but ashes. The flayed body of the holy man who had tended the shrine had been nailed head down to the charred trunk of the huge chestnut tree whose branches had once sheltered the shrine.

Brennen halted the ragged column of men and beckoned to Fyld. "Take him down and bury him properly beneath his chestnut tree," he said quietly. "With all the honor he's entitled to."

"But, my lord, the palace—" Fyld said.

Brennen looked westward, where Dun Eidon lay behind the trees, his face unreadable, his eyes hollow with grief and exhaustion. "There's time enough to give him properly to the Duality," he said. "We'll attend to our own people when we get there. First this, Fyld. A small task, but important." He touched Fyld's arm gently. "Do it, my friend."

When it was done, Brennen himself fashioned the hoop of ivy, representing the Unbroken Circle of birth, life, death, and rebirth, to lay upon the stone cairn the soldiers had raised beneath the chestnut tree. He bowed his head in a brief reverence to the soul of the holy man, then signaled his men to mount and led them to the palace.

The stench of death and burning came to them long before they saw what had been done to Dun Eidon. Once the ancestral home of the Princes of Skai had been a place of airy, open rooms, wide colonnades, spacious gardens, and graceful towers. The returning men of Skai found it a place of ruin and destruction, a place of desolation and death.

The towers still stood tall and slender, but they guarded only the silence of the dead. Bodies of men and women lay in the courtyard, where they had fallen to the swords and arrows of the Somber Riders.

"That troop of Somber Riders we met in the pass," Fyld said, his voice hoarse with horror. "They did this."

"Aye," Brennen said. "We were too late. We came only a few days too late . . ." His voice trailed off, and the lines etched by grief around his eyes and mouth deepened immeasurably. "By days . . ." he repeated hopelessly.

He dismounted amid the horror of the courtyard, and with only Fyld beside him, went into the Great Hall. More bodies lay in the burned wreckage inside. Carefully, numb with grief, Brennen searched through the charnel house of the Great Hall for the four bodies he dreaded to find. When he finally saw that they were not there, he began doggedly and methodically to search the rest of the palace.

He found his wife and daughter among their women, shut into a storeroom at the base of a little-used tower. Clearly, the Somber Riders had made great sport of the women before cutting their throats. They had all suffered before being granted the release of death. Lisle, Brennen's only daughter, had been eleven, barely on the threshold of womanhood.

Looking down at them, Brennen could not even summon tears from the hollow, aching anguish within himself. He turned away finally, his eyes burning in his gaunted face, and made a helpless gesture to Fyld.

"Please," he whispered.

Fyld understood. He straightened the limbs of the woman and girl, then spread his cloak over the two bodies. When it was done, he followed his prince to search for Brennen's two sons, Eryd and Gareth.

Except for the grisly evidence of splattered blood in the

chambers the boys shared with their nurses, they found no trace of Brennen's sons.

For two days, the men of Skai worked at the palace. They dug a long trench along one wall and went grimly and silently about the task of burying the dead. Brennen worked beside his men, asking no special consideration. Grief had wiped out any differentiation of rank among them. In their sorrow and anguish, they were all simply men of Skai, bereft and devastated.

Brennen himself brought down the bodies of his wife and daughter and laid them gently in the long common grave. Even then, he could find no tears for them, although his eyes burned in his bleak face.

On the morning of the fourth day, the last of the dead were placed in the trench. The men began the final task of filling the grave and raising a massive cairn of stones above it.

Only then did Brennen allow himself to take his grief to a solitary place. He went to the ruined shrine on the hillside above the palace and knelt before the altar. The old stone bowl, now cracked and broken, lay on the floor, dried petals of some spring flower still adhering to the curved fragments. A faint scent of incense and flowers lingered in the cool air, and the stench of burning and death seemed far away. He bent forward until his forehead rested against the cold marble of the altar and closed his eyes. He did not pray. His mind and heart were still too numb to search for words to offer to the Duality. Bereft and alone, he simply knelt in silence.

Fyld found him there shortly after dawn the next morning. Brennen knelt, still and quiet, with his forehead against the altar. For a moment, Fyld thought he might be asleep. Wearily, he rested his shoulder against the scarred pillar which had once supported the door and allowed his love and his pity for this man to flow through him. Brennen had taken no ease for three days. Even for such news as he now bore, Fyld was reluctant to disturb his prince when it looked as if he had finally allowed himself to rest.

Fyld had found no trace of his own wife and daughter, neither in Dun Eidon itself nor in the village below the walls. Their small stone-built house, once so comfortable and filled with love, was deserted and empty. He cherished a faint hope that perhaps Rhia had taken Tanyth into the mountains before the Somber Riders attacked the palace.

Brennen had allowed himself no such hope when the searchers had been unable to find the bodies of his sons. The overwhelming evidence of large pools of blood in the chambers the boys shared with their nurses pointed to the death of the boys, even though their corpses were missing.

Becoming aware of Fyld's presence, Brennen slowly and painfully straightened, then turned to look at the captain.

"Yes, Fyld?" he asked with all the quiet courtesy that had always been his.

"My lord Prince—"

Brennen shuddered. "I am no prince," he said harshly. "I've lost both my bheancoran and my sword to the Maedun. Without her—without Fiala—and without Bane, I can be no Prince of Skai."

Fyld was about to protest that there was far more to being Prince of Skai than carrying a Rune Blade or being served by a warrior-maid who acted as both guardian and confidante, but Brennen raised his hand abruptly to cut off the words.

"What do you want of me?" he asked, his voice quiet.

There was little use in arguing with Brennen now, Fyld thought. His loss was still too raw, too painful to allow him to listen to reason. Fyld stepped away from the pillar and pointed. "Down there, my lord," he said. "There's a ship in the

Ceg. One of ours, coming to the dock. I thought you'd want to know."

Brennen got stiffly to his feet. "Thank you," he said. "I'll come down with you now."

They reached the jetty just as the ship's anchor plunged down into the green water of the Ceg and the sailors finished furling the wide, blue sails emblazoned with the white falcon of Skai. The name of the ship — *The Skai Seeker* — glowed in gilt on the high, jutting prow and across the blunt stern.

As soon as the gangplank was in place, the ship's master and one of his men hurried down onto the stone jetty. They went to one knee before Brennen.

"My lord," the master said, "we have come to take you to safety. Even now, a company of Somber Riders comes this way. We've not much time. We've great need of hurry."

Brennen nodded to Fyld, who ran back to the palace, shouting for his men. Within moments, the first of the soldiers were boarding the ship. There was barely enough room aboard for the ninety-three men, and none at all for the horses. Regret plain in his face, Brennen ordered Fyld to set the animals free. Only when the last of his men were aboard did Brennen climb the gangplank to the ship. Fyld and the master waited for him on deck. As soon as he was aboard, the master ordered the gangplank taken up, and shouted to the sailors to weigh anchor and unfurl the sails.

"Where are we going?" Fyld asked, as the sails caught the wind and bellied out. Ponderously, the ship began to move, then gained momentum and quickly moved toward the open sea to the west.

"The fleet lies waiting in the shelter of the offshore islands," the master replied. "Four of ours and five Tyran ships." He glanced at Brennen, who stood watching Dun Eidon dwindle in the distance behind them. "Sent by your esteemed grandfather, Red Kian, my lord."

Brennen nodded in acknowledgment, but said nothing.

"How did you know we were here?" Fyld asked.

"I sent a man to watch from the ridge up there." The master pointed to the shoulder of the mountain where a rocky spur thrust out above the water. "He saw you arrive and rode to tell me where we hid in a small inlet. Along the way, he passed a company of Somber Riders moving inland. I thank the Duality we got here before they did."

"Four ships," Fyld murmured. Beside him, Brennen stood silent, unmoving. "That's better than we had hoped."

"We have survivors with us," the master said. "We picked up a little over two hundred people along the shores here shortly after the raid."

"Survivors?" Fyld asked. Silently, he sent up a brief prayer for his wife and daughter.

"Mostly women and children and old men, sir," the master said. "Very few men of fighting age. Aye, and most of those wounded. They're on one of the islands right now, being cared for by the Tyran sailors."

"Then we had best hurry to join them," Brennen said quietly. He stepped away from them and moved to the taffrail, watching his home disappear behind them.

The ship arrived at the offshore islands just before dusk. The islands were merely rocky outcroppings in the sea, tiny specks of land nearly lost in the sea against the brilliant flare of sunset behind them to the west. Only one of them was big enough to support trees and grass. It was there, in a small natural harbor, the nine ships lay at anchor. A small fleet of curraghs came out to meet *The Skai Seeker* as she dropped anchor beside a larger Tyran vessel. Women and children crowded onto the beach as the curraghs brought Brennen's men ashore.

Standing apart, Brennen watched as far too few

reunions took place. Too many of his soldiers stood bereft, and too few of the women found husbands, sons, or lovers among the soldiers. He saw Fyld find his wife and small daughter. The expression of joy on Fyld's face as he swept them into his arms made the backs of Brennen's eyes sting. Brennen turned away to look for the *Seeker*'s master.

Then Fyld was at his side. "My lord," he said softly. "Look." He pointed to a woman who walked slowly toward them, holding two small boys by the hand.

The unbearable pain of hope rekindled flared in Brennen's chest. A low, incoherent cry burst from his throat, and he began to run. He dropped to his knees before the woman and gathered the two boys into his arms. At last, he found his tears and let them flow freely. They washed unashamed down his face as he held his sons tightly to his chest.

Finally, he looked up at Fyld, who was unable to hold back his own tears. "We'll go to Skerry," Brennen said. "Tell the masters to prepare their ships. Those who wish to accept my grandfather's offer of sanctuary in Tyra may do so with my blessing. Those who wish to come with me into exile on Skerry are most welcome. Tell them we shall leave as soon as possible."

The islands of Skerry and Marddyn, located off the far north coast of the Isle of Celi, had been given to a Prince of Skai by some long-ago chieftain of the Veniani as repayment for a long-forgotten debt. One of Brennen's great-grandfathers had built a hunting lodge on Skerry, just off Skerryharbor at the foot of one of the three towering mountains on the island. It was said that he spent most of his summers there to escape a wife who had developed a tongue like a rusty blade once her children were grown and gone from the nest.

So it was to the big island of Skerry that Brennen took

the tattered remnants of his shattered people. The winters were long on Skerry, but were neither so bitter nor so harsh as in the north of Venia, thanks to a warm sea current that swept up and around the islands from the south. Trees grew thickly on the slopes of Ben Warden and Ben Aislin, and the forests were full of game animals. His people would be safe there, and crops of grains and vegetables would grow well in the rich soil of the glens.

On the voyage north, Brennen learned how his sons had survived. Gareth, the youngest, only three, had been hidden by his nurse in the cold ovens of the bakehouse. The elder son, eight-year-old Eryd, had been with his mother and sister when the Somber Riders fell upon the palace. Knocked on the head and left for dead, he had been stunned but awake, and he had watched as the Somber Riders made their ghastly sport with the women—including his mother and sister.

Emerging from her own hiding place after the Somber Riders left, the nurse had retrieved Gareth from the ovens. The child was frightened, but safe and unhurt. The nurse left him with another shocked survivor while she went in search of Eryd. She found him next to his mother and sister, staring at nothing, and slowly drawing circles on his arm with a finger dipped in his mother's congealing blood.

The boy had come out of his shocked trance eventually, but he had not spoken since. Nor did he ever speak again.

Brennen's sorrows did not end with the voyage to Skerry. The first winter on the island was a hard one for the displaced yrSkai. They lost too many people to hunger or illness brought on by the cold. Among them was Eryd ap Brennen, heir to the prince's throne.

Brennen buried his eldest son in the winter-hard earth. That night, he wept silently and bitterly for his murdered wife and daughter, and his lost son. Perhaps later he might find comfort or joy in the one son left to him. But not this night.

On the other side of the room, in a small alcove curtained off from his father's bedchamber, a small boy slept restlessly, dreaming of a sword.

It swam before his eyes, its outlines shimmering in the dim, green-tinted light. The light had a curious quality and texture to it, as if it shone through water. Shadows flickered across the unstained, glimmering metal, obscuring the line of runes that spilled down the center of the blade. Above the sword, slippery green vegetation bent low, as if to shield it from prying eyes. Something bright and silvery flashed and flickered among the leaves, hesitated for a moment above the blade, then darted away.

The child murmured softly in his sleep, fascinated by the play of light and shadow across the blade. He reached for the sword, his hands dwarfed by the ornate hilt, crafted by an artist in metalworking to fit a grown man's two hands. But even as the child's small fingers tried to close around the hilt, the sword faded and was gone.

The boy awoke in an unfamiliar bed, in a strange room. He called out in confusion to his mother. She didn't come to him, and he was too young to realize she would never come to comfort him again. Bewilderment turned to fear, and he cried for his father. But his father, lost in the morass of his own misery and grief, had turned away and didn't see the desperate need in the boy's eyes. Frightened and alone, the boy sobbed himself to sleep.

1

A raucous clangor shattered the dream image of a sword bathed in waterlight, and brought me leaping and snapping out of sleep like a gaffed salmon. Dazed and disoriented, my heart pounding wildly, I sat blinking into the candlelit dimness, gasping for breath. Someone close by called my name, both urgency and impatience in the voice.

"Gareth, get up! Quick! There's a ship aground in the harbor mouth. Get up!"

I stared at him blankly. So deep was the dream, so thick the fragments that swirled through my head, a long moment passed before I remembered I was in my small room in the barracks at Broche Rhuidh in Tyra, and another fled before I recognized the clanging as the alarm bell in the Clanhold courtyard. My cousin Comyn dav Kenzie, who shared the room with me, impatiently shook my shoulder. He was already half-dressed, struggling with his kilt and shirt, typically trying to do everything at once. His red-gold hair flew wildly about his face, gleaming in the light of the one small candle burning on the washstand. The single thick braid falling from his left temple bounced and swung, tangling with the golden topaz dangling from his earlobe on a fine, gold chain, as he hopped on one foot, pulling on his boot. He managed to get the boot on, then kicked at the bed. Not for the first time, I fancy.

"Hurry, Gareth," he cried. "Get up. We're needed."

My wits came back with a rush. I had forgotten we were standing as first rescue crew this fortnight. I swore and leapt from the bed, reaching for my kilt and plaid. Comyn was already on his way out the door as I thrust my feet into my boots. Buckling my kilt around my hips, dragging my plaid, I followed him at a dead run.

We found a wild night outside. A blast of wind spattered a sheet of half-frozen rain into my face and tried to snatch the flapping plaid from my shoulders as I ran out into the court-yard behind Comyn. I swore again. Why was it that when-ever Comyn and I were called to rescue duty, not only was the weather the worst it had been for several fortnights, but ships had the bad timing to go aground in the dark? Comyn always firmly declared that the gods conspired against us. He might have been right. Tonight's weather certainly seemed to prove it.

I swirled the plaid about myself, pinned it as securely as I could on the run, and ducked my head down into the shelter of its folds. Shreds of cloud scudded low above the trees, hiding all traces of approaching dawn. The fury of the wind bent the trees beneath its force, and the stark, bare branches rattled and moaned like live things in tor-ment. From far below, the rhythmic booming of the break-ers crashing against the black, broken rocks at the foot of the cliff reverberated through my bones like the cadence of an enormous heart, felt deep in the blood itself rather than merely heard.

I glanced up at the boiling sky. Vernal Equinox was still a little less than a fortnight away, but on a night like this, it was too easy to believe the Wild Hunt of Samhain raged through the sky, seeking the wretched souls of the hapless and the hopeless. I shivered and ran across the cobbled yard behind Comyn.

Comyn commanded one small boat this shift, and Govan dav Malcolm, youngest son of the Clan Laird, commanded the other. I was in Comyn's crew, so I stuck close to him as we hurried across the wet, slippery cobbles to the shelter of the gatehouse, where several of our crew were already assembled. More appeared quickly out of the gloom, and we all gathered into a tight little group around Comyn.

Behind us in the courtyard, streamers of flame trailed from torches in the wind, fluttering like flags, as men and women moved purposefully through the night. The healers who would tend to the survivors gathered near the infirmary across the courtyard from where we stood. They moved about, deftly collecting the supplies and stretchers they might need. Men hurriedly hitched mules to the trio of light, two-wheeled carts used to transport the injured or dead back to the infirmary. They worked swiftly and efficiently, with the ease of long practice, ignoring both the howling wind and the chill of the rain.

Comyn looked around, counting us over. When he saw we were all assembled, he nodded, then turned and hurried us through the gate. The fourteen of us fell in behind him in an orderly file, hastening through the predawn gray toward the cliffs.

The quickest way down to the harbor was by way of a narrow track plunging down the side of the cliff just below the forbidding gray-granite walls of the Clanhold. We slid and slithered down the treacherous path, buffeted by the rain and the wind that tried to pluck us off the cliff and fling us down into the shredded foam swirling around the rocks below. I followed blindly behind the dimly perceived plaid of the man ahead of me. The paling sky of approaching dawn gave barely enough light to see by, not yet enough light to distinguish color. It turned the men ahead and behind me into dark, anonymous shapes against the flying cloud, and made the drop-off only a deeper and darker area of amorphous shadow next to the paler stone and gravel of the path.

From out of nowhere, a strange image of a glimmering sword surrounded by wavering greenish light flashed into my head. An image from my childhood, so old, so well-known, I wasn't sure if it was a real sword I'd once seen, or merely from a dream that swept through my sleep so often that it became as real, as familiar, as other memories of Skerry. I could almost reach out and touch that sword, knew exactly how the hilt would fit itself snugly into the palms of my hands, knew how the crisply carved runes would feel under the pads of my fingers as I ran them down the deeply etched blade. And I knew how the sword would sing in my hands in defense of Celi.

Except that Celi was lost . . .

My chest tightened as a wave of pain and longing swept through me, tangled with the bitter taste of frustration and helplessness. If Celi was lost to the Celae, my father was lost to me in a different way. A curl of anger flickered under my heart. He was lost in a way I could not fight against.

Distracted, I put my foot down wrong on a slick patch of sodden grass and slipped. For one horrifying instant, I hung out over the edge of the cliff, arms flailing for balance, staring down into the blackness where the broken rocks waited a dizzying distance below. Before I could even cry out, Old Lachlan behind me grabbed me by the belt and hauled me bodily back onto the narrow path ahead of him. I nodded my thanks breathlessly, unable to speak, and he grinned cheerfully in acknowledgment.

"We need you to pull your weight on the oars, lad," he shouted above the howl of the wind. "I dinna wish to work any harder than I have to tonight."

I thanked him again—fervently—but he waved it aside, still grinning widely, and told me to save my breath for scrambling down the cliff, and to watch where I put my feet. It was sound advice. I saved my breath accordingly and watched closely where I put my feet.

• • •

The lookout who had sounded the alarm met us on the rocky shingle. Behind him, waves crashed against the long stone jetty, leaving it awash in foam and slippery with uprooted seaweed.

Comyn reached up and pushed the wet strands of red hair from his eyes. "Where are they?" he shouted. I stood right beside him but barely heard him above the roaring thunder of the storm and the pounding of the waves on the rocks.

The watchman gestured toward the amorphous gray mass of cloud, rain, and blown spume across the mouth of the harbor. "Out there," he cried. "North end of the Hook."

Comyn swore under his breath. I didn't hear the words, but I recognized the shapes his lips formed. He swore again, and his face settled into a wry, resigned expression. He had good reason. I looked out across the tortured water toward the invisible harbor mouth. It was a bad place to be, the north end of the Hook. In the summer at low tide, it was an easy swim from the harbor to the Hook through calm water. But with the turn of the season at winter, at low tide, the jagged rocks of the Hook were an effective breakwater, rising out of the sea to twice the height of a man. At high tide, the splintered rock lay awash in swirling whirlpools and turbulence created by the current and the tidestream. Until nearly a fortnight past Beltane, the storm winds came screaming out of the north to combine with the seasonal curve of the current sweeping close in past the mouth of the harbor. Add to this sorcerer's brew the pressure of the incoming tide, and the harbor mouth turned into a raging, boiling maelstrom. The helmsman of the ship foundering out there on the rocks didn't have to miss by much. Half a heartbeat off in his timing was all it would take.

This was not going to be easy. But we had learned never to expect it to be anything but difficult, dirty, and dangerous.

Comyn swore again and motioned the first crew toward their boat. Both boats were drawn up into the shelter of an open-sided shed tucked against the lee side of the jetty, well above the high-tide line. They were each about ten paces long, slender and graceful, with high, pointed sterns and jutting prows. Built of overlapping oaken planks and caulked with tar and hempen rope, they were sturdy and strong and tough, fully capable of standing up to the pounding equinoctial storms. Deft and maneuverable as eels, they could easily slip among the jagged rocks of the Tyran coast to pluck shipwrecked sailors to safety. Seven oarlocks per side held oneman oars, carved smooth and polished to silkiness by the sweat of men's hands over years of use. At the stern, a great steering oar lay ready to be thrust down into the water once the boat was launched. The helmsman stood braced in the stern, holding the oar, facing forward, exposed to the worst of the wind and rain. I was just as pleased that the helmsman's position was Comyn's place and not my own.

Govan urged his crew forward. They surrounded their boat, seven men to a side, and seized the wale, straining to get the boat moving down the gravel shingle toward the water. Slowly, the boat gained momentum. By the time the curving prow nudged the waves, the men were running alongside it, bent into the wind. The bow plunged into the foaming surf. Seconds later, the boat floated free, and the men near the bow made ready to leap into it.

The great ninth wave came out of the gloom, curling green water over a ragged edge of dirty gray foam. We watched, nearly frozen in shock and horror, unable to do anything. The howling wind drowned our warning shouts.

Govan's boat dipped as the wave broke over it and buried the bow, swamping the boat in churning, foaming water. The stern rose in an ungainly parody of a dancer's pirouette, spilling men like leaves from an autumn elm as it rotated. The boat made a quarter turn, presenting its flank to the sea, then fell. Another wave, smaller this time but still powerful, smashed into the helpless boat. The boat rolled, then capsized. As if it were of no more consequence than a small shred of driftwood, the surging wave tumbled it back onto the shore, grating and grinding along the gravel shingle.

Comyn shouted and ran forward, beckoning us to follow. We needed no urging. I plunged thigh deep into the surging water as the wave receded. Something tumbled against my legs. I reached down and grabbed a handful of soaked wool. Someone's kilt. It was Govan. He came to his feet, clutching the front of my shirt for balance, and together we crawled out of the foam. Around us, coughing, sputtering men stumbled toward the drenched shingle.

Still coughing and spitting out seawater, Govan gathered his men about him and took stock. We were lucky. Some of the men were obviously hurt, but apparently not seriously. All of his crew made it. None was sucked back out to sea with the retreating wave.

Behind me, Comyn shouted. I ran back up the shingle, dropped my plaid to the fine gravel, then bent with the rest of the crew to seize the wale of our own boat. We merged smoothly into a single unit at Comyn's command, put our backs into our work, and heaved at the boat. I closed my eyes as we reached the water, blinded by the stinging salt spray. We were luckier than Govan's crew. We hit the water just as a huge wave receded, sucking foam and floating debris back out to sea with it.

The boat became buoyant under my hands. I vaulted into it, fitted myself onto the thwart, and seized my oar. In seconds, we were launched and moving toward the Hook.

The wind, keen as a knife blade, cut right through my flesh to chill my bones. I ducked my chin down onto my shoulder, trying to shield my face from the rasp of the wind.

My hair whipped stiffly around my eyes in half-frozen strings. I could hardly feel the smoothly worn wood of the oar handle between my numbed hands. I began to doubt I'd ever be warm again.

Next to me, Old Lachlan sat stolidly working his oar, his face expressionless. He had five sons on the sea. I often wondered if he expected to find one of them drowned and dead when he brought this small boat out into the harbor to pluck sailors off the rocks. If he was thinking of his sons now, I couldn't tell. His face was blank and calm, filled only with the concentration necessary to keep the rhythm of the stroke.

We beat hard against the combined flow of tide, current, and gale. Flaying the driven foam to tatters, the wind swept over the tops of the waves and drenched us with icy spray. Blood and bone turned to ice, but we tucked down our heads and rowed harder.

A bucketful of spray lashed into my face. I gasped for breath and turned away.

Then I saw him. A man in the water. A young man, little more than a boy. He struggled in the heaving sea, his hands moving feebly as he tried to keep his head out of the water. Dark hair streamed across his forehead and cheeks. Pale skin, made paler by the wan gray light of approaching dawn and the dark smudge of a bruise high on his cheekbone. Mouth open in a shocked and silent scream. His eyes, wide and dark blue, fixed on mine as the current swept him past the boat, toward the jagged rocks at the base of the cliffs. Then, even as I watched, he slipped beneath the surface and disappeared.

I looked around quickly. Comyn stood clutching the steering oar between his arm and his body, bent slightly forward intensely, staring grimly ahead. Obviously, he had not seen the boy in the water, and neither had anyone else. When

I looked back, there was no trace of the young man where I had last seen him. Nothing marked the gray-green curls of water but flecks and broken streamers of foam.

There was no one else to go into the water after the boy. No one else had seen him, and in seconds it would be too late. Cursing, I pulled in my oar and shipped it so that it wouldn't tangle with the others. Stripping off my heavy woolen kilt and my boots, I stepped up onto the wale. Comyn shouted something—a question, I think.

"Man in the water," I shouted back, and launched myself into the sea after the boy.

The water closed over my head, cold as banished hope. I didn't think anything could be colder than the wind and the rain, but that water made them seem comfortable and warm. It forced every ounce of breath from my body. I surfaced, sputtering and coughing, and looked around. There was no sign of the boy, but I couldn't be far from where he had disappeared. I pushed the hair out of my eyes and let the current carry me.

For a moment, I bobbed on the crest of a wave. In the trough, far below me, I caught a glimpse of something pale, something too regular to be a fleck of sea-foam. I kicked out strongly, slithering down the slant of the wave like an otter, and lunged at the pale blob half hidden in the water. My fist closed over a handful of slick, slippery hair.

The boy was limp as a corpse as I turned him and pulled him against me so that the back of his head lay in the hollow of my shoulder. I felt no movement in his chest as I slipped my arm beneath his to hold him securely across the rib cage, but the cold water had robbed my hands of almost all feeling. I couldn't tell if he still lived, or if he were already drowned. When I looked up, the cliffs below the Clanhold loomed above us, and I had no more time to wonder whether I towed a dead man or a live one. If I couldn't break out of the current, we would both be dead men, smashed against the rocks at the foot of the cliffs.

I kicked hard, stroking through the water with my free arm. The boy's legs trailed slackly above my own, offering no help. A wave broke over my head, and I coughed and choked as I swallowed a pint of bitter salt water. When I looked up again, the cliffs looked closer, looming large above me. But we were too low in the water; I couldn't see the breakers pounding against the rocks, but I thought I could feel the rumbling vibration reverberating through the water. In only a few moments, the sea was going to throw the boy and me onto those rocks, smashing us to bloody flinders.

For a brief, panicky moment, I considered letting him go. Without his deadweight, I might be able to reach the gently sloping shingle near the jetty. If he were dead already, what sense was there in losing my life trying to pull a corpse from the water?

The bards sing tales of the legendary stubbornness of Red Kian of Skai, my great-grandfather. I may not have had a lot of Tyran blood in my veins, and Red Kian's blood may have been thinned after four generations of Celae, but all of his stubbornness had certainly been passed through my grandfather Keylan to my father Brennen and down to me. I gripped the boy more firmly and kicked out harder against the current, pulling with my free arm. I didn't bother wasting time or breath looking up at the cliffs again.

After an unmeasurable interval, my knees scraped against gravel. For a moment, I couldn't understand what was happening, or why there would be gravel in the middle of the harbor. Then somebody reached out and seized me beneath the arms to drag me from the surf. Willing hands took the boy from me as I stumbled out onto the beach. The wind plastered my wet shirt against my body like a wrapping of ice, and I began to shiver. Someone draped a blanket around my shoulders, and I huddled gratefully into its rough warmth and comfort.

The healers had set up near the boat shed by the side of the jetty, where it was relatively sheltered from the wind and flying spray. The boy lay facedown on a blanket by one of the carts. A healer knelt before his head, hands to either side of the narrow rib cage, rhythmically pressing the seawater from the boy's chest. In the wan light of early morning, the boy's lips looked blue, matching the large bruise on his cheekbone. He looked like a corpse, lying there so still on the blanket. He was not much older than fifteen or sixteen, and was obviously Celae, with his dark hair and blue eyes.

As I watched, he coughed and moved his head feebly. A moment later, he coughed again, then tried to curl himself into a small bundle on the blanket. The healer looked up at me and grinned, relief in all the lines of his face.

"He'll live," he said. "You did a good job of work for him, my lord."

Before I could reply, someone called my name. I turned to find Govan dav Malcolm beckoning me as Comyn's boat swiftly approached the shingle. I dropped the blanket and ran across the gravel, then waded thigh deep in the breakers to help pull the boat ashore.

As soon as the boat grounded, Comyn leapt from his place in the stern. He gave me a grin that lit his face like a lantern. "I hadna thought to see you again," he cried. He pounded me on the back, nearly knocking me facedown into the sea. "I should have known the sea would spit you back, unpalatable as you are."

I grinned at him. "I have only what I learned from you," I said. I gestured toward the mouth of the harbor. "The ship?"

"Courier ship," he shouted over the tumult of the storm.

A wave lifted the boat and threw it toward the shingle,

lifting us with it. I grabbed on to the wale to catch my balance and glanced into the boat. Six sailors lay huddled together in the bottom of the boat, all of them exhausted, some of them injured. But six meant that Comyn had plucked all of the crew of the courier vessel from the rocks. Not all our ventures ended this successfully. If the boy I had pulled from the sea were the only passenger, this time we had not let the sea take any lives. We didn't always win.

When I made my way back to the jetty, the healer's cart was gone, the boy along with it. By the time we had pulled both boats to safety and secured them in their shed, all the healers had left. They took with them four of Govan's crew who had sustained injuries when their boat capsized as well as the rescued sailors. The rest of us walked back, taking the road this time rather than the precipitous path leading up the cliff.

I had retrieved my kilt and boots from the boat, but my plaid was gone, probably wrapped around one of the survivors or dragged out to sea by a receding wave. The wool of my kilt was sodden and sopping with seawater, but it kept some of the wind off my legs and gave me the illusion of being a little warmer. My boots squished and sloshed unpleasantly as I walked. They were useless to warm my feet, but at least they protected me from the sharp rocks on the road.

It was nearly noon when we passed through the wide-flung gates into the courtyard of the Clanhold. The gray sky hung low above the crenellated walls, cheerless as ash. All I wanted was a hot drink in my belly and my bed for two days of uninterrupted sleep. My chest and belly trembled with a quiver that was partly from the cold, partly from reaction and exhaustion. Comyn looked to be in little better condition than I. His slack face and eyes dulled with fatigue must have mirrored my own. We were making our way to the barracks and our room when someone called my name.

Comyn went on without me as I turned to see who had called. My uncle Kenzie, Comyn's father, cut through the small throng of dispersing boat crews. He caught my arm, drawing me with him toward the Great Hall. A big man, was Kenzie. Tall and heavy-boned, muscles still tight and firm along his chest, belly, and thighs. Looking at him, I knew what Comyn would look like in thirty years.

"Malcolm would see ye, boy," he said.

"Right now?" I said. "I'm tired, Kenzie—"

"Aye, and little wonder," Kenzie said. "I heard what you did for the young lad, and I want you to know I'm proud of ye. This is important, though. The lad you pulled from the sea . . . He's a courier, and he comes from your father with a message for you."

I blinked in surprise. In the twelve years I'd been in Tyra, my father had all but ignored me. I thought that, to him, I was merely a painful reminder that the wrong son had died in the aftermath of the Maedun attack on Dun Eidon. Since coming to foster with Kenzie and Brynda, I'd had nothing but casual greetings from my father. Certainly nothing worth risking the crew of a six-man courier ship and a messenger to the worst weather of the year.

"Is something wrong?" I asked. This news of a message came oddly close to resonating with the remnants of this morning's half-remembered dream. A chill that had nothing to do with my frozen clothing or the weariness of my limbs rippled through my belly. "Has something happened to my father?"

Kenzie shook his head. "I dinna ken," he said. Concern tightened the corners of his mouth, and I was gratified to realize that it was as much for me as for my father. "But Malcolm has asked me to find you and bring you to him as soon as you came in."

I nodded, then turned to follow him up the wide steps to

the entrance of the Great Hall. I stumbled twice as we passed through the Great Hall, and Kenzie put out his hand to take my elbow, steadying me easily. He led me up the staircase to the solar tucked into the southwest corner of the Clanhold's second floor.

The family quarters looked out over the sea and the harbor, and were usually bright and airy. Today, the shutters were half-drawn across the windows against the storm, and candles burned in sconces around the walls. A fire blazed cheerfully in the hearth to take the damp chill from the room, and the air was fragrant, redolent of the scents of burning applewood and pine.

Malcolm dav Cynan dav Brychan, Fifteenth Clan Laird of Broche Rhuidh, stood before the hearth, his back to the door. His daughter Caitha sat at her loom between the hearth and the windows. The colors of the tartan she was weaving seemed preternaturally bright in the stormy light of the afternoon. On the bench by her hip lay the sett-sticks she used to count the threads of the pattern—each color wound an exact number of times around the stick to indicate the number of threads in warp and weft. I remember seeing the narrow band of yellow among the greens and blues and grays, and wondering if she wove the tartan for Govan.

Malcolm turned to greet me as I entered with Kenzie. He was a tall man, nearly as tall as Kenzie. His hair, once as brilliantly red-gold as Kenzie's, was now fading to gray. The single braid that hung from his left temple contained hardly a trace of youthful color. A large amethyst on a fine, gold chain dangled from his left ear. His eyes, gray as smoke and clear as water, met mine gravely as I crossed the room to stand before him. He held out a folded square of parchment wrapped in oiled linen.

"This is addressed to you, lad," he said. "Ye'd best read it without delay."

I looked at the packet in his hand and hesitated. I didn't want to take it, didn't want to know what it contained. Across the room, Caitha watched me intensely, then bit her lip and looked back to her weaving. But I had seen sorrow in her gray eyes. Sorrow and something else. Mayhaps fear?

"Take the letter, lad," Malcolm said gently.

I took it. It was addressed to me, but the handwriting was not my father's, nor was it sealed with his signet ring. I didn't recognize the seal. I slipped my thumb beneath the blob of wax and opened the packet. Seawater stains marred the upper edge of the letter, and the parchment had lost some of its crispness. But the rest of the letter was undamaged. The signature at the bottom was Fyld ap Huw, my father's Captain of the Company. The message itself, true to Fyld's character, was short, terse, and to the point. I read it quickly, then looked up to meet Malcolm's eyes.

"My father is very ill," I said hoarsely. "Fyld tells me I must return to Skerry now if I wish to see him again."

2

Kenzie's wife Brynda startled me badly by stepping forward and putting her hand gently on my arm. She had come in so quietly, I had neither heard nor seen her enter the room. My father's sister looked a great deal like him; both had the pale red-gold hair and deep brown-gold eyes that were legacies from their mixed Tyran and Celae-Tyadda heritage. Pain etched deep lines around her eyes now, making her look far older than she should.

"Does the letter say what happened to Brennen?" she asked quietly.

I shook my head. "No. Only that he's very ill." I handed her the letter. "It's from Fyld. He's never been a man of many words."

The ghost of a smile flitted briefly across her mouth. "I remember," she said.

"Mayhaps the courier will be able to tell us more," Kenzie said.

"Mayhaps," Brynda agreed. "But he's still unconscious and likely to remain so for a while. I did what I could for him, but he needs to regain his strength, and the only way he can do that is through sleep."

"Then we'll just have to wait," Kenzie said.

"Aye, we will," Brynda said. "I gave him deep sleep to speed his recovery. It may be a day or so before he wakes."

Brynda's Gift for Healing was nowhere near the legendary Gift that her own aunt had possessed, but it was a boon to Malcolm's Clanhold of Broche Rhuidh. Tyra was surrounded on three sides by the Maedun, the conquered lands of Saesnes and Isgard to the north and south, respectively, and Maedun itself on her eastern border. There were border skirmishes enough to keep Brynda's Gift in near-constant use Healing wounded clansmen.

Maedun had not given up trying to add Tyra to its empire. The Isle of Celi, our own homeland, was not so fortunate. The Maedun ruled it mercilessly. Tyra was the last bastion of freedom on the Continent and a refuge for many exiled Celae. Broche Rhuidh was an armed camp, watchful and alert. Half our men were on the border with the men of other clanholds, fiercely guarding the foothills of Tyra against the Maedun. All that stood between us and invasion were the Tyran mountains, which frustrated Maedun blood sorcery, and the ferocity of the Tyran clansmen themselves.

Malcolm turned from his place and went to the window. He stood for a moment looking out at the storm, his face grave. Beyond the rippled glass of the window, curtains of rain swept across the sea, dappling the pewter surface of the water in vast, random patterns of light and dark. The wind tore ragged streamers of foam from the crests of the muddled waves, blurring the definition between sea and sky. Tatters of cloud fled before the wind, their already shredded bellies fraying to wisps against the trees.

"Aye, well," Malcolm said, and turned to look at me. "In any event, you certainly can't take ship for Skerry until this storm dies down. It shows no signs of doing so for the next day or so, I'm afraid. I've nae wish to risk either your life or a courier ship by letting you set out while this gale blows, or there's a chance another will catch ye at sea and send ye onto the rocks off these shores. Or Skerry's either, come to that."

As he spoke, Caitha relaxed on her padded bench before the loom. A small smile curved her lips up as she picked up her shuttle again. She didn't look at me, but I could tell by the way she held herself that she was aware of my gaze upon her.

The idea of trying to penetrate that storm—or any winter storm—to the open sea in a small ship made my heart sink in the most dismaying fashion. The thought must have shown on my face, for Brynda looked at me, her eyes narrowed in speculation, and she frowned.

"You're exhausted," she said. "You should be in bed right now, resting and getting your own strength back."

Before I could properly protest, she and Kenzie had whisked me out of the solar, out across the courtyard, and into my own room. Comyn lay curled on his bed against the inside wall, snugged warmly under the blankets, deeply asleep. While Brynda made sure he was warm enough, Kenzie helped me strip out of my wet, clammy clothing and bundled me onto the bed beneath the blankets. Brynda brushed Comyn's hair back from his forehead in a tender gesture he surely would have protested had he been awake. It made me smile in spite of my fatigue. Brynda came to sit on the edge of my bed. She put her hand to my forehead and looked deep into my eyes. Her gaze was hypnotic, compelling, riveting. I couldn't look away.

"Sleep," she said softly.

Warmth, comforting and soporific, rushed through me, radiating from her hand into my head, then down into my chest and belly, driving out the trembling chill of the sea and the weather. My eyelids were far too heavy, and holding them open became far too much bother.

I slept.

I awoke to darkness and a strange, ringing silence. The storm no longer made grumping noises around the eaves. But it wasn't the silence that had wakened me. I thought someone had called my name, but not even a faint echo of the call remained in the room. I remembered the unmistakable tone of command in the voice—the voice of a man fully accustomed to immediate obedience. I rose from my bed and dressed quickly. Across the room, Comyn slept on undisturbed.

The stillness of a late-winter night met me as I stepped out into the courtyard. Cobblestones gleamed wetly in the warm, flickering light of the torches set in sconces around the courtyard, and frost rimed the fringe of grass that grew against the wall. No stars showed overhead through the thick covering of cloud, and no wind stirred anywhere. The stark, bare branches of the trees stood motionless and quiet in the night. Sometime during the night, the rain had stopped. The fresh, moist scent of awakening spring drifted through the still air despite the frosty chill.

The great main gates at the foot of the Clanhold courtyard were closed and locked for the night, but the small postern gate by the kitchen gardens was open, guarded only by one sleepy clansman. He nodded and stepped back as he recognized me, allowing me to pass unimpeded.

The postern gate opened onto the upper shoulder of the mountain, where the ground fell steeply to the meadow below the Clanhold. I scrabbled across the slope to the more gently tilted pasture close to the track, then turned to follow the track uphill. Wet grass swept against my boots, soaking the soft leather, as I made my way up the shoulder of the mountain, past the shrine, up to the gently dished hollow where a Dance of seven menhirs loomed up into the gloom and made darker shadows against the bulk of the mountain. Set in an open horseshoe shape, the menhirs surrounded a black-marble column that stood as high as my shoulder, the top flat and polished until it felt like glass beneath the pads of my fingers. I glanced at the empty surface and shivered as I remembered the last time I had been here.

That night, a small stone box lay on the plinth. Gabhain dav Wallach had charged me with the duty of seeing him home when a Maedun arrow struck him a mortal blow.

When he died only a moment later, I took his heart, his braid, and his earring, folded them into the square of oiled parchment all clansmen carried for just that purpose, and wrapped the package in his plaid. His only kin, his sister, asked me if I would consent to standing vigil with him on the night of his homecoming. I had placed the stone box containing his heart, his braid, and his earring on the plinth and stood guard over it. Halfway through the night, either I dreamed vividly, or his people from all the generations past came into the circle to guide him home. I'm still not sure which was the reality, but in the morning, the box on the plinth was shattered and empty, containing only a fine, gray ash.

Tonight the circle was empty of all ghosts but memories. The seven menhirs, representing the seven gods and goddesses, stood silent and still. No trace of magic sparked in the night. All was quiet and serene.

I placed one hand on the empty plinth and looked over my shoulder at the looming cliff beyond the circle. Long-ago craftsmen had carved a labyrinth of chambers out of the living rock of the mountain. Niches within contained all the generations of Broche Rhuidh, stretching back to the days when Tyra was little more than a collection of armed camps populated by warring tribes, before even the days when the Celae had broken from Tyra and sailed across the Cold Sea to the Isle of Nemeara, which they renamed Celi after themselves. My own great-grandfather Kian—still known as Red Kian of Skai from the time he stood as regent for my grandfather, Prince Keylan—lay in the crypts beside his wife and bheancoran, my great-grandmother Kerridwen. Close to them in his own place lay Kenzie's great-grandfather, Cullin dav Medroch—he who was foster father to Kian as Kenzie was foster father to me.

As I stood there, I realized I was wrong. The circle *was* filled with magic. It swirled and seethed in the air, thick as the springtime scent of blossoms and new grass. Soft magic. But powerful and vibrant. All-encompassing. It drew me into its center insistently, as easily as the current of a stream might draw a fallen leaf into a whirlpool. If I closed my eyes, I could see it flashing and flaring like the aurora across the sky. But this was the magic of history, of a sense of something anchored firmly in the distant past and stretching forward into the future, all connected, all inter-twined, all one vast tapestry woven of many lives, many events, many times. All the way down through the genera-tions to me.

My breath became suddenly too light to hold in my chest. *All the way to me . . .* I had my place in that far-flung net, just as my father had his. I shivered as the magic brushed against my skin like a cat's paw. And my children would have theirs. For the first time, it didn't seem to matter that perhaps my father thought the wrong son had died all those twenty years ago, that I, and not my brother Eryd, was the one who would carry his blood into the future. All that mattered was that our line *would* move into the future, and there would be a Prince of Skai for the next generation, even if he, too, was a prince in exile.

It was oddly comforting to stand there in the stone Dance and contemplate the endless Unbroken Circle of birth, life, death, and rebirth. Infants became children, chil-dren became young men, and young men became old men, and eventually the cycle began all over again.

A flicker of light came to life in the darkness beyond the stone Dance, out on the shoulder of the mountain just within the curve of the forest where the cedar and pine and leafless oak pressed close against the massive cliffs. Certain it had not been there when I walked into the Dance, I crossed the cropped grass that made the floor of the Dance and stepped between two menhirs to the matted grass outside the circle.

The light seemed brighter and wavered as if it came from a campfire.

Now, who would be camped so near the Clanhold? And why would the fire still be dancing so high at this time of night? Curious and mystified, I made my way quickly and quietly through the meadow to the trees. Oddly enough, I took few precautions but the careful placement of my feet. I had no sense of danger. Only interest.

Two men sat close to the fire, plaids drawn around their shoulders for warmth against the night. The elder of the two looked remarkably like Kenzie. He sat on a section of fallen log he had drawn close to the fire, leaning back, hands clasped around one raised knee as he watched the play of light and shadow from the fire dance across the bare trees.

The younger man, who might have been my age or a year or two older, sat cross-legged on a saddle blanket close to the fire. He held a naked sword across his lap, his polishing cloth by his knee as he honed the blade with a stone worn to a gentle curve from constant use. A frown drew his heavy brows together above his shadowed eyes as he concentrated on the smooth, clean sweep of stone against metal. The blade gleamed in the firelight. It was worthy of the meticulous care he took of it.

Runes spilled down the center of that blade, deeply etched, sparking with a life of their own in the fire-shot night. I knew their shape as intimately as I knew the shape of Caitha dan Malcolm's mouth, but I could not read the words they spelled out. Caught just beyond the circle of light cast by their fire, I hovered in the shadows, strangely unwilling to step out into the light, yet unable to turn back and return to the Clanhold.

The younger man plied the stone with concentrated diligence that looked to me almost like anger. One corner of the older man's mouth twitched, but he did not laugh.

The young man made a disgusted sound with teeth and tongue. He got to his feet, stretching out the kinks in his back. He was not as tall as the older man, and weighed mayhaps a stone or two less, but he was still much taller and heavier than I. He moved with all the natural, inborn grace of a mountain cat. It occurred to me that I would definitely not want to face the pair of them on the practice field, and certainly not if they were serious about using their swords against me.

He folded gracefully back into his cross-legged position and picked up the sword and the honing stone again. He swore softly. "There's enough magic around here tonight to light up the whole of Isgard," he said. "Gods, I *hate* magic."

"So you've told me, *ti'rhonai*," the older man said blandly, raising a hand to hide the corners of his mouth. Laughter bubbled just below the surface of his voice, but he spoke gravely. "Many times, in fact."

I stood staring, hardly able to credit what I saw. Surely I must be dreaming this, for how else could I be standing here, watching Kian dav Leydon, also known as Red Kian of Skai, as he sat by a fire with his foster father, Cullin dav Medroch. And how else could it be that Kian looked no older than I, and Cullin not as old as his own great-grandson, Kenzie dav Aidan.

Kian glanced up at Cullin suspiciously. "Is this your doing, *ti'vati*?"

Cullin raised one eloquent eyebrow. "My doing?" he repeated. "I? I have less magic than that stone you're abusing so enthusiastically. How could I have done this?"

Kian glanced up at him sourly. "Ye've done stranger things," he said. "I'd believe almost anything of you." Then he grinned suddenly, his teeth flashing white in the darkness. "Aye, well, as soon as accuse the stone, as you said." He bent his head to his work again. "I fancy it must be the lad, then."

"Aye," Cullin said. "His magic must be as strong as yours."

Kian grunted. "Stronger, if he can draw us here." He glanced over his shoulder at the shadows beneath the overhanging branches of the cedar and pine trees. I followed his gaze and thought I saw a figure hovering within the shadows, vague and undefined as a reflection seen in murky glass. The blurred, indistinct figure looked like a child of no more than twelve. But even as I looked, the shadow wavered, then was not there at all.

How very odd. For a moment, I thought the child might have been me, the child I had been. Not for the shadowed features I could not see, but for the tense and eager posture of the young body. A fierce yearning for acceptance warred with fear of rejection. My heart ached for the lad. I wanted to reach out to him, but he was already gone.

"He'll need the magic," Cullin said. "And sooner than we'd expect, I fancy." He got to his feet and went to get another log. Then he paused. "I believe we have company," he said softly.

Kian raised his head and looked straight at me where I stood in the shadows. His mouth twisted into a grimace of sorely tried patience, and he put away the honing stone. "There you are," he said, a trace of exasperation rasping in his voice. "Ye've kept us waiting, lad." He picked up the oiled rag that had been lying by his knee and put it to use. His arm made long, sweeping motions as he smoothed and polished the already gleaming blade. He looked up again. "Aye, well, don't just stand there like a lump of suet pudding, lad. Come here."

I stepped into the circle of light, and he got to his feet, unfolding in a swift, smooth movement. He seemed even bigger in the flickering night as he stood over me.

Cullin measured my worth with a careful eye. His teeth

gleamed with his sudden grin. "A likely lad, this, *ti'rhonai*," he said. "Not a fire-topped clansman, but he'll do. He'll do verra nicely, I fancy."

Kian stepped forward, holding the sword in his outstretched hands, the blade lying across his palms. "I've done half your job for you, lad," he said. "You should be honing this sword. It will be yours, not mine."

I looked down at the sword. The plain leather-bound hilt was long enough to be used two-handed, but a man like this clansman could have easily swung the sword with one hand. I had neither the height nor the heft to use it one-handed, but it would make me a formidable weapon even if I could only use it with both hands with any ease.

"My sword?" I repeated, my voice sounding odd in my ears, as if it echoed in the darkness of the forest.

"Aye, lad, yours. It was never mine, and never could be."

I stepped forward. The sword had all the beauty of a well-made and well-kept weapon, deadly and elegant. The runes along the blade glittered with a furious grace of their own. "My sword?" I said again, unable to believe him.

"It searches," he said. "But not for me." He thrust it forward at me. Involuntarily, I raised my hands and reached for the sword. But even as I touched the cold, gleaming metal, it fell through my hands. The blade flashed once in the darkness, then vanished. I didn't hear it hit the ground.

"Don't you lose it, too, Gareth," Kian said. "You'll be needing it verra soon." His voice grew fainter, as if he was moving away from me. "Verra soon indeed . . ."

I went to my knees, groping blindly on the ground before me for the sword. But it was gone. And when I looked up, so were the two men and the campfire. I was alone on the shoulder of the mountain, and the wind whipped freezing rain all around me, nearly blinding me as I knelt in the wet grass and shivered.

•   •   •

I awoke huddled on my bed in the small room I shared with
Comyn. Both the thick woolen blanket and the quilt had
fallen to the floor, and the temperature in the room was barely
above freezing. The fire in the brazier had gone out, and the
ashes lay cold and dark, almost damp to the touch. Shivering,
I built the fire again, then flung myself back onto the bed and
pulled the blanket and the quilt up around my ears. My wet
hair had made a clammy spot on the pillow, so I turned it over.

My breath caught suddenly in my throat and I reached
up slowly to touch my hair. Wet. With small bits of nearly
melted ice still entangled in the strands . . .

A dream . . . ?

I shuddered, and wrapped myself tighter in the bed-
clothes. This was something I could think about later, when I
wasn't fuddled with sleep.

Later . . .

I don't remember falling asleep.

•

3

The dream began before I knew I was asleep. The sword hovered just beyond the reach of my outstretched hands, the dappled shimmer of light bright along the deadly length of the blade, delineating the runes.

The sword was beautiful in the way that expertly crafted weapons are beautiful—the slender, deadly beauty of function and purpose. Honed to a lethal edge, and unmarred by notches or nicks, the blade shone with a muted glow of its own in the watery light. A delicate and complex network of braided-silver filigree twisted into an intricate knotwork design decorated the crosspiece of the hilt, and a smoothly carved ovoid of white quartz interlaced with narrow veins of gold formed the pommel. The hand-and-a-half hilt was made to be used either two-handed or one-handed, but it would take a larger, more powerful man than I to wield it efficiently with only one hand. A man like my grandfather, Keylan. Or my father, Brennen . . .

I reached for the sword, resignedly expecting it to recede as it always did. This time, it simply disappeared, startling me. The quality of the light changed, becoming painfully bright. Against the dazzling brilliance, shadows flickered and swayed. Half-blinded by the glare, I saw nothing but fractured images, like snippets hacked from a panoramic tapestry, vivid impressions of three men and a woman locked in mortal combat with an enemy I could hardly see.

. . . A bright blade glittering with engraved runes flashed as it rose to meet a dark blade . . .

. . . Sunlight caught on the gleam of red-gold hair and the swirl of a blue-and-green plaid as a man turned to engage a shadowy enemy . . .

. . . A double-edged Saesnesi war ax, swung by a tall, broad blond

*man, glinted furiously in the sun, then buried itself in the throat of a
black-clad man . . .*

*. . . A woman's face went taut and pale with urgency as she
spurred her horse forward to intercept a sword blow aimed at a man's
unprotected back . . .*

*. . . A gleaming sword went spinning off, runes glinting in the
sunlight as it fell, and the water closed over it with hardly more than a
ripple . . .*

*. . . A man crouched in shallow water near the edge of the stream,
clutching the body of a woman against his chest as tears ran freely
down his face.*

*Despair washed through me. Pain and grief so fierce and sharp it
threatened to shred my heart, my very soul. It wrenched at my guts,
tearing the cry of bereaved anguish from me, and I thought I would die,
too, as the woman died in my arms . . .*

I awoke with a start and stared out the window at a dim, gray
twilight. My eyes felt gummy and gritty, and I couldn't tell
whether it was dusk or dawn. Every muscle I owned
protested violently as I sat up. I felt as if I had spent the last
two days on the practice field, being pummeled over my
whole body by wooden swords.

Comyn's bed was empty, the blankets smoothed neatly
over it, the feather pillow plumped up. Comyn himself was
long gone. From the courtyard outside came the sounds of
voices and people moving briskly about on errands or business. I looked at the window again and thought the light was
brighter now than it had been a moment or two before. So,
the wan light was morning twilight, and I had slept half the
day and all the night. After sleeping like that, surely I should
have felt more rested and alert than I did—more eager to face
the new day.

My bones added their protest as I climbed out of bed and

searched through my clothes chest for clean clothing. I stretched to wring some of the kinks out of my back and succeeded only in causing a whole different set of muscles to creak and complain of the cruel treatment.

I groaned and reached down to rub the backs of my aching legs. Mayhaps I hadn't spent the night in the practice field after all. Mayhaps I had spent it running up and down the mountain . . .

A deep chill fizzed through me, and my breath caught in my throat as I remembered the strange dreams that had disturbed my sleep. I reached out and placed the palm of my hand against my pillow. I thought it might still be cold and slightly damp where it had absorbed the thawing sleet from my hair.

I shivered again, turned the pillow over, and made up the bed quickly. The dampness in the pillow was only my imagination. I had only dreamed; certainly I had not gone out onto the mountain in the dark of the night and met my great-grandfather. If I had been handed a sword, it had been in my dreams. Surely, had it been real, the sword could not have fallen through my fingers as if my flesh were of no more substance than smoke. I drew in a deep breath that was more shaky than I would have wished it to be. I closed my eyes and let the breath out slowly.

A dream. That's all it was. Only a dream.

My belly awoke and grumpily reminded me of the great expanse of time that had passed since I had last eaten. I searched for my plaid, remembered I had dropped it on the shingle during the rescue, and pulled an old blue cloak out of the wardrobe. It would have to do. But I didn't go straight to the kitchen for food to break my fast. I went to the infirmary instead.

The Celae boy was still asleep. One of the herbal healers

assured me that he was in no danger. There was no sign of lung fever, something that killed far too many men pulled half-drowned from the sea.

"The lad will recover," he said comfortably as he stirred a decoction brewing on a small charcoal brazier. "It will take time, but he'll recover well."

I nodded, then stood near the head of the boy's cot for a moment and studied his face curiously. He looked tantalizingly familiar. But I didn't think I knew him. I suppose there was no reason why I should. I had been nearly thirteen when I left Skerry for Tyra. That was twelve years ago. This boy would have been only three or four years old then, only a child and far too young to attract the notice of a lonely, withdrawn twelve-year-old.

On impulse, I bent over the boy and put my hand to his forehead. His skin was cool and dry beneath my palm. Then his lashes fluttered and he opened his eyes, startling me. He looked straight up at me, his dark blue eyes wide and uncomprehending.

"My lord Prince?" he muttered.

Something cold and shivery ran its fingers down my spine. *My lord Prince . . .* Not I. Not a prince. Not unless my father were already dead.

The boy raised a trembling hand to his face and pushed the dark hair from his forehead. He looked up at me again, slow comprehension dawning in his eyes, and wet his chapped lips with his tongue.

"My lord Gareth," he said. "You are Gareth ap Brennen?"

"Aye, lad," I said. "I am he."

"I'm Rhan ap Fyld," he said faintly.

"Fyld's son?" Startled, I looked more closely at him. The resemblance was obvious now that I knew. He looked very much like his father. "Aye," I said. "I can see that now."

"I've a message," he said faintly, his voice hoarse from swallowing all the seawater during the rescue. "My father entrusted it only to me. It's important—"

"We have the message, Rhan," I told him. "You rest and recover your strength. The message has been delivered safely."

Two splotches of hectic color stained the skin stretched taut over his cheekbones. "I'm to tell you something, my lord." His voice had dropped to the merest whisper. "I'm to say it was an accident, not an illness that struck your father. Fyld would have you know it was no weakness in your father . . ."

"No more, lad," I said. "There will be time to tell us more when you're better." I stooped and put my hand to his forehead again as he drew in a deep breath as if to continue speaking. "Sleep, now."

He looked up at me for a moment, then closed his eyes. In moments, he was asleep again. I straightened and stood for a moment, looking down thoughtfully at him, then turned to leave. The wind tore at my cloak as I walked out into the courtyard. I pulled the rough fabric closer around my throat and bent my head into the wind as I hurried toward the kitchens.

An accident. My father had been hurt in an accident and now lay near death. Fyld's letter urged me to come as soon as possible. I wondered how long my father had left, and would it be too late by the time the storm blew itself out.

Not until I sat down to a meal of hot oatmeal with honey and milk, bread, cheese, and dried fruit, did the fragments of the dream swirl back into my head. Like wisps of smoke from the fire on the hearth, they drifted in front of my mind's eye.

I had dreamed twice last night. And one dream was still so vivid, so detailed in my memory, it could have been real. How strange that I should dream of my great-grand-father. Not only my great-grandfather, but Kenzie's great-grandfather, too.

Dream piled on dream . . . I had been exhausted last night. And then there was Brynda's use of her Healing magic. Everything must have combined to make a jumbled tangle in my head. But not only had I dreamed of Red Kian of Skai, I knew I had dreamed again of the sword. And I had dreamed of my father.

The dream of the sword was a familiar one. Until I left Skerry in the far north of Celi, the same dream had come to haunt my nights time and time again as I was growing up. I remembered very little of the shape or substance of the dream. All that remained to me upon waking were images of the sword and the bright shards of waterlight flashing across the gleaming metal.

Now I knew the sword for what it was. Mayhaps it had taken the news that my father was dying to trigger the aware-ness of the truth of my dreams, the truth of the sword in those dreams.

My father's sword. The Rune Blade Bane. The sword he had lost in battle during the Maedun invasion of Celi all those years ago. The sword that should have been passed on to his heir.

His heir . . .

I was the only son of the Prince of Skai. That made me his heir. But more rightly speaking, I was the only *surviving* son of the Prince of Skai. There was a difference. And to my father, at least, the difference was apparently insurmount-able. In his heart of hearts, I knew he thought the wrong son had died those twenty years ago.

And now I had to return to Celi. Return to exile on Skerry . . .

The letter had come from Fyld. Not from my father.

From Fyld. Was my father too ill to write? Or was it Fyld who wanted me to come home, and not my father?

"Home," I whispered, then shivered. "But Skerry, not Skai . . ." It was certainly wrong that the heir to the throne of Skai could remember nothing of that beautiful province. My only memories of Celi were of exile in Skerry.

I didn't want to think of that. Not right now. I got up and went to the stable to saddle my horse. I still had a shift to stand on shorewatch, and I didn't want to be late.

The storm had not abated while I slept. The driving wind and rain matched my mood as I rode the headland, straining to see anything through the mist of rain and blown spume. It was fortunate that no other storm-tossed ship relied upon me this morning to watch for its safety in the storm. I looked toward the turbulent water, but I saw only my own musings.

The wind snatched at the braid by my left temple, whipping the hair into my eyes. I put my hand to the braid to push it back, then slid my fingers down to the blue topaz dangling on a fine, gold chain from my left ear. Brynda had chosen the topaz for me when I attained manhood. The color, she said, matched my eyes so well.

After twelve years in Tyra, I was more Tyran than Celae. Kenzie and Brynda had given me a home and raised me as they raised their own two children, Comyn and Eibhlin. They had given me love and protection and a place that was uniquely my own. In Tyran, the words for uncle and foster father were the same—ti'vati. As were the words for aunt and foster mother. Kenzie had been more father to me than my own father had been, and Brynda had certainly been more to me than the mother I could barely remember. I had come to manhood in Tyra, by Tyran rites. I belonged here far more than I could belong on that isolated little island where my father had taken refuge all those years ago.

And then there was Caitha . . . Caitha dan Malcolm, who had come so suddenly and startlingly to womanhood last spring. Caitha, who had danced so enticingly and gracefully between the Beltane fires and into my heart. We had not declared for each other, nor had we exchanged any promises, but it was understood between us that we would say our betrothal vows come this Beltane, only a little more than one season away. I knew Malcolm approved the match, but I had no idea how my father would feel about it.

But could I ask Caitha to leave Tyra and go into exile on Skerry? How could I ask her to leave her kin and all she had grown up with, and go with me to a place where she knew no one? And would she come if I asked her?

I turned the mare and guided her out of the trees onto a narrow strip of grass. I dismounted and walked to the edge of the cliff, drawn by something I couldn't name. Out there, a hundred leagues beyond Tyra's shores, lay the Isle of Celi, lost now in the mist and rain. Behind me, the trees moaned in the wind, and beyond the cliff, the gray of the sky blended with the gray of the sea, hazed by the rain and the blown sea spume. From here, the breakwater across the mouth of the harbor was invisible, obscured by the drifting mist. And even on the fairest of days, Celi was lost in the distance.

Someone moved quietly through the trees. I turned to see Kenzie ride around a low ridge of rock onto the gently sloped grassy ledge where I stood. He wore his plaid wrapped securely around his shoulders to protect himself from the mist and light drizzle, but he had left his head bare. Water beaded on his eyelashes and dripped from his beard and the strands of red hair hanging down around his chin. He dismounted and stood for a moment, looking out over the sea.

"I'd say a man on shorewatch today is wasting his time," he said at last. "Any ship out in that deserves whatever the sea gives it."

"Aye, you could be right," I answered.

He pulled the plaid up over his head, wiped the moisture from his face, and wrung the water from the braid hanging by his left temple. "Your shift was over more than two hours ago," he said. "Brynda sent me to make sure you were all right."

I looked out across the pewter gray of the sea and sky. "I've been thinking," I said. "I didn't realize how much time had passed."

"The evening meal will be ready soon," he said. "Will ye no come home now to eat it? Have ye eaten since breaking your fast this morning?"

I hadn't. I had completely forgotten about the packet of bread and cheese I'd stuffed into the saddle pack before I left the Clanhold. As soon as I remembered the food, my stomach took the opportunity to inform me that it was empty as a pauper's purse and began to demand I do something about it. Getting lost in long hours of introspection was not a habit of mine. Now that Kenzie had drawn it to my attention, I realized that it was near dusk, and I had no idea where the time between early morning and now had gone. For a moment, my head spun in a wave of disorientation as if I had been displaced in place as well as time. But the dizziness might have been only hunger, too, and that I could remedy easily enough.

Kenzie swung himself back into the saddle, adjusting the folds of his plaid around him. He gestured with his head toward the Clanhold.

"Let's go, shall we?" he said. "The mare's probably as hungry as you are. She deserves a good rubdown and some hot bran, then a warm blanket in the stables."

"Aye, she does," I replied. I mounted quickly, and we set out together through the dripping trees toward the track. I glanced over at Kenzie, hunched down into his plaid, and got a sudden flash of the sun glancing off bright hair of copper-

gold and the flare of a green-and-blue plaid. My hand tightened convulsively on the reins. "You were with my father
when he lost Bane, weren't you?" I said, startling myself
nearly as much as I startled him. I hadn't meant to say anything about the dream.

He stared at me in the gray light, an odd, listening
expression on his face, and I could tell that his head was as
full of impressions of that skirmish by the river as was mine.
"Aye," he said slowly in amazement, his voice soft with it.
"Aye, I was. How did you know?"

I looked down at my hands, knotted in the reins, the
knuckles white against the brown of the leather. "I saw it," I
said at last. "In a dream. Last night. This morning, rather."

He turned to study me, his eyes very green under the
fierce red-gold of his brows, even shadowed by the plaid.
Finally, he nodded. "Aye," he said. "Brynda dreams true
yet. And I'm told so did your father on occasion. It wouldna
surprise me if you've got the potential for magic, as Brynda
has. It runs deep in your family. And it's no surprising that
you've the Gift to dream true, too. What did you see?"

"Just flashes and impressions," I said, then told him all I
could remember of the dream. As I spoke, the images swept
past before my eyes again, and the hair on the back of my
neck rose chillingly. Kenzie said nothing, not interrupting,
merely watching me as I related the dream.

"And at the end," I said, my voice sounding hoarse to my
own ears, "there was only that bare glimpse of a man holding
a woman's body, and I felt as if my guts had been torn out of
my belly."

"Fiala," Kenzie said softly.

"Fiala?" I glanced at him questioningly. "My father's
bheancoran?"

"Aye, Brennen's bheancoran," he said, still quietly. "She
died there, taking a sword thrust meant for him."

I knew about bheancorans, of course. All the Princes of Skai were served by warrior-maids who acted as personal guards, confidantes, and companions. The bond between prince and bheancoran was for life. A bheancoran seldom survived the death of her prince, Brynda had told me. She, herself, had survived the death of Prince Tiegan only because she had sworn him a vow to see his widow safe to Sheryn's people should he fall. Even now sometimes, twenty years later, the pain of the broken bond showed in Brynda's face. And after experiencing the bleak despair and agony that filled me in the dream, I realized that it was not much easier for a prince to lose his bheancoran.

Some princes had married their bheancorans, as my grandfather Keylan had, and my great-grandfather Kian had. My father had not married Fiala, but the bond between them was deep and strong for all that. I, of course, had no bheancoran. Another blot on my escutcheon to confirm my father's belief that the wrong son had survived . . .

"They caught us there at the stream," Kenzie said, his tone conversational, but his expression remote and thoughtful. "Your father, Fiala, me, and Aeliegh, who was Celwalda of the Saesnesi of the Summer Run. It was almost as if the Somber Riders recognized your father, for they fought more to capture us than to kill us, I think. I remember very little of the fight. I had no immunity then to Hakkar's spell, and it nearly drowned me in its black horror."

"They captured you there, didn't they?" I said. "All three of you?"

"Aye." A slight, rueful smile twitched at the corner of his mouth. "And it was Brynda and Sheryn who freed us from the prison cells. You know the rest of the story, how we fled across the breadth of Celi and took Sheryn back to her people."

I nodded. I doubted there was a free Celae anywhere

who didn't know the story. We rode in silence for a moment. Then I said, "Kenzie, I dreamed of the sword. Bane. I saw it there in the water."

He glanced at me across the ears of his horse, one eyebrow raised quizzically. "It calls you?" he asked.

"Aye, I suppose it does," I said, slowly. Then, more positively, "It does. Ever since I was a child, I think. I can't remember the first time I dreamed of it. I can't ever remember *not* dreaming of it. And last night, I was told the sword searched for me."

His mouth lengthened into a thoughtful line. "It searches for you?"

"I believe it might. Either for me, or for my father." I hesitated, wondering how much I could tell him. "And I dreamed, too, of Red Kian. He told me the sword searches and admonished me not to lose the sword as my father had done. I suppose he'd know about Rune Blades if anyone does, and how they seek."

Kenzie nodded, but said nothing. His brows came together over his eyes, a deep furrow appearing between them. He glanced at me again, and I thought he would speak. Instead, he merely nodded again and hunched deeper into his plaid.

I could almost read his thoughts. The Rune Blades of Skai had the knack of finding the man who was born to wield them, even if it meant calling other men to do their bidding. The greatsword Kingmaker had called my great-grandfather Kian to carry it to the son who would become King Tiernyn. It was easy to see the direction of Kenzie's thoughts. He wondered if I were being called to bring the sword back to my father.

I wondered, too.

We came to the Clanhold, the horses' hooves clattering loudly over the cobbled courtyard. One of the stableboys came running to meet us as we rode through the wide-flung gates. He was barefoot and bareheaded, wearing nothing but a thin shirt and a stained, ragged kilt. When Kenzie chided him about being unprotected from the cold, he gave us a wide grin.

"It's no so cold and miserable as snow, my lord," he said cheerfully as he gathered the horses' reins. "Wi' this weather, I can feel spring coming, so I dinna mind the rain." He tugged gently at the horses. "Come along then, my sweets. There's a warm blanket for each of you and hot mash in yon stable." The horses followed him eagerly, their ears pricked forward, and they disappeared into the gloom toward the stable. Kenzie and I turned away and hurried up the broad steps to the entrance of the Great Hall.

Music and laughter met us as we ducked quickly through the doors. The rich aromas of roasting meat, mulled wine, and baking bread floated on the air, braiding through the subtle scents of beeswax tapers and burning pine and birch. The Great Hall blazed with light from torches burning in sconces on the walls and candles in the elaborate candelabra hanging from the heavy beams of the high ceiling. Flames leapt high from the hearths at either end of the long room, dispelling the damp chill of the evening. The air was full of the mellow tones of a knee harp and the thin, reedy piping of a pair of wooden flutes. Several couples whirled through a set-dance to the lively music, the bright colors of their plaids and arisaids, the light tartan shawls worn by the women, swirling in the warm light.

Scattered throughout the Hall were men and women of Celi, easily distinguished from the red-haired, green- or gray-eyed Tyrs. They tended to have dark gold hair and brown eyes, or, like me, glossy blue-black hair and deep blue eyes. Some had been born here in Tyra. But most were exiles rescued from the beleaguered shores of Celi nearly twenty years

ago by Tyran ships sent by my great-grandfather Kian, one of
the last services he had done for Skai and Celi.

Brynda sat with Comyn near the far hearth. Comyn sat
on the table, his feet on the bench by her hips. Brynda beckoned cheerfully to us as we came in. I followed Kenzie across
the room, then shook the water from my cloak and spread it
on a bench in front of the fire to dry. Someone handed me a
goblet of hot, mulled wine. I thanked him and climbed up to
sit beside Comyn on the table. He moved over obligingly to
give me room and grinned at me. The heat of the wine
through the heavy pewter of the goblet took the chill from my
stiff fingers, and the heady aroma of the rising steam
promised warmth to my belly.

"You're late," Comyn said. "Any trouble out there?"

"Not when I left," I said. "But it's shaping up another
wild night tonight."

"You were out very early this morning," Brynda said.
"Are you all right?" She studied me carefully, flickers of
worry darkening her eyes.

I gave her what I hoped was a reassuring smile. "I
thought I might as well go out early," I said. "An extra pair of
eyes in this weather never hurts. Besides, I couldn't sleep this
morning and—" I broke off as the expression on her face
changed. She had been about to return my smile until I mentioned that I couldn't sleep, then concern filled her eyes.

"Dreams?" she asked, her voice quiet.

I shrugged. "Strange dreams," I said. "But please don't
worry about me, *ti'vata.*"

She said nothing, but the skin around her eyes tightened,
and I knew she was worried in spite of my reassurance. She
dreamed true at times. But I didn't know if my dreams were
true dreams or not. While I had dreamed of the fight by the
stream where my father lost both his sword and his bheancoran, it might simply be an old memory, or a construction of

my sleeping mind to cover something I knew must have happened. It might not be a sending from the sword. But only the seven gods and goddesses knew where the dream of Red Kian of Skai had come from. I had never dreamed of my great-grandfather before.

"Do you dream true, Gareth?" Brynda asked again.

I looked up quickly and met her eyes in an unexpectedly unguarded moment. In their brown-gold depths, I saw reflected all the pain and agony of a broken bond, the same agony I had felt when I dreamed of my father holding Fiala's body. She masked it quickly enough, but I had seen it. She had been bheancoran to the Prince of Celi, and the breaking of the bond by his death had nearly destroyed her. But she had rebuilt her life with room in it for Kenzie and their children, Comyn and Eibhlin. My father had survived the pain of losing his bheancoran, but had not been able to rebuild his life with room for his youngest son—me—in it.

Of course, that small, maddeningly reasonable voice within me whispered, *my father had also lost his wife, his daughter, and his eldest son. How much of himself could a man lose and still have enough resources left to rebuild anything?*

But to ignore his only surviving son . . .

That was something I really didn't want to think about. Not now. I forced myself to grin at Brynda and gave her a glib answer.

"Dream true?" I repeated and laughed. "I doubt it. Probably just Caitha dancing through my dreams."

Kenzie gave me a sharp look and frowned, but he said nothing, understanding that I had no wish to worry Brynda any more than she was already worried. Likely I'd hear more from him later about my prevaricating.

Comyn made a rude noise. "Blaming Caitha, are you?" he said. "She'd be more likely to disturb your dreams if she did more than just *dance* through them."

Kenzie reached up with mock ferocity and gave him a swift, half-playful cuff to the side of the head. "Mind your tongue," he said severely, but the corners of his mouth twitched suspiciously. Comyn made a face, then grinned and ducked away from a second swipe. A small hook of envy caught at my belly. My father had never touched me in that amiable, almost indulgent way.

Brynda caught my arm, drawing my attention back to her. "Will you go home, Gareth?" she asked.

I looked at her blankly. "I don't know," I replied. "I suppose I must . . ."

"Aye," Kenzie said firmly. "Aye, I believe you must."

4

The dream had a different quality to it as it spread itself through my sleep, an oddly anticipatory texture that I could not quite grasp. The sword still lay on the stony bottom of the stream, quiescent and dreaming, hidden beneath the weed-choked overhang of the bank. But a sense of eager impatience fizzed around it, like the waters of a mineral spring. Broken shards of sunlight flashed down the blade and danced across the smooth, round stones on the bottom of the stream in random patterns of green-gold and silver.

Above the water, shredded clouds hung low, gray as pewter, heavy with moisture and threatening cold rain or snow. Here and there, a flash of blue showed where a break in the cloud allowed a spear of sunshine through. The silver water reflected the colorless sky as the slow slide of the river bisected the shallow glen and curved gently to cup a tract of rolling pastureland. The air of the small valley appeared to shimmer, as if with heat waves, even though frost rimed the tufts of grass. I wondered at the shimmer, then noticed a faint, overlying stench of carrion and knew what it had to be. Brynda had told of such a stench emanating from the Maedun blood sorcery that lay heavy over the Isle of Celi.

If the blood sorcery spell covered Celi, it did little harm to the land itself. The grass in the meadow to either side of the stream was now yellowed and dead, beaten down into the still-frozen ground. Bare stalks of last autumn's final flowers thrust up through the sodden mass, broken and black. A herd of cows, their brown and white hides gleaming in the wan, gray light, stood cropping the old grass. They looked as if they had weathered the winter well. Or at least better than the boy who tended them.

The young cowherd, a lad of hardly more than ten summers, stood in the mottled gray shadows of a thatch of willow, fingering a small leather sack of stones hanging at his belt. The pale late-winter sun hidden behind the clouds gave very little warmth so early in the day, and he huddled into a ragged sheepskin cloak. His bare legs, feet thrust into clumsy sandals, were red and raw, the skin chapped and rough. He moved his feet rhythmically to help keep the circulation going, his attention on the cattle.

A young heifer ambled toward the stream, away from the main body of the herd. The boy plucked a small, round, smooth stone from his pouch and hurled it with casual accuracy. It caught the heifer high on the flank. The heifer's ears flapped twice in confusion, and it stopped to consider. Then, forgetting what it had been doing, it turned and wandered back to the herd, lowering its head to graze again.

Hanging from a slender branch beside the boy was a cloth bundle containing bread and cheese and a wrinkled and withered apple for his midday meal. But he still had several hours to go before he could enjoy the food. It had been a long time since his breakfast of oatmeal gruel and milk. He pulled his cloak more tightly around himself, sighed, and stamped his feet.

The noise startled a ringdove. He looked up as it broke from the tangled willow and skimmed close above the grass, fleeing toward the river. With a sudden rush and flurry of feathers and wind, a falcon dropped out of the sky, wings folded back, talons reaching for the vulnerable back of the terrified ringdove. The dove turned frantically, but too late, for the bank of the river. The falcon slashed into its prey. The dove tumbled into the trailing grass on the riverbank and fell with a small splash into the water beneath the overhang, well out of reach of the falcon. Screaming its disappointment and rage, the falcon beat back into the sky.

The boy began to run almost before the dove hit the water. The soft gray gleam of its feathers showed pale against the shadows of the overhung bank. The dove wasn't very big, but it was certainly large enough to provide a few welcome mouthfuls of sweet, succulent meat after being roasted over a slow fire.

He went to his knees on the slippery bank, but could not quite reach the dove where it floated on the quiet surface of the stream. Cursing softly under his breath, he lowered himself into the icy water. It swirled around his thighs, soaking the hem of his ragged tunic. He lunged for the dove and scooped it up in one deft movement. But he had overbalanced and had to take a step or two deeper into the water to prevent himself from plunging belly first into the current.

Something knocked against his foot, and he caught the muted gleam of metal beneath the rippling surface of the water. For a moment, he hesitated. Metal was a rich find, but the water was cold enough to turn his lips blue. On the other hand, he had his flint and steel, and he had a dove to cook to take the chill from his bones. And the metal was valuable. Any metal . . .

He tucked the dove into the front of his tunic, then took a deep breath and ducked below the surface of the water. His hands scrabbled blindly among the stones at his feet. He found something long and slender and burst from the water, clutching it against his chest and gasping for breath.

It wasn't until he had climbed back up onto the bank and pulled his sheepskin cloak around him again that he looked closely at what he held. He stared at the sword in awe, shivering half from the cold and half from the sudden excitement of his discovery. It was the most beautiful thing he'd ever seen. Even as he marveled at its slender, deadly beauty, he knew it must be hidden quickly from the darkly cloaked men who ruled the land, or his father would suffer greatly for it.

The boy made sure of the dove tucked into his tunic and made his way back to the willow thicket. None of the cattle had strayed while he had turned his back on them. He hid the sword amid the tangled stems of the willow while he gathered together dry leaves and grass to start his fire. He glanced at the sword over his shoulder. The sun glinted on the smooth, unpitted, and rustless gleam of the silvery metal. He shivered again, and concentrated on building his fire.

And, half-hidden among the willow, the sword quivered eagerly. It was on the move, seeking. It would not rest until it had reached its goal.

● ● ●

I awoke with a start in the wan light just before dawn, fragments of the dream swirling through my head. Even as I tried to gather them together to make sense out of them, they dissipated like smoke seen through mist. I was left with nothing but a feeling that something important had begun, a sense of eagerness, of anticipation. At the same time, a sensation of deep relief settled under my heart. The time of waiting was nearly at an end.

Gradually, I became aware of a strange, rustling silence. I sat up blearily and suddenly realized that I could no longer hear the wind whistling around the eaves, or the continuous rattle of the rain against the shutters. The weather, true to its contrary nature, had proved Malcolm wrong. The gale had blown itself out during the night.

Comyn stood by the window, fully dressed and disgustingly wide-awake. He turned to look at me as I sat clutching the blanket to my chest, still stunned by sleep and the vanishing dream. He grinned at me, and I shuddered. I don't know how he did that every morning. People who were that cheerful this early were not entirely human.

"Wind's shifted," he said. "It's out of the west now, not the north."

I mumbled something that tried to sound intelligent. He didn't reply, but that was all right. Even I wasn't quite sure what I'd said. I stumbled out of bed and joined him at the window. The storm had left a pale, washed, cloudless sky in its wake. Wisps of mist clung in ragged tatters to patches of grass and bushes, and at sea, frayed shreds of fog drifted with the breeze above the glassy swells of the water.

"Good sailing weather." Comyn glanced at me, one eyebrow raised speculatively.

I stared at him blankly for a moment before his meaning sank into my sleep fuddled brain. "Sailing weather?" I repeated. "Oh. To Skerry, you mean."

He nodded patiently. He knew me well now. "Aye," he said. "To Skerry. Today and tomorrow will be good. Mayhaps even the next day. I think we should chance it."

Comyn's father was the best swordsman in Tyra—one of the best swordsmen on the Continent. My father had sent me to Tyra to learn swordsmanshp from Kenzie dav Aidan for that very reason. Comyn was a thoroughly competent swordsman, which was only to be expected, but his real talent—his gift—was in reading the wind and weather, and guiding a ship safely through the swells and billows of the sea. He seemed to become one with the ship, one with the sea, and find all the safest routes through the storms and shoals. He had been born under the sign of Adriel of the Waters, a Beltane child, lucky and blessed, and the sea was in his blood. There was no one I'd trust more to take me safely through the teeth of the winter storms across the Cold Sea to the Isle of Skerry.

I looked at him again. He stood watching me, the one eyebrow still canted in query. My brain creaked into motion like an old farm cart with one square wheel lurching forward in spring mud. I nodded. "Aye," I said. "Then let's do it. Soonest started, soonest done, they say."

"I can have a courier ship ready to leave in an hour," he said. "Meet me down in the harbor." He nodded once, then hurried from the room, his kilt swirling around his knees.

"Comyn!" I called.

He hung on his heel and glanced over his shoulder.

"Make that two hours," I said.

"But we'll miss the tide—"

"The tide will still be ebbing in two hours. I've a lot to do."

He laughed. "Aye, I suppose you do. Two hours, then." And he was gone.

I sat down on my bed and scrubbed my hands over my cheeks as the enormity of the decision swept over me. For a moment, I sat there, staring out at the swiftly lightening sky. In two hours, I'd be on my way back to Celi.

Two hours . . .

Two hours to pack everything I'd need, break my fast, and bid good-bye to everyone.

Two hours . . .

And I wasn't even dressed yet . . .

I swore, then lunged for my kilt and shirt. It was the work of only moments to scramble the things I was going to need into a carry-pack. Bidding farewell to everyone at Broche Rhuidh would take me much longer.

Caitha wasn't in the solar when I took my leave of Malcolm and Govan. I didn't see her until after I had said good-bye to Brynda and Kenzie in their chambers in the south wing of the Clanhold. Brynda wanted to come with me. The way she held her strong, brown hands clenched tightly told me louder than words how much she wished she would be with me in the small ship. But there was no room for more than one passenger in the little courier ships. Had she tried to come, the danger of overloading the ship and foundering in the great swells following the storm was very real. Perhaps she could come after the worst of the equinoctial storms was past. Neither of us mentioned that by then, it might be far too late. So she clenched her fists and schooled her face into a pleasant smile to wish me good speed.

Caitha intercepted me after I left Kenzie and Brynda's chambers and made my way down the corridor toward the staircase leading to the Great Hall. She reached out of the shadows of a doorway to catch my arm and drew me into one of the spacious dayrooms. A fire burned in the hearth to dispel the chill, but the draperies were pulled tight across the windows, dimming the room to a soft twilight. She came swiftly into my arms and lifted her face to mine to meet my kiss. She clung to me for a moment, then quickly stepped away.

"So," she said a little breathlessly, "you're leaving us." A touch of roughness rasped in her voice. It might have been a disguise for emotion she thought unsuitable to express as we weren't properly betrothed. Or it might have been a hint of challenge, a touch of disapproval.

I reached for her hand, but she eluded me deftly. She moved back gracefully, folding her hands behind her as she cocked her head and glanced up at me sideways, her eyes watchful and shrewd. I dropped my hand to my side, and the fingers clenched into a fist of their own accord.

"Aye," I said. "I must go. It's my duty . . ."

She raised one eyebrow slightly, still holding her hands behind her. "Duty, is it?" she said, the eyebrow canted quizzically above her dove gray eye. "And have ye then no duty to Broche Rhuidh where you've sheltered safe and been made welcome these last twelve years?"

I didn't know what I had expected from her, but this wasn't it. I drew back, straightening my back and shoulders so that I stood at my full height. Her eyes were nearly on a level with mine. Even in the dim light, the flecks of violet and gold around her dark pupils stood out plainly. I found no warmth there, no trace of the love or regard I'd hoped for.

"I've been with your brother Taggert to guard the border and fought at his side against the Maedun and the Isgardians," I said softly. "And I've watched the coast with Govan and Comyn, and plucked shipwrecked Tyran sailors from certain death among the currents and rocks. Does that not count as fulfilling a duty toward Broche Rhuidh?"

Her expression didn't change. Something cold wrapped itself around my heart. I took a deep breath, but before I could speak, she reached up and plucked disdainfully at the plain, dark blue cloak I wore.

"And where's your good plaid this morning, Gareth dav Brennen ti'Kenzie?" she asked tartly.

"My plaid?" I repeated. Her sudden change of subject startled me, and I blinked stupidly for a moment before I recovered. "My plaid? I left it on the shingle the other day when we launched the boats. It might be halfway to Laringras by now with the tide. Or to Celi, come to that."

She flicked a finger at my cloak. "This is no good," she said with more than a trace of asperity. "You'll need a good, thickly woven plaid to keep you warm on your journey. And in those cold, drear mountains of Skerry. You'll surely freeze solid in this and shatter to flinders."

I wasn't sure what she was trying to get at. "Well, this will have to do," I said. "I've nothing else."

She turned to pick up a bundle that had been lying on the bench beneath the window behind her, then thrust it all anyhow into my arms. "This is for you."

I shook out the heavy fabric. The light in the chamber was not good, filtered by the draperies across the window, but I recognized the pattern she had been weaving the other evening in the solar. Thoughtfully, I ran my finger along the narrow gold stripe among the greens, grays, and blues. I looked at her and met her wide, gray eyes—soft gray as the breast of a dove. Nothing but guileless concern showed there now—no censure, no condemnation, no blame. And no hint of a smile on her mouth or around her eyes.

"I've not the right to wear the gold stripe," I said. "I'm not a son of the house of the Clan Laird. I'm hardly even a kinsman." I put the plaid back down on the wide, padded bench under the window.

"No, not a son of the house," she said softly. "But you could be a kin-son."

I took a deep breath. "Then would you betroth yourself to me now, before I leave? This hour, in the Great Hall before your father and the rest of the Clan? And would you come to me in Skerry once the sea is safe after the winter storms are done?"

She hesitated a moment, then stepped forward and put her arms around my neck. "I want nothing more than to say betrothal vows with you, Gareth," she whispered. "When you come back, we can say them right here at Broche Rhuidh, in the Great Hall as you wish. Beltane would be a fine time, don't you think?"

"Caitha . . ." I closed my eyes for a moment and simply held her closer, breathing in the soft fragrance of her hair. She smelled of lavender and honey and violets. I put my hands to her shoulders and held her away so I could watch her face as I spoke.

"Caitha, if we can't say our betrothal vows here, today, before I take ship, there's nothing I'd like better than to say them here come Beltane. But—"

The skin around her eyes tightened, and the line of her mouth hardened. The muscles of her shoulders stiffened beneath my hands. "But?" she repeated.

"I may not be able to return for Beltane," I said. "I may not be able to come back here for far longer than I'd like to be away. If my father dies, I shall be Prince of Skai." Just saying the words caused a ripple of chilled disbelief to rattle down my spine. *Prince of Skai . . . Me!* I tried to ignore the odd sensation. "I may have to remain on Skerry."

She reached up and put two fingers over my mouth to silence me. "You could be Prince of Skai in exile here in Tyra at Broche Rhuidh just as easily as you could be Prince of Skai in exile on Skerry," she said. "And you'd be far more comfortable here. You'd be among friends and kin."

It would be so easy to agree with her. She was right. One

place of exile was just as good as any other place of exile. In relief, I opened my mouth to agree with her, to tell her I would come back here to be with her when my business in Skerry was complete. But what I said was something entirely different from what I intended, and it startled me.

"Caitha, my father chose to take his people to Skerry. And his people chose to follow him. Those people will be my people should it happen that I become Prince of Skai." All those years of Fyld's training before I came to Tyra, listening to him speak of duty and honor had impressed me far more than I had given it credit for. And the twelve years of training with Kenzie, watching him live those same ideals of honor and duty had more than left their mark, too. I hadn't realized how deeply they had planted their seeds within my heart and spirit.

Caitha stood watching me, sadness and something else in her eyes. I tried again.

"I could send for you," I said. "You could come to Skerry . . ." I let my voice trail off as I watched her. The light seemed to go out of her face, and something darkened in her eyes, something that could have been sorrow, or regret — or even anger.

"I'll not leave Tyra, Gareth," she said quietly. "This is my home. It will always be my home; it's where I belong. I could never be happy elsewhere."

"But you could be mistress of Skerry Keep," I said. "Wife to the Prince of Skai. Surely —"

She straightened her back and tilted up her chin. The skin was soft and smooth, but the jaw beneath it was iron in its pride. "I am daughter to the Clan Laird of Broche Rhuidh," she said, "daughter to the First Laird of the Council of Clans. I can aspire to nothing higher than that. You could be kin-son to him, and mayhaps next Master of Sword. For an exiled prince, that is high office indeed."

I shook my head in real regret. "No, Caitha. The yrSkai will expect me to be with them on Skerry. And they'd certainly expect—and have a right to expect it, too—that my children would be born in Celi. My son will be the next Prince of Skai, and he should be born on Celae soil, even if it's Skerry and not Skai."

"I'm not yrSkai," she said. "And neither are you, really. You're as Tyran as I am." She reached up and touched the earring that dangled from the lobe of my left ear, then ran her finger along the braid at my temple. It wasn't red-gold as were most Tyran clansmen's braids. Mine was as glossy as theirs, mayhaps, but it was black— midnight black that sent back blue highlights into the sun. Very different from a Tyran clansman's hair. "Look at you," she said, her voice low and intense. "You're Tyran, not yrSkai. And hardly the Prince of Skai. You have no bheancoran. You carry no Rune Blade." She put her hand to the hilt of the two-handed Tyran sword rising behind my left shoulder. "Even the way you carry your sword is Tyran."

I looked down at her. I saw love for me in her eyes, along with the regret and sorrow. But there was an implacability about the corners of her mouth that told me how it would be. "You won't change your mind?" I asked without much hope.

"No, Gareth, I won't. But I'll be waiting here for your swift return."

"And if I can't return swiftly?"

She laughed, the gaiety forced, almost harsh. "Then I shall probably become betrothed to Comyn at the Lammas festival after this Beltane," she said. "He's a braw and bonny man, and my father's near as fond of him as he is of you. He'd approve the match."

I dropped my hands to my sides. "I see," I said. My mouth felt almost too dry to form the words clearly. "Good-bye, then, Caitha." I added the traditional farewell. "May you go always in joy and light." I started to leave.

"Gareth —"

I turned. She lifted the bundle of the plaid from the bench and thrust it into my arms.

"Take this," she said. "I made it for you."

"I've no right to it," I said.

"I made it for you," she repeated. "And in Skerry, no one will care if you wear the gold stripe. Besides, this willna keep anyone but you warm." She fumbled for the edge of the fabric and held it up. In one corner, just above the fringe, a glint of red-gold caught the light, shimmering beside a smudged glimmer of blue-black. "See? I wove my own hair into the warp and yours into the weft, so you'll always think of me when you wear it. And you'll be warm in the cold because of it."

"Caitha, I can't accept it." I tried to give it back to her. She put her hands behind her back again and refused to take it. Finally, I nodded. I took off my cloak and laid it on the bench, then swirled the plaid around my shoulders in a swift, practiced motion. She produced a plain silver brooch and pinned the plaid securely. Before she stepped back, she stretched up to kiss my cheek. She looked at me, and for a moment, I thought she might say something. But she shook her head and hurried from the room, her back and shoulders straight and stiff.

I stood there alone, my fingers smoothing the thickly woven wool of the plaid. Then I squared my own shoulders and went into the corridor. There was no sign of Caitha. I hurried down the corridor to the staircase. Comyn was expecting me on the jetty even now. I wondered briefly what he would say when he saw the plaid.

The courier ship, not much longer than the lifeboats we manned to pluck men from wrecks along the coast, lay against the jetty, secured by a heavy hawser to a stone bollard. It rose and fell sedately with the rhythm of the sea swell, its bright sails furled against the swaying masts. The five men of the crew tended unhurriedly to the chores that would see the ship ready to sail in a few minutes. Comyn sat in the stern by the helm, poring over a sheaf of charts, his lower lip caught thoughtfully between his teeth. He looked up as I approached.

"You're ready?" he asked.

"I suppose so." I tossed my meager carry-pack aboard. "As ready as I'm ever likely to be, at any event."

I saw the moment when he noticed the narrow gold stripe in the plaid I wore. He said nothing, but one eyebrow rose in an eloquent and ironic gesture that made him look the image of his father. Something that might well have been the beginning of a smile tugged at the corner of his mouth, but was gone before I could be sure. With elaborately casual nonchalance he turned back to his study of his charts.

Before I could take him to task, someone called my name. I turned to see Eibhlin, Comyn's little sister, flying down the jetty, her rose-gold hair streaming behind her. I dropped to one knee to catch her as she flung her arms around my neck. She sobbed her farewells into the front of my shirt, her face buried in the soft wool of my plaid.

"Oh, Gareth, I shall miss you so," she cried, her lovely little face filled with heartbroken woe. Even at seven, she showed promise of becoming as beautiful as her mother.

I stroked her bright hair. "I won't be gone forever, Littlest," I said.

She looked up at me, her green eyes tragic and woebegone. "It will seem like forever," she said. "But don't worry, Gareth. If you come home and find that Caitha has married Comyn, I shall marry you, if you'll wait for me to grow up."

I glanced at Comyn over her head. His face glowed

bright scarlet, and he would not meet my eyes. I felt the corner of my mouth twitch, but I dared not laugh aloud. It was my turn to feign elaborate unconcern.

"It's very kind of you to offer," I said to Eibhlin, once I was certain I had my voice under control. "But I'm very much afraid even the gods and goddesses themselves would frown on such a union. You are, after all, my sister."

"Foster sister," she said defensively.

"Aye, true, only foster sister," I said. "But also first cousin." I hugged her, then held her away. "When you decide to marry, Littlest, the man you choose will believe himself the luckiest man alive."

She considered that, her tears forgotten. "Do you really think so?"

"Of course. How could he not? Now, give me another kiss because I've got to go so we don't miss the tide."

The crew launched the little courier ship. Deft and efficient, they pushed away from the stone jetty and raised the big, square mainsail to catch the wind. I tucked myself down onto the deck near the small cabin sitting amidships, not part of the crew and therefore left with nothing to do but stay out of the way.

Comyn didn't look at me, and a dusky color sat in his cheeks and throat. He stood near the stern, the wheel in his hands, an expression of concentration on his face as he guided the little ship across the harbor toward the gap between the Hook and the cliffs.

I said nothing and turned my attention to the sea ahead of us. Comyn took us smartly through the gap on a shallow tack that gave us all the impetus the tide and the southwesterly wind could provide. Beyond the harbor, the open sea rolled in huge, glassy swells that came from the northwest, still following the gale that had already dissipated.

Comyn glanced at the sky, then shifted his weight slightly at the helm. The ship should have wallowed and staggered among the swells, but it slid smoothly across the surface, climbing the waves and skating down into the troughs between like a water bug crossing a still pond.

Gradually, the tide turned, and the seas were steep and breaking. We altered course to the northwest, sheeting in the sails until they were almost flat as we came on to the wind. It was cold then, with the wind on our faces and the spray slatting against our skin as the little ship beat to windward, bucking the seas and bursting through the crests of the waves. Water cascaded from the bows, flinging spume back in drifts solid as sea mist.

I had seldom been at sea with Comyn, and now I thought I saw him in a completely different light. He was a competent swordsman among a people renowned for the excellence of their swordmasters. But it was here, at sea, among the swells and wind and tides, that he truly came alive. His body all but shimmered with the vitality and power flowing through him, as if he were working magic.

Magic . . .

It might not be such a far-fetched idea. Comyn was a descendant of Red Kian of Skai, a man who had wielded gentle Celae magic with enough strength to defeat one of the most powerful sorcerers of Maedun. And he was kin to the Enchanter Donaugh, who was brother to King Tiernyn and the most powerful enchanter in Celi. The magic had come down through Kian's blood to Keylan's and then through Brynda's to Comyn. Why should he not have magic, and why shouldn't his magic manifest itself as an affinity with the sea, which was in his blood just as surely as the magic?

I glanced down at my own hands. And I? Did I have magic? The only difference in my ancestry and Comyn's was our parentage. His mother was my father's sister. Could I have inherited any of the magic that flowed like music through our family? But what would it feel like to have magic? What was it like to know that the rhythm of magic beat within one like the cadence of heart or breath?

Fyld told me Eryd would have had magic. Even at eight, he showed signs of a remarkable ability to use the webs of magic that ran like streams through the air and the very earth itself in Skai. And there was, of course, a girl-child in the village who gave signs of growing up to be bheancoran.

The Maedun had finished all of that—Eryd's magic, a young girl's promise. All of it, gone. Nothing left but me. Only me, without magic, without a bheancoran, and caught between two peoples. One had to pity Skai.

5

Toward evening the wind died, and the seas calmed to a series of vast, rolling swells of glassy water. Comyn turned the wheel over to one of the sailors, then dropped into a crouch beside me where I sat in the lee of the low cabin, my back to the bulkhead. Two of the crew lay sleeping in the cramped little cabin. As the passenger, I was entitled to sleep in the cabin, too, but I always found the tiny space too airless. Rather than prove myself to be less the sailor than I fancied myself, I preferred to stay outside on deck.

"At this rate, we'll make landfall sometime near dawn," Comyn said. "And mayhaps Skerry by midafternoon."

"We've made good time so far," I agreed.

"Aye, we have that." He paused, and I got the impression he was choosing his next words carefully. "Gareth, I didna approach Caitha to court her," he said quietly. Even in the dim light, the dusky color in his cheeks was quite apparent. "I know you two are all but promised."

"Don't trouble yourself about it," I said more bleakly than I had intended. I quoted an ancient aphorism. "No woman is won until she's wed."

His teeth flashed white in the gloom. "Aye," he agreed. "And even then, sometimes not."

I laughed. It sounded bitter to my ears, but it was a genuine laugh. "Aye. Even then, sometimes not."

The wind dropped to little more than a breeze as sunset glowed in the west over the water. Night brought a mist that hazed the moon and obscured the stars. It rose around the little ship in wisps and tendrils at first, that soon braided themselves together into thick ropes. The ropes thickened into swirls, then into a dense blanket of fog. When I looked up, the mist had blurred the outlines of the masts and sails above my head. If it weren't for the gentle belling out of the sails and the occasional slap and splash of water rushing along the hull, I couldn't be sure the ship really moved at all.

Comyn took the helm as the fog thickened. A faint line appeared between his brows as he peered intently ahead, as if through his intensity, he could pierce the mist by the strength of his gaze alone.

The fog muffled the ship like a blanket, smothering all sound. Occasionally, water rippled beneath the hull, startling me out of my half doze into full wakefulness. Each time it happened, I looked toward the stern. Comyn hadn't moved. He still stood, hands firm upon the spokes of the wheel, his gaze fixed straight ahead. And all the while, that odd frown of concentration puckered his brow.

Some time after midnight, Comyn turned the helm over to one of the sailors. They spoke together in low murmurs for a moment or two, then Comyn dropped onto the low bench beside me. He leaned back against the bulkhead of the tiny cabin, letting his head tip back to rest against the smooth planking.

"Skerryharbor by midmorning, I think," he said quietly. "Noon at the latest. We've turned west above the shoulder of Celi now."

I looked up. Without the stars to give me a sense of direction, I was lost. In this fog, it would be too easy to lose the ability to tell up from down, let alone east from west, or north from south. I smiled and shook my head. "If you tell me so," I said. "We could be halfway across the tides of Annwn for all I can cipher."

His teeth flashed white in a grin as he reached into his belt pouch and pulled out his Wayfinder. Held within the hollow glass disk, a narrow sliver of lodestone swung from a slender thread. On the bottom of the disk, four lines dividing the circle into quarters had been etched into the glass, one for each direction. Comyn turned so he faced the bow of the ship, the Wayfinder held in the palm of his hand. The lodestone quivered, seeking the Nail Star, and pointed to starboard.

"That's north," he said, pointing. "And that"—he pointed to the bow—"is west. We turned across the shoulder only an hour ago." He put the Wayfinder back into his pouch and pulled his plaid around him, yawning. "Feargus will call me when the mist lifts after sunrise. I'll be able to tell you exactly where we are then." He curled down into the thick wool of his plaid and closed his eyes. In moments, his breathing settled into the long, slow rhythms of sleep.

I didn't sleep. I dozed, but fragmented, vivid images of gleaming and glittering swords and towering standing stones kept yanking me awake, and I was surprised to find myself still on the little ship in the middle of a fog-shrouded sea.

Dawn approached, and the mist lightened and took on a faint, pearly glow in the east. Still dazed and half-asleep, I watched it swirl gently, the light dancing and swaying along the line of the horizon. The swirling of the fog made the line of light along the horizon behind us appear ragged and frayed even as it glowed from within.

As I watched, half-mesmerized, I thought I saw figures appear in the eddying opalescence. A young boy carrying a sword half-hidden in his tunic threw a surreptitious glance over his shoulder as he crept through the tall winter-browned grass. Startled, I sat up straighter, then leaned forward to watch. With no warning, I fell right into the brightening whorls of mist and the pictures forming there . . .

The young cowherd hummed under his breath as he guided his charges home from the pasture. The cows moved lazily, but wasted little time as they ambled toward the byre and the relief of the milk pail. He held the sword, bundled securely in the tattered sheepskin cloak, snug against his chest and belly, arms wrapped around the bulky package. I was as aware of his heartbeat thudding against his ribs in excitement and hope as I was aware of my own pounding in my chest, and I knew his thoughts as well as I knew my own. His name, oddly enough, was Ralf, as a young friend of mine in Skerry had also been named.

The sword was truly a magnificent weapon—at least as magnificent as Kingmaker, the sword in all the stories about King Tiernyn. The boy knew he himself could not wield it against the Maedun, but certainly his brother Ban could. Ban was not yet old enough for the spell to twist him into knots of agony if he moved to harm one of the hated Maedun Somber Riders, but he was already big enough and strong enough to swing a sword like a warrior out of the songs. Nothing would ever bring his mother or his sister back, taken for sport and pleasure by the Somber Riders, but some small retribution would help ease the pain of loss.

Caught up in his dreams of vengeance, he didn't see the Somber Rider in the paddock yard until he was nearly past the byre. The Somber Rider stood leaning negligently against the split-rail paddock fence, watching Ralf's father, who was bent over the raised hoof of the big bay gelding. The Somber Rider wore the lightning-flash emblem of a courier on the shoulder of his tunic. A message pouch emblazoned with the same symbol hung across the horse's back behind the saddle. Around the man's neck hung an intricately worked silver talisman that allowed him to pass unharmed through the Dead Lands on the eastern slopes of the Spine of Celi.

Ralf's father, Biggen, worked diligently over the horse's hoof with a hoof pick, worrying at the sharp stone wedged into the tender frog of the foot. The Somber Rider made a restless gesture and said something to Biggen. Ralf couldn't hear the words, but the tone was obvious enough. The arrogant impatience and scorn were too familiar.

Biggen held himself completely motionless for half a heartbeat, then straightened, throwing the hoof pick to the ground. But even as he opened his mouth to vent his anger, Ralf felt the slithery quiver in the *air that meant the spell was working close to him. Biggen went to his knees, his mouth open, his eyes wide, his face twisted with agony although no sound escaped him. He wrapped his arms across his belly and folded himself around the pain, his breath coming in harsh, tearing gasps.*

Ralf stood frozen, frightened and angry both, but unable to move. Then Ban came running out of the byre, shouting incoherently. But even as he approached Biggen and the Somber Rider, the Somber Rider turned his opaque glance on the lad. Ralf felt that strange swarming sensation in the air again. Moments later, Ban lay writhing on the ground beside his father.

Sick with terror and the realization that Ban could not now use the sword, Ralf stared at the Somber Rider. The man turned and met the boy's eyes, and his hand went to the hilt of the sword he wore strapped to his left hip. Ralf's knees felt as if they had turned to water. Something fell with a clang and lay at his feet, gleaming in the gray light of the overcast day.

The Somber Rider took a step toward Ralf. The boy leapt back, only then realizing that he had dropped the sword in his terror. He backed away again as the Rider advanced. But the Rider had lost interest in him. The man bent and picked up the fallen sword, an expression of intrigued interest on his face. He held the sword up to the light, then tested its balance with two practice swipes through the air, forehand and backhand. The sword seemed too heavy for his hand, but he took it back to the horse. With a complete lack of concern, he stepped over the still-writhing form of Ban and tucked the sword through the straps that held the message pouch to the back of the saddle. Without a glance at either Ban or Biggen, he rode out of the paddock yard and onto the track that joined with the main road leading west into the mountains.

His back against the rough wall of the byre, Ralf stuffed his fist into his mouth to hold back the bitter tears of rage and shame and sorrow. Somewhere a long way away, a young man asleep on a ship cried out in horror that the Maedun now had in their possession a Celi Rune Blade. Bane. The sword of the Prince of Skai.

• • •

Comyn's voice shouting my name brought me out of my reverie with a start. I glanced around, dizzy and disoriented. So closely had I joined with Ralf in the dream, I almost expected to see the byre and the paddock yard, and my father and brother recovering slowly from the torture of the spell. Finding myself instead sitting amidships with my back against the cabin of the little courier ship made my head spin for a moment. I blinked, then shook my head to clear it.

The shining mist I had been watching blew away, evaporating into the rising fog. Nothing remained of the dream or vision but wisps of memory that blew away as quickly and as completely as the mist. In moments, they were gone, and I was left with only a vague sense of having dreamed, but unable to recall what I had dreamed of. A nebulous uneasiness stirred in my chest, but vanished too quickly for me to find a reason for its being there.

"How very odd . . ." I thought aloud, then stood to answer Comyn's impatient summons.

He stood in the bow of the ship, beckoning me eagerly. I made my way forward to join him.

"There." A wide grin split his face as he pointed. "See it? Skerryharbor. I've brought you home safe and sound, Gareth, as I promised I would."

And so he had. Even through the thick fog and the dark of the night. I glanced at him, then grinned, too. "Ye look a bit like that cat that filched the honey cake," I said. "Might it be that ye werena quite so sure what the lifting of the mist might show us?" But his gift had brought us unerringly through the mist and the fog to within a bowshot of the harbor mouth itself. I had no difficulty believing that Adriel of the Waters herself guided Comyn.

Comyn glared at me indignantly. "Not sure?" he repeated, then made a disgusted noise with teeth and tongue.

"Tcha-a-a-a. For a remark like that, you deserve to be thrown overboard so you can bluidy well swim the rest of the way." The corners of his mouth twitched, and he shook his head. "Well, no, mayhaps not. We wouldna want the salt water to ruin that marvelous new plaid of yours, would we?"

Skerryharbor had changed greatly in the twelve years I had been away. I don't know why that should have surprised me. Even as I was sailing out of the harbor all those years ago, teams of men had been at work getting rid of the old, temporary structures and building new, stout, solid ones.

When my father's people arrived here after the calamitous Maedun invasion, nearly the first thing they did was enlarge and rebuild the old hunting lodge already on the island. By the time I left, the lodge was no longer recognizable. It had become a stronghold, surrounded by high walls and towers and turrets. Within the cobbled courtyard lay barracks and stables, smithies and bakehouses, and all the other workshops to keep a lord's house running smoothly. For many years, the stronghold, now called Skerry Keep, or sometimes Dun Warden after the looming visage of Ben Warden behind it, had been the only structure in Skerryharbor not made of mud and wattle.

When I had left, most of Skerryharbor still had the seedy, dismal appearance of a temporary camp. Now, it had a substantial look, an air of strength and permanence. Stone-built buildings took the place of the wattle-and-daub huts, lying in a sweeping curve along the semicircle of the harbor. There were not only dwellings there, but shops and taverns and markets.

Behind the houses, neat, well-ordered fields climbed the lower flanks of Ben Warden, stretching north to the forbidding pinnacles of Ben Roth and south into the thick forests robing the slopes of Ben Aislin. Snow still lay thick and heavy in the upper reaches of the mountains, but was nearly gone by the harbor. With the winter, the fields were bare, all crops long since harvested and stored against the arrival of the cold and snow. Sheep round with thick fleece and lambs nearly ready to drop wandered in the pastures to the north of the tilled fields.

The exiled yrSkai had settled in with a will and a determination that was completely typical. My uncle Kenzie would have called it sheer, mule-headed stubbornness; my father would have called it courage and determination. I think they both would have been right.

Comyn took the helm to steer the tiny courier ship into the harbor. I stood in the bow, watching the details of Skerryharbor become more clear and distinct as we neared the long stone jetty thrusting out into the belly of the harbor. Behind me, the crew scrambled to take in some of the canvas, shortening the sails to slow us down for docking.

Three horsemen rode through the wide-flung gates of Skerry Keep and galloped down the wide road leading to the harbor. Even from here, I recognized the lead rider. The erect posture and forceful grace of Fyld ap Huw, my father's Captain of the Company, was unmistakable.

The horsemen reached the root of the jetty just as Comyn swung the bow around and let the ship drift up to the stone pier. The ship had barely enough momentum to close the final gap of less than an arm's length between its wooden hull and the jetty as one of the sailors stepped ashore with the hawser to secure the ship to the bollard. I bent to pick up the bundle containing my possessions. When I looked up again, Fyld stood waiting at the end of the jetty. I stepped out onto the solid stone, then hesitated.

Comyn jumped across the wale onto the jetty and caught my arm. "Give our regards to your father and all else," he said. "We'll not be coming to the Keep with you."

My heart sank at the thought of losing his moral support. I didn't want to face my father alone. "You can't stay?" I asked, dismayed.

He glanced over his right shoulder to the west. "There's more weather building up out there. If we're to get back to Tyra this season, we'd best be leaving with the outgoing tide. We've barely enough time to reprovision."

I nodded. "I can see that you'd not want to finish out the winter here." I took a deep breath. "I'll pass on your regards to those as should have them." I reached out and grasped his arm just below the elbow. He clasped my arm in return, and we stood for a moment, uncertain of what to say next. "Adriel guide your return, Comyn."

"And all the seven gods and goddesses be with you and your father, Gareth," he replied softly. "Take care, and come back to Tyra when you can."

I nodded again, then turned and walked to where Fyld waited for me. I looked once over my shoulder, but Comyn was already engrossed in conversation, with a man who was obviously the dockmaster, and wasn't looking at me. My heart thundered in my chest. All I wanted to do was turn, leap back into the little ship, and run as fast as I could back to Tyra, where I would not have to face my father or deal with the painful reality that I might become Prince of Skai far too soon.

But Kenzie had trained me too well. Duty above all. The need to carry out a duty could sustain where courage might fail. I straightened my shoulders and went to meet the man who had raised me in my father's stead.

Fyld ap Huw stood quietly at the foot of the jetty, watching me as I slowly made my way down the long, stone causeway toward him. A tall man, Fyld, and powerfully built. The hilt of his sword rose above his left shoulder, left free of the dark

Skai blue cloak he wore wrapped tightly around himself.
There might have been more strands of pure silver-white in
the blue-black of his hair now, but to my eyes, he had not
changed much at all in the twelve years since he had seen me
off on my journey to Tyra from this selfsame pier. He held his
body relaxed but alert, hardly moving except once to hand
the reins of his horse to the man who stood behind him to the
left. His face was as carefully expressionless as his posture; I
could gather no indication from Fyld of whether my father
still lived or not.

I stopped within arm's length of him and merely stood
there, watching him as intently as he watched me. When I was
a child, he had seemed the tallest and strongest of men. He was
perhaps not quite as tall as I remembered him, now only a fin-
gersbreadth taller than I, but his look of strength and determination had not diminished with time, nor with my gaining
inches of height. If he thought anything of my kilt and plaid, or
the leather-bound hilt of the hand-and-a-half sword made of
good Tyran steel that rose from behind my own left shoulder,
nothing showed on his face. Those shrewd, intensely blue eyes
of his flicked quickly from my head to my feet and back again,
taking my measure. If he judged me as a man rather than the
stripling of twelve he had last seen, no trace of his conclusion
showed in his face. Fyld ap Huw was not now, nor had he ever
been, a man one wished to face across a table at cards.

I broke the silence between us. "Rhan delivered your
message safely and I have come home as you requested," I
said.

He nodded gravely. "So I see," he said. He made the first
motions of dropping to one knee to honor me as the son of the
Prince of Skai. My heart leapt in my breast in something akin
to fear, and I reached out to clutch his arm.

"No," I blurted. "No, Fyld. You don't kneel to me. Never
you." I looked into his face, searching for a trace of the laugh-

ing man who had so often ruffled my hair in affection, or
swatted my bottom for much needed discipline. That was the
man I desperately needed to see right now, not this stiff and
distant soldier sworn to my father.

"Fyld?" I asked.

His expression softened, and he smiled. "Ah, lad," he said
quietly. "I've missed you so these last twelve years. You've
grown into a man, as I knew you would." He tilted his head
back and studied my face, then smiled again. "And you're the
image of your mother."

With that, he opened his arms, and I stepped into his
embrace as if I were still twelve.

"Welcome home, my lord Gareth," he said. "Now, we
must hurry to see your father. Brennen is waiting to see you
again." He stepped away and straightened, becoming again
the soldier. "I have a horse for you."

He didn't wait for me to reply, gave me no chance to ask
after my father's health. He swung himself into the saddle,
waited until I had mounted the horse he indicated was for me,
then set out at a gallop toward the Keep, where my father
awaited my arrival.

6

*I followed the bright Skai blue of Fyld's cloak as we rode at a hand gal-*lop up the gently curving track to the gates of the stronghold. Thin threads of smoke rose from the chimneys of the houses we passed and were lost in the low overhang of the clouds. Patches of grainy snow lingered in areas of deep shade where hedgerows or dry-stone walls met, dividing the tillable land into fields. I could not see the peaks of any of the three mountains on the island. Ben Warden, the nearest and the highest, had lost itself in the clouds that bulged so low the shrine only a bowshot or two above the Keep lay invisible in the shifting mist.

Fyld rode bent forward in the saddle, looking neither right nor left, intent only on bringing us to the house and to the chamber where my father presumably lay waiting for my return. I had not even had a chance to ask Fyld what ailed my father, what accident had struck him so low that he lay dying.

Even now, I found it difficult to believe that my father could be or might be dying. All through my growing up, he may have been a man with very little love to share with a small boy, but he had always been a strong man, a good leader to the yrSkai who had followed him into exile on these northern isles. He smiled very seldom and laughed never, but no one had ever seen him with his head bowed in despair or defeat, no one had ever seen him slump in resignation, nor had anyone ever had even so much as a hint from him that he might ever give up. It was hard to picture all that strength drained from my father's solid and muscular body. That unbending, unyielding strength had acted as a beacon for the exiled yrSkai, and they took it as their own. Mayhaps my aunt Brynda was right when she said that the yrSkai's intractable stubbornness is his greatest strength and, occasionally, his greatest weakness.

We clattered through the wide-flung gates and into the courtyard. It had grown since I had been here last. Fyld drew his horse to a halt and slid to the ground in one smooth motion, tossing the reins to a young boy who came running to catch them. I dismounted more slowly and handed the reins to the boy, who grinned widely and led the horses away. Fyld made an impatient gesture, commanding me to hurry and come with him, and started up the wide stone steps, taking them two at a time. I followed quickly.

Through an iron-grilled man-gate in the wall behind the bakeshops, I glimpsed the winter-seared remains of a garden. I thought I saw a graceful pattern of rosebushes and herbal borders, now dried to blackened sticks by cold. Someone had tried to bring some of the grace and charm of Dun Eidon to Skerry Keep. I wondered if it had been Fyld's wife Rhia, who had loved gardening almost as much as she loved her husband and children.

Fyld waited for me at the top of the steps, fingers tapping impatiently against his thigh. I hurried up the stone treads, and he whirled and led the way indoors before I had quite gained the top landing.

We entered the Great Hall, a long room with a hearth at either end. It was similar to the Great Hall of the Clanhold of Broche Rhuidh, but much smaller. Fyld didn't pause, but made his way across the tiled floor to a set of stairs leading up to a wide gallery overlooking the Great Hall. This was new since I had left. Work had just barely begun on the second level the spring before I took ship for Tyra. I assumed the family quarters and my father's solar were now located up here.

Fyld led me along the gallery. Several of the doors leading off the gallery were open, and I caught another glimpse of the garden through the window of one of the large rooms just before we turned a corner into another new wing of the Keep. Fyld stopped before the first door and raised his hand to knock.

My belly tightened into a hard, cold knot. I took a deep breath and found I hadn't enough moisture left in my mouth to dampen my lips. My heart made a creditable effort to tear itself loose from its moorings in my chest. Resolutely, I straightened my shoulders, determined not to quake in front of my father, or anyone else, for that matter.

I didn't recognize the woman who opened the door. She was Tyadda, one of the strange, fey race who had inhabited the Isle of Celi when the Celae came. This woman was pure-blood Tyadda, though, I thought. She was small and slender, her dark gold hair and golden brown eyes as delicate and lovely as a spray of blossoms. She stepped back to admit Fyld and me, glancing at me curiously as we walked past her. She crossed the outer room and put her hand to the latch of the inner door.

"He's awake and expecting you," she said softly. She looked at me again. "It's good to see you home again, my lord Gareth."

I was not used to be addressed as *my lord*. It startled me, but I nodded with what I hoped was suitable graciousness. I still didn't recognize her, but she wore the cinquefoil of a Tyadda herbal healer on the left shoulder of her gown. She opened the door and stood back, ushering us in with a grace-ful gesture of her hand.

Fyld's message to me in Tyra had told me my father lay very ill, and young Rhan spoke of an accident. Kenzie, Brynda, and I had discussed his illness and tried to assess his condition from the few words Fyld had written and the sketchy informa-tion from his son. The presence of the healer in my father's outer chamber reinforced the message of serious illness. But nothing, neither Fyld's message, nor the discussions with Kenzie and Brynda, nor the attendance of the healer, prepared me for what I saw when she opened that door.

Brennen, Prince of Skai, was a big man—a man in whom our family's Tyran heritage showed plainly in both his size and his red-gold hair. The man I remembered stood tall and broad, his hair aflame, webs of muscle woven tight and firm across the heavy bones of his chest, shoulders, arms, and thighs, his belly flat and strong. The sword I needed two hands to wield properly he could have swung easily with one hand.

When the door to the bedchamber opened, the man on the bed turned with painful effort to look at us. Gone was the gleaming red-gold hair, replaced by lank strands stained a pinkish gray. The dim light could not hide the shocking emaciation of his face and body. The skull-shape of his face and head showed plainly through the sallow, sagging skin. Only his eyes, still brilliantly golden brown, looked alive, blazing below the white ridge of his eyebrows. My father was three or four years younger than my uncle Kenzie; he appeared twenty years older.

"Gareth," he cried hoarsely, plainly startled to see me. "What are you doing here?"

Even now, I thought. Even now, he didn't want to see me. "I was sent for," I said.

"By whom? I didn't send for you."

"I sent for him, my lord Prince," Fyld said quietly. "I believed there was need."

My father sagged back against his pillows. "I told you not to send for Brynda or Gareth. The seas are still too dangerous."

"But I'm here, and I'm safe," I said.

He said nothing.

"What happened?" I asked, the question torn from me despite my determination to wait until someone offered an explanation. "By all the seven gods and goddesses, Father, what happened to you?"

A smile resembling nothing more than a rictus twitched at my father's pale lips. "Gored by a wild boar hunting," he said briefly, gesturing toward his left thigh.

"And wound fever?" I asked.

"So it seems," he said. His voice sounded rusty and hoarse, as if he seldom used it anymore. The rich resonance and timbre I remembered was gone. He lifted a skeletal hand and beckoned to me. "Welcome back to Skerry, Gareth. Come here and let me look at you. Let me see how much you've grown since you left."

I noticed he didn't say *Welcome home*. He had never looked upon Skerry as home, and never would. I crossed the room, my mouth still dry, my heart hammering in my chest. He pushed himself up into a sitting position and looked up at me, a frown drawing the heavy white eyebrows together above the bridge of his nose. A shadow passed across his eyes, and the skin around his mouth tightened and paled slightly.

"You favor your mother," he said at last. "But you always did."

I remembered little of my brother Eryd, or my sister Lisle, but I knew both of them had been born with our father's red hair and brown-gold eyes. Only I had inherited our mother's black hair and blue eyes.

My father fell back limply against the pillows, as if the last of his strength had drained from him with his words. For a moment, he lay, breathing shallowly. Only a faint twitching at the corner of one eye spoke of the power of the pain coursing through his body. The Tyadda woman glided between us and bent over him to hold a goblet to his lips.

He drank the potion and lay back, his eyes closed. His face gradually cleared as the medication in the potion took hold and eased his pain. He opened his eyes and looked at me again.

"Kenzie and Brynda raised you well, it seems," he said quietly. He gestured toward my kilt and plaid. "I sent Kenzie and Brynda a young yrSkai, and it seems they've returned to me a Tyran clansman."

At my side, my left hand curled into a tight fist. "Could you expect anything different from Kenzie dav Aidan?" I asked lightly enough. "I am as he trained me to be."

My father's expression did not change. He merely said, "I trust you use your sword as well as your uncle Kenzie, too?"

I reached up and touched the hilt of the sword behind my left shoulder. "I use it well enough," I said. "I havena the strength Kenzie has, but I'm smaller and more agile. I make him work for his victories."

My father nodded, then lay back against his pillows and closed his eyes. The bones looked too sharp beneath the wax-pale skin over cheek and forehead, as if they might pierce it through. "That was the reason I sent you," he said. "I knew Kenzie could make a swordsman out of you . . ."

His voice trailed off, but I heard the unsaid, "And a man . . ." What he didn't say, or even hint at, was who would make a prince out of me.

"He taught me well enough," I said. "As you knew he would."

He smiled faintly, but said nothing. His eyes had closed on their own, as if the lids were too heavy for him to hold open. Pain etched deep lines between his eyebrows, to either side of his nose, and at the corners of his mouth. I glanced up at the woman, then to Fyld.

"Is there not a Gifted Healer on the whole of Skerry or Marddyn?" I asked.

Fyld shook his head. "We have none but Meaghean here, who has done wonders for your father."

The woman made a helpless gesture and glanced at my father, who appeared to be sleeping. "He has forbidden us even to try to go to Skai to see if we can find a Gifted Healer."

My father opened his eyes then. "No yrSkai here shall risk his life on a fool's errand like that," he said, his voice hoarse and dry. "I forbid it."

"I could go," I said.

He raised himself on one elbow. The effort it cost him showed plainly on his face. The lines drawn there by pain deepened, and the skin seemed to stretch more tightly across his cheeks and temple, emphasizing the sharpness of the bones beneath.

"You will not go," he said firmly. "You will not risk yourself in such a foolish task. I forbid it."

I looked at him, lying wasted and worn and near death, and the anger that smoldered under my breastbone burst into flaring rage. "You cannot forbid me to try to save your life," I told him sharply. "I will go today."

"You will not . . ."

"How can you be so blazing stubborn?" I demanded. "Look at you, lying there nearly dead. And too cursed obstinate to ask for help, or accept it when it's offered freely."

"You dare to speak to me that way?" Two splotches of hectic color stained his sallow cheeks. He tried to raise himself off the pillow, but his strength deserted him. He fell back, his eyes blazing. "You're just as willful and headstrong as ever. Did Kenzie teach you no discipline at all, then?"

"Aye, he taught me all I needed. And he taught me to do my duty as I saw it, and not let anything stand in my way." A vision of the sword swimming in its waterlight flashed through my head. It glowed softly and gently in my mind, and

I could almost reach out and grasp the plain, leather-bound hilt. "I will go," I said.

He forced himself into a sitting position, gasping for breath, all the color draining from his face. "As Prince of Skai and your father, I deserve and demand your loyalty and obedience," he said harshly. "You will not go."

I took a deep breath. "As your son and heir, what do I deserve?" I asked. "What can I demand? Am I not entitled to serve where I think it best?"

"I forbid it," my father cried. He fell back on the bed, exhausted, his eyes closed. Meaghean hurried forward and held the goblet to his lips again. She didn't look at me as she tended to my father.

I settled my plaid about my shoulders and turned to leave. Fyld reached out and caught my arm.

"He has forbidden it, Gareth," he said softly. "You will not leave here."

"Are you content to stand here and watch him die?" I demanded.

Pain flashed across his face. He had been with my father for more years than I had been alive, and was as close to him as any man could be to a brother. "He has forbidden us to go," he whispered, then looked away.

The anger rose up in my chest again. I shook off his arm. "If I am to be Prince of Skai, I will want a Healer in my house, and I shall want the Rune Blade Bane. When he wakes, tell him I've gone to fetch both."

The woman glanced at me. "You might look for Tyadda fastnesses in Skai," she said softly. "There will be Healers there." She lowered her eyes, then turned her attention back to my father.

As I turned, Fyld reached out to take my arm to stop me, but I avoided him easily enough and strode out of the bedchamber. I found my way back to the Great Hall, then to the courtyard. The stableboy came running out as I hurried toward the stable. Moments later, I was on the horse and speeding down the track toward the jetty in the harbor.

What I had meant to do, of course, was go storming down to the jetty, climb back into Comyn's ship, and sail heroically out into the gathering storm to Skai, poised starkly and dramatically in the bow of the ship. However, it's extremely difficult to make an effective and dignified exit when the ship one had been planning to employ for all that high drama was a good two bowshots beyond the harbor mouth out to sea, and certainly well beyond hailing reach. And swim for it, I would not.

I swore softly under my breath, then turned and looked up at the stronghold of Skerry Keep, secure and dark on its high perch on the shoulder of the mountain. That same unreasoning anger churned in my belly again, and I tasted the sour bitterness of frustration in the back of my throat. I still wasn't certain where to direct most of the anger. Certainly part of it was at my father, unchanged in these last twelve years, and still unwilling to admit that, if I was all he had left, he needs must make the best of a bad bargain. And part of it was directed at Fyld and Meaghean, the Tyadda herbal healer, because they knew my father needed a Healer with the magic Gift for Healing, as my aunt Brynda had. Without that, he would surely die, despite the skills and potions and salves of the delicate Tyadda woman. And was I angry that he might die because I loved my father and didn't want him to pass to the shores of Annwn? Or because I simply was not ready to become Prince of Skai and doubted that I ever would be?

Standing here on the jetty in the bitter cold of a late-winter afternoon would not solve my problems; nor would it answer my questions. I glanced out into the harbor. Comyn's little courier ship was nearly out of sight beyond the harbor mouth, leaning well into her course, with the wind belling out her sails. No, I would not be using that ship to make good my escape.

I turned and looked up at Skerry Keep again. Nor would I return to my father's chambers, defeated and beaten. There must be another alternative, something that would help . . .

Inspiration struck like a blow to the heart. If I went to Skai, as I had threatened to do, I could find a Healer—perhaps in a Tyadda fastness as Meaghean had suggested. And, were I lucky, and truly guided by the sword as my dreams might lead me to believe, I could find Bane and bring it back for my father. If he had both the sword and his health back, he would once again be the strong, accomplished leader he had been. The man I needed him to be.

I turned on my heel and caught the horse I had left standing, bewildered, on the gravel shingle by the root of the jetty. I had been a small boy on this island, and small boys have secret places. My own secret place was a little cave in the rocks at the foot of Ben Roth on the western end of the island. It was more a protected hollow in the tumble of fallen boulders spilling down the western cliffs of Ben Roth's flank than a real cave, but I had hidden a small boat there before I left all those years ago. The boat might still be sound. Sound enough, in any event, to get me across the Skerryrace to the mainland of Venia. From there, I could make my way down through Brigland to Skai.

The boat, of course, was ruined. I don't know why I expected otherwise. Twelve years of the damp, salty air and the constant freeze-thaw-freeze cycle of the winters quickly turned uncared-for wood into a shambles of rotting splinters and insect-eaten sawdust.

I sat down on a rock scoured smoothly round by wind

and water, uncertain whether to gnash my teeth, laugh, or burst into tears. As a noble rescuer and hero, I was nowhere near the standards set by even the least critical and demanding bard. Although I hated to admit it, it appeared that my only alternative was to return to Skerry Keep and beg transportation from someone who was loyal to my father, not me. I probably had as much chance of persuading someone to take me in a boat to the mainland at this time of year as a mouse had of surviving a roomful of hungry cats.

I got to my feet, ready to admit defeat, and walked back to the steep path that led to the top of the cliff, where the horse waited for me, reins dangling to the ground. A flash of light reflecting from something near the water made me turn my head. I saw nothing that might have mirrored the light, but something odd about the shape of a seaweed-covered rock lying just above the high-tide mark caught my eye, and I hesitated, my foot on the beginning of the track upward. A sudden vision of the sword Bane surrounded by waterlight flashed through my mind. I turned and made my way across the broken rock and gravel of the shore. The seaweed covering the rock was brittle and dry, and there were no barnacles or oysters clinging to the rough surface beneath the seaweed, as there were to every other rock surrounding it.

I brushed away more of the seaweed and found wood, not stone, beneath the pads of my fingers. Wood—firm, solid, sound wood. Planks, they were, carefully smoothed and shaped and caulked.

A boat.

I fell to my knees and scraped the rest of the seaweed and debris from the boat, then sat back on my heels and stared at it. It was much bigger than the boat I had secreted away in the cave. This looked as if it might be a fisherman's boat, large enough to challenge the sea beyond the harbor, but small enough for one or two men to handle. It was a matter of only a few moments effort to turn it over. The two parts of the collapsible mast and the small, square sail were carefully stowed inside the boat.

I glanced at the sea. The tide was nearly at flood, lapping at the foot of Ben Roth, and gray waves curling white foam under small green crests lapped only a few paces from the sturdy prow of the boat. Launching the boat would not be difficult, even for a man alone.

The sea took the boat easily enough. I hardly got my feet wet as I thrust it down the shingle and into the water, then hopped lightly aboard. Moments later, I had the mast assembled and raised, and the sail belling out into the wind.

Pleased with myself, I sat back at the tiller and turned the prow southward to thread my way through the strait between Skerry and Marddyn, south into the Skerryrace, toward the shores of the Celae Province of Venia.

An hour later, when a wind storm blew up and carried my little boat southwestward whether I willed it or not, I had more than enough time as I clung to the useless tiller to reflect upon my folly. And I gained a deeper understanding of how a cork caught in the swift current of a river might feel.

If the gale propelled my little boat close to the shore of the island of Marddyn, I never saw the rocks and trees of Skerry's sister island. I was too busy holding on to the sides of the boat, praying for help from the Duality and all seven gods and goddesses—Adriel of the Waters in particular—and cursing my own incredible stupidity and arrogance. I had no idea where I was, or where the storm was taking me. I had not Comyn's gift of reading the sea and the sky, and in any event, clouds covered the sky so thickly, I could not even tell where the sun went down, and did not know east from west or north from south.

As darkness fell, the gale died down to a mild breeze.

With the calm came a fog so dense I could not see more than a handbreadth beyond the little boat in any direction. I had no idea where I was; the fog was too thick to allow me to see the stars above my head. The current to the west of Skerry and Marddyn flowed north and east, I remembered. That might mean that the first glimpse of land I had could be the barren coasts of Saesnes on the continent. Or I might end up swept ashore on one of the ice-covered little islands that lay scattered like a handful of grain off the west coast of Saesnes and the ice-locked northern lands.

The motion of the boat in the calm, gently rolling sea lulled me, and, despite myself, I dozed off. I don't think I slept, for I was still very conscious of the thick blanket of fog around me and the glassy swells of the sea slapping against the sturdy wooden sides of the boat. But it seemed to me that I saw the green mountains of Skai rising all around me.

I watched a dark figure on a dark horse as he rode hard through a glen, bent over the neck of his galloping horse. A muted glow came from the left side of his horse where he had tied a long bundle to his saddle pack. The courier had changed horses several times since leaving the small farm where he'd taken the sword from the young cowherd, but he'd always transferred the sword to the new horse when he transferred his saddle pack containing the dispatches he carried from Hakkar of Maedun's headquarters in Clendonan.

Even as he raced through the glen toward the next posting station where a fresh mount awaited him, the sword he carried filled his mind. It was a well-made weapon, and he thought it would make an excellent present for his grandfather, who collected fine weapons.

As he thought of his grandfather, I received a flash of a tall, dark man gone silver-gray, dressed in a cloak of warlock's gray, standing to the left side of a man dressed all in black seated on an ornate chair. The man on the chair was not old enough to be Hakkar of Maedun, but it certainly might have been his son Horbad. Caught up in the dream, I shuddered as a cold chill crept down my spine. This was Brynda's

nightmare come true—a Rune Blade falling into the hands of a
Maedun who knew all about its power. And not just any Rune Blade.
This one was mine. My father's. This one was Bane, sword of the
Prince of Skai. I had to prevent it happening. I could not let a Maedun
warlock get his hands on a Rune Blade. I could not let Horbad son of
Hakkar possess Bane. I could not!

The sword lay quiescent in its wrapping, strapped securely to the
saddle pack behind the courier. Its glow muted, its song silent and still,
it merely waited patiently, biding its time.

I awoke to find my tiny boat bobbing gently in a wide bay
under the clear, pale sky of early dawn, surrounded on three
sides by the black-green of winter fir and pine, and the pale,
bare trunks and limbs of birch and silver-leaf maple.
Mountains rose all around the bay, and one of them soared
higher than the rest, forming a snow-covered cone against the
bleached colors of the dawn sky.

I knew that mountain. I'd heard of it hundreds of times
from bards and minstrels in ballads and stories sung and told
around the fires of both Skerry and Broche Rhuidh. It was
Cloudbearer, the highest mountain on the Isle of Celi. The
bay my little boat floated so calmly in had to be where the
Llewen River flowed into the sea, draining Loch Llewen,
which lay at the foot of Cloudbearer.

Some aberrant swirl of the current that raced along the
west coast of Celi and curled around the islands of Skerry and
Marddyn must have brought me here and deposited me like
a bottle in the tide. The seven gods and goddesses had shown
me this little boat, and now they had brought me where I
wished to be.

I shivered, then hurried to raise my sail and bring the little boat to shore before the outgoing tide took me back out to
sea with it and out of the reach of help from the gods and goddesses.

7

By the time I got the boat ashore and hidden among the roots of the pines and winter-bare birch and oak trees, it was full daylight. I had taken off my boots, plaid, and kilt before jumping into the water to haul the boat in by the sturdy sisal painter attached to its bow. I dressed quickly once I was ashore, but even the dry clothing couldn't dispel the chill of the icy water. The wan, wintry sun had not yet shown itself above the mountains to the east, and a hard frost lay thick and gray on the stiff, dead stalks of bracken in the open areas along the bank of the river. There was no warmth in the morning air, and I shivered as I wrapped my plaid around me against the damp cold.

Part of the chill I felt might have been the spell that Hakkar of Maedun, who styled himself Lord Protector of Celi on his usurped throne in the city of Clendonan, had spread across the whole of the isle. I had come up against Maedun blood sorcery several times when fighting at the side of Taggert dav Malcolm on the border between the foothills of Tyra and Maedun-held Isgard. That was when I had discovered that I had enough Tyadda blood inherited from my grandmother Letessa to protect me from the worst of the foul Maedun magic. But I was certainly aware of the spell. I could feel it now, furring the skin of my arms and legs, and seeping like a trickle of chill water down my spine. If it followed the same pattern in Celi as it did in Tyra, the higher I moved into the mountains, the weaker the spell would become until it finally dissipated altogether.

Under the shelter of the trees, I stood rubbing my arms and looking around. This protected harbor formed by the small bay had once been a busy place. A wide track led down to the water's edge. Even overgrown now with grasses, bushes, and small saplings, it still showed signs of use. I found a hoofprint cut deep into the icy mud in the center of the track, frozen and frost-rimed but still as clear as the day it had been made. I held my breath as I crouched by the print and looked around quickly. But that print might have been made today. Or last Samhain. I had no way of telling.

To my left, the river wound through its small, marshy delta to empty into the bay. If my remembrance of the stories were correct, Dun Llewen, where my grandmother Letessa had been born, lay less than a league inland. It had been one of the last strongholds to fall to the Maedun invasion all those twenty years ago, but fall it had. Whether the Maedun had garrisoned it with their own soldiers, I didn't know. Little information came out of Skai these days.

It would, of course, be wisest to assume that Dun Llewen was definitely a garrison for the Somber Riders of Maedun, and that Hakkar had also provided the garrison with a warlock to keep the spell strengthened and in force. Although I knew the spell could not reduce me to writhing agony as it had Ralf's father and brother, I was not sure that it couldn't turn my own weapons back on me if I tried to use them against any Somber Rider I might encounter. That alone indicated the best course of action would be to avoid the Riders both earnestly and diligently.

To my right, the vast bulk of Cloudbearer thrust into the sky, huge and solid, dominating the small valley, and even the sea. Standing by itself in the middle of the wide glen, it was as impressive a tor as any I'd seen in Tyra. It would have dwarfed even soaring Craig Rhuidh behind the Clanhold. I stared up at the towering summit and something stirred in my chest that I had never felt before. My breath caught painfully in my throat as I realized for the first time that I was really and truly in Skai.

Skai, where my family had lived and ruled for generation upon generation. Skai, my legacy from all those generations of men with their fierce and binding love of this land.

And where I might find a Healer and my father's lost sword. Between them, they might restore my father to be both the man he had once been, and the prince he could be.

Drawing the folds of my plaid around me for warmth, I worked my way inland. I avoided the track entirely and kept to the shelter of the trees flanking it. Tired patches of grainy snow, peppered with seed husks and dead pine needles, lay in areas of deep and abiding shade beneath the trees. I stepped carefully around these, not wanting to leave any trace of my presence.

The sun lifted suddenly over the shoulder of Cloudbearer, setting the frosted trees to blazing like a field of crystals. At the same time, I rounded a bend in the track and found myself staring at the ruins of Dun Llewen.

As bleak and tragic a view as I'd ever seen met my eyes. The once-proud towers and spires lay tumbled across the ruined courtyard, the stones still blackened with the soot of the fire that had destroyed the buildings. Draggled stems of bracken, yarrow, and Tyran thistle clung to the meager pockets of soil between the stones. Nothing remained of the Great Hall but a pair of crumbled hearths. Drifts of last year's leaves lay sodden and moldering among the cracked and broken tiles. Young trees grew where once yrSkai had laughed and feasted and loved and lived. The only sign of life now was one red-and-white cow foraging among the winter-killed grass at the edge of the clearing by a clump of skeletal rowan trees. As I stepped out of the trees on the opposite side of the clearing, the cow looked up, caught sight of me, and darted away, quick and agile as a startled deer.

The faint scent of a charnel house drifted on the morning air. It might have been Hakkar's spell, or it might have been the ghost of the stench of death left after the Somber Riders swept through here. But it didn't take the stink to tell me that many people had died here. I could almost hear their cries of terror and pain. The horror of the slaughter had blighted the whole valley.

There is a tradition that the Princes of Skai are firmly and implacably bound to the land, and that the joys and sorrows of the land are embedded into the Prince of Skai's spirit. I had thought that was poetic exaggeration, a fable told by bards, but as I looked at the ruins of my grandmother's home, I knew the tradition was true. My heart began to break, and an overwhelming wave of sorrow and grief washed over me, powerful enough to knock me to my knees. Tears flooded my eyes and blurred my vision. I had not expected this reaction, and it caught me completely unprepared. I brought my hands up to block the sight of the devastation before me and gasped helplessly for breath.

Locked into the agony of the land, I didn't hear the three horsemen approach until they were nearly on top of me. The clatter of iron-shod hooves on stone finally made me turn, still on my knees. Three men riding dark horses flew across the shallow riverbed, swords drawn, wide grins of pure, joyful anticipation on their faces.

Only the instinctive reflexes Kenzie had drilled into me for twelve years saved my life. I was on my feet, my sword drawn, ready to spring to one side or the other, before I fully realized what was happening or what I was doing. The first horseman reached me, his sword swinging in a deadly arc straight for my head.

Stupid, he was. Or arrogant enough to believe himself invincible. Kenzie taught me better than that. A head was too small a target. Always go for the body. It was a lot easier to hit.

I swayed easily enough out of the way of the descending sword, and brought my own blade around. The edge caught the Rider just below the rib cage, sweeping him neatly out of the saddle as the horse thundered past. Blood burst from the crumpling body as the man fell at my feet. I leapt over him and spun to meet the next Rider. But even before I lifted my sword, I knew it was far too late. I could never avoid both of them.

The closest Rider had his sword raised, ready for the killing blow. His horse swerved around the body of the fallen Rider. I smelled the sharp, salty tang of lathered horse and sweaty leather. I raised my own sword, but before the Rider could start the downswing of his blade, the feathered shaft of an arrow appeared like magic in the hollow of his throat. The Rider's eyes widened in surprise, then went blank and empty. He dropped his sword and toppled from his horse as the last Rider scythed a blow at my back. I leapt aside, brought up my own sword, and swept it across. At the moment my blade bit into the Rider's side just above his hip, another of the small, feathered shafts appeared just under his collarbone. His horse shied and swerved, slamming into me hard enough to knock me sprawling into the wet grass.

I lost my grip on my sword, but came to my knees almost instantly and snatched it up again. For a moment, I knelt there, scanning the trees at the edge of the meadow, my breath coming in harsh, rasping gasps. But I saw no sign of the archer who had saved my life. A spot beneath my shoulder blade itched furiously, waiting for another of the arrows. Gradually, I realized that no more of the arrows were forthcoming. Whoever had shot the Somber Riders obviously had not assumed that I, also, was an enemy.

Silence ringed the clearing. I climbed to my feet, then

carefully and deliberately sheathed my sword. Still there was no sign of my rescuer. I took a deep breath.

"Thank you," I said aloud in a normal, conversational tone.

"You're most welcome, my lord Tyr."

The voice was male and held an underlying promise of humor and music. And it came from behind me, far from the place where the arrows had come from. I spun around to see a young man dressed in dark green and brown step out of the shadows of the forest. He wore a dark green cloak flung back to make room for the harp in a carry case slung over his shoulder. At his hip hung a long dagger in a sheath attached to his wide leather belt. He had no other visible weapon.

He was unmistakably Tyadda, but taller than most others I had met. About my age, or mayhaps a year or two younger. Dark blond hair hanging straight and shining to his shoulders, golden brown eyes. Supple, whippy strength to the slender body. Narrow, handsome face just barely containing his laughter. He carried no bow, no quiver of arrows. If he had been the archer, he moved more quickly and quietly than any man had a right to.

I failed to see what he found so amusing. Certainly not the three Somber Riders who lay dead on the colorless, sodden grass. He never once glanced at them. He watched me, and his laughter seemed to be directed at me.

I held out my open hands and inclined my head. "My lord bard," I said. "You have my thanks."

"Better that you should offer your thanks to the one who loosed the arrows," he said. He glanced at the forest to my left, still smiling, his eyes lit with laughter.

I turned in time to see someone step out of the shadows. For an instant, I thought it was a young boy, then realized it was a woman. She was small and delicate, Tyadda like the bard, and close to his age. Like the bard, she wore a tunic, trews, and cloak of dark, forest green. Her dark gold hair hung in a plait thick as my wrist across her shoulder. She, too, wore a long dagger in a sheath on her belt, but as well, she carried a quiver of arrows on her back and held a deadly little Veniani recurved bow in her hand.

She hardly glanced at the three dead Somber Riders as she crossed the clearing and came to stand beside the young man. He was perhaps as tall as I, but the top of her head barely came even with his chin. Small and dainty-looking she might be, but the evidence of her efficiency with that bow lay at my feet.

"You certainly have my thanks, my lady," I said.

She looked up at me, her delicate mouth drawn into a disapproving line. "You might also thank the Duality and all the seven gods and goddesses that Davigan and I were nearby to help," she said with some asperity. "What in the name of piety were you doing, kneeling there in the grass as if you were simply waiting for one of those dark swords to take your head? You certainly can't be that stupid and have lived to your age."

The bard—Davigan, she'd called him—grinned at me. "She's little, but she's fierce and feisty as a ferret," he said.

She shot a glance at him that should have set his eyebrows on fire and withered his lashes. He only turned that devastatingly charming grin on her, then shrugged. She made an odd little resigned gesture with her eyebrows and looked at me again.

"You dress like a Tyran clansman," she said. "But you look Celae. Who are you and how did you get here?"

"I *am* Celae," I said. "YrSkai, but I was raised in Tyra. I came here looking for something or someone."

She wasn't going to let me get away with a partial explanation. "You came looking for someone? But how did you get here? And who are you?"

Davigan raised one hand. "Perhaps we should tell him who we are first," he murmured. "After all, we do seem to be the hosts here and he the guest."

She turned on him. "Davigan, do shut up, will you?" she said in a tone of sorely tried patience.

He grinned at me again. "You must excuse my sister, my lord Tyr. She has a tongue like a fistful of rusty fishhooks." Bright, hot pink stained her cheeks as he spoke, but he hardly spared her a glance. Instead, he looked at me, still smiling. "And I, as she will be very quick to tell you, was dropped rather too often from my cradle to the floor on my head when I was but an infant." He looked pointedly around the clearing. "However, we probably shouldn't stand here waiting for another squad of Somber Riders to come belting out of the forest. I would suggest we vanish as quickly as we can."

Her mouth tightened, but she nodded. "Davigan's right," she said. She gestured to the horses. All three of them stood quietly, reins dangling on the ground. "Take the horses. They're good Celae horses, bred in Wenydd from stock developed by Connor, Duke of Wenydd. I'm loath to let the Maedun have them."

"Besides," Davigan said cheerfully, "I'm tired of walking." He made a deep, elaborate bow. "After you, my lord Tyr."

I caught one of the horses, a glossy bay gelding. It stood obediently still, ears twitching forward curiously. It certainly wasn't one of the heavy, blocky horses the Maedun used on the Continent in Isgard. As I took its reins, it bent the elegant curve of its neck and looked around at me as if judging me. I reached out to stroke the shining withers. The horse whuffled, then stood quietly. "What about them?" I said, gesturing at the bodies.

She made a face. "Leave them for the ghosts and the crows," she said.

• • •

Both Davigan and his sister were excellent riders. They clung like cockleburs to the backs of the horses, guiding them at a hand gallop through the trees. They obviously knew the track and knew where they were going. I followed somewhat more carefully, being unfamiliar with the countryside. The last thing I needed was to ride full tilt around a corner and get myself swept ignominiously out of the saddle by an overhanging branch. That certainly wouldn't impress the Tyadda woman at all. What surprised me was that it seemed important to me to have her good opinion.

We were well up the shoulder of Cloudbearer when the woman pulled her horse to a stop. She lifted her head as if listening for something, then nodded. "We're safe here," she announced.

I drew my mount to a stop beside her and knew she was right. The faint stench that had been prickling at my senses since I'd come ashore was gone. All I could smell now was the fresh, crisp scent of cedar and pine and damp earth. The rigid tension no longer knotted the muscles of my shoulders, and I was no longer aware of the overwhelming sorrow of the land. I drew in a deep breath and let it out slowly, realizing it was my first free breath since landing in Skai.

The bard stopped beside us, his horse dancing restively. He soothed it easily, stroking its neck and speaking soft words. Then he grinned at me.

"Allow me to introduce myself," he said. "I am Davigan called Harper, and this is my sister Lowra al Drywn, and we"—he made an elegant and sweeping gesture—"are on a heroic quest." His tone made light of it, but something moved in his golden brown eyes. In the shadows beneath the trees, it was difficult to see, but I thought it might have been pain. Well masked, but still apparent. It puzzled me because he certainly had not shown any signs of pain in the valley by Dun Llewen.

His sister gave him another one of those withering looks. "Davigan, do be quiet," she said softly. In spite of her expression and contrary to her words, her tone was gentle, offering comfort. "It isn't something to make silly jests about." She turned to me. "Who are you and why are you here in Skai? Where did you come from? What do you want?" No trace of the gentleness remained in her voice.

"Many questions, my lady," I said. "I think if I tell you who I am, the other questions will be answered. In Tyra, I'm called Gareth dav Brennen ti'Kenzie. In Skai here, I'm called Gareth ap Brennen ap Keylan."

Davigan stared at me. ". . . ap Kian, who was Red Kian of Skai," he said softly. "Are you then Prince of Skai, Gareth ap Brennen?"

"No," I said. "My father yet lives. Barely, but he yet lives. That's one reason I've come to Skai."

Lowra urged her horse forward until she was knee to knee with me. Without speaking, she reached out toward my forehead. I started to draw back, but something stopped me. I sat the horse quietly and let her put two fingers on my brow. For a moment, it felt as if a whole hive of bees were buzzing around inside my head, and the air between Lowra and me fizzed gently. Startled, I tried to pull away and found I couldn't. A curiously glazed expression stole across her face, then she dropped her hand, turned to Davigan, and spoke quickly in the Tyadda tongue.

I speak both Celae and Tyran, which are similar languages—the legends say that the Tyrs and the Celae were once one people. And I had learned the old tongue when I was a child. But I had not spoken it, nor heard it spoken, for nearly twelve years, and my ear couldn't follow the quick, liquid flow of the words. I heard my name, and my father's, but the rest was lost on me. Davigan looked at me, speculation and contemplation in his eyes.

"Aye," he said when she finished. "You're right." He turned to me. "Lowra and I think you should join us."

"I've come to find a Healer for my father," I said. "He's gravely ill and desperately needs one with the Gift."

Lowra smiled for the first time. "I think we can promise you a Healer," she said.

I looked at her, then at Davigan, and for no apparent reason that I could discern except that they had saved my life, I trusted them both. "I must also find my father's sword," I said.

"A Rune Blade?" she asked.

"Aye. Bane, it's called. It's searching now for the Prince of Skai, and I must be here where it can find me so I can return it to my father."

"We can't promise you the sword," Davigan said. "But we'll help you look for it. Will you join us and help us?"

"What are you looking for?"

Before Davigan could answer, Lowra threw up her hand for silence. Her eyes grew wide, almost glazed, and an intense, listening expression spread over her face. "They've found the bodies," she murmured. "They're coming after us."

"The Maedun?" Davigan asked quickly. He glanced at me. "Lowra has the Sight . . ."

Lowra nodded. "Aye, the Maedun. A large troop. With a warlock." Her face cleared. "We must hurry." Gathering her reins, she wheeled her horse and set her heels to its flanks. In moments, both Davigan and I had gathered our reins and followed her along the narrow track.

It occurred to me that I still knew nothing about this odd pair, but I found myself more than willing to throw my lot in with theirs. If they could help me find a Healer for my father, and mayhaps help me find Bane, then their own quest would also be mine.

8

We kept moving for the rest of the day, riding steadily along a faint
track that skirted the flank of Cloudbearer and stayed below
the snow line as we circled the mountain, moving always
south and west. Above us, the towering mountain bulked
heavy against the sky and showed us its massive bones as the
track passed beneath sheer granite cliffs rising steeply among
the trees. Occasionally, we came across places where the
cliffs had crumbled and tumbles of broken rock nearly oblit-
erated the track. I couldn't see which way the track went
through the scattered boulders, but Lowra and Davigan
obviously knew where they were going. I was content to follow. When dusk fell, Lowra led the way off the track and into
the forest.

The horses were drooping with fatigue as we led them
away from the track. Beneath the trees, the winter-dry grass
offered rough forage for them, but sufficient, I thought, to
satisfy their hunger. Not far away, I heard the faint, musical
sound of falling water.

We stopped beside a hollow in one of the broken cliffs
formed by a jumble of fallen rock. A dense thicket of hazel
clung tenaciously to the splintered boulders, screening the
hollow from the track. Davigan set to work immediately,
gathering wood to make a fire. Lowra unlimbered her bow
and adjusted the quiver of arrows more comfortably on her
back. She handed me a small kettle.

"There's water that way," she said, pointing toward the
sound of rushing water. "We'll want tea." She turned and
vanished into the forest with hardly a sound to mark her passing.

I stood for a moment, regarding the place where she had disappeared. Davigan merely grinned at me over an armload of wood. I shrugged and went looking for the water.

By the time I had fetched the water, Davigan had a respectable fire going. While he fiddled with the kettle to get it hanging properly above the fire, I saw to the horses. I rubbed them down with handfuls of the dry grass and made sure they had water, then left them to forage for themselves. They seemed content enough with only the matted grass, but I wished we had some oats to give them.

Lowra returned even before the water began to boil over the fire. She carried two fat rabbits, already skinned, gutted, and ready for roasting. Davigan produced several thick, fleshy roots that he wrapped in wet leaves and tucked down into the ashes at the edge of the fire.

The rabbits spit and crackled over the fire, and the tantalizing aroma of roasting meat filled the air, reminding me of how long it had been since I had eaten. The tea made with chalery leaf and rose hips, sweetened with a pinch of dried sugar-shoot, did little to appease my hunger, but tasted wonderful just the same. As we waited for the food to cook, Davigan took his harp from the carry case and sat on a section of fallen log we had drawn up to the fire for a seat, engrossed in tuning the instrument.

I reached for the kettle to refill the cup I shared with Davigan. Lowra made an odd little gesture with her eyebrows. Something glinted in her eyes. It might have been amusement, to go with the slight upward tilt at one corner of her mouth.

"You come all the way from Tyra in search of a Healer, yet you bring nothing with you but your sword," she said. "Are you always so unprepared for your tasks?"

Heat rose in my cheeks, and I was grateful for the darkness that hid it from her. Or if it showed, she might think it was only the reflection of the fire on my skin that made it glow so redly. "Coming to Skai was a spur-of-the-moment decision," I said.

"Aye, it must have been," she replied.

"The opportunity presented itself, and I took it without much thought of what I'd need when I got here."

Davigan looked up without pausing in his tuning of the harp. His grin flashed in the fire-shot darkness. "When the gods and goddesses give you a gift, it doesn't pay to hesitate or refuse it."

"Exactly," I said rather more effusively than I had meant to. I still wasn't sure why it was so important to me to appear in a good light to Lowra. I turned to her and changed the subject. "Davigan said you were looking for something, too. If I'm to join you in your search, might you tell me what you're looking for?"

Davigan bent his head to the harp. He began to reply, but his words caught in his throat. He smiled crookedly and turned away, but not before I thought I saw the gleam of what might have been tears in his eyes. His fingers tightened on the strings of the harp, and a harsh, discordant arpeggio stabbed across the hollow. Lowra looked across the fire at him. The flickering play of light and shadow on her face made her expression difficult to read, but I thought her mouth set into a thin and level line. She bent forward and poked at the roasting rabbits with a sharp stick to test their doneness.

"We're looking for our brother," she said quietly. "Daefyd. He's Davigan's twin, the elder by sixteen minutes. We think he was taken by the Maedun."

I glanced sharply at her, but she didn't look at me, intensely involved with testing the rabbits. I chose my words carefully, not wanting to rub salt into what were obviously open wounds in their spirits. "I see," I said. "But I'm unsure why you might think he's still alive. The Maedun have a certain reputation—" I broke off, hesitant to state the obvious. I spoke from knowledge. I had fought against the Maedun on the Tyra–Isgard border, and I'd seen what the Maedun did to prisoners. It wasn't a thing a man could harden his stomach against no matter how often he saw it. Nor would he want to. I could not imagine becoming accustomed to seeing horror like that.

Davigan gained control of himself. He turned one of the tuning pegs in the sounding board of the harp, the movement careful and deliberate. He managed a grin, although I sensed the effort it cost him. "Aye, they do have that certain reputation," he said. "But Daefyd and I shared a womb. I'd know if he were dead. The twin-bond tells me he's still alive."

"I've heard of the twin-bond," I said.

"It's a powerful bond," Davigan said. "Mayhaps not as powerful as the bond between bheancoran and her prince, but strong nonetheless."

Lowra glanced at him sharply, frowning, as he mentioned bheancorans. He ignored her and bent to rake the ashes away from the cooked roots. He scooped them into a wooden bowl and handed the bowl to her. She frowned at him again, but he ignored that, too. She leaned toward the fire and flipped the rabbits into another shallow wooden bowl, blowing on her fingers as the hot fat scorched them. The rabbits smelled pungently delicious with the baked roots.

"Davigan's already told you I have the Sight," she said as she set the bowl on a flat rock where we could all reach it. "It's true. It's not as strong as the Gift my grandmother had, but it's a handy thing at times. I haven't seen Daefyd dead, but I *have* seen him in the company of a man dressed from head to foot in drabbest black. He's in pain, and he's dreadfully miserable, but he's alive."

The rabbit tasted as wonderful as it had smelled, and the thick, fleshy roots were both savory and slightly sweet. An odd combination, but somehow perfect with the rabbit. Hunger, they say, is the best sauce for all food, and I was certainly hungry enough to do any meal justice. I don't remember the last time anything tasted so marvelously good and satisfying.

"How did it happen that he was taken by the Maedun?" I asked around a mouthful of rabbit.

They glanced at each other across the fire. There were, I noted with some annoyance, an awful lot of these significant glances being exchanged. I wondered if they were hiding something from me. If they were, they could certainly be a little less obvious about it.

Lowra nodded at Davigan, then glanced at me. "The story is a long one," she said.

I looked around. Full night had fallen. Above us, the moon had barely begun its journey across the sky, followed relentlessly by the Huntress Star, as always in dedicated pursuit. "We have all night," I said. "And I certainly have nothing I would rather do."

Davigan quickly finished eating his rabbit leg and wiped his hands on the thick carpet of hazel leaves on the ground beside him. He took up the harp and held it on his knee. His fingers brushed softly against the strings, and a bright glissando of soft notes whispered around the hollow. When he spoke, his voice had changed, fulfilling the earlier promise of trained musical resonance.

"To understand what Daefyd did," he said, "you must understand the way of the Tyadda people. We are not a warlike people. We never have been. When the Celae came to this island, which we called Nemeara, we did not fight them. We had our magic, but it wouldn't let us use it to kill, or to harm even an invader. Even when our magic was strong—at its strongest, it would not let itself be used for harm. At one time, it was more potent even than the sorcery of the

Maedun, but it had weakened over the ages we were isolated on this island. When the Celae came, we couldn't look upon them as invaders."

A smile touched his mouth, and a hint of laughter lilted in his voice. "The Celae didn't conquer us; they married us. If it was a conquest, it was a gentle one. Then, oddly enough, we discovered that our magic strengthened when it appeared in the children of mixed blood. It was still a gentle magic, and could not be used to kill. So we became known as a gentle people, and we found that it suited our ways. We lived apart from the Celae for the most part, withdrawing into our separate fastnesses, our hidden mountain steadings, high in the uplands of Skai. We served as seers and bards and Healers to the Celae, but not as soldiers. Mind you, legend has it that the first bheancoran to a Prince of Skai was a Tyadda woman."

Lowra had made herself comfortable with her back against the rock of the soaring cliff behind us, listening to Davigan with her head bowed. The glimmer of the fire cast warm highlights on the planes and hollows of her face, limning the clean line of cheek and brow, gleaming on the fine, firm modeling of her lips. She looked up as Davigan paused, a small smile curving across her mouth.

"An exception to the rule, that bheancoran," she said. "A Tyadda bheancoran is warlike enough when she needs to be. But a warrior and personal guard isn't the only thing a bheancoran is to her prince. Don't ever forget that."

Davigan grinned at her and plucked a quick series of two-note chords from the harp strings, making it sound uncannily like laughter. Lowra smiled again and settled back against the rock wall.

He drew from the harp another liquid glissando of sound that sparked and danced around the hollow like freshets from a clear spring. His voice flowed like liquid honey, the voice of a bard trained to harp and song from infancy.

"My brother Daefyd was another exception," he said. "Among us in our hidden steading were men of Skai who had taken refuge with us when the Maedun invaded those twenty years ago. These men, and their sons, thirsted for vengeance and hungered to take back the lands the Somber Riders had seized." The laughter drained from his face, and sorrow took its place. "But they had no magic to defeat the spell of the black sorcerer, and they had no leader. The Prince of Skai had taken refuge in far northern Skerry, and the Duke of Wenydd had fled with his people to Laurel Water in far Venia."

He plucked a series of low chords in a minor key and bent his head over the warm, honey-toned wood of the harp. "No leader and no magic." Again, his fingers swept gracefully across the strings of the harp, and the music welled up to shower around us like the sparks rising from the fire. "But my brother had been raised to be a leader, to be as eager as the Celae to wrest the stolen lands from the Maedun. So the Celae found their leader in my brother. Daefyd had some magic—not much, but enough that the Celae believed he could overcome the spell—and he, too, believed it to be sufficient. He led thirty Celae warriors out of the steading, bent on rallying the yrSkai still in the mountains here and building an army to take back Skai from the invaders."

I knew what was coming next. I had fought against the Maedun myself, and I had seen the power of the spell their sorcerers wove. But so caught up was I in Davigan's tale, I sat in the dark, barely breathing, waiting for him to continue.

"They failed." Davigan's voice was flat, colorless, and the simple statement was all the more powerful for the lack of emphasis. The harp spoke harshly—sharp, discordant notes that sounded like shattering glass. In spite of myself, I drew in a quick breath and leaned forward, waiting. Across the fire from me, Lowra sat back against the rock, her head tilted forward pensively, eyes closed. Her hair shadowed her face, hiding her expression from me, blurring the clear, clean lines of cheek and brow, but her mood transmitted itself to me in a hundred small ways. Pensive, sad, resigned, wistful. All these at once, and overlying it a sense of determination. Mayhaps a lot to read from posture and the tense curve of a clenched fist, but I knew I was right, just as I knew how Davigan's tale affected my own posture and expression.

"Half the men succumbed to Hakkar's spell and were taken prisoner, we think," Davigan said at last. He spread his hand across the strings, stilling the quivering echoes. "The other half fell to the swords and arrows of the Somber Riders. Only three of them returned, one of them carrying Daefyd, who had been sorely wounded." His eyes sparkled brightly in the fire-shot darkness. Tears will do that. In the dark, lit by firelight, they can look exactly like diamonds. "And when his body was Healed and strong again, his spirit still ailed. He blamed only himself, and cursed the pride that made him think he could defeat Hakkar and his son Horbad by himself. Finally, to ease his spirit, to appease his honor, he went out again. By himself. He left a message saying that he would either free the men who had been swept into bondage because of him or die in the attempt."

The harp fell quiescent, and Davigan's voice trailed off into the silence. For a moment, the hushed echo of the final notes whispered around the hollow, then faded gently to silence. The only sounds were the crackle of the fire, the distant chuckling of the trickle of water, and my own quick breathing.

"That was just before Imbolc," Lowra said. "He has never come back."

I looked down at my hands. They had clenched themselves into fists on my knees while I listened to Davigan's tale.

"But he didn't die," I said.

Davigan shook his head. "No," he said quietly. "I don't believe he's dead. I can still feel the spark of him along the twin-bond."

I glanced over at him. "And can you tell from the bond where he is?" I asked.

"No, unfortunately. A twin-bond isn't like the bond of bheancoran and prince. I can't tell where he is, only that he's alive. Mayhaps if we were closer ..." His voice trailed off, and he shook his head again. "Then again, mayhaps not. I never could tell where he was before. I expect that hasn't changed, no matter how I'd wish it to."

Lowra leaned forward and poured more tea, nearly emptying the kettle. "And speaking of bonds, are you able to tell the whereabouts of this sword you seek?" she asked me.

"No," I said. "I see it only in dreams. I think it's somewhere in Skai now. In the foothills, or along the coast mayhaps." I didn't say anything about my fears that it may be in the hands of the Maedun. Mayhaps it was because I didn't want them to abandon me, not when they had promised to take me to a Healer who would help my father.

She took a sip of tea. "We're a fine company then," she said. "None of us able to say the location of what it is we seek." She took another sip of the tea and made a sour face. "This has steeped too long. It's too bitter to drink." She emptied the cup in the ashes at the edge of the fire. A billowing cloud of steam rose, obscuring her face. "It's late. We should sleep. We need to get an early start in the morning."

"Where are we going?" I asked.

She pulled a blanket from her pack and wrapped herself warmly in both the blanket and her cloak. "We promised you a Healer," she said. "We'll keep that promise first, and see where we must go after that."

● ● ●

I awoke and sat up, alert and listening for the small sound that had startled me out of sleep. The promise of a clear day glimmered through the thin mist in the false dawn. The sky behind Cloudbearer glowed a wan, luminescent turquoise streaked with pale pink haze. The fire had died to soft gray ash, but the rocks around it still radiated a faint warmth.

Davigan slept in the shelter of a thatch of overhanging hazel boughs, but Lowra's place was empty. For a moment, worry gnawed at my mind, then I relaxed sleepily. I knew where she was. She had gone to the little freshet of water that tumbled across the stones near the track just beyond the camp. She had likely gone for water to make tea for breaking our fast. I pulled my plaid more snugly about me, making ready to curl back down into sleep on my bed of dry bracken. But if Lowra were up and about making tea, the least I could do was fetch more wood to build up the fire so we could boil the water.

Reluctantly, I climbed to my feet and pinned my plaid around my shoulders. The morning air held a definite late-winter chill. The snow might be melting, but spring was still a long way off, especially at this altitude on the flank of the mountain.

I had gathered only a few sticks of deadfall when the cry for help came through the mist, piercing my soul like an arrow. There was no sound, but I heard it within my heart and my mind as clearly as if it had been shouted. I responded automatically, without thought. I dropped the wood and spun around, instinct driving me forward. I leapt over the tumble of broken rock, stopped abruptly in the midst of a tangle of hazel.

Davigan sat with his blanket and cloak still wrapped around him, the harp he had been using as a pillow by his hip. A man dressed in black stood before him, sword and dagger in hand, and Davigan stared at him much as a bird stares

mesmerized at a cat. By the fire, another black-clad man
stood behind Lowra, one hand clamped across her mouth,
the other hand holding a dagger to her throat. She stood
utterly still in his grasp; both her hands clutched his arm but
she no longer tried to pull his hand away from her throat.

The stench of blood magic hung thicker than the morning mist around the campsite. I tightened my grip on the
sword hilt and gathered myself to leap out of the trees at the
two Maedun soldiers.

9

Something stopped me—some premonition of more to this than met the eye, of hidden dangers, of some peril I could not yet see. I dropped to one knee behind a boulder and studied the scene before me tensely, trying to sort out what had triggered the sudden sense of caution.

The two men holding Davigan and Lowra at dagger-point had not moved. They gave the impression of waiting for something. Or someone. But where had they come from? And how had they found us?

Some of the stiffness went out of Lowra's muscles as she stood in the grasp of the Somber Rider. His dagger moved fractionally farther from the pale skin of her throat. Without moving her head, she raised her eyes and looked directly at the place where I knelt. She knew I was there, but she gave no sign of it to the two Somber Riders. The one by Davigan said something in a low voice; the other laughed. I knew the Maedun tongue; I'd been taught to speak it as part of my education when I was young. But I couldn't quite catch what the two Riders were saying. They spoke quickly, slurring their words in a regional accent I was not familiar with. Their tone, though, was unmistakable. They were pleased with themselves and their catch.

I caught a whiff of the charnel-house stench of blood magic. It hung in the air, strong enough to make my belly clench in nausea. But neither of the Somber Riders wore warlock's gray. They both wore the unrelieved black of Hakkar's regular troops. They looked like common troopers, not even officers. The magic couldn't be coming from either one of them. So there had to be a third man nearby. A warlock. Or a sorcerer.

I lowered my sword and studied the shadows. If there was a third man, he was well hidden. And if he was hiding behind a warlock's illusion, the strength of his blood magic was shocking. We stood on the flank of Cloudbearer, the highest mountain in Celi, and Cloudbearer was sacred to all the seven gods and goddesses. No Maedun warlock, whose magic abhorred the high, sacred places, should be able to work blood magic strong enough to hide behind this high in the mountains, and especially not on Cloudbearer himself. No ordinary warlock . . .

A movement in a fragment of shadow under the trees behind Davigan caught my eye. Even as I looked toward it, I realized I was wrong. The movement had not been in the patch of shadow; the shadow itself had moved. A man stood beneath the trees, wrapped in a mist of darkness that moved with him.

A frisson of chill rippled up my spine, and I shivered as I watched the shifting mist and the still figure at its center. The shadow twisted itself around him, obscuring his face, blurring the outlines of his body.

Through the shroud of mist, I caught a glimpse of the swirl of a gray cloak. A warlock, then. But a powerful one. If he had power enough to draw that haze of blood sorcery around him, did he have power enough to turn my own weapon back against me if I attacked him?

Lowra glanced at me again, only her eyes moving. She blinked once, then looked at the warlock. Davigan had not moved. He sat, one hand protectively around the harp beside him, ignoring the point of the sword against his throat, also watching the warlock.

The warlock spoke, his voice muffled by the mist. Again, I didn't catch what he said. The Somber Rider who held

Lowra captive grunted. The other Somber Rider flicked the tip of his sword negligently against the skin of Davigan's throat. A bright bead of blood formed and trickled down to stain the collar of Davigan's shirt. "And this one?" the Somber Rider asked.

The warlock stepped closer and bent to peer intently into Davigan's face. Davigan drew back slightly, but didn't drop his gaze, staring back defiantly into the warlock's eyes.

The warlock straightened and turned away. "He has no magic," he said. "You may kill him."

My breathing went ragged in my chest. Warlock or none, working magic or none, I simply could not stand by and watch the Somber Rider kill Davigan. I had no choice in the matter at all. I tightened my grip on the hilt of my sword and rose to my feet, still hidden by the rocks and hazel trees. At the same instant, Lowra's glance flicked to me, and I knew she would act the moment I did.

"I think this has gone far enough," I said, and stepped out from behind the boulder.

Too many things happened at once to keep track of. Lowra clamped her hands around the wrist holding the knife against her throat, and bit down firmly into the flesh and bone. Davigan grabbed his harp and swung it in a wide arc, sweeping the feet of the Somber Rider who held the sword to his throat right out from under him. And the warlock spun, startled, to face me, the black mist seething around him like boiling pitch.

My sword wasn't a Rune Blade of Skai, but it was fashioned of good Tyran steel and made to fit my hand and my reach and my swing. It had been shaped by a master craftsman to balance perfectly in my grip, until it felt as if the sword itself initiated and followed through on the cut and parry of the deadly, stylized dance between two swordsmen. It didn't make the same fierce music as a Rune Blade, but it sang in my grip with its own voice. And I had been trained well over the past twelve years to use the sword as if it were naught but an extension of my own hands and arms.

That good Tyran steel in my hands began to sing even as I stepped out of hiding. I was barely conscious of Davigan rolling out of my way as I surged forward over the rocks. The warlock leapt away, his face contorted in shocked consternation. Warlocks weren't often attacked directly; they were too dangerous, but I had no choice. The mist writhed around him, and a sullen red glow formed between his hands. The blood sorcery spell that would turn my own blade against me . . .

A frigid, crippling chill ripped through my arms and hands. For a moment, I thought my muscles had been turned to ice. The sword quivered, then began to turn in my hands, the blade reaching back for the flesh of my throat. I closed my eyes and concentrated every ounce of my strength into my hands and arms, and spun around, using the sorcery-induced movement of the blade to help me. I carried it around in a complete circle and lunged forward as I came around to face the sorcerer again The blade's own momentum completed the sweep of the arc. The blade sliced into the black mist and bit deeply into gray-clad flesh. The warlock died, still caught in the throes of his surprise.

I turned quickly. Davigan crouched on the far side of the trampled fire. He held the harp tightly against his chest, cursing and muttering over a broken tuning peg. The Somber Rider who had been holding a sword to his throat now lay on that sword, Davigan's long knife buried in his belly and an expression of intense surprise on his face.

Lowra stood leaning against the rocks, blood matting one side of her head, more blood staining the right sleeve of her shirt. But the other Somber Rider lay at her feet, his throat opened by his own dagger. I cried out in concern, started to turn toward her. Her gaze went over my shoulder, her eyes widening. She shouted a warning.

Two Somber Riders leapt out of the trees behind me, swords drawn, faces pale and intent. They were on me almost before I could raise my sword in defense.

The tales in Tyra say that the Somber Riders of Maedun put too much faith in the ability of their warlocks to protect them and not enough faith in their own strength and sword arms. Kenzie had taught me to hope for that, but not expect it. He was right. These two looked like good swordsmen, determined and canny. But I had spent twelve years training under the best swordsman in Tyra, which meant probably the best on the Continent.

I faced the two Somber Riders, exhilaration pounding in my blood and skinning my lips back from my teeth. I lost myself in the rhythms of the dance. My body moved without thought through the sequences I'd practiced so often, they had become second nature, part of me, instinctive. The first Somber Rider, too eager to prove himself, ran right into my blade. I barely had to move the sword to open his belly for him. The other, a little more experienced and a lot more canny, hung back for a moment, sizing me up. He was bigger than I, his sword longer. He charged me, holding his sword more like a cudgel than a sword.

Steel rang against tempered steel. The force of his blows sent shocks all the way up my arms into my chest, jarring my spine. For the first moment, all I could do was parry the rain of blows. I was so busy simply defending myself, I had no chance to attack. But I found myself coldly studying his strengths and weaknesses, just as Kenzie had taught me to do. The man had little finesse and grace, but his strength nearly made up for it. I gave ground slowly and deliberately, drawing him away from Davigan and Lowra.

The Somber Rider surged forward at me, swinging his

sword in a deadly arc. I spun out of the way, dodging under the whistling blur of the blade. He had overbalanced. Even as he staggered to one side to steady himself, I swung my sword backhand. The blade caught him near the groin, opening the large vein in the leg. He fell, shock and consternation widening his eyes. I left him to bleed out into the carpet of last year's leaves and turned quickly toward Lowra.

She had lowered herself to the ground and sat holding her left hand to the wound in her arm. Davigan was nowhere to be seen. I crossed the clearing in two bounds and fell to my knees beside Lowra.

"Are you hurt badly?" I asked. The wound in her head had already stopped bleeding, but blood still welled through her fingers and oozed down her right arm.

She glared at me. "No, of course not," she muttered through clenched teeth. "I always sit here and bleed like this because I enjoy it."

I said nothing. The teakettle lay on its side not far from her. I reached out to snatch it up. About half a cup of the chalery leaf tea we'd had for our evening meal still remained in the kettle. I pulled her hand away from her left arm and poured the dark liquid over the wound. There's something in chalery leaf that's good for cleaning wounds and preventing wound fever from forming. There wasn't a lot left in the kettle, but it was a start. We'd need more, but first I had to get the bleeding stopped.

Davigan leapt over the tumble of stones behind Lowra and dropped to one knee beside me. He held a handful of leaves and stalks, most of them withered and brown.

"Yarrow," he said quickly. "It will help stop the bleeding. Hold it over the wound while I get more water and something to use for bandages for it."

I took the leaves from him and turned back to Lowra. The knife wound still oozed blood. There was so much of it, I couldn't tell how deep the gash was. Well, the first thing was to stop the bleeding. Then we could clean it up and see what else had to be done.

Lowra leaned back, tipping her head so that it rested against the rock behind her, her face pale and strained. She closed her eyes and sat quietly as I pressed the yarrow leaves against the muscle of her arm. I held the damp wad against her skin, pressing as hard as I dared, to help stop the bleeding. My hands tingled for a moment, then warmed as the chill left the wet leaves. The yarrow must have had some sort of pain-relieving effect, because the tightness went out of the corners of her eyes, and color returned to the skin around her mouth. She glanced at me, a spark of something I couldn't quite read glinting in her eyes, then dropped her gaze to her arm. She put her hand over mine, and the tingle rippled in my fingertips again, then disappeared.

Davigan came back carrying fresh water in the kettle. He had turned the chalery tea leaves out into a square of cloth for a poultice and found more clean cloths for bandages. They looked as if they might have been torn from the bottom of a shirt.

"Let's look at that arm," I said. "Then we'll see to your head."

Lowra made a faint gesture toward her head. "This isn't my blood. The Rider bled on me when I opened his throat for him."

When we got it cleaned up, the wound in her arm looked a lot better than I'd feared it would be. From the way it had bled, I was certain the dagger blade had sliced clean down through the muscle to the bone. But only the skin looked to be damaged. It would be painful and sore for a few days, but it would heal cleanly and leave no impairment to the strength of her arm.

"You're lucky," I said as I reached for the chalery-leaf

poultice to bind it over the wound. "This is little more than a scratch."

Lowra opened her eyes and looked at me, one eyebrow raised, one corner of her mouth lifted in wry amusement. "A scratch," she said, exasperation in her voice. She looked down at her arm. "Aye, I suppose it is. Now." She let me finish, then got to her feet and made her way to the spring to wash the blood from her hair.

I watched her go, then turned to Davigan. He had come through the fight unscathed. "She acts like a badger wakened before dusk," I said.

He grinned. "She can get that way," he agreed. "She always expects other people to see obscure things she thinks are obvious."

"Obscure things?" I repeated. "Obvious? I don't understand."

"Well, no, you probably wouldn't," he said. "Not yet, at any rate. But you will, eventually." He got to his feet. "We'd better get the horses ready to go. She'll want to leave again as soon as she returns."

"Go?" I said. "Go where?"

He had already begun packing up the camp. "We still need to find that Healer for you," he said. He glanced in the direction of the spring, where Lowra was still washing Maedun blood from her hair. "Aye, and probably for Lowra, too, come to that."

We set out quickly, breaking our fast with nothing but water in our hurry. The bodies of the Maedun Somber Riders and the warlock, we left for the ravens. Lowra led us higher up the flank of Cloudbearer to a track that was even more ill defined than the one we had been following.

I rode behind Davigan in silence, a headache throbbing behind my eyes. For some reason, too, I felt lethargic and exhausted. I had certainly fought longer and harder, both in practice on the training field and in deadly earnest on battle-fields of the Tyran–Isgardian borderlands, than I had in the early-morning skirmish by the campsite. Never before had it left me feeling as if all I wanted to do was curl up in a warm corner and sleep for half a day. I couldn't understand why this particular scuffle would affect me so strongly, and it left me frustrated and irritable.

At the same time, I was acutely conscious of a strange sensation bubbling and quivering in my chest, just below my heart. It felt like a combination of excitement, anticipation, resentment, and anger. Very strange. And disturbing. I had no idea what it meant, but it seemed stronger, more intense, when I looked at Lowra riding in the lead of our small column.

It made for a very strange morning.

At midday, we found a sheltered spot off the narrow little track and boiled a kettle for tea. Lowra went out with her bow despite protests from both Davigan and me that her injured arm was not strong enough to pull the bow. She simply made a rude noise and went anyway. From the expression of long-suffering exasperation on Davigan's face, the action was typical of her.

But she came back with a rabbit.

While I skinned the rabbit and prepared it for spitting and cooking, Davigan cut an ash twig and sat by the fire with his dagger, fashioning another tuning peg for the harp to replace the one he had broken that morning. Lowra sat on the other side of the fire from me, rubbing her injured arm and scowling into the flames. Occasionally, she looked up at me, her expression midway between speculation, exasperation, and something else I couldn't quite place. And every time she looked at me like that, the odd sensation in my chest churned again.

My headache began to dissipate shortly after we set out again after the midday meal was done, although I still felt listless and tired. I plodded along in Davigan's wake, concentrating only on staying in the saddle, hardly caring where we went. Then, late in the afternoon, we moved out onto the southern flank of Cloudbearer. The track descended toward the sea, passing from scattered clumps of hazel and ash into a thick forest of oak, maple, cedar, and ash. The bare branches tangled together above the narrow track, nearly forming a tunnel. With the leaves thick on the trees, the shade would have been deep and cool, even in the heat of high summer.

I urged my horse up beside Davigan's as we made our way down the slope of the mountain. "Where are we going?" I asked him.

"You wanted a Healer," he said. "We're going to get you one."

I nodded, naturally assuming we were making for a Tyadda steading. But I had always thought those fastnesses were hidden deep in the high mountains of the Spine of Celi, not down on the narrow coastal plain. My puzzlement must have shown on my face, for Davigan grinned.

"You'll see in a little while," he said. "We're almost there."

Lowra turned and glanced at me over her shoulder, her mouth drawn down into a sour line. "An hour at most," she said.

I nodded again and let my horse fall back into line behind Davigan. Lowra's sour mood and obvious exasperation puzzled me, too. I didn't know what I had done to deserve it, and she certainly hadn't bothered to explain my transgressions to me. Mayhaps she might deign to make it clear to me once we had reached this mysterious destination.

An hour later, we came out of the forest onto the coastal plain. Behind us, the white cone-shaped summit of Cloudbearer glowed soft rose and gold in the westering sun. Ahead lay the vast stone circles-within-circles I recognized as the Dance of Nemeara.

Lowra reined in and sat quietly, looking at the Dance in satisfaction. Davigan stopped beside her and glanced over his shoulder, waiting for me to join them.

I pulled my horse up and stopped between them. "That's where we're going?" I asked. "The Dance?"

Lowra turned to meet my eyes. "You wanted a Healer," she said. "In there is where you'll find one. And a lot more besides."

"In there?" I repeated. "A Healer?"

"Yes," she said.

The sun sank lower, nearly touching the sea. The Dance lay silhouetted starkly against it, the menhirs looming heavy and black against the flare of the sky. I shivered.

"I don't particularly want to go in there," I said diffidently.

Davigan didn't look at me as he spoke. "But you must."

"Who says I must?" I demanded irritably.

Lowra's gaze still held mine. "You wanted a Healer."

"For my father. Yes."

"Then go into the Dance. You'll find your Healer."

Still resistant, I shook my head. "There's nobody there. No Healer."

"There will be," she said quietly. "A very powerful Healer. You, Gareth. You're the Healer. And a great deal more, besides."

10

I stood staring at the Dance, Lowra's words ringing in my ears. But I seemed unable or unwilling to extract any sense from them. Surely she had not said I was a Healer. I could not believe I'd heard that. It was too ridiculous, too far-fetched.

The sun sank below the surface of the sea, leaving us in that mystic, transitional time between sunset and dusk when the sky was still streaked with light and color and the last rays of the sinking sun flared on the cone of Cloudbearer, making it appear as if the snow-clad stone were afire. Bands of red, orange, and rose flamed in the west, illuminating the triple ring of standing stones. The imposing menhirs of the outer ring stood starkly black against the luminescent sky, crowned in pairs by massive lintels to form trilithons. The middle ring of stones bulked slightly smaller, gracefully joined all round by capstones, polished like marble to reflect the incandescent sky. The inner ring, standing alone without lintels, was not really a ring at all, but a horseshoe of seven menhirs enclosing a low altar stone that reflected the burning sky like a mirror. I'd heard the altar described as a gem cradled safe in cupped and loving hands, and I saw now what it meant. The seven standing stones of the horseshoe—each representing one of the seven gods and goddesses—watched over and sheltered the altar stone, protecting it.

The wind howled through the bare branches of the salt-bitten trees clinging to the scant soil of the cliffs above the sea. The pounding of the waves on the rocks sounded like the beating of a giant heart in counterpoint to the low moan of the wind. My hair blew about my face, strands whipping into my eyes and stinging. Without conscious thought, I lifted a hand to brush the hair from my eyes, but I could not turn away from the awe-inspiring sight of the Dance.

Silhouetted against the sunset, the Dance was a place of immense power. The energy of the place prickled against my skin, flowing over me like water. It vibrated along my veins like music vibrates a harp string. Music and magic, the very soul of the Dance, thrummed in my body and quickened my breath, and I shivered with it.

"Can't you feel it, Gareth?" Lowra whispered softly. "Can't you feel the magic here?"

Oh, aye. I felt it, all right. It tingled and buzzed through me, akin to but different from the sensation that had been seething through my chest and belly all day. Without taking my eyes off the Dance, mesmerized by it, I tried to answer her, but could not find my voice. I had to draw on all the strength I could muster to close my eyes before I could turn away from the Dance.

"I am no Healer." My voice sounded hoarse and rusty, as if I hadn't used it for too long. "And I have no magic. Not I. No magic at all. I never have . . ."

Lowra tore the bandage from her arm. I stared at it and lost the thread of what I was saying as my voice trailed off into silence. Where this morning there had been a clean slice in the skin of her upper arm, now there was only a thin, white scar. "That Somber Rider's dagger cut this to the bone," she said softly. "Yarrow didn't heal it. You did. But because you've never been trained, because you've never been shown the strength of your Gift, it took time for the Healing to complete itself."

I stared at her arm uncomprehendingly, then stepped back, shaking my head, denying her words. "No—"

She reached out. Her fingers closed tightly about my wrist. "Look you," she said. "You defeated a warlock this morning, Gareth." Exasperation rasped in her voice, and she glared at me. "You overcame the spell that would have turned your own weapon against you. The spell dissipated before the magic you used. You used magic."

"No . . ."

"Do I need to slap you until your eyes cross? You *did* use magic."

My mouth was too dry to form words, and my chest was so tight that breathing hurt. I shook my head and tore my arm from her grip, then turned away from her, from the Dance, watching the fiery blaze slowly fade and die on the topmost cone of Cloudbearer.

"No," I whispered again, unable to believe, unwilling to believe. I had no magic. How could I have magic? In twenty-four years, I had never felt it stir within me, never had so much as an inkling that I could claim any magic at all, much less the powerful gift Lowra assured me I had. It was Eryd who had possessed the magic, Eryd, who lay cold and dead in his grave these last twenty years. Not I.

"Gareth." Lowra's voice seemed to come from a great distance. I turned slowly to look at her. She stood at my elbow, a petite, delicate woman, pretty as a summer wild-flower with her dark gold hair and her brown-gold eyes, her small, pointed chin and wide, clear brow. It was as if I was seeing her for the first time. So delicate she appeared almost fragile. Yet she had dispatched the Somber Rider with lethal efficiency. She used that deadly little Veniani recurved hunting bow as if it were part of her. And she knew how to use the long dagger that in Tyra we called a *cleddor bachen*, a small sword, usually held in the left hand behind the targe or small shield. Deft and agile, she was. And quick and deadly.

"Gareth, did you hear me?" she asked again. She still sounded faint and distant.

"I heard you," I replied, my voice sounding much calmer than I felt. That unsettled sensation churned and seethed in

my chest and belly like the water around the Hook in Broche
Rhuidh's harbor in winter.

"You know what this place is," Davigan said.

I didn't bother to look at him. I nodded. "I know."

And I did. I had been well steeped in the tale since the
day I was old enough to understand. The Dance and my family were inextricably connected, and both Fyld and Kenzie
had made sure I understood the implications of that. Oh, aye.
I had never before seen this Dance of stones, but I knew this
place very well, indeed.

Since long before the Celae had come from Tyra to this
island, the Tyadda had lived here. They recognized the high
places, Cloudbearer in particular, as sacred to the Duality
and the seven gods and goddesses. Even legend is vague
about the origins of the Dance of Nemeara, and who built it.
It goes back to the misty beginnings, but all agree that it was
at least as old as the Tyadda race on the island. The magic of
the place figures prominently in all the tales of Red Kian of
Skai, who brought the fabled sword Kingmaker back to Celi
when it had been stolen during a rebellion. Red Kian stood as
regent until his son Keylan grew to his majority and could
be invested as Prince of Skai. But Kian's second son was
Tiernyn, who became the first—and only—king of a united
Celi, and his third son was Donaugh, Tiernyn's twin, who
was the most powerful enchanter the Celae had ever known.
It was here at the Dance that Tiernyn received Kingmaker
from the gods and goddesses, and it was here that Donaugh
received his gift of powerful magic.

It was here, too, that Brynda had brought the shattered
remains of Kingmaker after the devastating invasion of Celi.
When she laid the broken sword on the altar, both Tiernyn
and his son Tiegan lay dead on the field of Cam Runn, and the
only hope for Celi lay hidden in the womb of Sheryn, Tiegan's
widow, who was pregnant. And it was here that Brynda

received the promise that Celi would rise again under a strong and powerful king and defeat the Maedun, aided by the powerful enchanter of the prophecy.

It was the Maedun's own prophecy that foretold the coming of the enchanter. That prophecy had been the cause of the struggle with the Maedun in the first place. Their whole campaign against Celi was fought because some long-ago Maedun seer had predicted that an enchanter rising from my great-grandfather's line would destroy Maedun, crushing them completely and eradicating every Maedun sorcerer.

"I can't go in there."

"And just why can't you?" she demanded fiercely. Her eyes blazed with an odd mixture of exasperation, anger, and concern. She planted both fists on her hips and glared at me again. "How can you deny your gifts like this? Don't you know how badly Skai needs them? And you? Or do Davigan and I have to drag you in there?"

"I'm not the enchanter of the prophecy," I said blankly. I looked at the Dance, then at Lowra. "I can't be."

"Perhaps not," she said, her voice softening. "But you are a powerful Healer. Or you will be. For your father's sake, you must go in there."

She had a deadly and accurate aim with that lethal little Veniani recurved bow. Her aim with the remark was no less exact and sure. And there was the sting of truth and inevitability in her words. I took a deep breath, settled my plaid more surely on my shoulder, then made sure of my sword. Not that I expected to need it in there—or expected it to be of any use to me if I did need it. But it was a comforting gesture. I was positive in my own mind that I had no magic, that I was no Healer, and the only way to prove it to both her and Davigan was to go into the Dance. The magic held within was Tyadda magic— gentle magic. As Davigan had so recently pointed out, it could not be used for harm. I would be perfectly safe in the Dance.

Just terrified enough to curl my toes. But I didn't want to tell them that.

For my father's sake rather than my own, I put one reluctant foot in front of the other and crossed the winter-killed grass. As I passed between the two massive uprights of the entry trilithon, the shadow falling across me felt black and cold as the winter sea. The sound of the wind died away as I stepped into the Dance itself. Outside, the trees and grasses bent and twisted to the surging gusts of the wind, but within the Dance, the evening became suddenly hushed and silent as a shrine. The texture of the air around me seemed to change, as if the Dance were a place apart from the rest of the world, a place untroubled by the turmoil and pain of the land. Even the padding of my footsteps on the beaten grass sounded different, cushioned and softened and muffled.

This place was the heart of Celi, and it was the very soul of Skai. I paused between the outer ring of trilithons and the inner ring of capped stones and looked up. Stars glimmered in the dark sky behind Cloudbearer's shoulder, but a faint glow of turquoise and gold still showed on the western horizon above the sea. The silence was complete. I could not hear the distant shushing of the sea lapping against the rocky shoreline, nor could I hear the horses tearing at the winter-pale grass where Lowra and Davigan awaited me. I pulled my plaid closer around my shoulders and stepped between the capped menhirs, into the central horseshoe of standing stones, and walked forward until I stood before the altar itself.

Without conscious thought, I went to my knees before the altar. The stone felt cool and slick beneath my hand as I stroked it. The stone was blacker than the night sky, and polished to such a gloss, I thought I saw the reflection of the stars glinting in its depths. As I watched, the faint light coalesced into a vague, slender shape. Then, with an almost audible snap, it was a sword, and I was once again watching Bane.

The sword lay on a wooden table, the planks waxed and polished and gleaming. A crystal pitcher of wine and two crystal goblets stood beside it, as if someone had pushed them carelessly aside to place the sword on the table. Tall, many-branched candelabra stood on the table, casting a warm light across the room. The wine in the goblets and the pitcher glinted like rubies, or blood, in the soft glow. The waxed and polished surface of the table reflected the silvery glimmer of the sword blade. The runes spilling down the blade glinted in the candle glow like sparking facets cut into a gem.

Two men stood by the table, one to either side, both of them fully intent on the sword between them. The younger man was the courier who had taken the sword from the young cowherd. The older man wore a robe of warlock's gray, and a faint, dark aura shimmered around his head.

The warlock reached out a gnarled and veined hand, the skin stained with brown age spots. He ran one finger along the runes etched into the blade. His mouth drew in on itself in deep contemplation as he examined the sword.

The courier spoke, his voice jarring in the stillness of the room. "Are you pleased with the sword, Grandfather?" he asked.

The old man looked up, his eyes a deep, drowned black in the soft light. "Tell me again where you got this," he said.

The courier reached for one of the goblets and stood watching the ruby swirl of the wine as he tilted the goblet first one way, then the other. "I took it from a young boy—a cowherd, I believe—in that province the Celae call Mercia."

The warlock nodded. "I see," he said. "And how far would that be from the palace at Dun Camas?"

The courier frowned thoughtfully. "I'm not sure," he said at last. "Perhaps three leagues? Certainly not more than four."

The warlock reached out and caressed the blade of the sword again. He smiled, revealing large, yellowed teeth. "I see," he said again. He touched the runes. "Can you see what's under my finger here?"

The courier leaned forward, peering intently down at the blade. He straightened and shook his head. "Just the blade, Grandfather. Very clean and bright, though, don't you think? Considering where I found it. I doubt that young farmer knew how to take care of a sword properly."

"You don't see the runes on the blade?"

The courier shook his head. Then he blinked in surprise. "Runes?" he repeated. "On the blade?"

The old man laughed softly, deep satisfaction in his expression. "You don't realize what a prize you've brought me," he said. "Only those with magic—even ours rather than the crude native magic—can see the runes. This is one of those swords they called a Rune Blade."

"A Rune Blade?" the courier repeated. He reached out to touch the blade, but changed his mind and simply let his hand hover above the rippled glimmer of the steel. "I've heard of those, I think. A sword of great power."

The warlock picked up a silver bell with a carved ivory handle and rang it once. The echoes of the chime had not faded before a servant stepped hastily into the room. He was Celae, his deep blue eyes fogged by the strength of the spell the warlock kept active on his estate. The warlock hardly bothered to look at him.

"Fetch me a blanket," he said. "One of the finest in the house." He touched the sword again, as the servant nodded and hurried away. "Great power, indeed," he said to the courier. "Power that can tap into the intrinsic magic of this ridiculous country where we cannot touch it. The Lord Hakkar has been searching for one of these for a long time. Think of how grateful he will be to both you and me if we present him with a genuine Rune Blade." He barely turned as the servant reentered the room carrying a softly woven woolen blanket. He took the blanket, dismissed the servant with a gesture with one finger, then gently and carefully wrapped the sword in the woolen fabric. "Just think," he said, smiling in satisfaction. "For this, I will surely be called to Court, and

will finally get away from this miserable frontier. And you — you may
get your fondest wish and be given a troop of soldiers to command."

I drew back from the altar stone, shivering. The vision of
Bane faded until only the faint gleam of the stars reflected
back at me from the polished jet of the altar. It was cold in the
Dance, and frost glittered on the grass and edged the stones
with silver. Deep, stark fear, colder than the frosty air, froze in
my belly.

Hakkar of Maedun holding a Rune Blade . . .

It couldn't happen. And this was my task, my responsibility. This was why I had been drawn to Skai. I had to prevent Bane from falling into Hakkar's hands.

A sound just below the threshold of hearing broke the
stillness. Something moved with a rustle just barely audible in
the night. I lurched around, startled.

A man glided silently as a shadow between the two
uprights of the gateway trilithon and across the frost-rimed
grass toward me. He moved easily, and so smoothly that the
grass seemed hardly to bend beneath his feet. No footsteps
showed in his wake; the hard sparkle of the frosted grass
remained undisturbed. He wore a long robe, pale in the deep-
ening night, girdled by something that glinted like gold. His
hair and beard, silver as the moon itself, framed a face carved
into austere planes and hollows, the eyes shadowed by silver
eyebrows. He gave the impression of vast age and wisdom,
but moved with the lithe grace of a youth. I drew back as he
approached the altar, but he held out his hand to me in welcome, and smiled.

"You are correct in your assumption, Gareth ap
Brennen," he said quietly. "At all cost, you must find a way to
prevent Bane from falling into Hakkar's hands."

"Who are you?" I asked, badly startled.

"Men call me Myrddin," he said. "I am the guardian of

this place. I am the one who led your great-grandfather to Kingmaker. I am the one who guided your great-uncle Donaugh to the place where he found Wyfydd the Smith to fashion Heartfire and Soulshadow. With those Rune Blades it was possible for him to defeat the father of this Hakkar of Maedun, who now sits in Clendonan and calls himself Lord Protector of Celi. And I am the one who received the shards of Kingmaker from Brynda al Keylan."

I took in a deep breath of the cold air. My belly still quivered in both fear and excitement. Of course he was Myrddin. Who else would come to me through the shadows of the Dance and speak to me of Rune Blades and magic?

"I must prevent Bane from reaching Hakkar," I said, then repeated his words. *"At all cost . . ."*

Myrddin stood before me as I knelt by the altar. He put out his hands to take mine and raised me to my feet. "At all cost," he said again. "But I would not send you unarmed and unprepared to face your tasks, Gareth son of Brennen. Look around you."

The moon lifted above the shoulder of Cloudbearer, washing silver along the stones of the Dance. The shadows played strange tricks on my eyes. For a moment, I thought I saw the figures of men and women carved in bas-relief into the tall stones of the inner horseshoe, carved with such clarity and precision, the figures seemed alive, breathing like real men and women. Startled at first, then frightened, I realized they *were* men and women.

And I recognized them.

Rhianna of the Air, her long, moon-silvered hair floating like a veil about her body. Cernos of the Forest, with the tall rack of stately antlers rising from his brow. Adriel of the Waters, carrying her enchanted ewer. Gerieg of the Crags, with the mighty hammer he used to smite the rocks and shake the ground, spilling great landslips down from the crags into the glens. Beodun of the Fires, carrying in one hand the lamp of benevolent fire and in the other, the lightning bolt of wild-fire. Sandor of the Plain, his hair blowing like prairie grass around his face. And the *darlai*, the Spirit of the Land, the Mother of All, smiling at me with compassion and tenderness.

"What's happening?" I asked hoarsely. I looked for Myrddin, but he was gone, and I was alone with the seven gods and goddesses.

11

I stood frozen in the center of the Dance, staring in awe at the silent figures revealed by the moonlight. Rhianna of the Air stepped forward. She crossed the stark black-and-silver shadows like the wraith she had to be and came toward me. Half-stunned in disbelief, I could only stare at her. Her bare feet did not quite touch the ground as she approached. The veil of her hair floated around her naked body, cloaking her in silver gilt, drifting on a gentle breeze I could not feel. The wind that had lifted my hair and fluttered my plaid beyond the circle could not enter here, but the air was still the cold of late winter. The chill that bit at my face and hands did not so much as prickle the smooth, warm flesh of her arms.

She stopped less than an arm's length in front of me and held out her hands, palms up.

"Give me your hands, Gareth Skaiborn," she said, her voice as soft as the breathy whisper of reed flutes, as gentle as quiet harp music.

I became aware that my mouth hung open, so I closed it. But I still could not move. To my chagrin, I seemed capable only of standing there, staring like a simpleton. I could not quite convince myself that I was dreaming, nor could I believe I was awake and this was really happening. Rhianna of the Air merely smiled.

"Give me your hands, Gareth," she said again, raising her own hands slightly to guide me. "Your hands."

I stood frozen. My mouth was dry. I could hardly speak the words that shamed me. "I'm afraid . . ."

"I know. Give me your hands."

I tried again, and found I could move. Dumbly, I placed

my hands in hers. Their warmth dissipated the chill of the night and made me think of midsummer, of rich, green grasses and sweet meadow flowers. The perfume of wildflowers and newly mown hay rose around us in the Dance. Energy surged from her hands into mine, then up my arms and into my chest. It smashed into my heart and my belly, snatching away my breath, filling me with something I could not describe. Pain. Pleasure. Both. Neither. I forgot to breathe.

As the odd surge of energy abated, a new awareness seeped into me, filling my head, my heart, my very spirit. In the air around me, bright threads of power braided together, flooded across my skin like sunshine in summer, tangible as wind or water. Beneath my feet, streams of power flowed like rivers through the earth, through the very rocks and soil of Skai. I felt as if I could trail my fingers through them the same way I could reach out of a boat and let the silken waters caress my fingertips.

My body began to quiver and shake, and my heart thundered and pounded in my chest as if it were bent on tearing itself loose. I took a deep, shuddering breath, then accepted the Healing magic pouring into me from the goddess's hands, from the very air around me and the ground beneath my feet. A vast, deep, slow calm settled over me. For the first time in my life, I felt as if I was in the place I was meant to be, and becoming and being who I was meant to be.

"Remember," Rhianna said, her voice lilting softly like music in the air, "if you don't want your own strength to dwindle and ebb away, the Healing power you use must be replenished from the power around you. You must draw strength from the one being Healed, too. If there is no strength left there because the wound is mortal, even all your magic cannot help. You must have the strength to help whom you may, but you must develop the wisdom to accept it when you cannot help."

"Wisdom," I repeated quietly. I looked at her, all the wisdom in the world shining from her eyes. "Will I ever develop enough wisdom? I despair of it, my lady."

"Balance," she said. "On this night especially, remember balance."

Balance . . . The night of balance between light and dark. Vernal Equinox? I hadn't realized the time had passed so quickly. It startled me, and I stared at her, dumbfounded.

"Do you understand what I mean?" she asked.

"I think so," I said hoarsely.

Smiling gently, she let go of my hands and stepped away. I didn't see her move back to her place in the circle, but she was suddenly no longer standing before me. I stood alone among the moon-washed silver and sharp, black shadows at the center of the Dance, the empty altar stone before me, the moon rising over Cloudbearer's shoulder behind me.

I let my hands fall to my sides. A soft sound made me turn toward the head of the stone horseshoe, across the altar from where I stood. She left her place in the circle and came slowly to me. The *darlai* . . . The Mother of All. If the Dance of Nemeara was the heart of Celi and Skai, the *darlai* was our fire and spirit. Silver streaked the dark hair that fell past her shoulders to frame a face I could not call beautiful, but which held all the love and understanding and compassion of a mother. She had seen much and endured much, had loved much and was loved much in return. Her aura seemed to reach out and wrap me in warmth and acceptance and all-encompassing love. I went quickly to my knee before her and bowed my head, a courtesy and obeisance she deserved and was no less than her due.

"Lady . . ."

She reached out and gently touched my cheek. Her fingers burned my skin like hot coals, were cold as the ice in the upper reaches of the headwaters of the Eidon. I closed my eyes as my breath caught in my throat. She stepped back, and when I looked up at her again, she was smiling.

"You know who I am, don't you?" Her voice was like the combined music of harp and soft, breathy reed flutes. It rang around the circle, chiming against the megaliths as if they were made of crystal and the words of silver.

"Aye, Lady," I said. "You are the *darlai*. The Mother of All, and I do you honor."

"I am she, and I have a gift for you, Gareth Skaiborn."

I shuddered, remembering the tales of Donaugh the Enchanter. She had gifted him with magic stronger than any man should have to bear by himself. I had not that strength. Nor had I the wisdom of Donaugh ap Kian, brother of King Tiernyn. I knew I could not bear the burden of magic like that. "Please, Lady," I whispered. "Oh, please, Lady. I don't want magic."

She smiled, both sympathy and amusement in her eyes. "You already have magic," she said. "You were born with it, my child. My gift is but its awakening, so that you might use it well in service of Skai and Celi."

I bowed my head, drew in a deep breath to control the quivering in my chest. Once again, that desolate feeling swept through me, the same sensations that had brought me to my knees by the ruins of Dun Llewen. If Skai could do that to me, then I needed all the strength, all the magic, I could get to serve her properly.

"If it means I may better serve Skai, I accept," I said. I had no other choice.

"I think you are very like him, Gareth son of Skai," she said. Something akin to amusement lilted in her voice. I glanced up at her in surprise.

"Like him, Lady?" I asked. "Like who?"

She reached out once more and drew a finger down the side of my face, tracing the line from cheek to jaw in a gentle, loving gesture. "Like the one you fear to be like. Your kinsman, Donaugh Secondborn. Oh, Gareth, would that your magic could be as strong as his. But even I cannot give that gift to you, as much as I would wish to."

"I would not wish it, Lady," I said fervently. Just the thought of wielding as much power as Donaugh the Enchanter, son of Red Kian of Skai, was enough to frighten me cold. I would never have the wisdom to use it as wisely and as well as he had.

"I could promise him only service," she said. "I can promise you little more, Gareth Skaiborn." She cupped her hands around my temples, then stepped back and made an eloquent and graceful gesture with one hand. "Watch. Learn."

Color and light flashed and flared brightly, and spears of blue and green and gold light crackled and leapt across the Dance. Music like the chime of harp and flutes and pipes rang around us until the air vibrated with it and my blood and sinews thrummed with the same rhythm. Music and magic, the very soul of the Dance . . .

The megaliths seemed to be made of crystal gems, and the light streaked from one to the next, glittering, leaping, growing, running like liquid fire from pillar to pillar, striking sparks of green and red and blue and violet. One standing stone after the other caught and erupted into evanescent light until I was certain we were trapped within a crystal that caught the sun and sent it sparking in shimmering rainbows of color and light to all corners of the immense Dance. The music swelled until it filled the Dance, and the very air quivered and shimmered with it.

Images spun and swirled in the coruscating light. Two swords wheeled past my dazzled eyes, one of them bright and gleaming, reflecting the liquid light and color, the other the darker shadow of the first. Runes spilled down the center of both blades like liquid, runes I could not read because neither sword was mine. But I knew them. Heartfire and Soulshadow, the swords that Wyfydd the Smith had crafted for Donaugh the Enchanter so that he might defeat the first Maedun invasion—the swords that were now lost.

Another sword spun through the wildly flaring light, and I knew this one, too. The plain, leather-bound hilt with its one crystal gem at its pommel was even more fabled than Heartfire and Soulshadow. This was Kingmaker itself that hovered before me, the runes along its gleaming blade glittering and sparking with a fire of their own. Kingmaker, which had broken on the field at Cam Runn during the second Maedun invasion—the successful one. Kingmaker, which had shattered in King Tiernyn's hand and spelled disaster to Celi. But now it was whole here in this Dance of stones, whole and strong and eager for the hand which must hold it to drive out the Maedun. But even as I reached for it, I knew it was not for me. It whirled away from me to become lost in the scintillating brilliance of the light.

Then, finally, there was another sword. And this one I knew, too. The runes flashing along the blade coalesced into words, and I read them aloud in wonder and awe.

"COURAGE DIES WITH HONOR," I whispered. "Bane . . ."

"Bane," the *darlai* repeated. "Your sword, Gareth. You have the magic to bond with it. Find it. You must find it . . ."

She burned before me with a radiance that filled the world with light and color. I closed my eyes against the painful brilliance. When I opened them again, it was to darkness and silence. The light and color were gone; the music had faded with it. I knelt before the cold stone altar within a silent horseshoe of standing stones, and the moon rode half-hidden in a stormy sea of clouds high overhead. Burning with fever, I bent forward slowly until my cheek rested on the smooth, chill surface of the altar stone.

I awoke to the sound of rain. I lay on something soft and wholly comfortable, wrapped warm against the damp chill in my plaid and a soft blanket. A fire burned nearby, spreading heat and flickering light into the dim space. Behind me, rain hissed as it fell, and a trickle of water made soft, musical sounds as it spattered against last year's sodden leaves. Music. It reminded me of the music of the Dance.

But I didn't want to think of that right now. Later would do. Later when I wasn't so sleepy. Much later.

Someone bent forward and put a hand to my forehead. It felt cool and soothing against the feverish warmth of my skin. I opened my eyes and looked up to meet a pair of golden brown eyes. The skin around those eyes was puckered with concern. For a moment, I didn't know her.

"Gareth?" she said softly. "How do you feel?"

Then I had a name. Lowra al Drywn. And all the rest of it. Small, lovely, delicate, and deadly. A Tyadda woman, like the first bheancoran to the first Prince of Skai. That odd sensation fluttered again in my chest.

"Where are we?" I asked thickly.

"In an old sheepherder's bothy," she said. "On the lower slopes of Cloudbearer."

"How did I get here?" I asked. The last thing I remembered was closing my eyes after all the gods and goddesses had disappeared back into the megaliths that represented them. And swords—many swords swirling through the flaring light and color. Heartfire, Soulshadow, Kingmaker. And Bane. I wasn't sure if I had dreamed the time in the Dance, or whether it was real. But if I concentrated, I could feel the magic and music humming softly along my nerves and sinews, singing in my veins and bones. It was real—far too real for comfort.

"Davigan and I brought you here," she said. "You weren't in much shape to bring yourself. A meeting with the gods and goddesses takes a lot of strength from a person."

I looked up at her. The dimness blurred her features, but I thought I saw a faint smile curve her lips back. "That sounds as if you speak from experience," I said.

She shrugged. "Mayhaps," she said. "Sleep now, Gareth. You need to rest to recover your strength."

I needed no more urging. I closed my eyes and slept.

When next I awoke, it was full daylight. Sun streamed in from behind me and turned the raw, undressed stone of the curving wall to brilliant gold. The tantalizing aroma of roasting meat filled the air, mingled with the scent of fresh kafe tea. I sat up.

The small, round bothy had only a little more than half a roof, but that half had kept us reasonably dry during the rain. Moss grew thickly on the bare, windowless walls. Outside the low door, sheltering thatches of hazel and willow clustered close. It was a snug, protected place, a good place to hide from the Maedun.

Davigan filled a cup with kafe tea and handed it to me. "Awake are you?"

"I think so," I said. "How long was I asleep?"

"Two whole days and nights," he said. "Enough to regain your strength, I hope?"

I nearly spilled the tea. "Two days?" I repeated, startled. "Two days? I had no idea it was that long . . ."

He shrugged. "You must have needed it."

I put down the tea and scrubbed my hands across my cheeks. "I feel as if I could sleep for another two days," I said.

He picked up his harp and ran his fingers across the polished wood. A whisper of music shimmered softly in the small room. "What did you learn in the Dance?" he asked.

"Among other things, that I must find my father's sword," I said. "The courier has given it to a warlock, and the warlock wants to make a gift of it to Hakkar."

His hand stilled in midair above the harp. He stared at me, his head cocked at a curious, listening angle, an odd expression stealing across his face. "A Rune Blade in Hakkar's hands?" he said slowly. "That could be bad."

"Very bad. But I don't know where to begin looking."

"They haven't many garrisons in Skai and Wenydd," he said. "They destroyed the strongholds like Dun Eidon and Dun Llewyn, and built their own of vitrified rock. Each garrison has a warlock, some of them more powerful than others. The one you faced the other day was among the strongest I've seen. But there are stories of another powerful warlock, an old man, in their garrison just north of where Dun Eidon used to be. On the coast about a league or two north of the Ceg."

"That must be the warlock I saw in my vision," I said. "He'd send the sword by courier, wouldn't he?"

Davigan nodded. "Probably. And likely a courier like the one who brought it here to Skai. One who has a lot of resistance to their spell to get through the Dead Lands."

"The Dead Lands," I repeated, and shuddered. I had never seen them and was quite sure I never wanted to. Because Hakkar's spell could not be forced into the high country, because the mountains themselves defied Maedun blood sorcery, Hakkar had deepened and intensified his spell along the eastern slopes of the Spine of Celi, and along the foothills that marked the border between Venia and Brigland. It was, I suppose, similar to the curtain of enchantment Donaugh raised to keep the Maedun out of Celi before he fell to treachery and the Maedun invaded. No Celae, even those with Tyadda blood, could safely penetrate the Dead Lands. Hakkar kept the spell active to be certain that the renegade yrSkai and Veniani were contained, and that no other Celae could run to the mountains to escape subjugation. The spell was powerful enough to affect even the Tyadda, who were mostly immune to the spell that prevented the Celae from attacking the Maedun. I had seen the agony inflicted by that spell—in my dream of Ralf, as his father and brother tried to attack the courier.

The sorcery affected the Maedun as well. Couriers who carried messages back and forth had to have a high level of resistance to the spell, and were often given talismans to help protect them. If the courier carrying Bane to Hakkar managed to get into the Dead Lands, we had very little chance of ever catching up to him and taking the sword. The Tyadda blood in our veins couldn't help us there. The Dead Lands would stop us even more quickly than an arrow.

"Is there any way we could make ourselves immune to the Dead Lands' sorcery?" I asked.

Before he could answer, a shadow fell across the door. I looked up quickly as Lowra entered the bothy. She glanced at me, nodded, then made her way across the small room to the fire and poured herself some kafe tea. She wore her bow slung across her shoulder and carried a quiver full of arrows at her hip. Small for a warrior, she was, but certainly no less a warrior for all that. Once again, that odd sensation fluttered in my chest, and this time, I knew it for what it was.

"Why didn't you tell me you were my bheancoran?" I asked thickly. It was suddenly an effort to speak.

She looked at me over the rim of her cup. Her eyebrows twitched. "So you know that now, do you?"

I nodded, unable to speak. My throat felt too dry and rusty.

She sat back on her heels. "I thought you should have

known who I was when we bonded on the slopes of Cloudbearer that first day."

Davigan's words came back to me, the amusement in them obvious now. *"She always expects other people to see obscure things she thinks are obvious."* So this was the obvious thing that Lowra knew and I did not.

"I've never expected to have a bheancoran," I said. "I was brought up believing I would never have one. Nobody told me how a bonding would feel. How was I to know? How was I to recognize a bonding when it happened?"

She was quiet for a moment, sipping her tea. Then: "You might have trusted your instincts," she said softly, amusement as well as exasperation in her voice. "We have much to talk about, I think."

"We do," I said. "And not just about the bonding. You might want to tell me why neither of you told me who you were. Or, more specifically, who Davigan is. Or should my instincts have told me that, too?"

12

Lowra sat back and stared at me. Except for the faint tilt of one eye-brow, her face was so bland as to be expressionless. But I had already learned to mistrust that look. "Whatever do you mean by that?" she said. "I don't have any idea what you're talking about."

I ignored her and watched Davigan. He leaned back against the wall of the ruined bothy and held his harp tightly to his chest, both arms around it as if it were a shield that could protect him from my knowledge. New-found knowledge. Come with the magic, mayhaps, in the Dance. He regarded me calmly enough, though, his brown-gold eyes glinting with something I interpreted as amusement. But he didn't speak. He merely sat there and looked at me.

My own gaze was as calm, I think, and just about as bland, as I looked back and forth between him and Lowra. Brother and sister, they called themselves. I had believed them, although they didn't look at all alike, even if I discounted the fact they were both Tyadda. Both of them had the characteristic dark gold hair and brown-gold eyes, but that was all they had in common. They shared no other features as did most other siblings I knew. While I had seen brothers and sisters with fewer features in common, most of them shared at least one family trait. In my family, it's the nose—strong, prominent, thin. Even Eryd and I, with our very different color hair and eyes, had shared our father's knife-blade-straight nose and his square chin.

Lowra's gaze didn't waver. "What do you mean?" she asked again, her voice as bland as her face.

"Lowra al Drywn," I said, watching her. "That's what you call yourself, isn't it?"

She nodded gravely. "That's who I am," she agreed.

I turned to Davigan. "Yet this man you call brother is not Davigan ap Drywn, is he?"

Lowra said nothing. One corner of Davigan's mouth curled in a rueful little half smile, but he, too, remained silent.

I glanced at him levelly. "Are you, Davigan Harper?" I said. I went to one knee before him, doing him homage. "Shall I offer service to the son of Prince Tiegan, grandson of King Tiernyn, Davigan ap Tiegan ap Tiernyn, even though you are not King of Celi, but brother to the King?" I drew my sword and held it across my palms, offering it to him. "Will you accept the service of Gareth dav Brennen ti'Kenzie, only son of the Prince of Skai?"

Lowra started to protest, but Davigan held up one hand to stop her. For the first time, she subsided, conceding to his wishes. It surprised me, but it probably shouldn't have.

"It's interesting that you style yourself in the Tyran way, but claim to be heir to the throne of Skai," Davigan said, the small smile playing around his mouth, amusement dancing in his eyes. "But you needn't offer me service, Gareth ap Brennen. I will, though, accept your service in my brother's name. How did you know who I was?"

It was my turn to smile, but my smile was far more rueful than amused. "You yourself told me in many little ways," I said. "And I think I knew before I went into the Dance. But when the *darlai* gave me magic, and I saw all the swords swirling through the Dance, the man in my vision looked like you holding Kingmaker . . . or reaching for it, I can't quite remember which. Since you're the younger twin, it must have been Daefyd I saw." I slid my sword home in its scabbard at my back and sat cross-legged under the sagging roof of the bothy, letting my hands rest on my knees.

Davigan nodded slowly. "So you have magic, too? As well as the Healing?"

"Aye," I said, my voice sounding glum even to my own ears. "Or so the *darlai* tells me."

Davigan grinned widely. "You look so immensely pleased with your Gift," he said. I shot him a sharp, nearly resentful look, which he blithely ignored. He glanced at Lowra, still grinning. "I told you so," he said.

She inclined her head in acknowledgment, but didn't take her eyes off me. "So you did," she agreed. "Indeed you did, Little Brother."

There she went, calling him her brother again. "Why did you tell me you were brother and sister?" I asked. "Was that just a ruse?"

"No," Davigan said. "We *are* brother and sister." He cut off my protest with a quick gesture. "My mother married Lowra's father when Daefyd and I were ten and Lowra was twelve. We grew up as brother and sister. By Tyadda law, we *are* brother and sister."

"Aye, well," I said. "And by Celae law, too." I glanced at Lowra. She sat with her knees drawn up and her arms around her legs, chin propped on her knees. "And you're my bheancoran?"

She nodded, unsmiling.

I wondered irrelevantly how Caitha dan Malcolm would react to Lowra, if I ever managed to return to Tyra. Caitha was hardly a woman to share a man, even if she could understand that the bond between bheancoran and prince was *not* a love bond. It could make my life far more interesting than I could be comfortable with.

"How did you know you were my bheancoran?" I asked. "Did you even know I had survived the attack on Dun Eidon all those twenty years ago?"

"I had to be your bheancoran," she said. "Not necessarily

yours, you understand, but to the son of the Prince of Skai. I knew from the time I could walk that I would be bheancoran. But I certainly wasn't Daefyd's bheancoran. The only thing left was bheancoran to the man who would become the next Prince of Skai." She shrugged. "We didn't know which of Brennen's sons had survived, but we knew one had. Otherwise, I wouldn't have grown up knowing I would be bheancoran to the Prince of Skai." She shrugged again. "If you had not come here, I would have gone to Skerry to find you."

"I was in Tyra," I said, then shook my head. "No, I don't suppose that would have mattered, would it? It wouldn't have stopped you."

"Hardly," Lowra said dryly.

Davigan laughed. "Stopped her? Not for a second."

Lowra grinned at me. There was more than a touch of grim determination in the expression, making it oddly thin and attenuated. "You may not want a bheancoran, my lord Gareth, but you've got one now. We're bonded, you and I, and you can no more send me away than I could go." She lost her smile, and her face became grave and remote. "I am committed to your quest now. I must go with you."

I looked back and forth between her and Davigan. A shaft of sunlight blazed down through a hole in the broken roof and slanted between them like a knife blade, turning their hair to molten gold. I raised both hands in surrender, palms up.

"Just as I am committed to your quest," I said quietly. "How could I refuse help to the son of Prince Tiegan?" I thought of my father lying in his chamber at Skerry Keep, in pain and close to death, and what he had already sacrificed for his king. I closed my eyes for a moment, but I could not block out the picture I had called up. Lowra leaned forward and put her hand on my arm, surprising me. A gentle, comforting gesture. Not something I had expected from one as fierce as she.

"I have the Sight, Gareth," she said softly. "I do not See you becoming Prince of Skai for a long time yet. When you become Prince of Skai, your hair will be silver. In my Seeing, you looked as old as your father is now."

I looked down at her. A hard, painful surge of hope slammed through my belly. "You know this for certain?" I asked.

She dropped her gaze. "No," she said. "Nothing is ever for certain. Even Donaugh the Enchanter said that."

I watched her for a moment. She looked up and met my eyes gravely. I had to take her word. What other choice was there? But now I had hope, and perhaps some assurance of a less terrifying outcome. Some of the tenseness drained from my shoulders as hope and relief flickered together in a warming flame beneath my heart.

"What's our first move?" I asked.

"Our first move?" Davigan rose and tucked his harp into its carry case. "I think we'd better see if we can intercept that Maedun courier and reclaim your sword. The best place to begin looking is probably their stronghold north of Dun Eidon."

I got to my feet and stooped to help gather up the utensils to pack them into Lowra's saddle pack. "The sword first?" I repeated. "Do you think that more important than finding Daefyd?"

Davigan was silent for a moment, his mouth drawn into a grim and level line. "I'm thinking of what might happen if we let a Rune Blade fall into Hakkar's hands," he said quietly. "Your aunt Brynda was right to worry about it. Only the seven gods and goddesses and the Duality itself know what might happen if Hakkar gets his hands on Bane."

Lowra tucked the last of the camp things into her saddle

pack. She turned to me, her face pale. "If Hakkar discovers how to use the magic in a Rune Blade, it might destroy us all," she said.

Brynda had told me how she fought to keep Whisperer, her own sword, out of the hands of the Maedun, and how she had worried about Bane when she discovered that my father had lost it. But I couldn't see how any Maedun, even Hakkar, could use a Rune Blade's magic against us.

"But a Rune Blade won't fight for anyone not born to use it," I said. "Each one was built by Wyfydd Smith for one man or woman, to be handed down to a rightful heir. How could Hakkar use it?"

Lowra shook her head. "Think about it, Gareth," she said. "Tyadda magic is gentle magic. It won't let itself be used to kill. A Rune Blade is imbued with Tyadda magic, and yet it kills—kills very efficiently and deftly, too. It's the exception to the rule. It will kill in defense of Celi; that's what it was made for."

"But Hakkar certainly won't be using it in defense of Celi," I said.

"No, he wouldn't," she agreed. She picked up her saddle pack and started for the door. Beyond, the horses stood already saddled and ready to go. I followed her and helped her tie the saddle pack across her horse's back. Davigan followed us outside and tied his harp carry case to his saddle on the opposite side from his saddle pack. He deferred to Lowra, ready to let her speak for both of them.

I waited for her to continue, but she stood watching a cloud creep out from behind a crag, her face remote and thoughtful.

I prompted her again. "If Hakkar won't be using a Rune Blade in defense of Celi, how will he make it work for him?"

"Think of what Hakkar's been doing these last twenty years," Lowra said.

I frowned blankly at her, not seeing where her reasoning was leading.

"Gathering up all the people he can find who have magic," she said patiently, as if speaking to a loved but slow-witted child. "Think of the implications."

I shook my head. "I don't understand."

"Think." She swung herself up into the saddle and waited for me to mount my horse. "Think of how they managed to finally invade Celi back then."

"Betrayal," I said immediately. The story of how Mikal, bastard son of Tiernyn by a Maedun sorceress, broke through the curtain of enchantment placed by Donaugh around the Isle of Celi was one of the most common stories told on long, cold winter evenings, both on Skerry and in Tyra. "Mikal the Bastard murdered Donaugh and dissolved the curtain of enchantment."

"Aye," Lowra agreed. "But how did Mikal get through the curtain in the first place?"

"He was Tiernyn's son," I said. "Of course he could get—" I broke off, and suddenly felt cold. "Of course," I said, but more slowly this time. "He had Celae blood. And because of his lineage, he had some Tyadda magic."

Lowra nodded. She was pale in the morning light, the skin around her eyes tight and drawn. "Aye, he did. And if Mikal could corrupt Celae or Tyadda magic and use it to kill Donaugh, the greatest enchanter on the Isle of Celi, think what Hakkar has been doing with those possessing Tyadda magic he's been capturing these last twenty years. It might well be he's bred a man or woman who could wield both Maedun blood sorcery and Tyadda magic. Someone who can corrupt our magic so it might kill. And because it would be Tyadda magic, would we still be immune to the spell?"

I shuddered. "I see," I said softly. "And if he could corrupt Tyadda magic, he might be able to corrupt a Rune

Blade." A sudden thought struck me. I turned slowly and
stared up at the towering bulk of Cloudbearer. All the Gifts
the *darlai* and Rhianna had bestowed upon me. All of them
were for one purpose. To stop Bane from falling into
Hakkar's hands. My responsibility. My heart leapt, then settled into a hard, painful gallop. The safety and survival of
Skai depended on *me*.

"He'd use it to kill every Celae and Tyadda on the island,"
Davigan said, startling me. I had almost forgotten he was
there. "So we believe. And Daefyd would also believe it to be
so. He'd tell us our first priority was to regain the sword, then
look for him." He put his heels to the flank of his horse. "We
had best hurry."

We moved inland. To avoid any encounters with patrols of
Somber Riders, we skirted the lower flanks of Cloudbearer
and climbed to the top of a ridge that connected the king
mountain to the westernmost range of the Spine of Celi. That
great wall of crag and spire had protected Skai and Wenydd
for centuries from the predations of the eastern provinces
before Tiernyn united all of Celi under one king. The Spine
now harbored fugitives from all over Celi, and sheltered the
hidden fastnesses of the Tyadda. I believed we were now safe
from the effect of Hakkar's spell. It could not penetrate the
towering, green-clad mountains. But if the spell could not rav-
age the land here, the Somber Riders could—and did. They
hunted the Celae who fled into hiding here—hunted them as
if they were little better than the beasts that inhabited the
forests. Even in Tyra, we heard tales of the depredations of the
Somber Riders as they scoured the mountains of Skai and
Wenydd, and the bleak ranges of Venia in the north.

The glory of the mountains of the Spine filled me with
something akin to reverent awe. I had thought Tyra was a
beautiful country, with its tors and crags and green glens, its

tumbling white rivers and high cliffs, and its still, blue lochs. Skai was easily as beautiful, although her peaks didn't tower quite so loftily as Tyra's. But her glens were as wide and would be as green as spring touched them, and her rivers were as wild and white, and her lochs as broad and calm. Tyra had never twisted my heart the same way as Skai's mountains did.

This was home. This was the land I was born to rule, as my father ruled now from exile on Skerry, and his father had ruled before him. Even caught in the bleak browns, duns, and grays of late winter, this land was beautiful. Soon the land would begin to green toward spring, and then, I knew, it would tear at my heart even more strongly.

The light made sudden bright spears in my vision. I blinked away the unexpected tears. This should have been Eryd's heritage, this physical and spiritual bond with the land. But Eryd had died at the age of eight, before he matured enough to be drawn to the land. Skai must have an heir to become prince when the prince was gone, so Eryd's heritage had become mine. I found it far easier to accept this fact now that I was here in Skai. I wondered if my father would have to come to Skai before he also accepted it—and me. Or would he always and forever believe that because the wrong son— Eyrd, not I—died as a result of the attack on Dun Eidon all those twenty years ago, Skai could not now have a proper heir after him.

We made camp beside a small burn rushing and tumbling its way down the side of the ridge in its hurry to join the River Eidon. All around us, the lofty crags soared up into the dark blue velvet of the evening sky. The days were becoming longer, the nights shorter. It wouldn't be long until the leaves budded on the trees. I thought I had seen a patch of snowberries blooming shyly in a sheltered sunny spot just before we stopped for the night. Spring would come again . . .

With a small shock, I realized that it already had. Equinox had passed. When I counted back, I knew that the night I had spent in the Dance was the Night of Balance. I shivered. It was no wonder the place was alive with magic that night. But how could Vernal Equinox have passed without my knowledge? And why had neither Lowra nor Davigan said anything about it? But as I pulled my plaid around my shoulders and settled for the night, I knew why. We had all been preoccupied that day, and certainly that evening. And why would they have reminded me of something I should have been aware of in the first place?

I laughed softly to myself and let sleep take me.

The full moon shining directly into my eyes woke me. Blinking in the brightness, I rolled out of my nest of spruce boughs and last year's bracken and climbed stiffly to my feet. Lowra and Davigan slept on, undisturbed, rolled in their blankets and cloaks around the subdued, banked fire. Dragging my plaid to my shoulders and buckling my kilt around my hips, I made my way deeper into the woods, following the overhang of the crag.

They were in a small clearing beyond a copse of rowan on the other side of the little burn, exactly where I expected them to be. Kian sat staring into the fire, his hands clasped between his knees. Cullin sat cross-legged, his back to the fire, honing and cleaning the Tyran greatsword he held across his lap. I recognized that sword. Kenzie carried it now. A legacy from his great-grandfather, he'd told me, passed down through Kian, who had given it to him when he returned to Tyra after seeing Princess Sheryn safely across Celi to her people.

Cullin didn't look up as I entered the clearing. "You're late, lad," he said.

"I came as soon as I could," I said defensively. "I'm unused to being summoned by the shades of my ancestors."

A brief half smile played across his lips. "I believe you might have to sort out just exactly who is summoning whom," he said.

"What do you mean?" I asked, startled.

He made an eloquent gesture with one eyebrow. I had seen that exact expression on Kenzie's face; it was decidedly odd to see where he'd inherited it from. Cullin ignored me and went back to his work with the whetstone and the oily rags.

Kian looked up, his face bleak in the reflected glow of the fire. "Come here, lad," he said softly.

I went to him as a child goes to its father, and fell to my knees on the brittle carpet of last year's leaves and pine needles. "What do you want of me?" I asked.

The ghost of a smile quivered on his mouth. "It's what you want of me that's important," he said. "Hold out your hands."

Obediently, I cupped my hands like a child expecting a Winter Solstice treat and held them out to him. He made no move to give me anything; he merely nodded and glanced up at the moon behind his shoulder. Moonlight streamed into the clearing, casting dark, sharp-edged shadows across the gleaming granite of the crags, etching the rowan branches with silver and ebon, and frosting the grass with silver light.

"Look at your hands," Kian whispered. "Can you feel it?"

I looked down. Moonlight ran through my fingers, like molten silver but cold and clean and crisp. It splashed, thickly liquid, onto the ground by my knees, leaving spots of brightness on my kilt. It felt cool and smooth and glabrous, slick and soft as spider silk, strong as good Tyran rope. I could weave it, braid it the same way I braided strands of my own hair. Or I could mold it like clay.

I hardly had to move my fingers. The moonlight coalesced, flowed together, formed itself into a perfect globe the diameter of my cupped hands. Light glowed from its center. Deep down in the heart of the globe, figures moved.

Frightened, I tried to pull away from the lambent flare of the globe, but my hands were frozen around it. I could not move. "What's happening?" I demanded, alarmed.

"You're learning how to use this new magic you've been given," Kian said, his voice distant and faint. "Watch, lad. And learn. There's so little time. Watch. Learn . . ."

Still frightened, but unable to resist, I looked down into the globe again. The glow in the center swept forward with a rush and enveloped me in its silver light. Someone cried out in alarm. It might have been me, but I couldn't be sure. I was caught in the swirl and sweep of a light storm, and I could not free myself.

13

The globe in my hands burned with cold fire, bright spears of light stabbing out like streaks of lightning all around me. A man stood in the center of the bright glow in the heart of the moonlight globe. He was a tall man, his once-black hair silvered and streaked until it gleamed like polished pewter. Even the heavy braid that fell from his left temple showed more white than black. He was slender, but it was not the willowy, limber slenderness of youth. His leanness had the quality of supple, strong leather, as if all the excess flesh had been burned off his bones until nothing remained but strength and resilience and toughness of spirit rather than mere flesh and bone and sinew. No matter what came to face him, this man would endure.

As I watched, he reached out and seized the moonlight, twisting it into thin, strong strands, like finely attenuated wire, which he braided into barely substantial, sinuous plaits. He left the delicate pattern fluttering like spider silk in the air as he turned to the other side of the globe, where the sun blazed brightly above the crags and snow-covered peaks.

He held out his hands and let them fill with sunlight, then wove it into ropes that shone like molten gold. My mouth dried as I recognized the magic; I had heard the bards tell of Tiernyn's sister Torey weaving sunlight into mirrors to reflect back the Maedun warlock's spells at them, incinerating them where they stood. Powerful magic, indeed.

Slowly, the man in the globe brought the silver strands of moonlight and the gleaming gold of sunlight together and wove them into an intricate pattern, a bright lattice of living light. This was not a mirror to thwart blood sorcery, though.

Within the weaving of sunlight, the barely discernible shape of a man moved, as if swimming underwater. A woman's delicate figure floated within the strands of moonlight. They reached toward each other and slowly came together. Their union formed other brilliant filaments of color—blue and green and amber. The colors of Skai. Of Celi itself. And deep within the dazzling pattern, two other nebulous figures floated, rocking gently as if safe within the womb of their mother.

The enchanter stood watching his handiwork for a moment. If he was aware of my presence, he gave no sign, and I could only stand silently, frozen in place, watching in awe. The breath caught in my throat as he spun two more strands of interwoven gold and silver. To either side of the glowing, flashing pattern representing the man, the woman, and the two children, two swords gleamed in the air.

And I knew them. Recognized them as surely as if I had watched their forging and held them in my hands. Two swords out of legend.

Heartfire and Soulshadow. The swords fashioned by Wyfydd Smith himself for Donaugh the Enchanter, swords blessed by each of the seven gods and goddesses who gifted them with some form of their own magic, swords that defended Celi from the first attempted Maedun invasion.

Heartfire and Soulshadow. All the bards sang the story. Both of them now lost, hidden by enchantment until a Champion and Kaith, a warrior-bard, came to claim them.

Then, deep within the twisting strands, Kingmaker himself glowed like a beacon lighting the way home. Or to freedom. And a young man reached out to grasp its hilt firmly in his hand.

The enchanter turned and looked directly at me. He was old. Older than the Guardian of the Dance, older than the magic that formed the Dance. Yet his spirit was still that of a young man. A young man trapped within an aging body. Far too old to produce the son or daughter who would bring forth the strand of color representing the man born to take Kingmaker and lead the Celae as they defeated the Maedun. The man to fulfill the Maedun's own prophecy of an enchanter rising to destroy them all.

Under the shaggy white eyebrows, the enchanter's deep blue eyes glinted with urgency and speculation as he looked at me, as if measuring my worth. Framed by the white hair, the planes and hollows of his face echoed the stringent need in his eyes, and worry etched deep lines that bracketed his mouth and plunged between his eyebrows.

I cried out, and the globe of moonlight shattered in my hands. The shards melted like ice and flowed away between my fingers to splash onto the ground in the middle of the empty clearing where I stood alone.

Frightened, I stared down at my hands. They still glowed softly with the residue of the magic from the moonlight globe. I shuddered and wiped my hands against my kilt, leaving bright smears on the wool. But I could not forget the face of the enchanter.

It was my own face.

I awoke with a start to a fine drizzle sifting out of the sky, beading my plaid with moisture as I lay curled on the cushion of spruce boughs and last year's bracken. Water dripped from the branches of the rowans, making the clusters of dead brown berries glisten in the wan light like the eyes of the birds that called halfheartedly from the depths of the copse.

Fearful of what I might find, I raised my hands and stared at them. But there was no trace of the powdery residue of magic in the lines and creases of the palms. I let out the breath I had been holding and rubbed my hands against my kilt, not sure whether I was relieved or disappointed.

I stretched to wring the kinks out of my back. My whole body ached as if I had spent the night on the practice field sparring with the weaponsmaster and coming out a poor second with the wooden swords. Or perhaps I had spent the night wrestling and being slammed onto the iron-hard beaten-earth floor of the games arena. If just dreaming about practicing magic did this to a man, I wasn't sure I ever wanted to make magic in earnest when I was awake. I might not survive it.

The drizzle turned to a soft, drifting mist as Lowra and Davigan rose from their blankets. Davigan made a sour face as he glanced up at the sky, then went off to search for dry wood to light the fire, which had drowned overnight. Lowra dug among the supplies for the remnants of last night's meal to warm for our fast breaking—provided Davigan could find enough dry wood. Hoping he could, I took the kettle and fetched water from the burn for kafe tea. The warmth of the tea would go a long way to dispel the damp chill of the rain.

Davigan returned with an armload of deadfall and managed to get a fire lit. The fire produced a lot more smoke than flame and heat, but eventually we got the water boiled for tea, and got the leftover rabbit warm enough to eat. I sat with both hands wrapped around my cup, breathing in the delectable vapors from the kafe tea. I felt myself slowly coming back to life. My joints didn't creak quite so alarmingly when I moved, and my muscles didn't protest quite so violently as they had when I first woke.

Lowra came to sit beside me, her own cup held tightly. She looked almost as wan as I felt. I noticed she had eaten very little of the leftover rabbit. Of the three of us, only Davigan seemed to have any appetite.

She muttered a curse as she rubbed a shoulder, then took a sip of her tea.

"Dreams?" I asked.

She nodded. "I don't know if they were Seeings or just dreams," she said irritably. "Sometimes, it's hard to tell."

Intrigued, I looked at her over the rim of my cup. Davigan's cup, actually, but he didn't need it right yet—not nearly so much as I. She frowned at me. "What did you dream?" I asked.

"Of an enchanter," she said. "And woven sunlight and moonlight and dancing colors and bright strands of power."

My heart leapt like a startled deer. "An enchanter?" I repeated. "A man with silver hair and a braid, like a Tyran clansman?"

She looked up at me curiously, then shook her head. "No. He had silver hair, but he looked Tyadda, I think. He might have been Donaugh, King Tiernyn's brother."

I swallowed some tea. It was too hot and scalded the roof of my mouth, but it spread its stimulating warmth through my belly and out into my limbs. "Donaugh the Enchanter? Surely an odd dream."

She nodded. "Yes, it was. But I don't know if it meant anything." She looked up. "You dreamed, too?"

"Aye, I did." I took another sip of tea, being more careful this time. "Of an enchanter, but not of Donaugh. This man looked something like me, although much older. Much, much older. Ancient, he was." I looked down into the tea as if it held all the answers had I but known how to read them "Ancient . . ."

She looked at me for a moment, her face pale. Then she got to her feet and brushed off the seat of her trews. "Well," she said briskly, "we should be on our way, I think. No sense in sitting around here brooding."

"None at all," I agreed. "We might as well be gone."

Between the two of us, we hustled and bustled a protesting Davigan through his kafe tea, onto his horse, and out onto the trail. I glanced over at Lowra as we set off down the sodden track. It would seem that I wasn't the only one who dreamed strange dreams and didn't want to think about them too much come morning.

Interesting . . .

The misty drizzle still had not quite made up its mind to become rain and floated in the air, soaking hair and clothing. Water dripped from the ends of the horses' manes, and their hides shone in the dull light. The bare trees to either side of the narrow track looked dark and bleak with the wet. Except for the soggy clopping of hooves on wet dead leaves and the steady drip of water from every conceivable surface, the world seemed quiet and withdrawn. The birds had retired to drier parts, or sat sulking in their damp, ruffled feathers in the drizzle.

There was room on the narrow little track for only one horse, so we rode single file. And because it was difficult to talk, we traveled in silence. Lowra rode in the lead, and I brought up the rear. Between us, Davigan sat his horse, hunched protectively over the harp in its carry case, his cloak wrapped around the oiled leather to help keep the moisture out of the harp. He used his left hand for the reins of the horse, and every once in a while, the fingers of his right hand moved in an odd, intricate pattern. I watched for a long time, puzzled, before I realized he was practicing the fingering for different songs, plucking imaginary strings.

Toward midday, the drizzle stopped, but the overcast still hung sullen and gray close above the trees. Davigan brightened with the day, smiling to himself as he practiced his fingering. I caught occasional snatches of music as he sang softly to himself. He kept his voice low. All I heard was a phrase or two of melody; I could not make out the lyrics of the songs. At least, not until he began the "Song of the Swords." He might have raised his voice as he sang, or I might have been overly sensitive to any mention of swords, the same way one can pick out the sound of one's name from a muttered conversation when one can understand nothing else.

> *"Armorer to gods and kings,*
> *Wyfydd's magic hammer sings.*
> *Music in its ringing tone,*
> *Weaponry for kings alone.*
> *He who forged the sword of Brand,*
> *Myrddin blessed it to his hand."*

The song was a long one, and told the story of how Heartfire and Soulshadow were made, how Tiernyn had died on the field of Cam Runn, and how a Champion and Kaith would arise to take up Heartfire and Soulshadow and a King arise to drive out the Maedun.

I shivered, and not entirely because of the damp chill of the day. If I closed my eyes, I could see Heartfire and Soulshadow dancing through the flaring twists of light in the midst of the Dance of Nemeara. Images of swords. I couldn't seem to escape from them. Heartfire. Soulshadow. Kingmaker. Even Bane.

> *"Blades to fill a kingly need.*
> *Royal blood and royal breed."*

The nearly whispered words described Davigan himself. Royal blood and royal breed. Grandson of King Tiernyn. The heroes in the song were twins; Davigan was a twin himself. Twins had already played a significant part in the history of Celi. The enchanter Donaugh was the younger twin brother of King Tiernyn. And now the song told of another pair of twins.

It struck a chord with last night's dream. Twins. Two

infants rocking in the quiet waters of a shared womb. There
was an answer there, perhaps. Twins to raise Heartfire and
Soulshadow. But who to raise Kingmaker?

> *"Music to the blades he gave*
> *With magic did the hilts engrave."*

Music and magic. The soul of the Dance. The heart of
Celi. Light and color and the chime of bell and harp. I felt as
if I could reach out and shape that amorphous blend of light
and color and music—make it into something beautiful and
potent and useful. But what? Tyadda magic was gentle
magic. It healed; it didn't harm. But there was something
there that could be woven together to form a weapon, if only
I knew which skeins to use, which strands to bring together,
and how to fashion them correctly.

Davigan finished the song and began another, a light and
airy love song about a young man who falls in love with a
swan. He longs for her until Adriel of the Waters takes pity
on him and turns him into a swan, too, and he and his love fly
away together. His song ended and, as if it were a signal, rain
began to fall steadily out of the gray sky.

I reached up and scrubbed my hands across my face. The
merry little tune about the swans had torn my thread of
thought. In frustration, I clenched my fist and beat it against
my thigh. I had the feeling that I was so close to discovering
something important—about my magic, and about the future
of Celi itself. But it was gone now. If I concentrated, I could
remember something about sunshine and moonlight, and
braiding different strands together for . . . for what?

But it was well and truly gone. Cursing softly under my
breath, I gave up and pulled my plaid closer around myself. If
this weather was any indication, spring was coming to the
Spine of Celi. And such typical early-spring weather it was,

too. Cold, gray, and wet. It made a man wonder why on earth anyone would leave the comfort of a Great Hall with not one but two roaring fires blazing on hearths at either end of the room. Warmth. Good food. Hot, mulled ale.

"Tcha-a-a-a," I muttered.

Davigan turned in his saddle and grinned at me. "Welcome to Skai," he said, raising his hands to the rain.

Just after midday, Lowra pulled her horse to a stop and pointed. "Smoke," she said. "Look."

As she pointed, I caught a whiff of it on the air. A wisp of blue-gray smoke rose from behind the next rise to blend with the overcast sky. There seemed to be too much of it to be just a cookfire, yet not enough to be a structure burning.

"What's over there, Davigan?" she asked. "Do you know?"

He shook his head. "I didn't think anyone lived around here anymore."

Lowra frowned. "We'd better see if we can take a look."

Had we not been looking for it, we would have missed the entrance to the tiny valley. Only the smoke rising serenely into the air gave it away. The track was no more than a faint deer trail leading around a stand of soaring fir trees. We rounded the shoulder of the hill and came unexpectedly on a small homestead.

. . . Or what had been a small homestead. The stone-built house and byre still stood, but the thatched roofs were both burned to piles of smoldering ashes. The charnel stench of blood sorcery overlay the stink of charred meat. This destruction had to be the work of Maedun Somber Riders. Accompanied by a warlock, too, judging from the stench. The fires must have been fierce, as blood sorcery fires often were. It had been raining all morning, and half of yesterday, and ruins were still smoldering.

We drew our horses to a halt and exchanged dismayed glances, wondering if the charred-meat stench meant the occupants of the steading were still in the byre — or the house.

Just then, a young boy appeared out of the trees beyond the burned-out house. He drove a thin milch cow before him. A scruffy-looking dog walked beside him, and he kept a hand on the dog's ruff. He seemed alert enough, unaffected by Hakkar's spell. I couldn't smell the stench of it here nearly as strongly as I had smelled it closer to the sea. But then, the boy wasn't much more than six years old, and Hakkar's spell didn't affect children or adolescents until they grew enough to pose a danger to the Maedun.

The child saw us and stopped dead under the trees. The cow ambled a few steps farther, then bent her head to tear at the brown grass by the edge of the clearing. The dog remained by the boy's side, lips drawn back in a silent snarl, hackles rising. The boy's gaze settled on Davigan, and his eyes grew wide with fear. He turned and ran, shouting, toward the byre. He disappeared behind it, still shouting for his father.

Davigan drew his horse to a stop and reached up to run his hand over his cheeks. He looked at me, puzzlement drawing his eyebrows together over his eyes. But amusement glinted in their depths.

"I realize my face will never be my fortune," he said quietly. "But I didn't think it was bad enough to frighten children."

"Perhaps if we dismount, we'll be less threatening," Lowra said. She swung her leg over her saddle and slid gracefully to the ground. Davigan and I dismounted and stood holding the reins. The horses whuffled and shook themselves, but stayed obediently still.

A man came cautiously around the corner of the byre where the child had disappeared. He appeared to be about my age, black-haired and blue-eyed, built with the sturdy stockiness of the mountain men. He stood for a moment, staring at us, his face grim and set. He made me nervous. There was something terribly disquieting about the intense expression in his eyes—anger or hatred or all-consuming fear. Or perhaps a combination of all three.

Instinctively, I raised my hand to the hilt of the sword above my left shoulder. The presence of that good Tyran steel was comforting. But it bothered me, made me warily uneasy. I shouldn't have to turn to the comfort of the steel to protect myself in my own land, from my own people.

Even as this thought scurried through my head, the man leapt away from the wall and hurled himself across the muddy yard. "Murderer!" he shouted. "Traitor!"

Before any of us could react, he threw himself upon Davigan and dragged him to the ground. Even as my hand closed again about the hilt of my sword, the man had Davigan sprawled in the wet ashes and mud, the blade of a long dagger against his throat.

"Murderer!" he shouted again. "Filthy traitor!"

14

Lowra reacted far more quickly than I. She had her bow drawn, an arrow nocked and aimed at the man's heart, before I could get my sword clear of the scabbard.

"Draw my brother's blood, and you die before it can splash on the ground," she said.

The man looked up and I read the expression in his eyes. Pain and anguish were there, certainly. But so were determination and hatred. Lowra saw it, too, and drew her bowstring back a further inch or two, her own face set coldly and firmly.

The man hesitated, his eyes darting toward the child, then back to Lowra. His hand on the haft of the dagger trembled, then moved fractionally closer to Davigan's skin. Before Lowra could make the decision to actually shoot the man, I reached out to the threads of power that spun through the air around me and flowed through the ground beneath my feet. The magic hardly needed my bidding to weave itself into a netting that I dropped over the man on the ground as easily as if he had been a bird and I a hunter. The netting tightened around him, pulled his hand away from Davigan's throat, bound him tightly at our feet.

He sobbed helplessly—hopelessly—and tried to bring his hands up to his eyes. But the netting of magic held him tightly. "Don't hurt the boy," he whispered. "Kill me if you must, but don't hurt my son. He's all I have left . . ."

Davigan got to his feet, then dropped to one knee beside the sobbing man. He put his hand to the man's shoulder—a gentle, almost brotherly, gesture.

"The child is safe," he said quietly. "I promise you. As are you. We'll not harm you." He nodded at Lowra. She unnocked her arrow and put it back into the quiver, then slung the bow across her back. "I am Davigan Harper." He gestured toward Lowra, then to me. "My sister Lowra and our companion Gareth of Tyra. Who are you?"

I loosened the magic and stood back, waiting. The man looked at me in disbelief, then at Lowra, and finally at Davigan. Bewilderment spread slowly across his face. He flexed his shoulders as I loosened the magic even further, then let it go. The threads snapped back into the flows I'd taken them from, the dissipating magic stinging like willow switches against my skin. I flinched away.

Davigan got to his feet and held out a hand to help the man up. The man hesitated a long moment before taking the offered hand and rising. "Who are you?" Davigan repeated.

"Margan," the man said hoarsely. "And my son Llew." He held out his hand to the boy, who still huddled by the wall of the ruined byre. The boy came forward slowly, obviously still afraid, but obedient to his father's gesture. He crept into the shelter of his father's arm about his shoulders and huddled against Margan's side. He watched Davigan fearfully. Davigan reached out to him, and the boy flinched back and squeezed his eyes shut as if expecting a mortal blow. Davigan drew back and let his hands fall to his sides.

"Why do you fear us so?" he asked, both pain and puzzlement in his brown-gold eyes.

Margan stared at him in disbelief. "You would ask that?" he said incredulously. "You? You, who were here not three days ago?"

Davigan and Lowra exchanged startled glances. I knew exactly what they were thinking. There was only one man living who could be mistaken for Davigan. If this man Margan claimed he saw Davigan three days ago, it had to be Daefyd he saw.

Davigan shook his head. "I give you my word it was not I you saw. I was with my friends here."

Margan held his son tightly to his side and shook his head. "No . . ." he whispered.

"If you won't take his word for it, will you take mine?" I asked. He looked at me, still skeptical. "I am Gareth ap Brennen ap Keylan," I said. "My father is Brennen, Prince of Skai, who is in exile on the Isle of Skerry."

He studied me skeptically for a moment. I had been raised in the house of the Prince of Skai, and later in the house of the Clan Laird of Broche Rhuidh. I knew how to look regal when I had to. I drew myself up to my full height and looked him in the eye. I saw the exact moment he began to believe me. Some of the fear melted from his expression, and his eyes widened. "My lord," he stammered. "How is it that you are here with this man . . . ?"

"He is a good friend," I said. "I trust him with my life."

Davigan stepped forward. "The man you saw was my brother Daefyd," he said. "He's my twin, and we resemble each other closely. We've been searching for him since just after Imbolc. Please tell us what happened."

Margan looked down at the boy. He blinked hard a few times, and his eyes shone suspiciously, as if he were holding back tears. "He came here three days ago," he said. "And he took my wife and my daughter."

Davigan jerked back as if Margan had hit him. "He took your wife and daughter?" he asked. "That's ridiculous."

"No, my lord," Margan said with dogged, exhausted patience. "It's the truth." He spread his hands before him in a helpless gesture. "He took my wife and daughter. Both of them had small magics, you understand. Just small magics. Nothing more than what it takes to make this place grow enough to feed us. Your brother came here with a troop of Maedun Somber Riders and took them away. Then they burned everything. Llew and I were lucky to escape with our lives. My wife's father was not so lucky. He was in his dotage, and became confused and ran back into the house." He made a gesture with his head toward the byre. "It's him I was burying when you came."

Davigan flinched again. Lowra reached out and put a comforting hand on his arm, her own face pale with shock and disbelief. "How could this be?" Davigan asked. "Daefyd riding with the Maedun?"

"This valley was protected by my wife's masking spell," Margan said quietly. "But he came straight here and pointed her out to the Maedun as possessing magic. He pointed out my daughter, too, and they took her as well. Baela was only nine."

"I don't believe it," Lowra said, still shocked. "Daefyd wouldn't do that."

Margan looked at her bleakly. "That may be, my lady," he said. "But I'm not lying to you. My words are the truth. I swear by the Duality and by all the seven gods and goddesses." He made the sign of the Unbroken Circle in the air before his forehead.

"I believe you," Davigan whispered. The expression on his face I had seen before—on the faces of men who had taken mortal wounds. But there was no use asking Margan the most obvious question—why in the name of all piety would the man born to be King of Celi be riding with the Maedun, betraying those of his own people who had magic? "Which way did they go when they left here?"

Margan waved toward the south. "That way. Toward the stronghold."

"Can we do anything for you?" Lowra asked. "Is there any way we can help?"

Margan looked at her, his expression wry. "I doubt it, my lady," he said. "All I want is to have my wife and daughter back. I doubt ye can help me there."

"No," she agreed. "Not yet." Then her eyes went all deep and drowned and dark, and she was looking at something far beyond us, both in place and time. "But I can promise you that your son will live to see the time when the Maedun are driven out of Celi. Llew will live to see Skai free again, a place where a man can raise his children without fear under the High King of all Celi."

Margan stared at her in awe. For a moment, none of us could speak, then Margan cleared his throat. "Thank you, my lady," he said, and sketched a small bow to her. "I believe you."

We left Margan to finish burying his kin-father and made our way back to the track. None of us spoke. No one mentioned Daefyd's name. Lowra and Davigan were obviously deep in their own thoughts, which shut me out completely. The silence had a shamed, almost guilty flavor to it. I could think of nothing constructive to say, so I kept silent as well.

We camped that night near the banks of the River Eidon. I had no appetite for the meal. I left it half-finished and went down to the river's edge to watch the water tumble and spill over the rocks as it made its way down to the Ceg.

The River Eidon. And at its mouth on the Ceg lay Dun Eidon, the ancestral home of the Princes of Skai—or what was left of it. I wondered if it would be the same as Dun Llewen, and whether the same atmosphere of tragedy and death hung over the ruins.

Sunset blazed in the clouds in the western sky, and the rushing water reflected back the brilliance in muted tones of turquoise, rose, and gold. I picked up a small stone—smooth and round and flat, pleasing to the touch. It fit my hand well. I hefted it, then hurled it at a calmer back eddy. The stone skipped three times across the glowing surface of the river before disappearing.

"I used to be able to make them skip five and six times," Lowra said at my elbow. She hardly startled me at all. I had almost been expecting her. She picked up a stone and sent it skipping across the water. It bounced five times before catching on a ripple and diving to the bottom of the river.

I smiled. "Not bad for a wee bit of a lassie like you," I said. I expected her to take umbrage at the remark and bristle like an outraged hedgehog, but she didn't offer the diversion I so desperately needed. She merely smiled, then stepped forward and put her hand on my arm. The touch was comforting and warm.

"What's bothering you, Gareth?" she asked gently.

I glanced down at her. "You mean besides the news about Daefyd."

She raised one eyebrow.

I looked out over the water again. The sun had gone now, and the colors were fading to deep blue and black. Trying to organize my thoughts, I picked up another stone and tossed it carelessly. It skipped six times before disappearing. I hardly noticed.

"I don't really know what's wrong," I said. "Meeting Margan today did something strange to me."

"Something strange? How so?"

I shrugged helplessly. "I dinna ken," I said, the accents of Tyra coming back because I wasn't thinking about it. What bothered me was far more than the disturbing tale he'd told about Daefyd, but I didn't know if I could put it into words. The sensation that battered my mind and soul was similar to seeing the star-gleam coalesce into the image of Bane as I knelt before the altar stone. But now, it seemed that all the nebulous bits of duty and honor had come together to form, not a sword, but something just as firm and sharp-edged. A sense of purpose. Of belonging.

Mayhaps even of destiny. Overwhelming, that. It could take a man's breath away should he let it.

I picked up another stone and rubbed the smooth surface with the ball of my thumb. It was cool and clean to the touch. "Let me see if this makes sense. Ever since I came to Skai, I've been acquiescing to one thing or the other for the good of Skai. Because I'm eventually going to be Prince of Skai, and these things are expected of me. Things like accepting the gifts of Healing and magic. I didn't want them, but I accepted them because with them, I could serve Skai better."

"Is that so bad?"

"I think so. I've been accepting them for Skai, but until I met Margan today, it didn't really mean much to me. But seeing Margan's grief and fear drove it home to me. *He's* Skai. He and all the others like him—the people of Skai. Skai isn't just a collection of mountains, glens, and seacoasts. It's people. My people . . ."

She tilted her head to one side and looked up at me. "And that never occurred to you before?"

I shook my head. "Much to my shame, no, it didn't," I said.

"They *are* your people, Gareth," she said. "Whether they're still here in Skai, hiding from or under subjugation to the Maedun, or in exile on Skerry or in Tyra. And they'll accept you and look to you for help."

"That's what frightens me. How could I help Margan? I'm as helpless as he is."

"Are you? It's not just because of your magic he'd look to you for help. You'll be Prince, Gareth. Men like Margan will look to you to lead them. You know you have the strength. And now you've got the sense of purpose."

I laughed without humor. "I wish I were as confident as you."

"What about Bane?"

I looked down at her. The light had faded, but the stars and the quarter moon gave enough light to show me the gleam of her eyes. "What about Bane? I don't know where it is."

"Did none of your visions show you anything about the place where the sword was?"

I frowned, then nodded slowly. "Yes," I said. "Yes, they did. Each time, I was completely aware of everything around the sword. Right from the beginning, when I saw the land around the stream where the sword lay since my father dropped it there after the invasion. And I saw the countryside when the courier rode through it. I saw the warlock's lodge, too—at least the room where the sword was."

"Then could you call up a vision of the sword and look carefully at where it is? If you described it to me and Davigan, we might know where it is, and we could go there."

"I—I don't know if I can call up a vision of the sword," I said. "I've never done it before. The visions come in their own time and on their own terms."

"Why don't you sleep tonight with the sword on your mind," she said. "Concentrate on the sword, on where it is, on what it's trying to tell you. In the morning, tell us what you saw."

"I'll try," I said. "I don't know if it will help, but I'll try."

I awoke with the full moon shining directly into my eyes. I sat up, knowing I had not dreamed at all. No vision of the sword had come to me as I slept. Disappointed, I sat up and threw aside my blanket.

Something about the night struck me as extremely odd. Different. Unreal. I looked around, frowning, wondering what it was. I had to blink the moonlight out of my eyes.

The moon . . . Surely it had been only a quarter moon when Lowra and I stood together down on the bank of the river. No natural moon could go from the last quarter to full in one night.

I got to my feet and turned toward where I knew they were camped. It startled me badly when Lowra shed her blanket and stood. She held out her hand, and I took it.

"Show me, too," she said softly.

We walked together through the trees and found the campfire burning exactly where I knew it had to be. Kian looked up as we entered the small clearing. Cullin continued polishing his sword, paying us no attention at all.

"Aye, well," Kian said. "I see you've found your bhean-coran, lad. It's about time."

One corner of Cullin's mouth twitched, but he didn't look up. "This from the man who fought so hard against his own bond," he murmured. Kian shot him a glance—half amusement, half exasperation—then looked back at Lowra and me, an expression of sorely tried patience spreading across his face.

"Ye've come to me for a vision of the sword, have ye no?" he said.

"Aye, we have," I said.

"Lad, you don't need me to show you how to do that," he said. "Have ye no paid attention to anything I've shown you?" He gestured toward the moon, which stood over his left shoulder. "Look there, lad. Look and remember."

I looked up at the moon. Unthinkingly, I formed my hands into a cup to hold the moonlight streaming through my fingers. A globe formed within the hollow of my palms. I glanced up to thank Kian, but both he and Cullin were gone. I thought I heard a faint echo of Cullin's chuckle.

I looked down. The moonlight felt cool and smooth in my hands. I was conscious of Lowra leaning against me, peering around me down into the globe. I lowered my gaze and looked deep into the globe.

There was the sword, wrapped in soft wool and lying by the saddle pack of a courier. The Maedun slept in a small room of a structure that had to be a posting station. Outside were paddocks and stables where horses slept, guarded by grooms. The sword and the saddle pack lay on the floor by the head of the bed where the courier slept. Even through the wrapping, the gleam of the blade was strongly apparent.

I reached out and discovered I could touch the bundle containing the sword. A small shock jolted through my body, as if I had been walking across a carpeted floor and touched a metal sconce on the wall. A picture formed in the air above the sword. A narrow track led through a mountain pass where a thin jet of water shot out of a cleft in the rock of the cliff above it, and tumbled briskly down to join the river below.

"Where?" I whispered. But the vision was gone.

And I was standing in the empty glade, the nebulous substance of the globe flowing swiftly through my hands to splash on the ground by my feet. I looked up to meet Lowra's wide, startled eyes. Even in the wan light of the quarter moon, she looked pale.

"I know the place," she murmured. "There's a bog just to the east of the falls. It's not that far from the steading. Less than a day's ride from here. If we hurry."

In the morning, I awoke with a headache. Lowra looked in little better condition. I didn't have to ask. I knew she had shared my dream—or whatever it was—and that we were truly bonded as firmly as any prince and bheancoran could ever be. One soul, two bodies. A sobering realization.

15

The little glen was eerily familiar. The track ran along the crooked little burn, just as I had seen it in the globe of moonlight the night before. Almost directly overhead from where we stood, a thin jet of water hurled itself out of a narrow cleft in the rock wall and shot out in a graceful arc before tumbling a good bowshot distance into a deep pool. The water left the pool and bounded over its stony bed toward the river to the west.

To the east lay a small meadow that was the best part of a bog, filled with half-grown saplings, tangled brambles, and puddles of brackish water. The track skirted it handily. Some of the saplings were tall enough to be called young trees, and bent over the track in what would be a modest canopy of leaves in the summer.

We dismounted in the screening shelter of a tangle of willows, where we could look down the track for the first sign of someone approaching. Davigan took the horses well away, where they would not hear the other horse coming and betray our position, then posted himself in a tall pine a little more than a furlong down the track to give us early warning of the courier's approach.

Lowra and I hid ourselves within the thatch of willow and settled down to wait patiently. Still, every time I looked around and saw how my vision in the moonlight globe had detailed this place precisely, it sent an icy chill shivering down my spine. Lowra seemed to be taking the whole thing much more matter-of-factly than I, taking it all in stride. Well, she was Tyadda, and had probably grown up with magic. But I hadn't, and I found the matter decidedly disconcerting. I wondered if there might ever come a time when I didn't find it so.

It remained to be seen, however, whether the courier would come by this way. Or if he had already passed and what I had seen was a vision of what had already been. Somehow, that possibility was far less disturbing than the thought of glimpsing the future. Tyadda seers and Lowra's Sight notwithstanding, I wasn't sure anyone but the gods and goddesses should know what was to come.

I had a feeling it was something that I had to get used to, like it or not.

The morning passed slowly. Clouds gathered more thickly and turned the sky a dull pewter, but the rain held off. Lowra and I huddled in our little hollow among the willow stems, trying to make ourselves as comfortable as possible. The ground was damp and cold, and the chill seeped into our bodies despite every precaution we might take. When I looked up, I could barely make out Davigan's figure perched within the boughs of the pine tree. If I tried to look at him with an unprejudiced eye, he resembled nothing more than the nest of a largish sort of bird. Which, I suppose, was a good thing. It was, of course, what he wanted to look like. Or at any rate, if not that, then something else as completely innocuous.

Around midday, Lowra brought out our share of the remains of last evening's meal, and we chewed on the cold rabbit in silence. I was beginning to despair that we had missed the courier and the sword. We had seen not so much as a hint of anyone using this track. Perhaps I was right when I thought that the moonlight globe had shown us where the sword had already been, not where it was going.

Davigan arrived in a rush, slithering through the willow thicket noiselessly. The pine tree had pulled up a small forest of snags in his cloak, his tunic, and his trews, and his hair looked as if he had brushed it with a pitch-filled pine bough. Two deep scratches marred his cheek, and he was out of breath.

"They're coming," he said. "They're about a furlong or two down the trail."

"They?" I repeated, startled. "What do you mean, 'they'? Couriers ride alone—"

"Not this one," he said positively. "There are at least a dozen Somber Riders with him. Not a score of them, mind you, but certainly more than a dozen."

"Do they have a warlock with them?" I asked.

Davigan shook his head. "I couldn't tell."

Lowra's mouth lengthened into a thin, grim line, and she reached for her bow. I put out a hand and grasped her wrist, restraining her.

"No," I said. "We can't fight a whole troop of Somber Riders. You're very good with that bow, but you aren't good enough with it for that. Even without a warlock who could turn the arrows back on us, they'd ride all of us down before you could get more than a few of them."

"What do you suggest we do, then?" Lowra asked, her voice tinged with asperity. "We can't afford to let that sword get into Hakkar's hands. Or Horbad's, either, come to that. Once it gets past us and into the Dead Lands, we have no way of fetching it back."

I looked thoughtfully up the track toward the marshy area. Those young trees were supple . . . The idea that blossomed fully formed in my mind was sheer madness. But it might be just insane enough to work. Childhood tricks might turn into useful devices in adult warfare, sometimes. And I could think of no other way of stopping a small troop of Somber Riders—not without the overwhelming risk of all three of us getting killed. At least this way, Lowra and Davigan would be safe, and have a chance at rescuing Bane.

"I have an idea," I said. "But I'll need one of you to take the horses over there to the other side of that boggy area. And someone to create a diversion to draw off some of the Somber Riders."

"I'm not much of a warrior," Davigan said without apology. "I'll take the horses."

"And I can draw off some of the troops," Lowra said. "A couple of arrows coming from a direction they don't expect should do the trick. If I'm up a tree, they probably won't see me and ride by right underneath me. How much time do you need?"

"Not much. Just a few minutes before they come by here."

"Right," Davigan said. "I'm off then." He reached out, and we grasped each other's forearms in a warrior grip. "Luck of the gods and goddesses be with you, my friend."

"And with you."

He grinned, then turned and vanished into the trees with hardly a sound to mark his passage.

Lowra touched the bow slung over her left shoulder as if to assure herself that it was there and in good condition. She turned to go, but I stopped her with a hand on her arm.

"Be careful," I said, and my voice sounded strange in my ears. Harsh. Rusty. As if I hadn't used it enough lately. "I don't know if I could bear it if something happened to you."

She looked up at me gravely for a long moment, and the air between us fizzed gently, disconcertingly. Then suddenly, she gave me a smile so brilliant, it nearly reflected on the trees around us. "I think we both feel the same way," she said. She reached up on tiptoe abruptly and kissed my cheek quickly. "I'll be with Davigan and the horses on the other side of the bog. Be careful."

I watched her disappear into the forest, then turned and loped down the track and around the bend to the place where a thick stand of young trees clustered, bent low after the winter's snows. I paused for a moment, studying the way they hung over the track. I needed one that was springy enough, yet solid. I chose the best one, and had to leap up to catch hold of a branch sturdy enough to use to draw the tree down across the track, then back until it was cocked like a crossbow aimed at the track. Hanging on tightly to the tree, I got myself into a position where I could watch and wait without being seen.

The courier and the troop of Somber Riders were taking it easy through the narrow pass. Well, even Hakkar's men couldn't expect a good horse to race all day through the mountains and not drop dead beneath its rider. I had been hiding for more than ten minutes before I heard the shouts go up. Moments later, the clatter of hooves on rocky soil echoed through the pass.

The courier and four Somber Riders thundered around the bend. At about the exact moment they saw me, I let go of the branch I was holding. The trick couldn't have worked better if all the seven gods and goddesses had been standing behind me, assisting me.

It was like throwing a weasel into a crowded henhouse.

The supple young tree snapped back, sweeping across the track about chest-high to a mounted man. It caught the courier across the throat and swept him cleanly out of his saddle before he knew what was happening. His horse shied and reared, plunging into the two horses behind it, which promptly threw their riders. The last two Somber Riders had their hands full trying to control their own mounts. Their horses reared and plunged, the whites of their eyes showing. The horses obviously wanted nothing more than to get away in the quickest and most direct way they knew how.

In the confusion, the courier's horse snorted and reared out of control, nearly trampling his rider, who was frantically squirming around on the track, trying to stay out of the way of the hooves. The bundle containing the sword flapped and bounced across the horse's back. It certainly didn't help calm the horse down. The terrified animal spun and kicked out, its hooves catching a second horse directly in the ribs. The sword bundle snapped away from the saddle and landed with a dull thump near the edge of the track.

I darted out onto the track and snatched up the blanket-wrapped sword. Someone shouted behind me as I turned and sprinted for the boggy ground to my left. One of the Somber Riders threw himself from his saddle, sword drawn, right in front of me.

I dropped the sword bundle and my own sword all but leapt from the scabbard on my back into my hand as I turned to meet him. Roaring a Tyran war cry, I swung my sword to meet his as it whistled in a deadly arc toward my head. Steel met steel with a clang and a slither and a shock that traveled up my arms and into my spine.

The staccato clatter of approaching hooves announced the arrival of more Somber Riders. I glanced quickly back over my shoulder. The troops that had split off in response to Lowra's diversion rounded the bend at full gallop, swords and bows at the ready.

I pressed forward, disengaging my sword from the Maedun sword, then swung it in a swift arc, aiming for his belly. The Rider staggered back, off-balance. I leapt to one side, sweeping the sword into a slicing curve. The blade caught him just below the rib cage. His eyes widened in shock. His own sword fell from nerveless fingers as he died before he realized he was hurt. I snatched up the blanket-wrapped bundle containing Bane and ran for the boggy ground, sheathing my sword as I ran.

The rest of the troop exploded around the bend and plunged into the confusion on the track in a welter of screaming horses and cursing men. I left them merrily to it and concentrated on running.

The scrub willow and berry bushes offered scant cover from arrows, but I was counting on the confusion lasting long enough to let me lose myself in the labyrinth of low brush. The Somber Riders wouldn't dare take their horses through this mess behind me—not if they didn't want to risk their mounts breaking their legs.

I stopped worrying about where the Somber Riders might be and put all my concern into my own legs. The ground beneath my feet was soft, a thick tangle of brambles and uneven tufts of grass. It trembled as my footsteps thumped against it. Twice, I tripped and measured my length on the wet ground, but I didn't lose my grip on the bundle. And, if the Somber Riders managed to use their bows, none of their arrows found my back.

My breath came in sobbing gulps as I struggled through the bog, clumsily leaping clumps of tangled bramble and broken branches. When I snatched a glance back over my shoulder, the willow scrub and berry bushes hid the track from my sight. I breathed a little more easily. If I couldn't see the Somber Riders on the track, they couldn't see me. And if they couldn't see me, they couldn't send their arrows after me with any accuracy.

I plunged out of the boggy meadow into the forest by the burn. My footsteps sounded solid and firm on the hard ground. I dodged around a pine tree and through a copse of leafless rowan, then had to lean against the solid trunk of an oak to catch my breath.

Slow surprise grew in my chest as I got my breathing under control and my heart stopped galloping like a runaway horse. It worked! By all the Seven, it had worked. A child's trick, and it had worked against a whole troop of Somber Riders. I began to laugh, and nearly choked trying to laugh quietly. I leaned up against my oak and laughed until tears came to my eyes. There may have been an overtone of hysterics in the laughter, but the cathartic effect was wonderful.

Davigan and Lowra stepped forward from between two holly bushes. I gasped for breath and tried to stop laughing. Both of them appeared to be unharmed and in one piece each.

"I am truly pleased to see both of you," I wheezed.

They exchanged glances, possibly wondering if I had lost my grip on my wits. Davigan shrugged and grinned, allowing me my moment of gleeful folly.

"Have you got Bane?" Lowra asked.

Hardly able to speak, I held up the blanket-wrapped bundle. "Right here," I managed.

"What happened?" she asked.

I told her, unable to keep the glee out of my voice. Grinning widely, I said, "I haven't had so much fun since I was a knee-child."

She made a wry face. "You took a terrible chance, Gareth," she said. "It wouldn't have been much fun if it hadn't worked."

"Aye, well," I said. "You're right, of course. But it did work, and I've got the sword right here." I put my hand on the bundle.

She stepped forward, put her hand out to touch it, then stopped short, her nose wrinkling.

"Faugh," she said. "You stink as if you took a bath in a midden heap."

I brushed at the bog mud on my kilt and plaid, but managed only to smear the mess over a wider area. "You can toss me into the river later," I said. "Right now, we had better put as much distance as possible between us and those Somber Riders."

Davigan made a face. "If your horse will let you within a bowshot of him, smelling like that," he said, then grinned.

"When the bards sing of the Rescue of Bane, I think they'll leave out the bog stench."

There may have been a touch more sarcasm in my voice when I replied than I had meant to put there. "That's dashed decent of you," I said.

"More than you could know," Lowra muttered with heartfelt sincerity, her nose wrinkling. "Come on. We'd best hurry."

I strapped the sword bundle to the back of my saddle, then stood for a moment with my hand resting on the wool. I fancied I felt a faint quiver in the bundle, as if it contained something live, something that wanted to be free of its bindings, something that fervently desired to be *doing*.

I reached up and touched the hilt of the good Tyran sword that rose above my left shoulder, then dropped my hand. That sword had served me well these last ten years. It would serve me well for the next while. Bane was my father's sword, not mine. It might fight for me well enough in my hands, but it would not be completely right until my father himself handed me the sword and commanded it to serve me.

I swung onto the horse, painfully conscious of Bane behind me. But until the day the sword was commended to my hand, I would not use it. This way was better.

16

We traveled hard for the rest of the day, urging the horses to the edge of their endurance. I'd wager my last silver that those Somber Riders were extremely upset, and we wanted to take ourselves as far out of their way as possible as soon as we were able. They'd be searching through the mountain passes and all the glens for us, and it wouldn't take them long to call in reinforcements.

Lowra and Davigan knew the country well. They guided us along tracks that looked like little more than game trails, hardly open enough to give passage to a horse and rider.

All day, as we rode, I was conscious of the sword strapped to the saddle behind me. Every time I put my hand to the bundle, a driving sense of restless urgency surged up through my hand, along my arm, straight into my heart and spirit. The strange sensation sent shivers along my spine, but I couldn't help reaching back often in fascination and touching the sword.

We made camp before it was too dark to see the track. Davigan found a shallow cave just off the trail with ample room for us and the horses. The interior was dry, the floor rock and sand. We decided we could risk a fire if we kept it small and built it in the back of the cave so that the smoke would dissipate before it reached the outside. I saw to the horses while Davigan went in search of firewood.

Lowra pulled a blanket from the camping supplies and rooted through her saddle pack. She found what she wanted and turned to me, handing me both the blanket and a small cake of yellow soap.

"There's water just beyond that spur of rock," she said,

pointing. "Don't come back until you've washed both your-self and your clothing. I don't think any of us could sleep with that horrid bog stink."

I took the soap and the blanket. I hardly noticed the rank, fetid smell radiating from my kilt and plaid, which had stiffened as the slimy mud dried, but when I did get a whiff of it, I could understand Lowra's insistence on my bathing to get rid of it.

"Need any help?" she called after me, as I turned toward the spur of rock.

I paused and glanced back at her. She knelt by the saddle packs, her hands on her knees. There wasn't a lot of light from the fading sunset, but there was certainly enough to show me her wide grin. I made a wry face and shook my head.

"I've been doing for myself for many years," I said. "I'm sure I should be able to manage this."

She merely raised one eyebrow, still grinning, then shrugged.

The little stream leapt and bounded over the stones in its bed, and was as cold as the snow it came from higher up the mountains. I washed my kilt, plaid, and shirt, and all the while, images of the sword flashed through my mind. Twice, I found myself staring off into the black sky, lost in a reverie with a picture of the sword before my eyes. All those years, it lay lost. Then, within a season of being brought out of the stream where it had lain hidden, it found me. Or I had found it . . .

I had thought the legend of Rune Blades finding the hand born to wield them was just that—only legend. I'd heard the legend all my life, but hadn't really believed it. Until now. Bane had set out to find my father, and here was I, ready to take the sword to Skerry and place it back into my father's hand. After twenty years . . .

I finished with my clothing, then plunged my cringing body into the icy flow to make a lightning quick job of scrubbing my skin and my hair. But even then, the sword refused to stay out of my mind.

I returned to the cave, wrapped in the blanket and shivering, certain that my lips and fingernails were blue with cold. The small fire made a comforting warmth in the depths of the rocky hollow, and I settled gratefully before it after spreading my clothing to dry. Four good-sized trout lay on a flat rock at the edge of the fire, sizzling gently as they cooked.

My appetite had fled, and I picked at the meal that Davigan and Lowra had prepared, hardly noticing what it was that I ate. Finally, I set my bowl aside and drew the blanket-wrapped sword to me. I laid it across my knee and stared down at it for a long time before I began the painstaking chore of unwrapping it.

It shouldn't have startled me—but it did—to see the sword and realize it looked exactly as it had in my dreams. The delicate tracery of silver on the stained leather of the two-handed hilt—stained by the sweat of my father's palms—the downward-curving handguard, the long, glimmery length of the blade itself . . . All were shockingly—almost disturbingly—familiar. I had seen just this so many times—so many nights in so many dreams. It gave me a hollow, dreamlike sense of unreality to look at it.

My father had lost this sword twenty years ago. For all those twenty years, save part of the last season, it had lain on the bed of the stream where he fought the troop of Somber Riders that captured him, Kenzie, and Aellegh, Celwalda of the Summer Run. And where he had lost Fiala, his bheancoran. Yet not a fleck of rust showed on the bright surface of the blade. It was smooth and clean, and I could detect no discoloration at all. It was as bright and gleaming as if it had just come from the armorer's finishing shop.

The runes carved into the blade glittered in the firelight like facets of a gem. They spilled down the center of the blade, sharp and clear and distinct. I ran my fingers along them, and the edges of the figures felt crisp and precise against my skin. I knew what the runes spelled out because I had heard my father say the words often enough. COURAGE DIES WITH HONOR. And I knew what the words meant. Two meanings. A man who has courage will die with honor. And, when honor dies, courage dies with it.

But I could not read the runes. They would not sort themselves into words for me. I knew what that meant, too, and I wasn't sure if I was disappointed or relieved.

Bane was not my sword. And no man could read the runes on a sword not his own. If I were to use Bane, it would have to be given to me by my father's hand.

Or my father would have to be dead.

That was comfort, in its own way. As long as I could not read the runes, I knew my father still lived. That meant, of course, that I would not have to take up the torc and coronet of Skai and become a reluctant prince.

I put my hand to the hilt of the sword. As my fingers closed around the silver and leather, that rush of restless urgency surged through me again, a yearning to go home, to fit again into the hand of the man born to raise the sword.

Bane was, indeed, not my sword, but that didn't stop it from using me to gain its own ends as Kingmaker had used Red Kian for its own ends all those many years ago.

Preoccupied with my examination of the sword, I didn't notice the silence for a long time. When it finally penetrated that no one had spoken for a while, I looked up to find both Lowra and Davigan watching me gravely. They exchanged glances, then looked back at me. Davigan sat back, as if to make himself more comfortable against the rock wall of the cave, and cleared his throat.

"You'll be wanting to return to Skerry now that you've got what you came for, I suppose," he said quietly. His hands lay clenched into fists on his knees. He held his body as stiff and rigid as the rock behind his back, his shoulders hunched and tense.

"Back to Skerry?" I repeated, still half-immersed in my reverie about the sword. "What do you mean?"

He gestured toward the sword. "You have your father's sword, and you've become a Healer. That's what you came for, isn't it? There's no reason for you to stay here."

It took me a moment or two to realize what he'd said. I looked down at the sword in my lap. The knuckles of my hand were pale and tight on the hilt, and the soft vibrations shivering under my palm reminded me of one of Davigan's melancholy laments in a minor key. Bane wanted to go home. Its need to go home was nearly an irresistible demand. Its duty was to my father, and to Skai. Not to me.

I, however, had another duty.

Davigan and Lowra sat across the fire from me. The firelight made brilliant red-gold glints in their hair, but couldn't disguise the tight pallor of their faces. They waited, not moving, for me to reply.

"I'll be staying," I said softly. I stroked the blade of the sword, trying to soothe its driving need to return to my father. It had waited these twenty years. A fortnight, or even a season or two, would make little difference after all that time. "How can I desert you in your search for Daefyd after all my father sacrificed for his king?" I shook my head. "No, I shan't be returning to Skerry yet. My father is safe for the time being, and he certainly wouldn't thank me in any event if I turned my back on my duty toward you and Daefyd." Bane vibrated like a swarm of bees against my fingers. Aye, well, it was built to guard Skai. It could hardly be expected to understand a duty to a man born to be King of all Celi.

Davigan's posture did not change, but the tension went out of him. He smiled. "Thank you," he said.

"What for?" I asked, surprised. "You could have ordered me to help you. Instead, you let me choose."

He nodded. "Aye," he said. "If you were to help, it had to be of your own will."

I put my hand to the hilt of the sword again. My skin tingled where it touched the leather and silver filigree. "My own will," I repeated. "I wonder . . ."

Lowra tilted her head to one side, her eyes shadowed and dark. "The sword?" she asked.

I shook my head. "No. It wants only to go home."

"It's enough that you'll help." Davigan reached for his harp and drew it onto his knee. A bemused half smile touched the corners of his mouth as he brushed his fingers across the strings. A whisper of music breathed around the cave, murmuring of gods and kings and swords.

I pulled the blanket more closely around myself. "Where should we start looking for Daefyd?" I asked, trying to be practical.

"Can you use your magic to show us where he might be?" Lowra asked. "As you used it to find the sword?"

I hadn't thought of that. It was an intriguing possibility. The night seemed suddenly colder. And a frightening possibility. "I don't know," I said. "But I'll try."

We waited for the moon to rise, watching the wedge of sky we could see out of the entrance to the cave. All day, clouds had covered the sky, but as I watched, occasionally a star glimmered against the black of the sky as a tatter of cloud blew away in the gentle breeze.

Moonrise was a wan affair. At first, all that was visible was a faint glow through the clouds. I stepped out of the cave and watched the sky. The moon flitted in and out of the clouds, casting only pale, intermittent light across the trees and rocks.

No help was forthcoming tonight from Kian or Cullin, I realized. Not tonight. I had no sense of their presence, no certain knowledge they were near. This time, I was on my own. The fledgling had been shoved out of the nest to fly on its own.

Lowra put her hand on my arm as I cupped my hands and held them out before me. I glanced down at her, grateful for her support, but her gaze was fixed on the sky, the moon absorbing her attention. I took a deep breath and looked down at my hands.

Gradually, slowly, the moonlight filled my cupped palms. A globe formed, wavered, melted, then formed again. "Please," I muttered, hardly knowing whom I asked to help. The globe firmed, became solid and smooth and cool in my hands.

Images formed in the globe, blurred and indistinct. For a moment, I thought I saw the ancient enchanter watching me over his shoulder, his face lined and seamed, his eyes incredibly penetrating. Then cloud or smoke swirled through the globe, obscuring everything.

I concentrated, and again, figures and patterns took shape in the misty center of the globe, and I saw a crude homestead huddled beneath the overhang of a soaring crag. Smoke poured from the burning thatch on the low, stone-built house. A young man stood holding the reins of his horse as he watched two Somber Riders struggle with an old woman. The body of a man lay on the ground between the young man and the hut, and two children cowered beside a man dressed in unrelieved black.

Beside me, Lowra gasped as the young man came more clearly into focus, and my own breath caught in my throat. I had never seen Daefyd, but I recognized him immediately.

He was the image of Davigan. But he was a Davigan curiously devoid of expression. His face was as blank and expressionless as an unmarred field of snow as he watched the old woman writhing in the grip of the dark-clad Riders.

With surprising strength, the old woman threw herself at Daefyd, breaking the grip of the men who held her. She raised her fist and shook it in Daefyd's face, then spit at him.

"Murderer," she screamed. "Traitor! Murderer!"

One of the Somber Riders raised his sword and slashed at her, opening her throat. She fell, and her blood poured out to stain the trampled grass. Daefyd hardly moved. His face still impassive, he drew his foot back, without a trace of distaste or concern, so her blood would not touch his boot and stain the leather.

Lowra cried out, startling me. The globe shattered in my hands, the shards melting and splashing like water onto the ground by my feet. Dizzy and unsteady, I wiped my hands on the blanket wrapped around my waist, and closed my eyes for a moment. Lowra swayed and might have fallen had not Davigan leapt out of the cave and put his arms about her.

"He looked dead," Lowra whispered, her voice tinged with horror. "What have they done to him? His face . . . He looked as if he were dead even as he stood there."

"Where is he?" Davigan asked urgently. "Did you see where he was?"

She shook her head. "All I saw was a burning homestead beneath a cliff," she said. "I didn't recognize the place."

"West," I said with sudden, certain knowledge. "West of here. Near the coast."

They both looked at me. "How do you know?" Davigan demanded.

I looked down at my hands. Residual brightness from the globe marked the lines in my palms. Again, I wiped them on the blanket, leaving two softly glimmering smears on the wool.

"I don't know," I said. "But I do know it was west of here. The enchanter in the globe told me . . ."

I sat cross-legged near the back of the small cave with my sword across my knees, keeping my hands busy with the whetstone and oily cloth. The blade was clean and sharp; it didn't need cleaning, but I needed something to concentrate on besides what I had seen in the moonlight globe. Kenzie always used to say that one can't take too good care of one's sword. I don't know how many times he'd told me that if I took good care of my sword, it would take good care of me.

Davigan sat huddled around his misery by the fire, his cloak wrapping his shoulders. His harp lay by his hip, untouched. He stared into the fire, engrossed by the changing pattern of red chasing black through the embers, a frown drawing the golden brows together over his eyes. Lowra sat with her arms wrapped around her upraised knees, her gaze concentrated on the fire, too.

"Daefyd wouldn't do that," Davigan said, his voice rusty. "He just couldn't stand there and watch the Somber Riders kill someone."

I didn't answer. The whetstone made a soft hissing sound in the silence as I ran it along the edge of the blade. The fire popped and crackled quietly, intensifying the night silence.

He pounded his fist against his thigh. "I don't believe it," he said. He looked up at me, his eyes wide in the fire-shot dimness. "Are you certain what you saw was a true Seeing?"

"No," I said. "I'm not certain at all. All I know for sure is that the other night the globe showed me where we could find Bane. And tonight it showed me where Daefyd was. One was definitely a true Seeing, but the other may have been false."

"It was true," Lowra said, not looking away from the fire.

"How can you doubt it, Dav? You heard what Margan said. If Daefyd could betray people with magic to the Maedun, he could stand and watch impassively while they killed an old woman."

"But Daefyd's not like that," Davigan protested.

She slowly raised her eyes and looked at him. "Whoever he is right now—" She paused, a catch in her voice, then cleared her throat. "Whoever he is, he isn't the Daefyd we know. They've done something terrible to him. Didn't you say you could feel something like that along the twin-bond?"

He nodded. "Aye, I did," he said softly. "I was hoping I was mistaken. I thought it was pain."

"It is," I said softly. "But not the kind of pain you thought."

"Soul pain," he whispered bleakly.

I nodded. "Aye. I believe so."

"They're using him to track down anyone who has magic," Lowra said. "We know they've been trying to stamp out every trace of magic in Skai and Wenydd. They—" She broke off, and her eyes became wide and startled. The blood drained from her face, leaving her chalk-pale. "Oh dear gods and goddesses," she whispered.

I dropped the whetstone, sensing her sudden, chilling fear. "What is it?"

She made a visible effort to control her terror. "The steading," she said. "What if they can make Daefyd show them where the steading is? What if they attack the fastness?"

Davigan stared at her. "He wouldn't—"

"Wouldn't he?" she asked fiercely. "He betrayed Margan's wife and daughter, and he betrayed those people we saw in the globe. The Maedun want to get rid of the Tyadda. If they can use him to track down people with magic, they can use him to show them where the steading is."

Davigan didn't want to accept the knowledge that his brother could be forced to do that. But he knew as well as we did that the Maedun had done something terrible to Daefyd. Denial and acceptance warred on his face for a long moment before acceptance won.

"We have to warn them," he said. "We have to warn them now."

17

We set out early in the morning, going west with the rising sun to our backs. My shirt had dried overnight, but my kilt and plaid were still damp and clammy. They would dry soon enough in the sun. It seemed spring had come while we slept.

The sun shining gloriously through the bare branches of the trees made an almost tangible, pleasant weight on my back as I rode behind Davigan. Above us arched a sky that was as clear and heartbreakingly blue as I could ever remember seeing anywhere. But that might have been simply that I was so grateful for contrast of the sunshine after all the damp misery of the drizzle and rain. The air was thick with the smell of damp earth and waking vegetation. Even the horses sensed the change and pranced friskily in spite of the hard use we had made of them yesterday.

I couldn't see Davigan's face as he rode in front of me, but his shoulders were hunched and tense, and he carried his head bent low. For once, he paid no attention to the harp slung carelessly across his back. At the head of our little cavalcade, Lowra bent forward over the pommel of her saddle as if she could make the leagues go by faster if she leaned into them. Her worry thrummed and quivered along the bond between us until my belly churned with it, too.

As we cantered the horses, their hooves drummed a reverberating tattoo on the rocky ground, splashing through puddles and sending a spray of tiny rainbows into the air. The sound echoed from the crags around us. But today, we were more concerned with speed than hiding from the Maedun.

We rode through an awakening forest, opening to the welcome stirring of spring. The newly warm sun heated the soil, banishing the last abiding chill of winter. If I listened carefully, I could almost hear the sap rising in the trees, like water bubbling in a cistern. The air smelled fresh, redolent of the scent of green and growth.

Toward midmorning, we stopped at the edge of a small meadow to rest our mounts and cool them down. After giving them a good rubdown, we let them drink a little from the burn bubbling along beside the track and gave them a moment of freedom in the meadow. The horses nosed aside the dead, brown grass and found themselves sweet, green shoots that sprang up among last year's dry, withered detritus. Birds called insistently from all the trees surrounding the open, sunny meadow.

I stretched to wring the kinks out of my back and legs. "Where are we going?" I asked.

"To the steading," Davigan replied.

"Aye, so you said. But where is that?"

His grin flashed across his face, then disappeared back into his worried frown. "I keep forgetting you weren't born and raised here, and you don't know the country very well," he said. He pointed to a ridge of mountains to the northwest. "Up there. There's a hanging valley in the midst of those crags. It's almost in Cloudbearer's shadow, hidden well from those we don't wish to find us. Two days' ride at this pace."

I let my gaze follow his pointing finger. I couldn't see where there might be room to put a valley among the crags up there. If there was an opening in the unbroken line of towering crags, I could not detect it. They looked solid as the rock wall of a fortress. Part of the camouflage was the natural formation of the mountains, but part of it had to be Tyadda magic—masking spells placed to fool the eye. But a masking spell was a useless defense against a man born in the hidden fastness and raised knowing how to penetrate the magic.

"Telling my mother about Daefyd is not something I'm

looking forward to," he said bleakly, still looking at the crags.

An odd little shiver fluttered through my chest. His mother was Sheryn, wife of Tiegan, who was son to King Tiernyn. I knew the story so well—how Brynda, Kenzie, and my father had fled through Celi with her, taking her to safety with her people. The idea of meeting her myself was strangely exciting, as if I were going to meet someone in the epic tales the bards spin of the heroes of centuries past.

"Your mother, the queen . . ." I murmured.

He glanced at me, then shook his head. "No," he said. "She isn't the queen. She prides herself on being the widow of Prince Tiegan, but she says she can never claim the title of queen. Tiegan died before his father, so he was never King."

"But Daefyd is King," I said. "Or would be if Celi were free and he were crowned."

"Aye," he said. "If we were free . . ." His voice trailed off, and pain clouded his eyes.

"Do you have warriors there to defend the steading should the Maedun find it?" I asked quietly.

He looked at me, his mouth a grim and level line. "We aren't warriors, Gareth. You know that. We have only the remnants of the band Daefyd himself led out against the Maedun. Perhaps a dozen men. Perhaps a little less."

"A dozen men?" I repeated. "To oppose a troop of Somber Riders, who might have a warlock with them?"

He shrugged. "The warlock's sorcery won't work that high in the mountains."

"No? What about that sorcerer we met on the flank of Cloudbearer? His sorcery worked well enough to nearly kill all of us. And on Cloudbearer himself, a place sacred to all the gods and goddesses."

"But you overcame it," he said obstinately, determined to hope for the best.

"Aye, I did. But he didn't have a whole troop of Somber

Riders behind him. Only four of them, and there were three of us."

He didn't reply. He looked again at the granite spires of the ridge, then turned away. Lowra murmured something to Davigan, and he nodded and went to collect the horses.

"Davigan's right," she said to me. "We are not a warrior people. And you know that our magic cannot be used as a weapon. But we have other ways of defending ourselves. If we know what we have to defend against." She bit her lip and looked bleakly at Davigan. "And protecting our fastness against one of our own is certainly not something we've ever had to do before."

I reached out and put my hand to the side of her cheek. "Lowra, you said it yourself. Whatever Daefyd has become now—whatever the Maedun have done to him—he's not one of your own anymore. They've made him into something else. Something that may resemble the Daefyd you know, but it certainly isn't him now. I don't know what he is."

"A weapon," she whispered. "He's a weapon. They've taken my brother and made him into a weapon aimed straight at our hearts."

Bane warned me, but I paid it no mind. Perhaps I ignored it because I had heard all the tales of how Red Kian had argued with Kingmakor when his duty led him in a different direction than the sword's quest for the man who would be king. All I could think of was that I was kiting off in the opposite direction Bane would have me go, and the sword was making its displeasure known. I shrugged off the discordant vibrations radiating from the sword. Sourly, I reflected that owning a fabled Rune Blade could be singularly uncomfortable at times.

I could not stop the annoying whining sensation emanating from the sword. It got worse as the day wore on, and it didn't help my own mood much, either. Every furlong we traveled seemed to shorten my temper, and the buzzing of the sword became more and more irritating.

The narrow track we followed wound through the towering cedars and firs at the base of the cliffs. It followed the course of the river through the spur of mountains thrusting south and east from Cloudbearer to curve eventually around the Ceg at the mouth of the River Eidon. We rode through a deep valley between the river and the cliffs that rose in a series of staggered steps toward the towering peaks. The trees clung tenaciously to pockets of soil along the cliff, reaching greedily for the sunshine that spilled over the edge of the crags. Ahead, the valley narrowed where an ancient landslip had tumbled down the mountain, nearly forming a dam to the river.

As we approached the middle of the tumbled rock of the landslip, the sword howled and whined and grumbled, wrapped in its muffling woolen blanket. I put my hand to the bundle strapped to the saddle behind me. It was as if I had thrust my hand into a hive of bees. I thought it had been pierced by dozens of needles. I snatched it back and stared at the palm, but no punctures marred the skin. Muttering heartfelt curses, I rubbed my hand against my kilt.

Lowra turned in her saddle to stare at me, a frown drawing her eyebrows together above the bridge of her nose. She pulled her horse to a stop and waited as Davigan and I pulled up beside her.

"What's wrong?" she asked me. "You've been agitated about something all day. You're even making me upset."

"The sword," I said, and put my hand to the bundle again. A clamor like a thousand bees buzzed angrily through my body. "I don't know what it wants—"

The words clogged in my throat as the realization burst upon me like a flash of summer lightning. I knew what the sword wanted, and I cursed myself for being seven kinds of fool. Even as the thought formed, the sword's shrieking rose into an ear-shattering crescendo that nearly deafened me and set my teeth on edge, and I knew.

We were no longer the hunters; we had become the hunted. I had no time to wonder how it had happened, to wonder if Daefyd had sensed the magic I'd used the night before, or if he sensed Bane's own magic. It was far too late for that.

"Ambush!" I shouted. "Back! We're riding into an ambush!"

I was wrong. We weren't riding into an ambush. We had already blundered into it. My fault. All of it my fault. I had blindly and willfully ignored Bane's warning.

They burst out of the trees and rocks around us, nearly a score of Riders dressed in black, their hair and eyes as dark as their clothing. An odd mixture of fear, excitement, and anger slammed into the pit of my belly. I don't remember reaching for the sword at my back. It seemed as if the hilt leapt into my hand of its own accord. Roaring a Tyran war cry, I put my heels to my horse's flanks and charged forward to meet the black Riders.

One of the Somber Riders surged directly into my path. I kneed my horse sideways, and its shoulder slammed into the flank of the Rider's horse, knocking him off-balance. The Maedun grabbed for his saddle horn, and I relieved him of his head, then whirled to meet the next ambusher. Out of the corner of my eye, I saw Lowra wheel her mount, fitting another arrow into the string of her bow.

I ducked as another Maedun whirled ahead of me and swung his sword. His lips drew back over his teeth in a snarl, and he twisted in the saddle to avoid my counterthrust, then ducked and slashed his sword at my belly. I barely got out of the way in time by hauling my horse around and sliding side-

ways in the saddle. I turned back to the Somber Rider to find
his blade slicing toward my neck. I ducked and managed to
get my sword up to parry his. Sparks flew as the blades met.
The Somber Rider yanked his sword back, but overbalanced
and nearly fell from his horse. I slashed backhand and opened
his belly for him.

I had completely lost track of Davigan, but I had no time
to search for him among the confusion. "Davigan, run," I
shouted. "Back down the track!" I thought I heard his voice
call a reply, but I was too busy to understand what he said.

Lowra shouted something and urged her horse closer to
mine. I was only subliminally aware of her presence as I swept
my sword into the mass of Somber Riders surrounding us. I
felt the blade bite deep into flesh and bone, then swung back in
my saddle as another Rider attacked me from behind. The
sword in the Rider's hand whistled, gleaming dully in the
bright sunlight. I swept my sword backhand. My blade caught
on the hilt of the Rider's sword. The shock of the impact shivered all the way up my arm to my shoulder. The sword spun
out of the Rider's hand. He roared, reaching for a dagger at his
belt. The shout trailed off into a gurgle as the shaft of one of
Lowra's arrows found his throat.

Something tugged at my plaid. I caught a glimpse of the
blade of a dark sword as it tore through the hanging end of
the fabric. Caitha would strangle me if I ruined this plaid, I
thought incongruously. I swept my sword sideways as the
Maedun struggled to free his sword from the folds of the
plaid. The shoulder of my blade just beneath the hilt caught
him on the temple, splitting through skin and bone and spray-
ing blood and brains over the saddle cloth.

Davigan broke clear of the confusion and kicked his
horse into a gallop back to the east, the way we had come. I
wheeled my horse, reached for the bridle of Lowra's mount,
and pulled it around.

"Go," I shouted. A Somber Rider lunged at us, and I whirled, swinging my sword. The Rider swerved away. "Follow Davigan. Get out of here!"

"Not without you," she cried. Then her eyes went wide and every trace of color drained from her face. I could not hear her voice, but I saw the word her lips formed. "Daefyd," she whispered.

I spun around, following her dazed look. He sat his horse at the edge of the track, looking as if he watched no more than the water rushing over rocks. No concern for his sister or brother showed on his blankly calm face. In fact, if he recognized them—or even saw them at all—he gave no sign.

"Go!" I cried at Lowra again.

She gave Daefyd one last agonized glance, then pivoted her horse and followed Davigan. He was nearly out of sight around a bend in the track. I ducked away from another Rider and wheeled my horse to follow her, bending low over the horse's neck.

I didn't see the archers among the Somber Riders. But I heard the twang of bowstrings, and the whirring of an arrow as it sailed past my head. Before I could shout a warning, Davigan stiffened in his saddle, then tumbled to the track and lay still. I saw the arrow hit Lowra. It took her in the shoulder, and she nearly fell. She would have kept her seat, but in her concern for Davigan, she pulled her horse to a stop and slid to the track. Davigan did not move, and I could see the shaft of an arrow protruding from the small of his back.

The Riders were close behind me as I fled down the track, and I had to make an instant decision. I chose Lowra.

My horse thundered past her as she knelt by Davigan's side. I bent low in the saddle, gripping with my knees, and reached out an arm. I caught her around the waist and swept her off her feet and onto the saddle ahead of me. Her weight, slight as it was, nearly tore me off the horse, but I managed to keep my seat and not lose my grip on her.

"No," she cried. "I can't leave Davigan—"

I didn't bother to reply. We rounded the bend, and I hauled in the horse to a slithering halt. I slid to the ground, pulling Lowra with me, pausing only long enough to yank the blanket-wrapped sword from behind the saddle, then sent the horse skittering and curvetting down the trail by giving it a solid smack across the haunches with the flat of my blade. It disappeared, and I crouched in the shelter of a tumble of boulders, drawing Lowra in close beside me.

"What—?"

She struggled in my arms, but I held her tightly and clamped my hand over her mouth to quiet her. I couldn't let her inadvertently betray our presence to the Somber Riders as I reached out desperately for the flows of power that Kian had showed me. I found one and grasped at it, drawing it around us like a cloak. Clutching Bane between us, I bent my head and pressed my forehead against hers.

"Rocks," I whispered fervently. "When they come around that bend, let them see only two more rocks here."

18

The troop of Somber Riders came around the bend like an avalanche, bent low over the pommels of their saddles, intent on the chase. My horse had long since disappeared down the trail and around the next bend, but the clatter of its pounding hooves still echoed and reechoed off the walls of the gorge, sounding like half a dozen horses. I pulled the threads of power more closely around Lowra and me, concentrating on appearing to be only two more splintered boulders among the dead leaves and sprouting grasses.

It must have worked.

The Riders clattered past us without so much as a glance in our direction. In seconds, they had disappeared around the bend at the eastern end of the landslip behind my horse. It was a shockingly direct way of driving home the fact that I really *did* have magic after all.

I'd counted ten Riders. I wasn't sure how many we'd left dead on the trail by the ambush site, but I was certain it wasn't more than four or five. That meant there were still five or six Riders close around us. I didn't move, and I didn't let go of the web of power. It wrapped itself tightly around us, making my skin feel as tingly as a limb that has fallen asleep and finally begun to waken. The air around us felt charged as the air just before a thunderstorm. Wrapped tightly in its woolen blanket, Bane shrieked like a grindstone against iron.

Lowra quivered against me, making soft little sounds of annoyance, her lips moving against the palm of my hand. Her face held the pallor of chalk, her eyes wide and shocked. Blood oozed from the arrow wound in her shoulder, smearing bright red across my shirt. She glared up at me, and I removed my hand from her mouth.

"I know enough to stay quiet, you half-wit," she snarled, but so softly her voice didn't carry beyond my ear. "You don't have to muffle me like a gods-cursed dog."

"I'm sorry," I said. "I could think of nothing else on the instant. Things got a little chaotic there for a moment." I touched her injured shoulder. "Let me see if I can Heal that."

She twitched away and grimaced. "Later," she said. "When there's not so much danger. I can live with it for now."

She was obviously still in the time after wounding when the pain of the injury had not yet made itself agonizingly apparent. That worried me. Men die of wounds they hardly feel. "Are you sure?"

"Aye. It hurts, but not as much as I expected it to." She broke off and looked back down the trail. "Davigan —" she said, and bright tears sprang into her eyes.

"Still back there," I said. "Was he still alive?"

"I think so," she said. "The arrow took him in a bad place — in the small of the back. But I think he still breathed."

I tried to tell her how I'd needed to make an instant decision. I couldn't take both her and Davigan as I swept past. I'd chosen her because I knew she was still alive. And because she was my bheancoran, and therefore the other half of my soul. She may have seen it in my face, though. Pain still clouded her eyes, but she reached up and touched my face gently, and she tried to smile to show me she understood.

I learned something about myself in that instant. Something I'd never expected to learn, but before I could do anything about it, the blanket of power around us quivered and fizzed, stinging my skin like nettles. We heard horses approaching. Seconds later, the Somber Riders appeared, leading my horse. They didn't look at all happy.

Lowra stiffened against me, going still as a deer sensing a

hunter. I ran my fingers across the threads of power surrounding us, and thought hard about boulders and cliffs and sodden, dead leaves.

Daefyd and a Somber Rider rode back to meet the returning Riders. They stopped their horses no more than five paces from where we crouched among the dead leaves and scattered rocks. I looked at the man with Daefyd, and my blood froze in my veins.

He appeared to be only a few years older than I, a startlingly handsome man with a face that reminded me of a hawk. Deep lines plunged from either side of his nose to bracket his mouth, giving him a cynical, sardonic expression that was somehow both attractive and repellent at the same time. Unlike the other Riders, he wore no insignia. Nothing relieved the all-over black of his superbly cut and fitting shirt, tunic, trews, and cloak. His hair hung thick and coarse to his shoulders, and was blacker than the darkest night, absorbing the sunlight rather than reflecting it back. His eyes were darker than his hair, giving the impression of having no iris, only wide, empty pupils.

But he rode forever cloaked in shadow of his own making. Around his head, trailing around his shoulders and down his back, a black mist floated gently in the bright sunlight. I knew what that mist meant. He was a warlock. No, more than a warlock, this man. An adept at working the blood magic. A sorcerer, and a powerful one at that. That age, that powerful, there was only one man he could be.

I was staring straight at Horbad, son of Hakkar of Maedun, who was self-styled Lord Protector of Celi and usurper of Daefyd's throne.

Bane's whining rose to a shrieking howl, and the bundle vibrated between Lowra and me like a whole grove of aspens in a high wind. I could do nothing to stop it. Lowra heard it, too. Not hearing it would be difficult. She would have had to be deaf as a stone. She went rigid against me, staring in horror from the sword to Daefyd, who sat his horse calmly beside Horbad, and back to the sword.

I looked back at Horbad, terrified that he could hear it, too. He had magic. Blood sorcery it might be, but it was still magic. I couldn't understand how he couldn't hear the clamor and tumult Bane sent up.

Unless it was really true that a masking spell holds all magic within it, and contains it as a stoppered bottle contains wine.

The troop of Somber Riders leading my horse joined Horbad and Daefyd, forming a tight, disciplined knot around the black sorcerer's son. Horbad asked the leader something I couldn't hear. The man gestured back down the track in the direction they had come and shook his head. Horbad asked another question, and the troop leader shrugged and shook his head again. Horbad's face tightened, anger glinting in his black eyes. He turned in his saddle and called out.

I had learned the Maedun tongue when I was a boy, training with Kenzie. But Horbad was too far away, and I could not understand the words he spoke. The language spoken by his stiff body and glaring, narrowed eyes, though, was completely unmistakable. He was furious, and meant to find us.

Four more Riders joined them from the other direction, moving slowly with their burden. Lowra made a soft, horrified noise beside me, and I bit my lip to prevent any outcry.

Davigan sat slumped astride one of the horses. A Somber Rider straddled the horse behind him, holding him firmly in place. Blood stained the side of Davigan's tunic and trews, but he was obviously still alive. He was unconscious, though, and didn't move as the Rider guided the horse into position with the troop. Daefyd looked at his brother with no change of expression. He might have been looking at any stranger. At something less than human for all it affected him.

Horbad spoke again, then gestured in a wide circle. Again, I caught none of the words, just the commanding tone of his voice. The troop of Somber Riders dismounted and fanned out in all directions, obviously searching for Lowra and me. Horbad apparently wanted us badly. Or perhaps he only wanted the sword and its magic. He dismounted and paced impatiently as the Riders searched. Daefyd merely sat astride his horse with uncanny stillness, impassive as a well-trained hound.

The Riders searched for a long time. The sun was touching the western rim of the mountains when Horbad, in a foul temper, finally called them back in. Two of the Riders walked past us so close, their cloaks brushed against us. Lowra closed her eyes and bit her lip, and I shivered. A masking spell will fool the eye, but not the touch. Had those Somber Riders put out their hands to touch the "rock" they passed, they would have put a palm down directly on my shoulder. And since a man feels nothing like a rock, they would certainly have found us.

The Riders gathered in their horses and mounted. At Horbad's command, they formed themselves into two neat ranks and rode off westward down the track.

Daefyd wheeled his horse to follow, then paused as the breeze changed direction. We had been downwind of him. But now the breeze blew across the track, and we were upwind. His head went up, like a hunting dog scenting a deer. He turned in his saddle and looked straight at the place where Lowra and I crouched, wrapped in the threads of the masking spell. He frowned slightly, the first trace of expression I had seen on his face.

He looked directly into my eyes. A cold chill rippled down my spine and settled in my belly. Those eyes were the same brown-gold as Davigan's eyes, as Lowra's eyes, but no spark of humanity showed in them at all. I'd seen more compassion and empathy in the eyes of a wolf. Looking into Daefyd ap Tiegan's eyes was like looking down into a well of icy water. Whatever makes a man a man rather than an animal that walks upright on two legs was gone from his eyes. Daefyd didn't live there anymore.

For an instant that became an eternity, we locked gazes through the web of magic. How could he fail to see us crouching there? Any moment, he would call to Horbad and the troop of Somber Riders and betray us as he had betrayed Margan's wife and daughter, and those people at the homestead.

Then the breeze shifted again, and he looked away. For one more instant, he sat motionless, then put his heels to his horse's flanks and cantered after Horbad and the Riders. In moments, they were gone around the westward spill of the landslip.

Lowra shifted her weight against me. "Are they gone?" she asked.

"I don't know. I think so. We'll wait and see for sure."

"Daefyd was with them," she said.

"Aye, he was. He looked straight at us. He must have seen us. Or sensed the masking spell."

"He's always been able to sense magic," she said. "He says it has a scent that's unmistakable."

I'd smelled the stench of blood sorcery. I could believe that other magics had their own characteristic scent. "Do you think he smelled the masking spell?"

She shook her head. "He shouldn't have been able to," she said. "Not if you did it properly. All the magic should have been directed inside the spell. At us. There shouldn't be any outward sign."

"Still, he looked straight into my eyes." I shuddered at

the memory of those flat, dead eyes. Like two dull brown stones in the expressionless face.

"But he didn't betray us."

"No, he didn't."

She hesitated, her unwillingness to believe her brother could betray her plain in her voice when she spoke. "Mayhaps Horbad couldn't force him to betray kin . . ."

"Mayhaps," I said noncommittally. But I had seen Daefyd's eyes, and I could believe almost anything of Horbad's blood sorcery.

I held the masking spell around us for a long time after Horbad had taken Daefyd and the troop of Somber Riders down the track. Only when I was certain they were gone, and would not come back, did I let the web of magic dissipate and snap back into the ground and the air around us. The electric feel of the air subsided, and the disintegrating magic stung like sleet against my skin as it scattered. Exhaustion swept through me, and I sagged against the boulder for support.

Lowra cried out in pain as I moved to shift the sword from between us and the shaft of the arrow in her shoulder caught on my plaid. She clutched her shoulder, then pulled her hand back quickly as the point of the arrow protruding from the front of her shoulder scratched her hand.

"Let me see it," I said, and bent to examine the wound. She winced away from my touch, then bit her lip and stiffened herself to endure it.

The arrowhead had entered the back of her shoulder, penetrated the soft tissues just below her collarbone, and exited very close to the hollow of her throat. Nausea crawled through my belly as I realized how lucky she was. The point of the arrow missed the large vessel in her neck by less than the breadth of two of my fingers. A lot of blood stained her shirt and tunic, but it only oozed from the wound; it didn't spurt with each pulsebeat.

"I think I can Heal this," I said. "But I'll have to take the arrow shaft out first."

She made a muffled noise in reply. I unsheathed my dagger and used it to snap the arrowhead from the shaft. Her face went the same color as milk, the taut skin around her mouth tinged with pale green. I muttered an apology, then, before either of us could think too much about it, I seized the fletched end of the arrow and yanked briskly. I had to use far more strength than I expected to pull it from her flesh.

Lowra cried out, then slumped against me. Fresh blood oozed from the wounds, front and back. I opened the throat of her shirt and slipped it and her tunic down, exposing her shoulder. The wounds weren't big—two blue-lipped punctures, oozing blood and surrounded by bruised flesh. I hesitated, wondering if I needed to clean the injuries first, then put my hands to her shoulder, one hand covering each wound. If I Healed it properly, there should be no need to worry about wound fever.

I hoped.

Using all the concentration I had, I bent my head and reached out again to the flows of energy around me. They surged through the ground beneath me, as I knelt beside Lowra, and swirled in the air around us. Bright strands, the color of moonlight and sunlight and sea and sky and verdant glen. I drew the flow into myself and sent it through my hands into Lowra.

Her patterns were all there for me to see. Beautiful and delicate and fragile. Patterns that made a life—a person. Everything fitted neatly and precisely into everything else. I sensed the breaks in the patterns that were the wounds and directed the Healing energy toward the disruptions. Gradually, almost imperceptibly at first, the pattern began to rebuild itself. Slowly, so slowly, the broken lines realigned and re-formed, coming together to mend the disruption until it was as perfect as the rest.

I took my hands away from Lowra's shoulder and swayed dizzily. I had to reach out and steady myself against a rock as I looked down at the wounds. Nothing remained but two small, circular scars, slightly indented, and white where the rest of her skin was a warm, golden tan. Gently, I pulled her shirt up over her shoulder and tied it at her throat again, then adjusted her tunic.

She sighed as if coming out of a long, refreshing sleep and opened her eyes. Wonder flashed through her eyes as she reached up to touch her shoulder, then she smiled.

"You really are a powerful Healer, Gareth," she said.

I still was not sure enough of my balance to let go of the rock. "And a dizzy one," I murmured.

"Reach back for the power," she said. "Use it to replenish your strength. Otherwise, you'll have to sleep for nearly a day to get it back."

It was easier than I thought. Energy poured into me through my knees, which were pressed to the ground, through my skin where the air swirled around me. In moments, I felt better, but still somewhat giddy and weak. Rhianna had warned me that I would use my own strength in Healing. Holding the masking spell for so long had probably contributed its fair share to the sense of overwhelming tiredness. But we had to go on; we had to follow the Somber Riders. I got to my feet and held out my hand to help Lowra up.

"We'll follow them to see where they've taken Davigan," I said.

She nodded. "Let's check back there where they ambushed us," she said. "They weren't leading any extra horses. The other horses may have bolted, but they usually don't go far if they do. If we can find two, it will make it a lot easier to follow the Riders."

Luck deserted us, along with any of the horses that might

have bolted during the fight. We found none. But we did find dead Somber Riders.

I put Bane down and bent over one of the Somber Riders. He looked to be about my height and build.

"What are you doing?" Lowra asked.

"I want this uniform," I said, as I struggled to strip the corpse. "It might come in handy."

She made a distasteful face, but stooped to help me. All I wanted was the shirt, tunic, and cloak. It didn't take us long to collect them and stuff them into the bundle with Bane. I took the belts from two other bodies and used them to make a sling by looping the ends through the buckles and cinching them tight around each end of the bundle, then tying the two loose ends together. Now I could carry the bundle slung over my shoulder, leaving both hands free to use my sword if necessary. I adjusted the bundle comfortably against my hip, made sure it wouldn't get in the way if I needed to draw my sword in a hurry, then readied myself for a long trek on foot.

Lowra stopped abruptly as we passed the place where Davigan had lain after the arrow knocked him from his horse. She dropped to one knee and picked up his harp in its carry case. Blood stained the smoothly tanned leather and the harp itself was smashed. One of the plunging horses had put its foot down in the middle of the fragile instrument. No more sparkling music would come from the carefully tuned strings, no more bright, scintillating glissandos of notes.

Lowra smoothed the torn leather of the carry case, then slung it over her shoulder. "Even if it's broken, he'll want this," she said quietly. "He made it himself when he was only fifteen. Mayhaps he can repair it."

"We'll find him," I said. "And we'll get him back."

She turned a pale, determined face to me. "Aye, we will," she said. "I only hope we can get him back before they do to him what they've done to Daefyd."

19

Nearly a score of men on horseback, one of them bleeding, make an unmistakable trail. Even on foot, Lowra and I had no difficulty tracking Horbad's troop through the fading light. We stood a reasonable chance of catching up to them sooner or later. One thing working in our favor was the fact that urging a horse any faster than a brisk walk over these trails was begging for a nasty spill. And, eventually, unless Maedun blood sorcery had some way of turning dark into daylight, they were going to have to stop for the night. Riding mountain tracks in darkness, even if there had been a full moon, was not something a wise man did. I didn't think that Horbad was a fool. He was soldier enough not to risk his men unless he could gain something valuable in exchange. Riding at night wasn't worth the risk.

That, unfortunately, was a two-edged sword. Lowra and I could not charge around blindly after dark, either. Far too many unexpected cliffs led to sudden, icy rivers. Our only consolation was that it would not be difficult to pick up the trail of the Somber Riders in the morning. And we should be able to get an earlier start, too. It is a lot easier to get two people up and ready to go than it is to organize a troop of men to get them on the trail.

The weather wasn't helping much, either. The clear skies of day slowly filled with clouds as the sun set behind the mountains. Color blazed in the west—red and gold and orange and purple. But as the last of the light faded from the sky, the clouds thickened and lowered, allowing not the slightest glimmer of starlight to show. There should have been a moon in its last quarter rising shortly after sunset, but we never saw it at all through the clouds.

We followed Horbad and the Somber Riders until we began to stumble over roots and rocks on the track, bending almost double to make sure we could read the signs left by the troop of Maedun. As the shadows of the mountains closed about us and the night deepened, even walking slowly became dangerous. We could see little or nothing in the darkness of the night.

"We have to stop for the night," I said. "We'll kill ourselves wandering around here like this."

Lowra looked up at the sky. "The clouds will go away soon," she said. "Then we'll be able to see better."

I glanced up. Overhead, a solid, impenetrable black blanket of cloud choked off any light at all that might have come from stars or moon. Not a single break or thin spot anywhere indicated a chance of clearing up. We'd be lucky if we didn't get soaked by rain before daybreak.

"Lowra, no," I said. "Don't be foolish. I know you're anxious to find Davigan, but we can't stumble around here in the dark. We won't be any use to Davigan—or Daefyd either, come to that—if we blunder off a cliff and end up drowned in the river, or smashed to flinders on the rocks."

"We can't stop yet," she said. "We have to find them."

"If we kill ourselves, we'll never find them."

She turned on me. There wasn't enough light to see her expression, but her voice was fierce and taut and grating with obstinacy. "We can't stop," she insisted. "They're my brothers. You don't know what it's like to lose a brother—" She broke off as she remembered. I'd lost a brother, a sister, and my mother, too. "Oh, Gareth, I'm so sorry. Forgive me. I didn't mean—"

"I was four when it happened," I said softly. "The grief has dimmed with time. It's all right. There's nothing to forgive."

She slumped against the trunk of a tree, pressing her cheek against its rough bark. "No," she said. This time, tears choked her voice. "No, it isn't all right. I'm just so tired and so angry and so —"

"I know." I reached for her and drew her into my arms. All the women in the tales who were bheancoran to the Princes of Skai, or to King Tiernyn, were tall, big-boned women, all of them capable of swinging a sword nearly as long and heavy as the one I wore. Lowra was so small, so fragile, so delicate. I might have been cradling a bird to my breast.

She raised her head to say something. Instead, I kissed her. And, surprisingly, she kissed me back. It wasn't what I had meant to happen, but it was unexpectedly sweet and comforting and stirring.

The last woman I'd held like this was Caitha dan Malcolm, a tall, strong, Tyran clanswoman. Lowra was so very different, but she fit into my arms so well. We stood together for a timeless moment, then I let her go. She stepped away from me, and her hand went slowly to her lips, tracing their outline as if the shape of my mouth were still imprinted on hers.

"I — I'm sorry," I said. "This is hardly the time or the place for that."

"No," she agreed. "Not the time and place, but don't be sorry." She was quiet for a moment. Then: "You're right. We have to find a place to camp overnight. We can't —"

Something drifted to me on the light breeze. I lifted a hand imperiously to cut her off. "Smell that?" I asked.

"Smell what?"

"Smoke." I sniffed again. The faint scent of woodsmoke

rode on the wind from the west. "I smell smoke. Woodsmoke. A cooking fire?"

"I smell it, too." Subdued excitement tinged her voice. "That must mean they've camped somewhere around here. Can we follow the scent?"

"We can try," I said. "Be very careful where you put your feet. We don't want to announce our arrival for all to hear. Sound travels too well at night." I made sure Bane was secure in its sling around my shoulder, and took Lowra's hand. "Let's go."

With no warning at all, the forest opened into a clearing. We nearly walked right into it before we saw it. I stopped so suddenly, Lowra trod on my heel. She made a soft exclamation of surprise, then we both ducked back into the shadows of the trees.

A small, squat building stood in the middle of the uneven circle of open space. The house was a good-sized building. Stone-built and thatched with bracken and straw, the building was larger than most farmhouses I'd seen in Tyra. Smoke rose from the chimney, and warm, yellow light glowed in the narrow windows. It didn't look like a farmhouse even though the faint light spilling from the windows showed the outlines of a paddock yard behind it, and farther back in the shadows a byre or stable. No kitchen garden grew by the door. No attempt had been made to make the place look homey or welcoming.

"A posting station," Lowra whispered. "I'd forgotten this was here. I didn't realize we were so close to it."

"It seems quiet enough," I said. "I'd think the troops are bunked in the stable, and probably asleep." A shadow moved across one of the windows of the house. "Someone's awake in there, though. A man of Horbad's rank and stature wouldn't be sleeping in any stable. He'd be in the house. Probably well guarded, too."

As I spoke, a shadow moved near the paddock. The shadow turned into a man as he walked through the light of one of the windows. He carried a sword and a bow, a quiver of arrows clipped to his belt. A sentry.

"I don't think Daefyd and Davigan would be in the stables," she said. "They'll be in the house, too. Do you think we can get closer to take a look?"

The sound of a door opening and closing came to us on the breeze. We stepped back into the shadows as a man came out of the house and walked over to the edge of the trees. He relieved himself, then made his way back into the house. As the door opened, and he entered, the silhouette of a sword at his hip was plainly outlined by the light in the room.

"They're awake and alert in there," I said. "I don't think I'd want them finding us out here."

"We have to see if Davigan's in there," she said.

"I know. Let me think." I worried at my thumbnail with my teeth for a moment before an idea occurred to me. "A masking spell?" I said. "Can I make us look like Maedun Somber Riders so we can get over there and see if Daefyd and Davigan are in there?"

"That's an idea," she said, subdued excitement in her voice. "We might even be able to walk right in and take them out if we looked like Somber Riders."

It was well and truly a brilliant idea. But unfortunately, like many wonderful new ideas, it didn't work. I could use the magic to work a masking spell to give myself the appearance of a Somber Rider. Or I could use it to give Lowra the semblance of a Maedun. But not both. Try as I might, I could not manipulate the strands of power flowing around me to disguise both of us. I was ready to snarl with frustration. When I gathered the magic to try one last time, Lowra reached out and stopped me.

"It's no use, Gareth," she said. "It won't work."

"But it's *got* to work," I replied, foolishly close to tears of frustration. "I could work the masking spell to cover both of us back where we were ambushed. Why can't I make it work here?"

She shook her head. "Mayhaps you need more practice," she said. "You can't help being new to your magic."

I turned away and slammed my fist into the trunk of a tree. That was a mistake. I muttered curses under my breath and shook my hand to shake away the pain. I cradled my hand against my chest, trying to contain and confine the pain so I wouldn't cry out with it.

Contain and confine . . .

Then I knew why the spell wouldn't work on both of us. A masking spell contains magic, confines it within the boundaries of the spell. Back at the ambush site, it had formed a barrier that wouldn't let Bane's magic out to alert Horbad. Or Daefyd, either. I could give both Lowra and me the semblance of a pair of rocks because we were both inside the spell at the same time. If I worked the spell around myself to make myself look like a Somber Rider, none of my magic could penetrate the masking spell to transform Lowra.

Only one of us could go into the clearing to look for Davigan.

"There's no help for it," I whispered. "You wait for me here. I'll go and find Davigan."

She bristled like an outraged hedgehog. "Don't you *dare* try to treat me like a helpless child," she said stiffly. "I don't need protecting. I'm your bheancoran. If you go, I go."

"It's not that," I said quickly, and explained my theory about the masking spell. She didn't like it, but it made sense to her, too. She was reluctant to accept it, but she had to. Finally, she nodded.

"I think you're right," she said at last. "I don't like it, though. I don't like leaving you here by yourself."

"Do you want to try walking up to the house as you are and peering into the windows?" I asked. "You'd only be a little less conspicuous than a sheep in a den of wolves."

She made a soft, irritated noise in the back of her throat. "Very well," she said. "I'll wait. But you be very careful."

"Very careful, indeed," I assured her. "We'll meet back here when I've got Davigan."

I had thought to use the stolen clothing from the Somber Rider to help disguise myself. I pulled the black shirt and tunic out of the bundle, and rewrapped Bane carefully. The time spent wrapped in the blanket had not improved the clothing. Both shirt and tunic were ripe enough to make my eyes water, and the situation wasn't helped by the dried blood crusted on the shirt. Lowra coughed and made a disgusted noise, then stepped away from me, waving her hand in front of her face.

"Surely not," she said. "With that pong, they'd smell you coming a league or two away."

"I think you're right," I said. In the long run, it would probably be no harder to place the masking spell to disguise my kilt and plaid than it would be to mask the blood stains on the shirt and tunic. I dropped the shirt and tunic in relief.

"What about Bane?" she asked, gesturing toward the bundle.

I looked at the blanket-wrapped sword thoughtfully, suddenly and unaccountably reluctant to leave it behind, even with Lowra. I wondered if the reluctance was prompting from the sword, or my own need not to let it out of my sight. Obviously, it would be safer hidden here with Lowra. But even as the thought formed, Bane set up a screeching howl like the rasp of a file on the teeth of a saw, loud enough to alert Horbad in the posting station, and mayhaps even Hakkar in Clendonan. The howl set my teeth on edge and I leapt to snatch up the bundle. The moment I had it safe in my hands, the screeching stopped. Bane was not about to be left behind.

"With me, I think," I said breathlessly and slipped the bundle over my shoulder, snugging it against my hip. The straps held it securely enough, and it didn't interfere with my movements. I could easily hide the sword within the masking spell so it couldn't be seen. It would be safe with me. "I'll meet you back here later."

She nodded, then vanished like mist in the morning.

I heard nothing as she slipped away into the night, but suddenly she was no longer by my side. I took a deep breath, then put my hand into the flows of power that surrounded me in the night and wove them around myself. A Somber Rider, I thought. I'm a Somber Rider . . . And not just any Somber Rider—the leader of the troop . . .

My instinct was to creep into the clearing, ducking from one minuscule piece of cover to the next. I had to force myself to walk upright, proudly and arrogantly, as if I had a perfect right to be there. A cold patch formed on my back under my shoulder blade, waiting for the sentry's arrow to take me.

I was nearly to the house when he noticed me and called out a challenge. I muttered something and waved my hand in an irritated gesture, and kept walking. He watched me for a moment, then went back to his post in the shadows. Somber Riders were not men to question their superiors. I let out the breath I was holding and willed my knees not to buckle as I moved quickly around to the side of the house away from the paddock where the sentry stood.

The windows were narrow, more like arrow slits than windows to let in light and air. I slipped through the night and pressed myself to the rough stone of the wall by the nearest window. Carefully, I craned my head and peered into the house.

The window was glazed with thick, rippled glass, distorting my view. But I was able to see into the room reasonably well. It was obviously a bedroom. Candles stood on a table by a box bed, spreading a soft light over the turned-back quilt. A brazier by a desk shed cherry red warmth against the chill of the night. But the room was empty. In the wall opposite the window, a door led to what was probably the main room.

I ducked under the window and crept around to the other side of the house. Three windows faced out toward the forest. The Maedun had cut back the undergrowth so there was a good bowshot distance between the house and the trees, but the grass was high and thick. The spill of light from the windows reached less than half the distance across the tangled grass to the trees.

No glass covered these windows. They were unshuttered, open to the night. Cautiously, I peered around the stone coping and into the room.

Three men sat on comfortable chairs before a hearth. One of them was the leader of the troop that had ambushed us. The Maedun wearing the dung-coated boots was obviously the keeper of the posting station. The other was Horbad.

I recognized him immediately, of course. He sat with his feet on a hassock, slumped gracefully, holding a goblet of wine against his chest. The firelight sparked in the deep red wine, making it glitter like a bright ember in the night. He watched the fire, idly listening to the other two men, who were speaking quietly.

Behind the men, a solidly built table held the remains of a meal. Wax dripped from the stubs of candles and congealed on the rough wood of the tabletop. A wolfhound lay half-asleep beneath the table, contentedly gnawing on a bone.

Daefyd sat at the table, his eyes unfocused, his body slack, as if he were a cloak that had been discarded and left where it fell. He didn't move, didn't pay the slightest attention to the three men by the fire. He stared straight ahead. Wherever his attention was, it wasn't in the room. He didn't even seem to notice Davigan, who lay on a rough pallet near the door.

Except for a hectic flush on his cheekbones, Davigan was pale as milk, and his lips looked faintly blue in the flickering light of candle and hearthfire. His chest rose and fell quickly, as if he panted for breath. He wore no shirt or tunic. Someone had wrapped a dirty bandage around his back and hips. I recognized the signs of wound fever. Unless the wound was washed and treated, or I could Heal him, Davigan would die of it. Painfully, but not quickly.

Plans swirled in my head even as I caught sight of him. All I'd need would be a diversion of some sort. It would take hardly any time at all to open the door, seize Davigan, and be out of there. Surely Lowra could provide the diversion . . .

Daefyd lifted his head and sniffed the air like a hound on the spoor of a boar. A faint frown drew the golden eyebrows together above the bridge of his nose, and he looked straight at me.

"Ho," the troop leader said, pointing at Daefyd. "My lord Horbad, look. I believe your hunting dog smells a partridge."

Horbad came to his feet in one swift, fluid motion. He turned quickly and looked at the window Daefyd stared at. If it startled him to see the face of the man he knew to be beside him by the fire, he didn't show it. I leapt back into the shadows, but not quickly enough.

"You," Horbad shouted. "Who are you?" He snatched up his sword from where it lay at his feet and sprang for the door, vaulting the troop leader's feet.

I spun away and sprinted for the shadows of the trees.

20

The welcome shadows of the trees closed around me. I found an oak *with low, overhanging* branches, and swarmed up the thick trunk like a badgercat with a pack of wolves on its tail. I found a perch high in the branches and eeled around, losing some skin to the rough bark in the process, until I could see back into the clearing and the yard of the posting station.

Behind me, pandemonium erupted all through the clearing. Someone had roused the Somber Riders quartered in the stable. They poured out into the paddock yard with weapons clashing and clattering, shouting to each other. Torches burst into flame, throwing leaping shadows across the ground as men ran with them. The troop leader leapt out into the yard, buckling on his sword as he ran and shouting orders. The men with torches fanned out and began systematically searching the clearing, weapons held ready. There were probably not more than a score and a half of men at the posting station, including the stable men, but they were all in the yard, and looked as if there were nearly a hundred of them, the way they scurried around. Archers held arrows nocked against their bowstrings as they followed the men holding torches. Other men held naked swords, poised and ready to strike.

Daefyd had come out of the house with the troop leader. He stood for a moment outlined by the rectangle of golden light cast by the candles in the main room, his head cocked as if listening. Or sniffing the air. He moved quietly as a wraith around to the back of the house and stood in the spill of light from the window. The slight frown still creasing his brow, he stared intently, unblinking, at the grove of trees where I crouched in deep shadow, partially hidden by the trunk and branches of the oak.

The masking spell. He sensed the magic.

Quickly, I let go of the flows of power. They snapped back, stinging, as the spell dissipated. The shards sparked for a moment, falling in a bright shower around me, then vanished into the dark. Daefyd stood for a moment more, the light from the window glinting in his dark gold hair. The frown evaporated, and his face became as bland and expressionless as before. He lost interest in the shadows that hid me and turned to make his way back into the house.

I let out the breath I hadn't realized I was holding and closed my eyes, pressing my cheek to the rough bark of the oak. If Daefyd could sense the magic of a masking spell, his gift for perceiving magic was a powerful one, indeed. We were going to have to be very careful around him. No magic at all. Not if we didn't want him betraying us to the Maedun.

The Somber Riders ran around like ants after someone has kicked their nest. Bright sparks trailed from the streaming flags of flame as they ran with the torches, searching all sectors of the clearing. Several of them crashed through the forest, thrusting their swords into clumps of bushes. But men seldom look up when they run. And in the dark, I hoped I looked like nothing more than a knot of tangled branches. I dared not use a masking spell to ensure that a knot of tangled branches was exactly what I resembled. Not with Daefyd so close by.

The Somber Riders searched for the thick end of an hour. They hadn't found Lowra, either, as far as I could tell. But she was completely familiar with the forests of Skai and how to hide in them. She could easily make herself invisible, part of the forest. All she needed to do was to melt farther back into the shadows beneath the trees, and they'd never find her. I hoped.

Midnight had come and gone when the last of the men carrying torches returned to the paddock yard. Horbad stalked around, stiff with anger and frustration, questioning each man as he returned. Again, I was too far away to hear what he said. But I had the feeling that if I were closer, I might be able to add several interesting colloquialisms to my limited Maedun vocabulary.

Presently, the paddock yard was again empty except for half a dozen armed sentries posted around the clearing in the shadows. They carried bows and swords, and the alarm had obviously made them alert as startled deer. The men who tended the horses had soothed the restive animals in the paddock and returned to their beds in the stable. Quiet descended over the yard, broken only by the occasional snuffle of one of the horses. I waited, tucked into the shelter of my oak, treed like a badgercat with a whole pack of hounds nosing back and forth in the forest below.

Horbad had gone to his room. I saw his shadow moving back and forth across the glazed window, distorted by the rippled glass. The light became dimmer in the windows of the main room as someone extinguished most of the candles, but Horbad's window remained bright for a long time. If I concentrated, I thought I could see him sitting at the desk, working. But eventually, that light, too, went out, and the posting station slept in silence.

My arms and legs ached from clinging to the tree, and the bark had removed large patches of skin from them. Kilts are comfortable garments to wear for almost any activity, but tree-climbing wasn't among them. Bane's weight hung heavy from my shoulder, threatening to pull me backward out of the tree.

The sentries posted in the yard had not moved for a long time. I didn't think they were asleep. Surely Horbad would have their heads if he caught them asleep on duty, and they knew it. But I thought enough time had passed to take the edge off their wakeful vigilance. The hours after midnight are the most difficult in which to maintain alert wariness. Even the best of soldiers has to fight to remain awake as the body decides it must sleep.

I let myself down carefully from the tree, losing more skin on my arms and legs in the process and bruising my ribs as Bane rapped against me sharply. Slipping quietly through the trees, I found a niche of dark shadow at the edge of the clearing and stood watching the house and yard. Rescuing Davigan now looked like an impossible task. I began to wonder how I would even find Lowra again.

As I thought of her, the place in my chest where the threads of the bond nestled stirred. The sensation was calm and soothing. The knowledge came to me all of apiece—she was not hurt, or in any immediate danger. But she was awake and active.

I had hardly begun to wonder what she was doing when she announced her location in no uncertain terms. A sudden ululating cry shattered the quiet of the night, and the whole paddock full of horses burst into frenzied panic. A slight figure ran around in the paddock, still shouting, and flapping something that snapped and cracked. The horses seethed back and forth in the small enclosure, trying to escape that appalling shriek and the horrifying, flapping thing. The split rails of the paddock shattered as the horses plunged and wheeled against it, spilling terrified horses out onto the beaten earth of the yard.

Almost simultaneously, the haystack behind the stable burst into flame, sending great tongues of fire leaping up into the dark. The fire finished the job of panicking the horses that the cry of the mountain cat had begun. Blindly, they scattered in as many directions as there were horses and pounded away into the night.

Men blundered out of the stable, most of them half-dressed and obviously still half-asleep, weapons at the ready. They had to duck back into the protection of the sturdy wooden building to save themselves from being trampled as more than a dozen terrified and determined horses swept past them and away down the track leading eastward out of the clearing. The flickering light from the burning haystack outlined a cloaked figure clinging to the back of one of the horses.

Light appeared in the windows of the house. The station commander, the troop leader, and Horbad all tumbled into the yard at the same time. Only Horbad was fully dressed. One of the sentries shouted something about a man on one of the horses. Horbad hesitated only a moment, then waved the news away and pointed to the burning haystack. In moments, if the fire wasn't contained, it would spread to the stables.

I would never have a better chance to snatch up Davigan and run. I settled Bane firmly on my shoulder, then sprinted for the back of the house, away from the hive of activity in the paddock yard. A quick glance through the narrow window showed me only Daefyd and Davigan left in the room. Daefyd sat by the fire, his hands in his lap, staring down into the embers. Davigan had not moved on his pallet by the door. If either of them heard the tumult and confusion outside, they gave no sign of it. And Daefyd might have been alone in the room for all the attention he paid to his wounded twin brother.

Horbad, the troop leader, and the station commander were still in the paddock yard, snapping out orders to the Somber Riders who were trying to organize buckets of water to quell the fire in the haystack. There was a lot of shouting and confusion out there. No one seemed to be paying any attention to the prisoners in the house. Of course, they thought their intruder had vanished with the horses. Lowra had been sly and clever, careful to let them catch a glimpse of her, but not a clear enough glimpse to allow them to aim any weapons at her.

The window was narrow. I hesitated for a moment, unsure how Daefyd would react to an intruder. But I had not heard him say a single word, nor had I seen him actively signal to Horbad of magic nearby. He had been completely passive. I had to bet he would not cry out and raise an alarm as I entered the main room.

I was not a big man, but I had scant enough room to clamber through over the stone sill. Daefyd turned to stare at me as I ran across the room and bent over Davigan on his pallet. But he said nothing, as I had hoped. He watched me, but his face was as bland and uninterested as if I had been nothing more than a cat crossing the room. He didn't look away, nor did he cry out a warning to the Maedun. He merely sat passively and watched.

Davigan lay on the pallet, breathing shallowly. His face in the dim light of candle and banked fire was pale as chalk. I reached out to touch his shoulder. His skin burned with fever, and he didn't move. He was deeply unconscious. Wound fever had set in, and I could not waken him. He needed help quickly if he was to live.

I snatched a quick glance out the door at the paddock yard. The Somber Riders and stable men had formed a double line from the well to the fire, passing buckets of water from hand to hand. Great gouts of sparks and steam erupted into the black sky every time the man at the head of the line threw a bucket of water onto the fire. Other men threw water on the thatch of the stable roof, all of them shouting orders and encouragement at each other.

Davigan still had not moved when I turned back to him. There was nothing else for it. I would have to carry him. Bending, I scooped him up into my arms. He was a tall man, but slender and slight, almost delicate, as are a lot of Tyadda men. I could manage his weight well enough unless I had to carry him a great distance.

Daefyd watched me with no trace of interest or curiosity on his face. I stood up, Davigan in my arms, and turned to Daefyd.

"You'd better come with me, too," I said.

He didn't move—didn't reply.

"You want to get away from the Maedun, don't you?"

For all the reaction I got from him, I might not have spoken. He merely sat there.

"Please, Daefyd," I said. "Come with me. Lowra's out there, waiting for us. Come with me. Let's get away from Horbad."

The tumult in the yard was quieting down. The men were organized and working with practiced precision. Any moment, Horbad would come back into the house.

"Daefyd, come with me," I said, using my best command voice. Kenzie had taught me well. Tyran clansmen leapt to attention when I spoke like that to them. It affected Daefyd not at all.

"Please," I said.

He ignored me, his face bland as suet pudding, unblinking. He said nothing.

I couldn't wait. I had already stayed overlong. Making sure Davigan was secure in my arms, I scuttled across the room to the window. Davigan fit through it easily. I lowered him as carefully as I could—as far as I could—to the ground outside, then let him drop the rest of the way. He hit the ground like a limp bundle of wet clothing. I scrambled through the window after him. Something caught on the rough stone of the sill—the end of my plaid, I thought. I yanked at it frantically. It came free suddenly with a tearing sound, and I sprang to the ground beside Davigan. The fall had opened the wound in his back. Fresh blood seeped through the dirty bandage, staining it dark red.

The door of the house banged as someone opened it. An instant later, a man shouted, obviously noticing that Davigan was gone. I had run out of time. I picked him up, slung him across my shoulder, and ran for the woods.

It wasn't until I was under the shadows of the grove of oaks that I realized that Bane in its bundle no longer hung from my shoulder. A cold chill settled over my heart. The scramble through the narrow window must have broken the straps, and I had not noticed in my haste to get Davigan out of the house. I remembered the tug as I struggled through the window after Davigan. That must have been when I lost it.

That meant Bane was back in the house with Horbad. And I had failed the *darlai*. I had lost the sword again. And worse—far worse—had let it fall into Horbad's hands.

21

Dismay flooded through me as I stood in the shadow of the trees, holding Davigan's still body over my shoulder. Duality help me, I had lost the sword. Bane was back in the house. On the floor under the window in the main room. Horbad would surely find it as soon as he entered.

Horbad, son of Hakkar, with a Rune Blade. Not just any Rune Blade, but Bane, sword of the Prince of Skai. Cold fear settled in my belly, and I shuddered.

Indecision tore me in two. Take Davigan away to safety? Or return to find the sword? I couldn't leave Bane in the house for Horbad to find. But neither could I abandon Davigan to go back and retrieve Bane. And I certainly couldn't take him with me if I went back for the sword.

Myrddin's words echoed through my head. *At all cost, you must prevent Bane from falling into Hakkar's hands.*

Now Bane lay within Horbad's grasp. And if in Horbad's hands, surely it would not be long until it was in Hakkar's hands.

At all cost, Myrddin had said. I put my hand up to Davigan's back. The slow rise and fall of his ribs told me he still lived. Did *all cost* mean abandoning the man who was brother to the uncrowned King of Celi?

Gods and goddesses help me. What ought I do now?

Anger replaced the despair and dismay. How could I have been so incredibly stupid! I should have hidden Bane somewhere before I started prancing around the clearing, putting myself into danger. How could I have thought the sword could possibly be safer with me than well hidden somewhere? I had no business carrying Bane with me while

I ran around pretending I was the hero of one of Davigan's exaggerated bardic sagas. The arrogant stupidity of it was staggering—appalling. And the price exorbitant. The cost of stupidity was always far too high.

I wanted to hit something, to tear something to pieces, but there was nothing nearby but myself. And it was my fault Bane fell into Horbad's hands like a ripe apple from an autumn tree. Taking my anger out on some innocent surrogate wasn't going to help the situation.

Davigan moved feebly against my shoulder and made a soft sound of agony. That decided me. There was nothing for it but to take care of him first, then see about reclaiming my father's sword.

Horbad pulled a few men from the fire-fighting detail to search for me. I condemned Daefyd's ability to sense magic to the deepest pits of Hellas, and drew the power around myself to give Davigan and me the semblance of naught but shadows moving through the trees. If Daefyd sensed the magic, by the time he wandered back out into the paddock yard—and by the time Horbad noticed he was on the spoor of magic—Davigan and I would be well out of their way.

At least I hoped we would. But there was little choice. If I wanted to take us undetected through the searchers, I had to use magic.

I wrapped Davigan in my plaid for warmth, got him draped around my shoulders, and set out through the trees at a brisk walk. It took me less than a quarter of an hour to find the place where Lowra and I had agreed to meet. Carrying Davigan with me, I moved well off the track, deep into the shelter of the trees, then let the masking spell dissipate.

From where I stood, I could just see the place where the track curved westward away from the clearing through the trees. I had barely begun to wonder where Lowra might be when she materialized at my side like a mist wraith seeping out of the ground at dawn. She startled me badly, and I leapt to one side, nearly spilling Davigan to the ground.

"Where did you spring from?" I demanded, trying to catch my breath. "You nearly startled me out of my boots."

"I'm sorry," she whispered. Sorry was the last thing she sounded. "You've got him?"

"Aye," I said. "Right here. He's hurt badly, though."

She wore something dark, something that blended with the shadows behind her. It made her face look eerily as if it floated disembodied in the night. Then I realized she wore the Somber Rider's shirt. It hung past her knees, and the sleeves hid her hands. She laughed without humor, then stripped quickly out of the shirt and tossed it into the shadows behind her. "It still stinks," she said. "The horses hated it, too. I think they ran as much to get away from that stench as anything." She stepped forward and put her hand to Davigan's forehead. "He's burning with fever," she said, anxiety clear in her voice.

"Aye, he is. Wound fever, I think." I shifted his weight to lie more comfortably over my shoulder. How comfortable it was for him, I didn't know. But I had no time to worry about that right now. "We have to find a place where I can Heal him. And quickly."

"You can't Heal him here?"

I glanced back over my shoulder. The sounds of the tumult and frantic activity came faintly through the trees. But just because the Somber Riders were busy now didn't mean that Horbad might not send a few of them looking for us. "If I'm interrupted, it might kill both Davigan and me," I said. "We can't take the chance. We need a safe place."

"What about Daefyd?"

"He wouldn't come. And I couldn't drag both him and Davigan from the house."

"He refused to go with you?"

"He didn't refuse. He just didn't move when I spoke to him." My frustration reflected clearly in my voice. "It's as if he's not even there in that body anymore. As if something stole his soul and replaced it with something else."

She bent her head. I felt the sorrow coursing through her as strongly as if it had been my own. "Blood sorcery," she murmured.

"Aye, blood sorcery. Curse it."

"I believe it's already cursed," she said with a glint of wry humor.

"Lowra . . ." I hesitated.

She looked up at me, one eyebrow quirked.

"I—I lost Bane. It's back there at the house . . ."

"Oh, Gareth, no—" Dismayed disbelief tinged her voice. She stared at me, openmouthed. "You didn't—"

"Aye, I did. It got caught on the window as I was getting Davigan out. I didn't realize it was gone until I got to the trees."

She shuddered, then straightened resolutely. "Aye, well," she said at last, "we'll just have to make the best of it. We can come back for the sword when we've done with everything else. Bring Davigan. I have horses for us hidden up the track."

She had, at that. Three horses, saddled and ready to go. They stood quietly in a small meadow just off the track, waiting patiently, reins dangling on the ground.

"When did you have time to do this?" I asked, surprised. She had fled the paddock yard riding bareback when I had seen her—when she had let the Maedun see her. She could easily have brought the horses with her. But before that, Horbad had posted sentries all around the clearing. She would have had little difficulty getting herself past the sentries—not with her ability to blend into the night as she could. But even that ease of disappearance could not smuggle three complete sets of tack out from under the noses of the Somber Riders.

She laughed softly. "While they were all bounding all over the place, haring around trying to chase you down," she said. "Everyone seemed preoccupied in searching for you. Nobody thought to watch the tack room." She shrugged. "It wasn't all that difficult to bring the equipment out during all the confusion, and the tack room in the stable is near the back door."

I stared at her in honest awe and admiration. "You're incredible," I said.

"Not really. It's just that like most Tyadda who venture out of the steading these days, I've had to learn the art of invisibility. Seeming invisibility, at any rate." She picked up the reins of one of the horses and glanced at the sky. It was already beginning to lighten toward dawn. "We'd better get Davigan out of here and to somewhere relatively safe. He doesn't look good."

"He's not," I said. "He's burning with fever."

"We'll come back for Bane. Somehow, we'll get it back."

I hoped we could do it before Horbad—or worse yet, Hakkar—sorted out how to use it against the Celae and the Tyadda.

We rode until nearly midday. Lowra led us to a cave hidden in the seamed face of a tall crag, large enough to take us and the horses comfortably. From the track, all an observer could see was a tumbled pile of jagged rocks that had fallen from the cliff face. The entrance to the cave lay hidden behind the spill of rock and a tangle of hazel clinging tenaciously to pockets of soil between the boulders. The climb up the hillside from the narrow little trail was precipitous. We had to dismount and lead the horses. Davigan hung sprawled across the saddle of my horse like baggage. It couldn't have done him any good, but there was no other way to get him to the safety of the cave mouth.

The interior of the cave was mostly dry. Lowra spread her cloak on the sandy floor, and I laid Davigan on it, still wrapped in my plaid for warmth. Even snugged in the warm wool, he shivered. At the same time, he burned with fever. It was truly a wonder he had survived the ride here. It most certainly had done him no good.

"You'd better Heal him quickly," Lowra said. "He looks terribly ill. I'm worried that the fever might be mortal."

She had voiced my fears. Wound fever was not a pleasant or easy way to die. I hoped I could save Davigan from it.

I knelt beside him and turned him onto his side so I could take a good look at the wound. Lowra helped me remove the dirty bandage. She caught her breath as she saw Davigan's back. I was right. Pockets of pus ringed the flesh around the puncture, and angry red streaks radiated out from it.

I muttered a short plea to the *darlai*, and to Rhianna of the Air that this would work. But I still wasn't sure it would when I put my hands over the wound and closed my eyes. Calling up the power from the flows around me was easier now. I concentrated, directing the surging power through my hands into Davigan.

But something was wrong. Dreadfully wrong. This didn't feel right. Healing Davigan shouldn't have been that much different from Healing Lowra. I was sure there was more here than a serious wound. I had been expecting the patterns of his being to be disrupted by the injury and the fever. I knew it was those disruptions that I had to look for with the Healing power so I could realign them, fit them back into the pattern. This felt wrong. Horribly, sickeningly skewed, out of focus.

Nothing about Davigan's patterns felt right. It was more than the chaotic misalignment of the patterns caused by the wound and the fever. There *were* no patterns. Nothing I sensed was right. All wrong. *Wrong!* Nothing but chaos and random scatterings of something that might once have been Davigan but now were only shards and remnants.

What had happened? Surely just a wound couldn't do this to a man. Where were the patterns that made Davigan himself rather than someone or something else? How could this be? How could a man's patterns be so misaligned, so disrupted, and he still be alive?

The black mist came at me out of nowhere, wrapping tendrils of itself around my throat, my heart, my very soul. I cried out and flung myself back from Davigan. The mist tore away with a ripping, sucking sound that made my stomach churn. It retreated back into Davigan and left me gasping for breath.

I turned away, retching. Lowra fell to her knees beside me. She reached out and grasped my shoulders, steadying me.

"What is it?" she cried. "Gareth, what's wrong?"

"Bespelled." My voice came out a raw croak. "He's bespelled. I saw it in him."

"Bespelled?"

I nodded. "Horbad must have done it," I said. "It's strong, and it's vicious."

She looked at me, bewildered. "You speak of it as if it's alive," she said. "Can it be?"

"I don't know." I wiped the back of my hand across my mouth and looked down at Davigan. He lay exactly as I'd left him, on his side, his eyes closed, his fever-raddled skin dry and hot. "I don't know if it's alive or not," I said. "It attacked me. Tried to choke me."

She put her hand to her mouth, eyes wide with horror. "What can we do? We can't leave him like that."

No, we couldn't leave him like that. But I was at a loss to know what we—or more correctly, I—could do about it. I stared down at Davigan, nausea still churning in my gut with the memory of that black mist.

Something niggled away at the back of my mind — something important. Something to do with fighting a bespelling. I tried to clear my mind, then seized the thought when it skittered past again. I had it!

A memory. A piece of the legend of Sheryn's escape.

When Brynda, Kenzie, and my father had snatched Sheryn out of the clutches of the Maedun and spirited her away across the country, Kenzie had been bespelled, drowning in Hakkar's blood sorcery. Under the spell, he would have betrayed them to the first Maedun Somber Rider they encountered. Between them, working together using Brynda's Healing power and Sheryn's Tyadda magic, Brynda and Sheryn fought the spell, cleansed Kenzie's spirit of the cloying, strangling black mist.

That bespelling must have been similar to this. Brynda spoke of a black mist tangled around Kenzie's spirit, and how it had tried to drown her in itself as it had engulfed Kenzie. But she fought it. She and Sheryn fighting together as a team overcame it and gave Kenzie back his spirit.

We had no Tyadda magic — at least not the kind Sheryn used to free Kenzie. But my Gift for Healing was stronger than Brynda's Gift. She had often lamented that hers was a meager Gift. I knew mine was strong. Mayhaps my own magic, combined with the Healing, would be sufficient to rid Davigan of that revolting, obscene black mist.

Aye, well, I thought. I had little choice in the matter. Lowra was certainly right. We could not leave Davigan like this.

"I'll try again," I said. I took a deep breath and steeled myself to meet that nauseous blood sorcery.

"Can I help?" Lowra asked.

"I don't know. If our bond will let us share strength, I might need your help."

"When you need it, you'll have it," she promised.

I went again to my knees beside Davigan. Lowra moved aside and I put the palms of my hands against Davigan's temples. Concentrating, I gathered my Gift around me, and projected it into him.

. . . And met blackness. The same thick, dark mist that had met and attacked me the first time I tried to Heal him. It surged outward, seized me, and tried to drown me, too, in its darkness. I fought it, but it was like wrestling with the night itself. Smothering, hungry, clutching, it was all around me. I could not find anything to hold on to. It slipped through my fingers like quicksilver, only to wind tendrils of itself around my throat. I tore away wisps of it, but could not loosen its hold, neither on me, nor on Davigan. Choking and gagging on the foul stuff filling my nose and mouth, I struggled to breathe. I could not cry out, could not break away from the link with Davigan that lashed me to the dark and formless enemy. Someone sobbed harshly. It might have been me. I couldn't tell.

My strength ebbed quickly. I would not be able to fight much longer. In despair, I felt the sense of triumph throbbing and pulsing through the black, formless entity invading Davigan.

Then suddenly, more strength poured into me. Vaguely, I realized that Lowra had put her hands on my shoulders, willing her own strength into me. The bright stream of her energy joined with mine, and together we fought the blackness.

The brilliant Celae magic flashed and flared, meeting the black mist in an explosion of heat and light and color. Searing heat. Blinding light. I had been dropped into the heart of a forge, white-hot—incandescent. Pain consumed me as if the warring of the magics tore the very flesh from my bones and sundered the bones themselves beneath. Behind me, Lowra made a soft sound of horror, but her grip on my shoulders did not slacken. Instead, she tightened her hands, pressing them firmly to my shoulders, joining more fully with me.

Terror and rage suffused me. Not mine. Not Davigan's, nor even Lowra's. It emanated from the dark mist itself. In one last burst of passionate fury, the mist blew apart, fragments raining like splinters of rock around me.

But even the shards and scraps were dangerous and deadly. In the hot, shadowed darkness of Davigan's fever-ridden spirit and body, I fought a grimly silent battle. Dregs of the blood sorcery scuttled like huge, vile spiders as they fled the glowing lance of bright Celae magic. Doggedly, I hunted down each hideous fragment and impaled it on the point of my magic. Even as I destroyed them with the light of air and earth magic, they turned on me with unexpected strength, reaching out to wrap tendrils of black around my throat. But even as my strength ebbed, the searing brightness of my own magic scorched them to flakes of ash.

When, finally, the last of the blood magic was cauterized and rendered harmless, I sat back on my heels. Sweat streamed from my forehead and down into my eyes. My chest ached, and my belly spasmed painfully. With one last burst of strength, I sent the Healing power lancing down into Davigan's wound. Like dry tinder bursting into flame, the energy flared around the suppurating wound. The damaged flesh blew away as if on a raging gale, and new, healthy flesh grew in its place. The brilliant flash of power seared my eyes, hammered in my chest, and took away my breath.

I fell away from Davigan, aching in every joint. Gasping for breath, I knelt with my head bent, my hands braced on the ground before me. Davigan lay, still as death, on Lowra's cloak, but the wound in his back was gone, Healed cleanly, leaving only a faint, white scar. His eyes were closed, his face calm and composed as if in peaceful sleep.

Lowra made a strange, gasping sound behind me. "Gareth?" she whispered, her voice tinged with both awe and horror. "Gareth? Are you all right?"

I looked down at my hands, and recoiled in revulsion and horror. Those weren't my hands. They couldn't be. They were the hands of an old man, the skin wrinkled, the tendons knotted, the knuckles enlarged. Stunned with disbelief, I raised them and turned them over, front to back, back to front, before my eyes.

Lowra reached out and put her hand to my cheek. I raised my head and stared at her. A cold lump of terror lodged itself under my heart. Silver streaked the dark gold of her hair. Her skin had lost the dewy bloom of youth, and fine lines surrounded her eyes, bracketed her mouth. She was no longer the young woman I had met by Dun Llewen. She had aged ten years.

I raised my hands to my own face and found rough, wrinkled skin. When I pulled strands of my hair forward, I saw white. Not black dark enough to flash blue highlights back into the sun. Not even black streaked with silver-gray. White. Whiter than the silver in Lowra's hair. If she had aged ten years, I had aged at least twenty.

"What happened to us?" I whispered. "Oh dear gods and goddesses, what's happened to us?"

But even as I asked, I knew. The bright flare of the warring magics had burned us. Burned the youth from us and seared our spirits as well as our bodies. I didn't have to look into a mirror to know what my face looked like. It would be the face of the enchanter I saw in the moonlight globe. The young man trapped in the aged body.

22

Davigan slept peacefully, curled in my plaid. A weariness I could not
fight settled over me, weighing me down like blocks of stone.
My eyes stung as if I had poured sand into them, and I could
hardly keep them open. My head ached abominably, as if it
had been torn in two and nailed back together with iron
spikes. I wanted to crawl into a warm corner, pull darkness
around myself, and sleep for a whole season.

Lowra scrubbed her hands across her cheeks and brow
and recoiled in shock at the unfamiliar sight of her hands, the
feel of her own skin under the pads of her fingers. She stared
at her hands, then at me, shaking her head in incredulous
awe.

"Can you Heal us?" she asked, her voice low and rusty,
as if she hadn't used it for too long.

I tried to lift my hand to my forehead, but it was too
heavy. I hadn't the strength to move it. I looked at Lowra,
marveling at the changes in her. But if she was no longer
young, she was still lovely. It was a mature woman's loveli-
ness, though. The fine bones in her face would keep her looking beautiful even when she was eighty.

And me? The enchanter in the globe was ancient, but he
still had his power—my power. That hadn't burned out of me
when the magic flared so brightly and so hotly.

But Heal us? I didn't know.

"Can a Healer Heal the ravages of age?" I asked.

She raised her lovely, brown-gold eyes to meet mine. A
world of despair and misery filled them. Tears welled up; two
of them spilled over her lashes to roll down her cheeks, leaving shining tracks through the grime left by an active night. I

thought she was crying for what she had lost until she reached out again and touched my cheek with gentle fingers. Gentle as the brush of a moth's wing.

"Oh, Gareth, what it's done to you," she whispered, her mouth twisted with grief and pain.

I swayed on my knees as lethargy sticky as treacle flowed through me. I saw the same weariness in her face. Sleep would restore us—at least as far as restoration was possible. It would never make us young again, but it was what we needed most right now. Without a word, I reached for her and drew her against me. She came eagerly, and we curled together down onto the sandy floor of the cave.

I awoke once to the chill of night. Lowra and I huddled together for warmth. I put my hand to her head and stroked her hair, once again noticing how well she fit into my arms. I believe that, in spite of everything, I smiled as I fell asleep again.

Morning light streaming in through the entrance of the cave woke me. Lowra still slept curled in my arms, her head on my shoulder. My bones creaked as I sat up, and I remembered with a start what had happened to us. I wondered bleakly if this painful stiffness and creaking of bones was the harbinger of what all my mornings were to be like from then on.

Lowra woke when I moved. She moved with less stiffness than I as she got to her feet, but the lively spring to her step was absent. She crossed the cave to look down at Davigan where he lay wrapped in my plaid.

Davigan still slept. I crawled over to him on hands and knees and put my hand to his forehead. No trace of the fever remained. His brow was cool and dry beneath my palm. His chest rose and fell evenly, peacefully, slowly. I shook his shoulder, but he didn't move.

I frowned in concern. He should have had some reaction to my touch on his shoulder. Even if he were determined to sleep longer, he would have shifted his weight to dislodge my hand, or muttered a protest. He did neither.

"What's wrong?" Lowra asked.

"I can't waken him. He should be awake now. His wound is Healed, and he should have rested enough to recover his strength." I gathered the Healer's magic around me, relieved to find it as strong as ever, despite my aging bones. I put my hand to his forehead again and probed with the Healer's Gift. A startled cry burst from my throat.

Nothing. It frightened me badly. There was nothing there still. No patterns unique to Davigan. Nothing at all. Had the magic burned him, too, as it had burned Lowra and me?

He retained his youthful appearance. If he had been burned, it had not affected him in the same way it had affected Lowra and me. Was this lack of spirit within the living, breathing body a result of the warring of the two magics?

"He's not there," I muttered. "It's as if he's not even there. I can't find any trace of his patterns. None at all."

Lowra bent over Davigan, frowning. "He's gone away," she said softly. "Horbad hurt him so badly when he bespelled him, that he's just gone away." She gently smoothed the dark gold hair back from his forehead. "We'll have to take him home." She straightened up and climbed stiffly to her feet. "We have to go back to the steading to warn them about Daefyd. We'll take Davigan home, and they might help him there. We aren't far from home now. A day's travel. No more."

Lowra followed a trail discernible to her eyes only. Most of the time, I could barely make out an open area between the trees and rocks. To Lowra that was as good as a highway. Even as twilight fell across the land, she guided her horse with no false steps, confident in her route.

Behind her, I kept my eyes on the ground, watching each

step carefully as I carried Davigan before me on the horse. I could see no evidence that any man had trod this ground before us. When I looked up, as far as I could see were only tall, rugged crags, trees, and rocks. Lowra led us straight at a sheer granite cliff which rose several hundred feet straight up from the forest ahead of us. Unless there were caves in the cliff which were her destination, I was at a loss to see any way past or through the forbidding rock face of the mountain.

She drew her horse to a halt just below the narrow cleft in the rock where a little stream burst forth in a foaming white arc to fall noisily into a deep pool below the rock. Rainbows shot through the purling mist where the setting sun's rays sifted through it. She turned to me.

"Follow carefully," she said in a quiet voice that somehow carried easily over the tumult of the water. "Whatever you see — or think you see — just follow. Wait for a moment on the other side. They'll send someone up to meet us."

I nodded, thinking, the other side of *what*? All I saw ahead was a solid rock wall.

She nodded, then stepped forward and melted right into the rock. I shivered. A masking spell, then. But even knowing the rock wall was only a masking spell, it gave me a cold sensation in the middle of my gut to watch her disappear.

Holding Davigan tightly against me, I urged my horse forward. It didn't hesitate at all — simply stepped into the solid rock. We met a slight, springy resistance, and I urged the horse to push a little harder. My skin tingled, and, for an instant, a momentary flash of dizziness and disorientation swept over me. Then we were through. I looked back over my shoulder. Behind me, the trees and rocks were still there, but it was as if I looked at them through a thin sheet of shimmering water.

Definitely an odd sensation.

The valley spread out below us was wide and already

turning green with spring, nestled snugly among a circle of tall peaks. The little stream meandered through it, glinting brightly in the last rays of the sun. Near the center, pleasantly surrounded by tall, lush trees, stood a village. The houses were small and well tended—not many more than two dozen of them, all stone-built, some roofed with tile and some with thatch, but all surrounded by neat gardens. Dry stalks of what would become flowers and flowering shrubs in the summer clustered abundantly along walls and hedges.

Off to the left of the village stood a graceful, white structure that could only be a shrine to the Duality. Behind it on the flank of the hill was a small Dance of stones. Seven menhirs carefully set in a horseshoe shape around a low altar—one stone for each of the seven gods and goddesses. And behind the shrine and the small Dance, stretching high into the evening sky, loomed Cloudbearer. The valley lay in its shadow, protected and hidden.

I could only stare in fascination and amazement as Lowra led us down the track to the village. This was the very place that Sheryn had come to for safety after the Maedun invaded Celi and murdered Tiernyn and Tiegan. A piece of legend come to life before my very eyes.

As the light faded, a woman left the village and began climbing the track toward us. No longer young, she still retained her beauty. Her carriage was proudly erect, her movements graceful and serenely lovely. She was a tiny, delicate little thing, no taller than Lowra, but she looked taller because of her erect carriage. She wore her silvered-gold hair in a long plait wound around her head like a crown. She shook her head and hurried past, intent upon Davigan, as Lowra began to make obeisance to her. She came straight to me as I held Davigan ahead of me on the saddle, putting her hand to his limply dangling hand, frowning worriedly.

"It's well you brought him home," she said to me. "I am

Sheryn al Wallach, widow of Prince Tiegan, and wife of Drywn ap Iowalch. You are well come here, my lord Tyr." She studied my face curiously, her head tilted to one side. "I know you, don't I?"

I shook my head wearily. "No, my lady," I said. "But you know my father and are kinswoman to him. My father is Brennen ap Keylan, Prince of Skai, and I am Gareth ap Brennen."

She paled and lifted a hand to touch my face, then drew it back. "But you look—" she broke off.

"As old or older than my father," I said bitterly. "Aye, I do. It was—"

"It was the magic, Mother," Lowra said. "It burned us, and it stole our youth."

Sheryn stared at her, then drew back, her hand going to her mouth in shock. "Lowra?" she asked faintly. "Is that you? Oh dear gods and goddesses . . . The light isn't good but . . . How can this be, child? What has happened to you? I didn't recognize you."

Lowra closed her eyes for a moment and sighed wearily. "Mother, believe me, we hardly recognize ourselves. But we've brought Davigan home, and we have dire news of Daefyd."

A man toiled up the hill to meet us. He gave us a bright, sunny smile. "Is someone ill?" he asked, then he frowned. "Oh, it's Davigan. Let me take him. I'm strong. I can carry him." Before I could gainsay him, he had reached up and taken Davigan from me. He held him as easily as if he had been a small child, still smiling that brilliant smile.

Startled, I stared at his tar black hair, his darker eyes. He was Maedun. Automatically, I reached for the sword at my back. Sheryn put her hand on my knee.

"Hold," she said. "Mikal will not harm you."

I could not hide my shock. "Mikal?" I repeated hoarsely,

incredulously. I stared at the black-haired, black-eyed man who held Davigan so easily. "The man who murdered Donaugh the Enchanter and left Celi open to invasion? And he won't *harm* us?"

Mikal gave me another sunny smile, and for the first time, I saw the soft, almost innocent expression around his eyes. No trace of guile or slyness showed on that face. He was older than my father, yet his face was as smooth and unlined as a child's. A glimmering of understanding blossomed slowly in me as I remembered all the stories about him—about his upbringing by the sister of Hakkar of Maedun, how she used him and shaped him as a weapon, and gave him nothing a child had a right to expect from his mother.

Sheryn nodded. "Yes," she said. "You see what happened, don't you? Magic burned him, too. Blood sorcery mixing with Tyadda magic. It burned in him hotly enough to consume all the evil in him, and left him as sweet and innocent as a child. Up here—" She touched her forehead. "Up here, he's no more than three or four years old."

I let my sword slip back into the scabbard. I looked down at Mikal. He stood holding Davigan, cradling him gently in his arms. He made crooning sounds, as one might to a sick child, and began to walk back toward the village. Sheryn was right. That man was most certainly no danger to anyone now. Not anymore.

I wondered which of us had been left better off by the consuming blaze of the magic.

Sheryn put Davigan to bed—his own bed in the room he had shared with Daefyd. She made sure he was as comfortable as he could be, then she herded Lowra and me to the main room and sat us at the table. A meal appeared on the table before us in an incredibly short time. Lowra's father, one of the elders of

the village, joined us, and, while we ate, we told him what had
happened. Drywn ap Iowalch listened without interruption,
his face grave and grim.

Lowra began to droop before the meal and the tale were
done, and I wasn't far behind her. I kept forgetting what I had
already told Drywn and repeated myself too often, and
Lowra often lost the thread of what she was saying and ended
up staring off into space as she tried to remember what she
wanted to say.

Drywn held up his hand to stop us. "I think you've told
us enough for now," he said. "You're exhausted, and we're
keeping you from your rest." He beckoned to someone in the
shadows.

They put us to bed, too. I lay on a feather bed, covered by
a down quilt, wondering if I had passed the portals to Annwn.
Only Annwn could be this comfortable, I thought sleepily. If
my days were counted and totaled, and I had been judged by
the Counter at the Scroll, I was not about to quibble. If it was
this comfortable to be through the Portal, then I was content.

Lowra slept in another room. Only the thin barrier of a
wall stood between us. I was pleasantly conscious of her presence nearby. The bond between us thrummed and murmured
and shimmered in my chest. A good thing, indeed, that. I was
content.

I awoke once to hear the hissing of rain as it drummed on
the roof of the cottage. The gentle patter seemed to become
tangled with the hissing of the fire on the hearth, then
sounded like whispered conversations, too soft to make out
words. But it was comforting. I drifted back to sleep, grateful
for the warmth and the softness of the bed.

*The sword came silently and softly into my dreams. I saw it again
lying on a table while a man dressed in unrelieved black stood back*

*with a glass of wine in his hand and studied it with a careful and spec-
ulative eye. I recognized both the man and the surroundings. Horbad
was still at the posting station.*

*That surprised me. I had thought he would have moved on days
ago. Why would he still be there when Lowra and I, and Davigan, too,
were long gone? What reason had he to stay there?*

*I received my answer when he picked up the sword and took it to
the bedroom in the back of the posting station. This was his room. His
desk, his bed, his temporary headquarters. It made sense. Com-
munication between the posting station and Clendonan, where
Hakkar made his headquarters, was swift and efficient. And the posting station was close to the mountains where the free yrSkai still lived,
hiding from him and his Somber Riders. From there, it was a simple
matter to ride out with Daefyd playing hunting dog for him.*

*Horbad placed the sword on his desk and sat studying it carefully,
still sipping his wine thoughtfully. He reached out and ran a finger
down the center of the blade where the runes sparked in the light of the
candles on the desk. He glanced at Daefyd, who lay curled in sleep on a
pallet under the window, and an odd expression stole across his handsome face. He looked at the sword again, then back to Daefyd.*

*"Perhaps you can bring its magic to me, my little hunting
hound," he whispered aloud. "Can you wield a Rune Blade? Can you
show me how to use its magic for my own purposes? My father would
be so pleased if I could show him I am master of a Rune Blade." He
smiled and stroked the blade. "We'll see. Yes, we'll see."*

23

I stood before the hearth in the main room of Sheryn's cottage, watching my fingers flex as I made a fist, then relaxed my hand again. Such a simple thing, opening and closing a hand. What had been so simple was now suddenly complicated by the enlarged knuckles on both my hands. Tiny pains shot through my fingers as I tightened my fist. This would affect everything from the way I picked up a piece of bread to the way I held the hilt of a sword. I wondered if my father—or Kenzie—were bothered by this ridiculous manifestation of an aging body.

"What are you doing?"

Sheryn's pleasant, melodious voice behind me startled me. I turned to see her standing with her hands behind her back, head tilted to one side, gazing up at me. Her posture reminded me suddenly of Caitha dan Malcolm, and I couldn't help wondering what she would think of this suddenly aged body of mine. I was no longer the supple young man she had thought to betroth herself to come Beltane. If, of course, I was back in Tyra by Beltane. It was beginning to look as if I wouldn't be. And, oddly, I had less desire to be there than should be apparent in a young man wishing to persuade a young woman to be his wife. And I had a flash of how sweetly and neatly Lowra fit into my arms.

I looked down at Sheryn, almost surprised to find her still there. "What am I doing?" I repeated. "Letting my mind wander, I suppose. Watching my hand hurt as I make a fist. My lady, I'm afraid I don't really know what I'm doing."

She smiled, then reached out with both hands to take one of mine between them. Gently, she worked her fingers, massaging the backs of my hand, the soft places between the fingers. As she worked, I felt the stiffness abating.

"You'll get used to this," she said, her eyes on her work. "With most of us, it creeps up so gradually, we have time to become accustomed to it and compensate for it. It happened very suddenly with you, so of course you notice it. You'll be able to adjust to it soon."

"But it hurts when I grip a sword, my lady," I said. "How can I use my hands to fight?"

She laughed softly. "Gareth, King Tiernyn was nearly eighty when he was killed. His hands were swollen with the swelling sickness, but he had no trouble swinging Kingmaker." Her eyes clouded with the memories. "It was the sword itself that let him down in the end. Not his aging body." She took my other hand and began massaging it. "A man of middle years—a man in his prime—still has much time left." She looked up at me. "The blood sorcery may have stolen twenty years from you, but don't let it steal your whole life. Your life is a long way from over."

I clenched my fist. She moved her hands before I could trap them. But my fingers didn't hurt so much anymore. Nor were they so stiff. "You may be right," I said slowly.

She smiled. "But you're reluctant to admit that yet," she said. "I understand."

"Did you want me for something, my lady Sheryn?" I asked.

"Yes, actually, I did." She looked up at me, her lovely face grave in the flickering light of the fire. "We want to do a soul retrieval for Davigan later this evening. Would you help us? You're a powerful Healer, and we need someone who not only has a lot of power, but knows Davigan's patterns. Would you help us?"

I stared at her. "A soul retrieval?" I repeated. "What's that?"

"Have you never done one, or seen one done?" she asked.

"No, my lady. I believe I've heard the term, but I don't know what it is. Not something we've done in Tyra, I think."

"We do it when persons have lost a part of themselves. Sometimes they lose all of themselves, especially when something evil or completely devastating has happened, and they simply can't face it. They go away somewhere. Somewhere far away so they don't have to remember what happened."

I thought of Briga, wife of my friend Weymun. Three days after I brought her news of his death fighting against the Maedun, their cottage had burned with her children trapped inside. Briga had been forced to listen to her two children screaming as they died. All that kept her from rushing back inside the burning cottage to be with them was one of the neighbors holding her tightly imprisoned in his arms. After the funerals, she had simply gone away. The priests and priestesses of our shrine took care of her now. They said she had retreated so far into her own spirit, she might never find her way out again.

I told Sheryn about it. She listened, nodding as I spoke.

"Is that what you mean by losing yourself?" I asked.

"Yes," she said. "Briga needed—or still needs—a soul retrieval. She lost herself because she could not face the pain of losing everyone she held dear. And who could blame her? But with help, she could find herself, and there are ways to help her past the worst of the pain."

"Do you think that's what Davigan has done?"

"Yes." She raised her hands in a helpless gesture. "Lowra believes they hurt him badly—so badly that the only way he could survive was to retreat so far back into himself, they couldn't find him."

"But he lost himself in the process and can't find his way out again. Is that it?"

"Yes. Just as Briga lost herself."

"But what does a soul retrieval do?"

"If the person is still in the spirit—hiding and afraid, but still there—a soul retrieval can show him the way out again." She made that helpless gesture again. "If he wants to come out, that is. It doesn't always work. But we need to try."

"Do you think we can do it? Show him the way out, that is?"

"I think we can. It's not an easy thing to do, though, Gareth. You must be very sure you want to do it before we start. We cannot force you to do it. You must be willing to try of your own free choice. You mustn't do it if you really believe you cannot do it. If you try under those circumstances, you can do more harm than good."

"But don't only priests and priestesses do that?"

"We will have priests and priestesses present," she said. "But we need a Healer, and we need someone familiar with Davigan's patterns. He's my son. I used to be very familiar with all of his patterns. But I have no Gift for Healing, and you've Healed him recently. You're more familiar with his—his lack of patterns now."

I hesitated. "My lady Sheryn, if you think I can help," I said, "then I'll certainly try."

"Thank you," she said simply. "We'll call you when we're ready." She turned to go, then glanced back at me over her shoulder. A smile turned up one corner of her mouth. "Are you going to marry Lowra?" she asked.

I jumped, startled. "Marry Lowra?" I repeated, stunned. "I—I don't know. She's my bheancoran, and I hadn't really thought about it—" Flustered, I stared at her. "I don't know."

"Well, don't wait too long before making up your mind," she said. "I'll call you when we're ready for you to start." She hurried away before I could reply again. I turned back to the fire with a lot more to think about than some insignificant little pains in my fingers.

Night had fallen when Sheryn appeared at the door to the main room. "We're ready for you now," she said. "Will you come?"

I rose from my chair by the hearth, took a deep breath to steady myself, and followed her into the bedroom where Davigan lay. The air in the room all but fizzed with magic. Only two candles burned on the small table by the hearth. Leaping shadows danced across the walls and floor as the breeze from my entry met the candle flames and made them flicker softly. Sheryn knelt by the head of Davigan's bed, her hands resting gently on his shoulders. Around her and behind her, twelve shadowy figures stood—the priests and priestesses from the shrine—a living wall of gentle magic.

I hesitated by the door and glanced at Sheryn. She smiled reassuringly and nodded, then made a graceful gesture, indicating I should kneel beside her by the bed.

I went to my knees on the stone floor and took a deep, calming breath. Magic swirled thickly all around me, cloaked me in welcome, passing me its warmth and strength. I gathered it around myself, then put my hands to Davigan's temples, cupping his head between my palms, and willed my Gift into him. I closed my eyes and sent my spirit to find his, following after the Healing power, deep into the complex structure of his spirit.

All the patterns that made up Davigan's body were whole and perfect in every way. The wound in his back had Healed completely, leaving not so much as a scar to mar the perfection of the physical pattern. But nothing remained of the part of the pattern that made Davigan himself. Gone were the delicate scrollworks that were his love of music and his talent with the harp. Gone were the interchanges that made his sense of humor. Davigan himself was not there anymore. This was just a hollow shell, empty as a blown egg.

It was akin to walking into a house the occupants had fled in panic. Everything was in perfect working order, but there was a ghostly feeling of leftover terror, a residual taste of fear. It was the eeriest sensation I'd ever experienced. There were none of Davigan's patterns left at all. This was abandoned, completely unoccupied, and it frightened me.

I tried calling out to him. *"Davigan?"*

There was no answer. Only the uncanny sense of echoing hollowness. Concentrating more intensely, I took a deep breath and went deeper. Behind my concentration, I was frightened that I might go too deep and never be able to find my way out of the barren labyrinth that had been my kinsman.

I don't know how long it went on. I had no sense of time, no sense of anything except the overwhelming need to find Davigan. And, in the back of my mind, there was the underlying feeling of panic that I, too, would become as lost as he was.

Then, quite suddenly, I found something. A hard knot of resistance so deep down, so tightly clenched and hidden, that I didn't realize what it was at first. I circled it, looking for an opening, and found none. But I was sure I had found Davigan.

I touched the knot. It was hard and smooth and flawless as a cabochon gem. There was no surface to get a grip on. I could find no way to penetrate it, to communicate.

"Davigan?" I called again.

No response.

I tried once more. *"Dav?"* An infant name. A name his brother and sister had called him as he was growing up.

Something loosened subtly, gave way so slightly, I almost

missed it. I wrapped the Healing power around the knot, trying to infuse whatever was inside with a sense of my presence.

"*Davigan, it's Gareth. Let me in. I want to help. Let me in.*"

Again, a meager loosening, a scant relaxation in the knot.
Then I heard him, so faint, so distant, it was less than a whisper.

"*Gareth?*"

"Here. I'm here."

"*Is it really you?*"

"*Really me.*"

"*Not another trick?*"

"*Not a trick. It's me. Touch me. See for yourself.*"

A sudden spasm and a tightening again of the knot into
an impenetrable sphere. A sensation of fear. The ghost of terror and pain.

Patiently, I began again, soothing, assuring, comforting.
It was difficult not to try to hurry, to try to subdue my own
sense of horror and outrage at what had been done to him. I
lost all sense of subjective time. I tried to reassure him by
infusing my presence, the Healing power, into the impervious
shell of the knot—afraid of failure, afraid of what I might find
if I succeeded.

Then, abruptly, I broke through. He opened to me, suddenly and completely.

"*Gareth! Here!*"

And he thrust something toward me—a small kernel of
memory. With it came a blinding, smothering explosion of
pain and terror, a burst of total humiliation and revulsion so
strong that it flung me back, mentally and physically.

I found myself huddled on the polished slate floor by
Davigan's bed, my arms wrapped around my head as if for
protection. My head ached severely enough to blur my
vision, and nausea churned uneasily in my belly. Sheryn

knelt beside me, fright and concern on her pale face.

"Are you all right?" she asked breathlessly. "You were so still for so long. I was frightened."

"They did something to him," I said hoarsely. "They did something to him so terrible . . ." I raised my hand to my aching head. "I can't reach him. I couldn't get through whatever they did to him so I could Heal him. I can't do it . . ." My voice cracked, and I fell forward. I think someone caught me before I hit the floor, but I'm not sure.

I came back to myself lying in my own bed. Sheryn bent over me, her face softly lit by a candle by the head of my bed. Behind her, the shadowy figures of the priests and priestesses hovered like disembodied wraiths in the flickering light.

"Are you all right?" she asked, concern making her voice rough and rasping.

I felt surprisingly well, but so weary I could hardly lift my head. "Just tired," I said.

"The priests and priestesses gave you the strength of such Healing power as they had," she said. "We could do little else."

"They have my thanks," I said hoarsely. "I'll be much better if I can sleep for a while."

"Yes," she said. "You need sleep."

"And Davigan?"

"Sleeping. No change in him."

I closed my eyes, frustration quivering in my chest.

"Did he give you anything?" Sheryn asked anxiously.

I became aware that my fist was closed tightly around something. I raised my hand and opened it. Nestled in the palm lay a small, ovoid object that looked something like an opal. Colors swirled and gleamed within it, catching the light and glinting back every color from green to blue to red to purple to gold. It felt warm in my hand, the surface almost oily, like ivory. Surprised, I stared at it. It seemed right, somehow, that Davigan's spirit should look like a flawless opal. I held it out wordlessly to her.

She took it, cradling it gently in her two hands. She smiled. "Thank you, Gareth," she said softly. "You've given me my son's soul back. We can help him put himself back together now."

"Will it be soon?" I asked hoarsely.

She looked down at the jewel in her hands. Tears formed in her eyes. "No," she said. "Not soon. But eventually he'll be Davigan again. He'll be my son."

"And Daefyd?" I asked.

She met my eyes. "We'll do what we can for Daefyd when you and Lowra bring him back here," she said.

24

My dreams took me to strange places, places not conjured up by Bane. I stood at the foot of an almost symmetrical hill in that mystic, transitional time between sunset and dusk when the sky to the west was still streaked with light and color. Bands of red and orange flamed behind the hill, illuminating the triple ring of standing stones that circled the summit of the hill like a diadem. Imposing menhirs arranged in an outer ring stood starkly black against the luminescent sky, crowned in pairs by massive lintels. The middle ring of stones bulked slightly smaller, gracefully joined all around by capstones, polished like jet to reflect the incandescent glow of the sky. The inner ring, standing alone without lintels, was not a ring at all, but a horseshoe enclosing a low altar stone. This was the Dance of Nemeara, but transformed. It was not my dreaming place I had come to. Someone else fashioned this landscape, familiar but just skewed enough to be completely mystifying.

Behind me loomed the vast, cone-shaped bulk of a mountain, taller than any of the other mountains in the soaring, crenellated ridge beyond it. Cloudbearer in his glory stood tall above the mountains of the Spine of Celi, majestic and regal. I did not have to look at it to know it was there. Cloudbearer dominated the landscape. His shadow touched and protected all of Skai.

I waited at the bottom of the mound, conscious of the light weight of the empty scabbard on my back. The air was warm as spring, and the fresh scent of crushed grass beneath my feet rose strongly around me. A breeze stirred gently and ruffled my hair. Casually, I lifted an unhurried hand to brush away a lock of hair that fell into my eyes.

A man appeared in the opening in the foot of the horseshoe, dwarfed by the giant stone Dance. He came forward slowly to look down at where I stood at the bottom of the hill. As he approached, I recognized my father. He looked as he should have looked, with no trace of the wasting fever about him. A man just past his prime, but still a strong man, tall and straight. He carried a sword in his hand, the naked blade flashing and flaring as it reflected the brilliant light of the sky.

My father stopped within arm's reach of me and looked around himself. "Where is this place?" he asked. "Is this your dreaming place?"

"Not mine, my lord," I said. "Is it not yours, either?"

He shook his head. "I have never dreamed true before," he said. "I am amazed to be here." He looked at me and paled. "Who are you? I look at you and see my own face."

"I am Gareth, Father," I said gently. "I'm your son."

"My son?" My father shook his head again in bewilderment. "No, you can't be. My son is a young man yet."

"Three days ago, I was a young man," I said, bitterness flowing thick in my voice. "The mixing of blood sorcery and gentle Tyadda magic burned me to make me what you see now. I am still your son."

Again, my father studied my face. "Aye," he said slowly. "Aye, I can see it now. For all those years, I saw your mother reflected in your face every time I looked at you. And now I see myself. How very odd."

I allowed myself a smile. "And I see you when I look into a mirror," I said. "And I wonder how it is that my father is in the mirror—then I remember what happened. Why are you come here? Why did you call me here?"

"I? Call you here? No. You called me, I believe."

We were being stuffily polite and correct to one another — so brittle it was a wonder we didn't both shatter like glass. I looked around, but there was no one else in sight. Just my father and I. No sign anywhere of Kian or Cullin—or of Myrddin, the Guardian of the Dance, either. I gestured to the sword he still held naked in his hand. "Perhaps Bane called us here, Father," I said.

He looked at the sword as if startled to see it in his hand. "Ah," he said at last. "Yes, of course. The sword. I wanted to give you the sword. There's a long and tedious ceremony for this, but we haven't the time right now." He held out the sword. *"I commend Bane to your hand, Gareth, that you might use him in defense of Skai."*

My heart made a hard, thumping leap in my chest. I stepped back, away from the offered sword. *"No!"* I cried. *"No, I won't accept it, Father. I can't."*

"Take it," he said again, and thrust the sword at me.

"No," I repeated.

He glared at me. *"You are as stubborn as a rock,"* he roared. *"Take the sword."*

"If I'm stubborn, it's a trait I inherited from you," I shouted back. *"And learned from you, too—I learned from a master of the art."*

He made a low, frustrated growling sound, and pushed the sword at me again. *"You must take it, Gareth."*

"No. If I take it from you now, like this, you'll die. I don't want you to die."

He didn't move. He stood on the small patch of grass, the sword held out before him. *"Do you not want to be Prince of Skai?"* he asked.

"No," I said. *"That is, yes, I do. Someday. But not now. I don't want you to die."* Desperately, I searched for words to convince him that he must live. *"Do you really want me to be Prince? I'm not Eryd. You always thought he should have lived all those years ago, and not I. Do you really want to commend Bane into my hands when I'm the wrong son?"*

He stared at me blankly. *"The wrong son?"* he repeated. Slowly, he lowered the sword and peered intently into my face. *"Could it be?"* he murmured. *"Could it really be?"*

"Could what really be?"

"I look into your eyes and I see no condemnation there as I always saw before. No blame. Could it be that you've forgiven me?"

It was my turn to stare blankly. *"Forgiven you? Whatever for?"*

Pain filled his face, twisted his mouth into an anguished line. *"For not being there when you needed me—you and your mother and your sister and your brother. When you needed me, I did not come to you because I put other duties ahead of my love for my family."*

It was as if the sun had come up between us. *"You had sworn an oath to protect your king," I said. "Did you not think that I could understand that?"*

"You were a child . . ."

"Who became a man," I said. "I thought you could not forgive me for living when Eryd died."

Pain clouded his eyes, and he shook his head. "No," he whispered. "Never that. I grieved for Eryd as I grieved for Mai and Lisle. But I rejoiced that you still lived. I still had one son. But I thought I had lost you in a different way."

I looked at the sword he still held. "Father, I will not accept Bane from your hand. Not now. Not for a long time. There is too much between us we must settle."

"You must take the sword, Gareth," he said softly. "You shall need him to fight for you if you wish to survive this venture." He held out the sword. "Take it."

Like a small, stubborn boy, I put my hands behind my back and stepped away from him. "No," I said. "I will regain Bane for you, and I will bring him to Skerry and place him in your hand. Then, if you wish, you may commend him to my hand. But not now. Not like this."

"But you must . . ."

"No," I said again. "Not like this." I made a wrenching effort to waken myself . . .

And woke, drenched in sweat in the bed in the small room in Sheryn's cottage. I shuddered, then put my hands up over my eyes and wept because, after all these years, I knew my father truly did love me, even if only in that strange dream landscape.

The bond between Lowra and me vibrated gently beneath my heart, and I took my hands away from my eyes as she came to me softly in the night. She fitted me in every way a woman is supposed to fit with a man, and I believe I pleased her as much as she pleased me. I took her into my arms and into my bed, then into my heart as well as my soul.

●   ●   ●

We lay in the dark in each other's arms, weary and spent, but not sleepy. I smiled up into the dark.

"Your mother asked me tonight if I was going to marry you," I said in amusement.

She raised herself to look down at me. The embers in the hearth gave just enough light to limn the soft line of her cheek and brow with warm gold. "And what was your reply?" she asked.

"I said I didn't know," I said.

"An honest reply," she said, and laughed softly. "If not a very flattering one."

"It was honest then," I said. "Now, my response would be this. Lowra al Drywn, my soul lies cupped within the palm of your hand."

She looked down at me, her face grave and solemn. For a long moment, she was silent. Finally, she smiled. "Gareth ap Brennen, your soul is sheltered safe within my hands and my heart."

I pulled her down against me and kissed her. Things became rather complicated for a while after that. When we had finally sorted it out and lay quietly again, she came into my arms and tucked her head into the hollow of my shoulder.

"What about the woman who waits for you in Tyra?" she asked.

"Caitha?" I smiled. "Caitha won't wait for me. As well she shouldn't. She knew it when I left, and I think I knew it. I shan't be returning to Tyra. She knew a long time before I did that my loyalty lay with Skai and Celi, not Tyra. And I think she knew that my heart didn't really lie with her, either. She'll be very happy with Comyn, he'll be happy with her, and they'll produce many happy and handsome Tyran children. Besides, she didn't bargain on marrying an old man."

Lowra laughed softly. "Gareth, my love, you are not nearly so old as you fear you are," she said.

There was no good response to that remark, so I let it go past without comment. After a decent interval, I said, "I shall be going back to reclaim Bane. I'll leave tomorrow."

"Not without me, you won't," she said.

"I thought so. I was, in fact, counting on it. We can get ready and leave tomorrow morning."

She snuggled down into the circle of my arms. I smiled and pressed my cheek against her hair, breathing in its fragrance. I was almost asleep when a sudden thought struck me and threatened to turn my blood and bones to ice.

Lowra's Seeing. She said I would not be Prince of Skai until my hair was silver and I was as old as my father was now. Years of time, I had thought. But no more. I was that old man now.

Did that mean my father would die before I could get back to Skerry?

"At all cost you must prevent Bane falling into Hakkar's hands . . ." Myrddin's words echoed in the darkness around me.

"All cost," I whispered aloud into the night. Dear gods and goddesses, did *all cost* mean asking my father to sacrifice not only his wife and daughter and eldest son, but his life as well?

My duty was clearly defined, but how could I simply turn away and let my father die?

Lowra raised herself on one elbow and looked down at me. I didn't have to tell her what caused my turmoil. She knew. Her sympathy vibrated gently along the bond between us, but there was implacability there, too. If she knew my turmoil, she also knew as well as I where my duty lay.

"I'm sorry," she murmured. "Oh, Gareth. I'm so very sorry."

"Will he die?" I asked.

"I don't know." Her voice broke. "I just don't know."

25

I stood before the polished bronze mirror in the small bedchamber and regarded my reflection with some amazement. That couldn't be me. It had been so long since I had seen myself in anything but a Tyran kilt and plaid that it was hard to recognize the man wearing the shirt made of fine Tyadda linen in a soft brown, the wide sleeves gathered to snug cuffs at the wrist, and dark green tunic and trews. Even the tall boots of supple leather were new. He looked nothing like a Tyran clansman—nothing like the man I had been accustomed to meeting when I looked into a mirror.

No, that wasn't quite true. I raised my hand to touch the thick braid hanging from my left temple—silver now, not black. I still wore the braid and the earring of a Tyran clansman. Twelve years of ingrained habit and belief were difficult to shed. A clansman's braid is his strength, both in war and in love. He gives it up only in death. I had unplaited the braid when I washed my hair, but even though I thought I would leave the hair free, I couldn't. I found my hands automatically replaiting the braid without any conscious thought on my part. In the end, I decided my instincts were right. The braid stayed, as did the earring. I might be the son of a Celae prince, but part of my spirit was Tyran. To honor that part, I kept the braid and the earring.

As for the apparent age of the man in the mirror . . . I could deal with that later. In time, I would probably become accustomed to seeing my father's face in every mirror I gazed into. Right now, the less I thought about it, the more comfortable I was.

Lowra's image appeared behind mine in the mirror, her

fists on her hips. She, too, wore a new shirt, tunic, and trews in similar colors to mine. We would blend in well with the forests of Skai, the pair of us, as the forests came back to life with spring.

"Had I known you were the sort of man who enjoyed admiring himself in mirrors this much," she said, "I might not have been so eager to bond myself to him as bheancoran."

The mirror was a good one—good enough to show me the subtle lift at the corners of her mouth and the light of laughter in her eyes. I turned and gave her an elaborate bow.

"How could I but admire the fine suit of clothing I've been given," I said. "I wonder if it's true that clothes make the man."

She folded her arms across her chest and looked me up and down, eyes narrowed, mouth held in a speculative line. "Well," she said at last, "you look more like Gareth ap Brennen now than Gareth dav Brennen ti'Kenzie. That may or may not be an improvement."

"The night spent together gave you the right to be impudent and flippant, did it?"

She considered that carefully, then shook her head. "No," she said contritely. "Of course not." She put a hand up to her mouth to hide her smile. "I've always had that right."

"Had I known that, I might not have been so eager to accept you as my bheancoran and soul's companion."

She put a hand to her breast in shock. "You'd abolish a tradition set generations ago?" she said, eyes wide, eyebrows raised. She did a fine job controlling the corners of her mouth. "Why, all you need do is look back to the tales of Kian and Kerridwen to know a bheancoran's rights in that direction."

"I see. Lies the wind in that quarter, does it?"

"Of course," she said. "I believe in tradition." She lost the twinkle of humor. "Are you ready to go?"

I took one last look at my reflection. Someday, I'd become accustomed to that man. A quiet chill shivered down my spine. But not today. I turned to face her. "As ready as I'll ever be. Are the horses ready, too?"

"Aye," she said. "Everything is packed. All we have to do is say good-bye to Mother and Father, then we can leave."

I picked up the dark brown cloak and swung it around my shoulders. My kilt and plaid were in the hands of a Tyadda sempstress, who might or might not be able to repair the damage of hard wear. In scrambling through the window carrying Davigan, I had torn away the corner of the plaid where the blue-black of my hair blended with the red-gold of Caitha's in the warp and weft of the fabric. An omen, mayhaps.

The sempstress had admired Caitha's expert work in the weave of the plaid and assured me she would do her best to mend it properly. They would be ready and waiting for me when I returned. She had given me a bright, cheerful smile, certainly far more sure of my return than I was. I wondered if I would ever wear the kilt and plaid again. Assuming I did manage to return here after all.

Lowra and I walked outside into spring. Under a clear, deep blue sky, the valley opened itself to the warmth of the sun. Buds were already swelling to bursting on the trees. High up on the slopes of the mountains, where patches of snow still remained in areas of deep and abiding shade, the white blossoms of snowberry starred the ground, giving off their honey-sweet perfume that drifted downhill with the gentle breeze. Beneath the trees surrounding the village, young, green bracken had pushed through the blanket of last year's dead stalks, unfurling their pale green heads to the new warmth of the sun. Soft green grass sprang up eagerly beneath the hedgerows, and birds greeted the new warmth enthusiastically.

We mounted our horses and turned them uphill out of the village, riding quickly to the valley mouth.

We camped that night in the shelter of a copse of hazel and beech beside a small stream. By the time we had everything set up and a meal made and eaten, it was late. A faint sliver of new moon hung in the clear sky, caught between two tall peaks. Lowra and I talked desultorily for a while, then curled down together in our blankets. If magic happened, it was the magic of two people who suited each other so well, they blended to one with fire and passion, and with grace and elegance and warmth.

She slept with her head on my shoulder, her breath moving against my throat, her hair soft against my cheek. I looked up at the sky for a while, watching the slow wheel of the constellations, and thinking of as little as possible. Eventually, sleep took me.

My dreams drew me back to the strange landscape that both was and wasn't the Dance of Nemeara. But before my father could appear to try again to give Bane to me, I wrenched myself awake and came convulsively to my knees beside the pallet Lowra and I shared. She murmured a sleepy question. I assured her I was all right, then got up, careful not to disturb her further, and picked up my sword.

Just beyond our little hollow, the stream chuckled and bubbled along on its way to join the river. It made a broad, sweeping turn, leaving a wide, flat strand of fine gravel on the inside of the curve. The night was clear, the sky full of stars. The slender crescent moon had not yet set. There wasn't much light, but there was more than enough to practice by.

I unsheathed the sword, held it out before me, staring at the gleaming blade while I centered my concentration. Then I began the first of the series of exercises Kenzie had taught me over the years. Ideally, one began slowly, then increased the tempo with each set until reaching the fastest speed possible. The steps were a graceful and stylized dance, ordered and sequenced to practice all the different movements of the sword, one sweeping into the other as one movement of a piece of music segues into the next movement. Attack, defense, evasion—all performed with a precise rhythm and flow that could have been set to music and looked right . . .

Or it should have. I stumbled more than once when an unfamiliar stricture of tendon caught me unawares. I hesitated too often when a stiff muscle protested violently to the rapid stretching and pulling. My speed was ludicrous in its lack. I fumbled through the last of the steps, slower and clumsier than a rank beginner, then stood panting on the gravel strand in the faint moonlight, appalled at my performance.

Kenzie would not be impressed. Not one whit would he be impressed. He would have let me feel the flat of his sword in some tender places had he seen that performance. Surely I could do better than this. Disgusted, I straightened up, held out the sword again, and centered myself to begin the next exercise.

"Guard yourself."

The voice behind me startled me badly. I spun around just in time to see Cullin's sword descending on me. I had barely enough time to raise my sword in the answering block. He twisted aside and glided into the next motion of the sequence, moving with liquid grace. I followed, trying to ignore the sudden shooting pain in my knee.

Out of the corner of my eye, I caught a glimpse of Kian standing with his arms folded across his chest, shoulder propped against the trunk of a young birch. He watched with a critical eye as Cullin and I danced through the formal, elegant exercise.

"I thought you'd finished with me." I swung my sword up in a high block to meet Cullin's descending blade, then swept it to one side and sliced at his feet. He sidestepped sinuously, spun, and came back at me with a backhand slice at my knees.

I leapt back out of the way of Cullin's blade, more desperate now than graceful, and managed to block his sword. The blades slithered together, sending a shower of sparks down onto the gravel strand. We disengaged and stepped back — a breathing space.

"We only come when we're needed, lad," Kian answered calmly. "Careful. Watch the stone there —"

"Do I need you now?" I asked.

Cullin lunged forward, blade sweeping around in a gleaming arc. I tried to turn into the block, but stepped on a round rock and stumbled. Cullin took full advantage and beat me back across the gravel. My heel caught on a protruding root and I fell sprawling onto my backside, bruising my hip. The flat of his sword came down with a crack on my shoulder.

"Killing blow," he announced, and stepped back.

"You may not need *us*, precisely," Kian said judiciously. "But it's glaringly apparent you need something. At the very least, a good sparring partner and a lot of practice."

I sat there on the gravel, rubbing the point of my shoulder. I'd have a fine and colorful bruise there come morning. My legs ached, my back ached, my arms ached, and my hands hurt. If this was age, I could definitely do without it, thank you very much.

"I can't get used to the changes," I muttered angrily. "It's just too frustrating . . ."

"You'll get used to it, lad," Cullin said. "You need look no further than your uncle. Kenzie isna exactly a young man anymore, yet he's still as deadly as he ever was with a sword, is he no?" A trace of pride lilted in his voice. Kenzie was, after all, his great-grandson.

"Aye, he is," I said. "But he's had a chance to get used to the changes."

"As will you," Kian said. "With practice."

"If I manage to live through the process," I said glumly. "The evidence here seems to indicate the worst."

Cullin put out a hand. I caught it, and he hauled me unceremoniously to my feet.

"I promise you, it will become easier with practice." He raised his sword again. "Guard yourself."

My muscles screamed in protest as we danced the second sequence. I thought my arms would fall off and the rest of my body would break in two. Cullin pressed me hard, demanding speed and precision. I fought desperately to give him both, determined not to fail him. Or Kenzie. Or myself, either, come to that. Then, about halfway through the sequence, I noticed something strange happening. The pains in my body lessened, and I moved with more ease. I was still nowhere near my former level of performance but, for the first time, I began to believe that I really would become accustomed to this suddenly aged body, and perhaps use it as well and as gracefully as Kenzie used his. It was heartening.

We finished the sequence, and Cullin stepped back, raising his sword in salute. "Much better," he said. Genuine approval lilted in his voice. It gratified me immensely to hear it. "I believe there might be hope for you after all." Barely enough light fell from the stars and crescent moon to show me the tilt at the corners of his mouth.

"Thank you," I said, and sheathed the sword on my back. "I almost believe you may be right." I went to sit on the grass beneath the tree where Kian stood. Cullin followed and sat on a water-smoothed boulder.

"You're going to fetch back Bane, are you?" Kian asked.

"Aye. And Daefyd, too, if we can."

"D'ye have a plan?" Cullin asked.

"Well, no, not exactly," I said.

"Does the lass?"

I shook my head.

Cullin raised an eloquent eyebrow. "Surely one of you should have a plan," he said.

"We'll scout out the lay of the land when we get back to the posting station," I said. "Something should suggest itself. There's no sense in formulating a complicated plan before we see how things are."

Cullin glanced at Kian. "Aye," he said. "Definitely your seed, *ti'rhonai*. Kiting off into the teeth of the enemy without so much as an idea of what to do."

Kian grinned lazily. "Aye," he said. "And wise it is, too. If you depend too much on advance planning and something goes wrong, it can be verra difficult to improvise, ye ken."

Cullin said nothing, but the eyebrow rose again, arching high above his green eye.

"When you find Bane, he'll fight for you," Kian said.

I shook my head. "No," I said. "I refused to take it from my father's hand when I dreamed true. It's not my sword."

It was Kian's turn to lift an eyebrow in wry amusement. "Do you think that refusing to take the sword means it hasn't been commended to your hand?" he said. "Ye're wrong. The sword is yours now."

A cold chill rippled down my spine. "Does that mean my father is dead?" I asked. "He can't be . . ."

"And he isn't," Kian said. "He hasn't given you the sword except when you dreamed true."

"I don't understand," I said. "If it was a true dream, and he dreamed true as I did . . ."

"Then the sword is yours in the dreamscape."

"But not in the waking world."

"Well, aye, it is. In a way."

"You're confusing me."

"It's perfectly simple," Kian said.

"Gareth?"

I turned quickly to look over my shoulder. Lowra stepped out onto the gravel strand. "I thought I heard voices here," she said. "Who are you talking to?"

When I turned back, both Kian and Cullin were gone, and I sat alone under the birch tree. It was patently obvious that they wouldn't be back tonight. Whatever Kian was about to tell me—the explanation that was perfectly simple—was not something I was going to learn yet. Frustrated, I turned back to Lowra and shook my head.

"Myself," I said. "Arguing with myself about a plan to retrieve Bane."

"We'll have to see what things are like when we get there," she said. "Come back to bed now. It's late."

I looked around. There was no sign of Kian or Cullin. Only the churned gravel where my own feet had disturbed it.

"Aye, you're right," I said. "It's late."

26

Shortly before midday the next morning, we drew our horses to a halt on a low ridge overlooking the clearing where the posting station stood. We were less than a furlong from the clearing and just barely high enough to see into it over the trees. Had the leaves been fully out on them, we wouldn't have been able to see anything at all.

We left the horses a hundred paces back among the rocks and pine trees and crept to the edge of the ridge, taking full advantage of the newly leafing burrberry bushes for cover. A few early blossoms had already bloomed where the sun warmed the branches, and the delicate perfume drifted around us as we studied the clearing below our perch.

Smoke rose serenely from the chimney of the house, rising straight up into the still air. The horses in the paddock stood dozing in the warm spring sunshine. Except for an occasional flick of a tail, nothing moved in the clearing below us. There was no sign of any Somber Riders, nor of any stable men.

"It looks different in daylight," Lowra murmured. "Smaller than I remember it."

"Things always look bigger when you have to bound around them in the dark, tripping over things," I replied.

But she was right. The posting station and the yard looked a lot different by daylight. For one thing, the grass between the house and the trees looked shorter, as if it had been recently mown. Someone had become thoroughly industrious with a scythe. I could imagine Horbad's annoyance when he realized that I managed to get away with Davigan. He would have ordered the grass cut back for better visibility. I wished he'd done it earlier. It would have saved me some scratches and bruises.

The paddock looked different, too. I couldn't quite sort out what the difference was, and I frowned as I considered it. What about it was strange now—unlike it was before? I stared at it for a long time before the answer dawned on me, and I had it.

"Look at the paddock," I said. "Last time we were here, there must have been a score of horses in it. Look now. Mayhaps half a dozen."

She chuckled softly. "I wonder if they caught all of them after I stampeded them," she said.

Still frowning, I watched the clearing. Something else about it was different, too. Something besides fewer horses in the paddock.

"Horses don't run that far, once they've managed to get past what frightened them," I said absently. "They might have lost one or two of them, besides the three we took. But not so many that they're left with only half a dozen." Something batted against the back of my mind the same way a fly bats against a window. Something important, but I couldn't quite pin it down.

A Maedun dressed in black trews and an open-necked shirt, his sleeves pushed back to his elbows, came out of the stable carrying a saddle slung over his shoulder. He heaved it onto the split-rail fence around the paddock, then stretched mightily and looked up at the sky. The sun stood very close to zenith. Midday. Mealtime, mayhaps. He made his way to the house. The door slammed closed after him.

Lowra and I waited and watched. The clearing and the posting station lay placid and peaceful in the sunshine.

The men inside the house had barely had enough time to eat the midday meal when the clatter of an approaching horse being ridden hard shattered the tranquillity of the day. The door of the house opened, and a man walked unhurriedly to the paddock and entered it. He chose a horse and led it outside. The horse danced and sidled around exuberantly. It seemed eager for the chance to run on such a fine spring day.

The stable man had nearly finished saddling and bridling the horse when a courier galloped into the clearing from the west, drew his lathered horse to a skidding, slithering halt, and threw himself from the saddle. As the stable man finished tightening the cinches on the fresh horse, the courier tore his dispatch pouch from the saddle of his blowing and exhausted horse and threw it across the saddle of his new mount.

The stable man gestured toward the house, obviously offering refreshment and perhaps food to the courier. But the courier shook his head, then stretched to wring the kinks out of his back, vaulted into the saddle, and put his spurs to the horse's flanks. Moments later, all that remained of him was the sound of galloping hooves fading to the east.

"In somewhat of a hurry, wasn't he?" Lowra murmured.

"Looks as if he was on his way to Clendonan with a message for Hakkar," I said. "Those couriers don't waste any time."

Then I had it. I knew what was so importantly different. It was obvious now that I realized what it was. Angry with myself because I should have seen it immediately, I swore under my breath.

"Horbad," I whispered, more to myself than to Lowra. "Horbad isn't there."

Lowra looked at me, startled. "What do you mean?"

"The horses," I said. "He's taken his troop of Somber Riders and gone. There aren't enough horses in the paddock. He's gone."

"Gone?"

"Aye, he's gone, and he's taken Daefyd with him. And Bane. He's taken Bane away."

Lowra made an odd little sound on an indrawn breath, then hesitated as if she were afraid to voice what we both feared. "To Hakkar?"

I took a deep breath and let it out with a shudder. "Aye. I'm afraid so. To Hakkar."

I lay there under the berry bushes, silently pounding my fist into the yielding ground, my stomach churning as I muttered curses under my breath. I had a strong enough bond with Bane through the dreams and Seeings it had sent me. Its absence, now that I recognized the sensation, was so obvious, I could not see how I had misunderstood at first.

"What will we do now?" Lowra asked.

"Find out where Horbad went." I got stiffly to my feet. The ground was still damp and cold, and my bones complained of the chill. "He can't have more than a day or two lead on us. If we hurry, we might be able to catch up to him."

"Not if he rides like that courier," she said doubtfully, her face pale. "We'd not have a chance."

"He won't ride that fast," I said. "He can't. He's got his troop of Somber Riders with him, and he's got Daefyd with him, too. A score of men can't ride at full tilt all day long like a courier. No posting station would have enough horses to keep them supplied with fresh ones. If they tried to ride like that courier, they'd kill the horses under them and end up walking. I can't see Horbad son of Hakkar walking, can you?"

She allowed a hint of a smile to hover at the corners of her mouth. "I shouldn't think so," she said with a faint chuckle. "But how will you find out where he went?"

The corners of my own mouth quirked slightly. "Magic," I said. "I've got all this burden of magic. I'm going to put it to good use. Especially since Daefyd isn't there to alert anyone to it." I pulled the threads of power around myself like a cloak and thought hard about Maedun couriers. I knew it had worked when Lowra involuntarily drew in a sharp little breath and stepped away from me.

She shook her head. "Even though I know that's you," she said a bit breathlessly, "it almost frightens me. You look so dreadfully real."

I thought about the lightning flash on a courier's shoulder, then masked the hilt of my sword. Couriers rode unarmed.

"How do I look?" I asked.

"Terrifying," she replied. She put a hand to her mouth, then laughed a bit nervously. "Like a Maedun courier."

"Then I've done it right. That's exactly what I want to look like." I grinned. "Suppose a courier comes bursting into the posting station with an important message from Hakkar for his son. Do you think they wouldn't tell the courier where he's gone?"

"They might," she said. She studied me and shivered. "You look almost exactly like that courier who just left. It could really frighten me if I didn't know it was you."

"Good," I said. "I need to look authentic. Let's get back to the horses. I have to come into the station from the east."

"Gareth?"

I paused.

"Do you speak Maedun well enough to fool them?"

My Maedun was not as fluent as my Tyaddan. But first Fyld, then Kenzie, had insisted I learn the language thoroughly. They both maintained stoutly that it would one day be useful. Aye, well, I suppose this was the day. My vocabulary was somewhat limited, and I didn't know all the colloquialisms, but I thought I could pass. Especially as a courier in a tearing hurry. I had a slight accent, but I hoped it wasn't much different than some of the regional accents in Maedun itself.

"Let's hope so," I said.

She looked at me doubtfully.

"What other choice do we have?" I asked.

She considered that for a moment, then nodded. "You're right," she said. She unlimbered her bow and made sure of the arrows in the quiver at her hip. "I'll move down to the trees just beyond the house, where I can see the paddock yard. If it looks as if you're in trouble, you can be sure that at least the Somber Rider who greets you won't carry the tale. Nor will the next if they try to rush you."

I grinned at her, then kissed her quickly. "I'll meet you back here," I said. I turned to run back to the horses.

"Gareth?"

I paused, glanced at her over my shoulder.

"Be careful."

"Oh, aye," I said. "Always. And you, too."

"I always am," she said.

In moments, she had disappeared into the trees. I heard not so much as a rustle of dead leaves to mark her passing. I wasted a moment wishing I had her grace and dexterity in the forest, then ran for the horses.

I didn't have to work very hard to give the horse the semblance of a courier's horse. The horse had come from the paddock in the clearing, though, so I had to disguise it with the masking spell, too. If one of the stable men recognized the horse as one that was stolen the other night, that would finish everything rather too quickly—and quite probably very unpleasantly. As long as I stayed on the horse, the masking spell would cover both of us.

I kept to the forest just behind the crest of the ridge. It took the best part of an hour to work my way around the posting station so that I could come in on the track from the east, the way a courier would come from if he had been sent from

Clendonan by Hakkar. I found the track leading into the post-ing station and kicked my horse to a gallop. At the last moment before we entered the clearing, I remembered to make the horse look sweaty, as if he'd run a long way. And I put the sem-blance of Hakkar's personal emblem on the sleeve of my tunic.

A stable man came running to meet me as I thundered into the paddock yard. I recognized the station commander. He still had horse dung on his boots. Either he never cleaned them, or he worked as hard as his men mucking out the sta-bles. Somehow, I rather doubted the last. The Maedun were extremely prickly about who was superior to whom. A supe-rior officer *never* did a trooper's job.

He waited for me by the paddock fence, a look of puzzle-ment on his face. Obviously, he wasn't used to unscheduled couriers pounding through his well-ordered posting station. I pulled to a skidding halt beside him. The horse pranced and curvetted, most unlike a tired, hard-used horse. I stilled it with a sharply curbed rein.

"My lord Horbad," I cried. "Where is he? I have a mes-sage for him from Clendonan. Urgent."

The station commander caught the reins of the horse and calmed it easily. "He's not here," he said. "He's gone to the west."

"How long ago?" I demanded.

"Two days," he said. "But he should be back within the fortnight. Give me the message. I'll see that he gets it."

I looked down at him, unlimbering my most haughty, supercilious expression and trying it on for size. It must have fit nicely, because the station commander took a step back.

"This message is for my lord Horbad's eyes only," I said. "I'm charged with delivering it personally into my lord Horbad's own hands. Tell me quickly. Where did he go?"

"West," the station commander said again, gesturing

with his chin. "To the rock—" He used a word I was unfamiliar with.

I made a bad mistake. "The rock what?" I asked.

His eyes narrowed in sudden, dawning suspicion, and he
tightened his grip on my horse's bridle. "How many days ago
did you leave Clendonan?" he demanded.

I tried to do a lightning quick calculation in my head, but
I wasn't completely sure of the distance between Clendonan
and here—mostly because I wasn't precisely sure where *here*
was. "Six," I replied.

Another mistake, obviously. The suspicion bloomed full-
blown, narrowing his eyes to mere slits. He quickly tried to
hide it. "Interesting," he said. "But the last I heard, the Lord
Hakkar was taking his ease in Honandun in Isgard." He
turned his head and shouted to someone in the stable, holding
tight to the reins of my horse.

I reached up behind my left shoulder for the hidden hilt
of my sword. Before I could get it clear of the scabbard, something went past my ear with a swift, fluttering hiss. The feathered shaft of one of Lowra's arrows appeared in the hollow of
station commander's throat. He let go of my reins and
clutched at his throat, making horrid little choking sounds.
Even as I watched, his eyes went all strange and glazed and
empty. He was dead before he hit the hard-packed ground.

Near the stable, someone shouted. I didn't wait to see
whether it was simply another stable man, or an armed
Somber Rider. I put my heels to the horse's flank and bent
low over the pommel of the saddle as it leapt into a gallop. I
turned the horse to the west and let it have its head. I thought
I heard an arrow sail past me, but if I did, it missed, and I
didn't have time to worry about it.

Moments later, we were out of the clearing and around
the bend. Not until we had covered another furlong did I pull
the horse to a stop. I could hear no sign of pursuit. But

Maedun troops are not encouraged to think for themselves. With the station commander dead, it could take them a while to organize themselves—if there was a man at the posting station who might take the initiative. I waited another minute to make sure, then urged the horse off the track and up the slope to the ridge where Lowra waited.

That had been a close thing. But I had learned two important facts. The first was that Horbad and the sword weren't any more than two days ahead of me and Lowra. The second—and most important—was that Horbad would definitely *not* be taking Bane to Hakkar. At least not yet. Hakkar was not even in Celi, but in Isgard, across the Cold Sea. And likely to remain there until the last possibility of violent storms had passed. Except under the most dire circumstances, I could not imagine Hakkar risking his life on an unfriendly sea.

I allowed myself to believe that Lowra and I now stood a reasonably good chance of recovering Bane. And, mayhaps, of rescuing Daefyd, too.

27

Lowra was nowhere in sight when I reached the place we'd agreed to meet. I pulled the horse to a stop and looked around for any sign of her, but found none. Just as I began to worry, she stepped out of the trees, bow drawn, arrow nocked, point aimed directly at my heart.

"Gareth?" she asked.

I hadn't realized I still held the masking spell. I let go of the threads of power, letting them snap back into the air and ground I'd taken them from. The dissipating magic stung against my skin, but was gone in an instant. Lowra allowed a relieved expression to cross her face and lowered her bow.

"What on earth happened down there?" she demanded. Her worry made her voice sharp, scratchy, as if it hurt her throat. "It looked as if you were doing so well, then that Somber Rider became all upset and nasty. What did you do?"

I dismounted and scrubbed my hands across my face. "I made a mistake," I said. "He said Horbad had gone to rock something-or-other. I didn't quite catch the word and asked him to repeat it."

A stricken expression stole the color from her face. "Oh, Gareth, I'm sorry," she said. "I should have told you."

"Told me what?"

"Rock," she said. "That's what they call their fortresses. The one a league south of Dun Llewen, near the Wenydd border, is called Rock Vanizen, after one of their kings. The one north of where Dun Eidon used to be is Rock —" And she said something that sounded like a series of unrelated gutturals.

"That's what he said," I told her. "What's the word again?"

"Greghrach," she said slowly. "Named after one of their major warlocks, I'm told."

"Aye, well, whoever he was, he tripped me up, and no mistake about it," I said. "Thank you for being quick and accurate with that bow."

She slipped the arrow back into the quiver at her hip and slung the bow across her shoulder. "That's what the ceremony in the shrine was all about," she said. "Or don't you remember?"

"I remember well enough," I said. "Horbad has taken Daefyd and Bane, and gone to Rock whatever-that-word-was."

"Greghrach."

"Greghrach, then. That was two days ago. Hakkar himself is enjoying a holiday in Honandun, I was told. If that's true, we've been given a reprieve. We'd do well to make the best of it."

"West, is it?" she said. "He'll take the main track. If we take some of the ridge trails, we might be able to catch up with him."

So we took to the ridge trails, the narrow little tracks that sometimes seemed to go straight up one side of a mountain and straight down the other. Game trails, mostly. Old hunting trails that for more than twenty years had been used only by hunted free Celae and Tyadda. They were rough, nearly nonexistent in places.

We could not hurry the horses past a brisk walk, not if we didn't want to risk exhausting them, or breaking a leg on the rough tracks. But we saw no Somber Riders, and we saw no sign of Horbad and Daefyd. Twice, we made camp in hollows in the very bones of the mountains themselves, screened by thickets of willow or hazel. They were cold camps. We wanted no scent of smoke to give away our location.

Occasionally as we traveled, far below us in the valley, we caught sight of the main track winding wide and clear along the bank of the River Eidon. And in the far distance to the northwest, there was the hard, blue sparkle of the sea.

"The Ceg," Lowra said. "Dun Eidon used to stand at the mouth of the Eidon at the eastern end of the inlet."

"But no more," I said softly.

"No," she said. "No more. It's in ruins. The Maedun took it apart, literally stone from stone, brick and board. It's a sad and desolate place now."

"Like Dun Llewen?" I asked, remembering the overwhelming sense of devastation that engulfed me as I looked at the ruins of my grandmother's birthplace.

"Worse," she said. "Much worse."

Dun Eidon. Where my father and my aunt Brynda were born and my mother and sister died. I remembered it not well at all, and I had no desire to see it to refresh my memory. Seeing it as a decayed ruin might well break my heart. My mother and my sister were buried there in a long common grave near where the walls had once stood. I needed no such reminder of my loss. It lived in my heart and in my spirit, and that was reminder enough.

"Rock Greghrach is that way," she said, pointing to the northwest. "The main track divides about a league from here. West takes you to Dun Eidon, northwest takes you to the Maedun fortress. The other track goes southwest. It used to go to Wenydd, straight to Dun Wenydd."

"Where the Duke of Wenydd lived."

"Yes. But Connor and Torey fled with their sons to Laurel Water in the northwest of Venia," she said. She made the sign of the Unbroken Circle in the air before her forehead. "Torey was the only member of King Tiernyn's family to survive the invasion."

I knew the story. Torey al Kian was King Tiernyn's young sister, the youngest of Red Kian's children. She, her husband Connor, and their three sons were rescued by one of Red Kian's ships. Like my father, they didn't go to Tyra, but settled in Laurel Water because Connor could not bear to leave Celi. He accepted exile in Venia, as my father accepted exile in Skerry.

Late afternoon of the third day after leaving the posting station, Lowra spotted a column of smoke rising into the calm twilight air. She drew rein and looked down into the valley, biting her lip, her face pale. I could see nothing through the trees, but the smoke made it obvious something the size of a house or byre burned below us. The smoke was so pale a gray, it was almost white. Not black with soot and lit within by flames. Whatever burned no longer blazed fiercely.

"There's a farmstead down there," she said softly. "Or there used to be."

"Who lives there?"

"An old man, his wife, their daughter and kin-son, and three grandchildren. The Riders in the fortress take most of what the farm produces for themselves—grain, fruit, vegetables, fowl. The family barely subsists under the spell on what's left."

The last thing I wanted to do was go down into that valley and see what had happened. But they were my people, and there was nothing for it but to see if we could help. I turned my horse and guided it down the slope toward the valley.

We left the horses in the trees a good furlong from the farmstead and made our way through the forest, slipping from shadow to shadow. Lowra moved silently as a wraith. Not so much as the snapping of a twig gave her away. I made a little more noise, but I was learning. I had to watch more carefully where I put my feet as I followed her.

The farmstead lay in the wide curve of the silver thread of a river. It had once been a very pleasant little place. Low dry-stone walls outlined a series of small fields. Several of the fields had already been tilled in preparation for the spring planting. One large one had obviously been used as meadow for the milch cows. But two cows now lay stiff and stark in the middle of the meadow, slaughtered where they stood.

The house and byre stood close to the riverbank. The soil in the kitchen garden, like the fields, had already been prepared for planting. But no one would ever lay seed in that ground.

The house looked relatively undamaged, but the byre, timber-built and straw-thatched, had burned to the ground. The ruins still smoldered, sending up the thick column of smoke we had seen from the ridge. The fetor of blood magic lay heavy over the reek of burning, but I could detect no sickening stench of charred flesh.

We watched for a long time, hidden in the trees at the edge of a carefully tilled field. The light faded slowly as the sun sank behind the low ridge of mountain between the farmstead and the sea. Nothing moved but a scrap of rag hung on a bush by the door, fluttering in the faint breeze. The Somber Riders had done their murderous work and moved on. When we were sure the Maedun were gone, we crept cautiously closer.

The first two bodies lay behind the stone wall edging the garden. One of them was a woman, young, probably pretty at one time. She held a child—a small boy of mayhaps four—clutched tightly in her arms. Both corpses fairly bristled with black-fletched arrows, obviously cut down as they tried to flee. The woman had been trying to shield the child, but several of the arrows had pierced both her body and the child's.

No Healer's Gift in the world could help them. My stomach turned over uneasily as I looked down at them. All those arrows . . . It was as if they had been used for target practice. Lowra, her face pale and set, her eyes bleak, made the sign of the Unbroken Circle above them.

We found the woman's husband a moment later. He lay by the byre, and he had died harder than she. His corpse was hacked nearly to pieces. Swords, I thought remotely. Any one of the blows would have killed him. The rest were sheer bloodlust.

The old man's corpse had been thrown into the bushes beside the door of the house. What we had thought was a rag set to dry was a scrap of his shirt. He, too, was quite dead. We searched the yard, but could not find the old woman, nor the other two children.

"There was no need for this," Lowra whispered, as we stood by the low garden wall. "They were under the spell. They couldn't have fought back if they wanted to. This was sheer, wanton destruction for the pleasure of killing." Her voice quivered with anger, disgust, and grief. "They're all animals. Bloodlust-crazed animals."

"Animals don't kill for pleasure," I said. "That's a depravity reserved for men."

"The house," Lowra murmured. "We haven't looked in the house yet."

"Aye," I said. It was the only place left—the only place we had not searched, except the burned-out byre. But nothing had died in that fire, animal or human. The fetid odor of blood magic was sickeningly strong, but there was no reek of charred meat in the air. I didn't want to enter the house. The stench of death in the open air was sickening enough. Confined within the walls of a house, it would be overwhelming. But we had little choice.

The house was a typical farmhouse—one large room with a fireplace and hearth at one end that served as kitchen, living room, and work area. Above the far end, a loft served as the sleeping area for some of the family. Beneath the loft in an area just barely high enough to allow a man to stand erect without ducking stood a worktable, a few chests for storage, and a box bed set into the wall. Someone had been repairing a harness at the worktable; the leather straps lay tangled where they had been dropped.

The old woman was slumped across the table in the kitchen area. Lowra reached out a gentle hand to brush the white hair back from the bloodied forehead, then jumped back when the old woman moaned.

"Quickly, Gareth," she cried. "Help me with her."

The old woman's body felt as if it were made of bird bones and parchment when I picked her up. She weighed next to nothing. Blood oozed from a sword cut just under her ribs. I carried her to the box bed beneath the loft. As I set her down, she moaned again, and moved her head feebly. Lowra bent over her and smoothed back her hair.

"It's all right," she murmured soothingly. "We're friends. We won't harm you."

The old woman opened her eyes. They were faded blue in the dim twilight coming through the unglazed window. She looked first at Lowra, then at me, standing behind Lowra.

"The children," she muttered, her voice wheezing and faint. I had to bend close to hear her. "They took the children."

"The Somber Riders?" Lowra asked.

"Aye. And that turncoat Tyadda man who rides with them. The children—They had a little magic. Just a little—" She closed her eyes again and turned her head away.

"Gareth?" Lowra said. "Can you Heal her?"

"I'll try." I sat on the edge of the bed and put my hand to the wound in her side. The old woman's blood had caked and dried on the thin fabric of her gown, but no more oozed from the sword cut. Gathering the threads of magic around myself,

I closed my eyes and concentrated on sending the Healing power into her frail body.

I met cold emptiness. The old woman had no strength left that I could call on to assist with her Healing. Her strength was spent. Gone with the blood that had seeped out of her body. The cadence of her pulse was almost too faint and weak to detect. Bile rose in my throat as I felt the chill of death creeping over her. A mortal wound. Rhianna had warned me of this, but I hadn't realized it would be so bleak and lonely, or leave me feeling so helpless and utterly useless.

But I couldn't simply let her slip away without trying. I gathered more of the power around me, but even as I tried again to pour the Healing power into the old woman, she died. The flickering thread of her pulse simply stopped between one flutter and the next. I felt her life ebb away like water between my fingers, and nothing I could do could prevent it. Her spirit slipped away quietly, fluttering for a moment in my hands like a small bird, then it was gone. I pulled my hands away and looked down at her helplessly.

"She's gone," I said softly. "I couldn't help her."

Tears formed on Lowra's lashes. She closed her eyes, her face twisted in grief. "Daefyd," she said. "Dear gods and goddesses, this is Daefyd's work."

"The children had magic," I said, shaking my head in horrified awe. I couldn't keep the disgust out of my voice. "Children. Their magic couldn't have been more than just bare glimmerings still."

"Yet Daefyd found them and led Horbad here," Lowra said. "Oh, my dear brother! How could you do this to your own people?"

I shuddered as I remembered what I found—or didn't find—in Davigan when I tried to Heal him. Daefyd would be like that. Only worse. Much worse. He had been in Horbad's clutches for a long time. Anything at all that was left of

Daefyd's spirit must surely have long ago been burned to sere ash and cinder. "Lowra, they're not his own people," I said. "Not anymore. Because he's not Daefyd anymore. He's Horbad's creature. Not Daefyd. Just a construct that looks like him."

She closed her eyes briefly. Slowly, the pain cleared from her face, unclouded in her eyes. "You're right," she said wearily. "My brother is not in that shell. Not anymore." She reached down once more to smooth the old woman's hair gently back from her forehead. "We can't leave these people like this. We have to bury them, Gareth."

She was right. We couldn't leave them like this for the animals. They were my people. I couldn't protect them, but I owed them at the very least proper preparation to meet the Counter at the Scroll.

The ground was soft in the garden. It didn't take long to dig a trench deep enough to take all of them. When we finished, we took some of the rocks from the dry-stone walls to make a cairn over them. Lowra gathered what greenery she could find and made a hoop to place on the cairn.

"May your souls be brightly shining so that the Duality find you quickly," she murmured as she stepped away from the cairn. She turned to me, her expression bleak and lost. "I feel I should be placing a hoop for Daefyd, too," she murmured. Her face seemed to crumple. She put her hands up to cover her face and sobbed into them. "Whatever shall we do, Gareth? Daefyd's lost to us. The Maedun own his soul and his spirit as well as his body. He's well and truly lost completely."

The sound of a footstep on the hard-packed earth behind me made both of us spin around. My hand went automatically to the hilt of the sword behind my left shoulder, and Lowra unlimbered her bow in one swift, fluid, practiced motion. She had an arrow nocked and ready before my sword was halfway out of the scabbard.

But we were too late. Too slow. Far too slow.

Horbad stepped out into the yard from the shadows behind the house. At the same time, his troop of Somber Riders moved out into a wide ring around Lowra and me, bows and swords drawn. Horbad smiled.

"Lost?" he said pleasantly. "Oh, I shouldn't think he's lost. I know exactly where he is." He raised one hand and snapped his fingers. Daefyd drifted out from the shadow of the house to join him, his face blank and vacant. Horbad put his hand to Daefyd's shoulder, and Daefyd winced away so slightly I wasn't sure I'd actually seen the motion.

"We were several leagues away, but he led us straight back here," Horbad went on, still smiling. "How cooperative of you to use such strong magic. But you mustn't use it again."

I let go of the hilt of my sword and felt the blade slide back into the scabbard. Out of the corner of my eye, I saw Lowra lower her bow. She knew as well as I that we stood little chance against twenty armed Somber Riders. But if we could not hope to overcome them with weapons, mayhaps I could use magic, were I quick enough. The same snare that had held Margan when he attacked Davigan might work here to snare the Somber Riders.

Carefully, I began to gather the threads of power that flowed around me through the air and the ground beneath my feet. But even as I drew the first threads to me—before I had a chance to work magic from them—Daefyd stepped forward, frowning darkly.

Horbad raised one hand. "I'm disappointed in you," he said softly. "I told you not to use magic." One finger made a small gesture. "You shouldn't ignore my warning."

I hardly felt the blow to the back of my head that turned everything dim and soft and blurred and very, very far away . . .

28

Dazed, half in a stupor, I hardly noticed the twilight turning to deep night, and I was only vaguely aware of what was happening to my body. I was far away, standing on soft grass, surrounded by nebulous, indistinct shadows that might have been standing stones, or they might have been people. As I stood there, half-bemused and surrounded by the green perfume of growing, awakening plants, and the fresh scent of nearby water, I thought they all came to me. Kian. My father. Myrddin. Rhianna of the Air. All of them trying to tell me something important—something about the flows of power that ran like rivers throughout this land. But if I tried to listen to them rather than simply standing still and breathing in the springtide fragrances, my head ached abominably, and I could not hear them over the roaring in my ears caused by the pain. It was far more pleasant to concentrate on the coming of spring and ignore the urgency in their voices and etched in their faces.

But I could not stay forever in the peaceful, quiet surroundings of the Dance. The pain in my head intruded, throbbing and pounding with each beat of my pulse. It brought me back to myself. At first, all I knew was that I was inside an enclosure, not out under the open sky. The air smelled used and stale. I lay in an uncomfortable heap on what felt like cold, hard-packed earth. My neck was bent at an awkward angle, and my cheek pressed against something rough and gritty. I tried to move to a less cramped position and found I couldn't. My right wrist was bound to my left ankle—manacled firmly by iron—forcing me into a stiff curl.

My eyelids felt gummy and sticky. It took a long while to force them open.

Firelight flickered dimly in the darkness, sending faint shadows dancing across my eyes. The light, wan as it was, sent sharp, stabbing pains through my head. I had to concentrate to focus on the source of the light. Eventually I realized it came from a hearth and two smoky torches thrust into sconces on a rough daub-and-wattle wall.

For a long time, I lay there, blinking stupidly, trying to sort out where I was and why I was here. Something very bad must have happened to give me this blinding headache. And leave me trussed like a game bird ready for the oven. Compared to the pain in my head—bad enough to leave my belly queasily uneasy—the why and how of it seemed like a trivial problem.

Gradually, memory returned, and I realized where I had to be. I lay in the farmhouse against the far wall, under the sleeping loft. The narrow, unglazed window must have been nearly directly above my head. But my head hurt too much, and I could not twist my neck around that far to look up and see for myself.

Slowly, I took stock. My head ached fiercely enough to blur my vision. But once I got past the miserable headache, the rest of me seemed reasonably undamaged. And deep under my heart, the soft, comforting thrumming of my bond with Lowra fluttered gently. She was alive and not far away. Some of the fear left me then.

The farmhouse was quiet. Someone slept noisily in the box bed where I had tried in vain to Heal the old woman. His heavy breathing was the only sound in the house except for the soft popping and crackling of the carefully banked fire on the hearth near the door.

My head still hurt. My left hand was free, so I raised it to my forehead. It didn't help any. Pain still pounded through my skull. It made it difficult to thread together a coherent thought. But I knew I had forgotten something. Something very important.

A movement nearby startled me. I turned my head quickly toward the sound, then wished I hadn't. For a moment, I thought my head was going to fall right off my shoulders and into my lap. I swore softly.

"Gareth?"

Lowra's voice. Again, I turned toward the sound. She sat curled in an awkward posture, her back against the wall, less than an arm's reach from me. She had been similarly bound. Her face in the fire-shot dimness was only a pale oval as she looked at me, but I felt her anxiety shivering along the bond between us. She hitched herself along the beaten-earth floor until her shoulder and hip pressed against mine. I put my free arm around her shoulders and hugged her to me.

"I'm all right," I said softly. "Except for this headache."

"They hit you terribly hard."

"Aye, they did that. But I'll survive that. Are you all right?"

"Pretty much," she whispered. "Just uncomfortable. All Horbad did to me was have me manacled and thrown in here like a sack of grain."

"Where is he?"

"In the loft," she replied. "Probably asleep. There are guards posted at the door. One inside and one outside. And one of them asleep in the box bed."

"Where's Daefyd?"

"In the loft with Horbad."

I managed to ease my head into a position so that it no longer felt as if it would wander off by itself. "I suppose it's significant that we're both still alive," I said wearily. "That must mean Horbad wants something of us."

She was quiet for a moment, contemplating the idea.

"Don't be such a ninny," she said wearily. "He's been taking prisoner everyone, man, woman, and child, he can find with magic. He wants your magic."

"Well, he shan't have it," I said with far more confidence than I felt. It was difficult not to remember the blank shell that was now Daefyd, or the bleak, echoing emptiness in Davigan that Horbad's black sorcery had put there. I couldn't let him do that to me. Not even if I had to die to prevent it.

Lowra said nothing. She shuddered and tucked herself closer under the shelter of my arm.

"Come morning, we'll see what he wants," I said. "We have until then to think of something that might help."

"Not much time," she murmured.

"No. Not much time."

We lapsed into silence. I sat taking comfort from her closeness, letting my mind drift. The streams of intrinsic power flowed around me, moving like rivers through both the air and the earth. At the end of the room, the fire in the hearth shimmered as red-and-black shadows chased themselves across the banked coals.

I found myself thinking about water. The cool, clean tumble of melted glaciers and snow over smooth stones.

Air. Earth. Fire. And water.

The Healing power, the gentle magics that produced masking spells and other common spells, came from the earth and air. Woven sunlight and moonlight globes were fire magic, borrowed through Rhianna of the Air from Beodun, Father of Fires. Was there a water magic? Did Adriel of the Waters have a special magic that was her own? I couldn't remember ever hearing of it. Surely there must be water magic, if there were magics of earth, air, and fire. How curious that I couldn't remember. But it wasn't water magic—if such a thing existed beyond Comyn's uncanny ability to find his way around the seas—that I needed. It was something else. Something different. But I could not remember what it might be.

Then an odd idea came creeping in from nowhere in particular and lodged itself in the middle of my aimless musings. Earth and air magics, wrought from the threads of power. And Daefyd's ability to smell or sense magic. I thought I had an idea, but I would have to wait until morning to test its accuracy.

Morning came sooner than I expected. No light of dawn filtered through the unglazed window above my head when the guard at the door plodded across the room to waken the Somber Rider asleep in the box bed. Between the two of them, they dragged Lowra and me outdoors and removed our bonds long enough to allow us to relieve ourselves, but not long enough to wring the kinks out of our cramped backs and legs. When we had finished, they bound us again, hand and foot, but using plain rope this time, and left us to our own devices near the ruined byre in the chill air of early dawn.

Presently, the sky brightened to daylight, and we heard sounds of activity coming from the farmhouse. An hour later, two more Somber Riders emerged from the house, loosed the bonds from our ankles, and yanked us ungently to our feet.

My guard dragged me through the door of the farmhouse and threw me onto the floor. With my hands bound before me, it was difficult to break my fall. I landed bruisingly hard on shoulder and hip. My head hit the stone of the hearth hard enough to reawaken my headache. It blurred my vision and set my belly churning uneasily. Behind me, Lowra cried out in pain as the other Rider threw her onto the floor beside me.

My head cleared a little, and I struggled to sit up. The interior of the farmhouse was dim, but I had no trouble recognizing Horbad sitting at the table, smiling in sardonic glee.

The remains of a meal lay scattered on the table before him. Two empty chairs faced him across the table. Daefyd sat on a small stool at Horbad's feet, for all the world like a trained hound. He looked at me incuriously, a slight frown creasing his forehead. Once again, I stared into those cold, empty eyes. I shuddered.

"Be welcome here, my friends," Horbad said pleasantly enough. His hand moved in an elegant gesture toward the two empty chairs. "Please be seated."

Lowra and I had no chance to accept or reject his cynically gracious offer. A pair of Somber Riders seized us and unceremoniously dumped us each onto one of the chairs. Lowra landed gracefully enough, but I nearly overbalanced. I managed to catch myself by clutching at the table with my bound hands, and straightened up before I toppled to the floor. I left my hands on the table before me, fingers intertwined. The ropes around my wrist cut into my flesh, and my hands were already swelling. Lowra kept her hands in her lap.

Horbad barely glanced at Daefyd. "Does he have magic?" he asked. A shaft of sunlight slanted through the window behind him. It grazed his shoulder, limning the black shirt with a faint, bright haze, and splashed onto the table between us just beyond my reach, turning the planks of the table a glowing silvery gold.

Daefyd said nothing. He simply continued to stare at me with that small vertical crease between his eyebrows.

I flinched away from that soulless stare, tore my eyes away, and looked at Horbad instead. He sat with casual grace in the rough-hewn chair. A small, easy smile stretched his mouth but didn't reach his eyes. I might never have a better opportunity to test the conclusion I had reached during the night.

The flows of power moved all around me. Gingerly, I

reached out into the stream and drew the power to me, but I attempted no magic. I simply diverted the power around myself, watching Daefyd carefully all the while. He had lost interest in me, but the instant I reached into the flow of power, his attention snapped back to me, like a hunting dog scenting a covey of pheasants.

Horbad gestured to one of the Somber Riders who stood guard by the door. As casually as if he swatted a fly, the man stepped forward and brought the flat of his hand against my face hard enough to knock me backward, chair and all, against the stones of the fireplace. I tasted blood as my lip split against my teeth. The Somber Rider let me lie there for a moment to contemplate my sins, then righted the chair, with me still in it, and pushed it back to its place by the table.

"You were warned about trying to use magic," Horbad said mildly. He dismissed the Somber Rider with a wave of his hand. "Please don't do that again, or the punishment will be far more painful next time. Do you understand?"

I nodded. But I wouldn't need to try it again. I had proved my theory to my satisfaction. Daefyd could not actually smell magic. I had deliberately refrained from using the power I gathered. I had made no magic with it. I thought mayhaps what he sensed was the disturbance in the flows as they were diverted. That being the case, could he sense other magics besides earth and air magics?

Casually, Horbad swept the meal debris from the table with his arm. He pulled the sword from the scabbard he wore at his belt and laid it on the scrubbed planks of the table. The black blade might have been made of polished black anthracite, or obsidian. Instead of reflecting the light, it seemed to absorb it. Darkness seeped from it like water from a broken pitcher, repelling the light.

"Do you like it?" he asked.

I didn't bother to answer, but I couldn't take my eyes

from the black sword. Darkness swirled like a veil around it. Cold and dank.

"It was my father's," he said. "Imbued with magic, just as this one is." He reached down, pulled Bane from the bundle lying at his feet, and laid it on the rough planks of the table.

"A different magic," I said hoarsely.

"To be sure," he agreed. "But magic nonetheless." Bane sat before him, gleaming softly in the dim light. For a moment, I thought the two swords shuddered as they lay side by side on the table. Bane's blade sparked with the light, the runes spilling along the blade glinting as the light caught them. The runes refused to come together into legible words. A small ripple of relief fluttered in my chest. If I could not read the runes, my father still lived. I was yet only heir to the Prince of Skai and not the Prince as I had feared.

But Kian had told me that in the dreamscape the sword was mine to use. There, my father had commended the sword to my hand, whether I wished to accept it or not. In the dreamscape, Bane would fit itself sweetly and solidly into my hand, and it would sing for me as we danced together. But not here. Not in this small farmhouse. Not here in the very shadow of Cloudbearer.

Daefyd got to his feet and moved to the edge of the table. He placed his hands on the wood and stared down at Bane. Something like longing flickered briefly across his face. Horbad brushed him away. Daefyd moved back half a step, but didn't take his eyes off the sword.

"Now, who do I have here?" Horbad asked softly, measuring me carefully with his gaze. He glanced at Lowra, then back to me, a small, three-corner smile twisting his mouth. "A man served by a warrior-maid." He raised his hand and stroked his chin, feigning a thoughtful expression. "Could it be that I've snared the man who claims to be born to be king of this pathetic, benighted island?"

The realization burst on me like a flash of lightning. Horbad did not know who Daefyd was. For all of his ensnaring Daefyd's spirit with his blood sorcery, he didn't know! I remembered that hard, impenetrable knot in the center of Davigan's empty spirit. Was it possible that Daefyd, too, had retreated into himself still guarding the secret of his parentage? Did that mean there might be something in there that was still Daefyd? Still resistant to Horbad's choking blood sorcery? I dared not look at Daefyd when I replied.

"I am not he," I said.

"Not a king?" Horbad said. "Oh dear. What a pity." He put out a hand casually to stroke the hilt of the sword, and his lips drew back from his teeth again in a parody of a smile. "Then you are of the Tyr's get. The so-called Prince of Skai."

"No," I said again.

He raised one hand languidly and pointed at me. A thread of black mist spun away from his fingertip and snaked its way through the air above the table. It wound itself around my throat, cold as banished hope—cold enough to burn. I choked and coughed, reaching desperately for my magic to tear it away. But I couldn't reach the flows of power through the black mist. My magic lay buried under the blood sorcery.

"Don't lie to me," Horbad said gently. "I very much dislike being lied to. It makes me very angry. I ask you again. Are you the Prince of Skai?"

"No," I said again, choking through the black mist. "Not the Prince. But I am his son."

Horbad lowered his hand, and the mist around my throat disappeared. "Ah," he said. "I see. Not the Prince, but the whelp. Nearly as valuable a prize as the Prince." He put a hand again to Bane's hilt. "This, I believe then, is yours, is it not?"

"No."

He merely glanced at me, and a lash of pain whipped through my guts. I doubled over, my eyes closed, biting my lip to prevent myself from screaming with the pain. The planks of the tabletop were rough and cool beneath my cheek. Beads of cold sweat broke out on my forehead, and my belly lurched dangerously.

"My father's," I gasped. "The sword is my father's. Not mine." The pain faded, and I got my breath back. I managed to open my eyes and straighten up again to meet Horbad's cold, black eyes. Between us on the table, the splash of sunlight had moved closer to my clenched hands as the day crept forward toward midmorning. Light flared on the hilt of my father's sword, turning the silver filigree on the haft to blazing white fire.

Sunshine . . . What was it about sunshine I had to remember?

Horbad rose to his feet. "The sword," he said. "They tell me a Rune Blade won't fight for a man not born to wield it."

"It's the truth," I said. I edged away from him, letting my hands move closer to the narrow shaft of sunlight coming through the window. I could almost reach it now without being too obvious about stretching toward the light.

"But you can tell it to serve me," he said. "You're the son of the Prince of Skai. You can place the sword in my hand and command it to serve me."

"No . . ."

He resumed his seat. Without looking away from me, he snapped his fingers. One of the Somber Riders dropped to one knee beside Lowra. He snatched up a handful of her hair and yanked her head back. Slowly and deliberately, he drew his dagger and placed the edge on her throat.

"You have two choices," Horbad said. "You will commend the sword into my hand, or you will watch as the woman dies before your eyes."

I leaned forward another inch or two. The sunlight streamed through my fingers, warm and thick as honey, pliant and strong as silken rope.

"Let her go," I said breathlessly. "Let her go, and I'll do it."

Lowra made a strangled sound. "No, Gareth . . ."

Horbad sat across the table from me, a little more than an arm's reach away, smiling that sardonic smile of his. Behind him, to his right, Daefyd stood beside the table, staring down blankly at the sword. Lowra sat stiffly in her chair beside me, her head thrown back, the Somber Rider behind her gripping her hair tightly. The blade of the dagger moved closer to the pale skin of her throat.

The sunlight. I had to do something with the sunlight. Desperately, I reached into the flood of dazzling light. Daefyd didn't so much as twitch as I gathered the golden light to me. I spun it into strands, wove it into a shimmering net, moving so quickly, the startled Somber Rider had no chance to do anything but stare at me. Even as his fingers tightened on the haft of the dagger, even as Horbad began to rise from his chair in anger and alarm and a filament of black mist curled out from the ends of his fingers, I spun the delicate, glowing web about the four of us—Lowra, Daefyd, Horbad, and myself—and *yanked*.

29

We were on a vast and empty plain, a place out of time. Above us, black-green storm clouds boiled and seethed across the sky. The air smelled scorched and burned, the land charred by the fury of the lightning that split the clouds. And when the thunder followed the dazzle and flash of the lightning, the ground shook beneath my feet. Thick, sinuously twisting bolts of godfire lashed the earth, illuminating everything in livid blue-white light, leaving the stench of seared, incinerated earth behind it. Far away, tiny on the horizon, visible only when the lightning flared, stood something that might have been the Dance of Nemeara.

The fury of the storm raged around us. I had never seen a storm like this one before, but I had never seen the visible manifestation of two warring magics clashing furiously before, either. If I had no sunlight here to work with, Horbad had no source for his blood sorcery, either.

My magic had brought us to this place, but it had not removed the bonds from my wrists. Nor had it eased the pounding headache that throbbed behind my eyes. But I had removed us from the farmhouse, and no Somber Rider's blade now threatened Lowra's throat. Horbad now had no lever to force me to commend Bane to his hand.

We stood, Horbad and I, facing each other across a small arena of fused sand, smooth as ice, gleaming like polished silver. Between us, both Bane and the black sword stood, points buried in the clouded glass, rising like young trees. Behind me, to one side, Lowra crouched in the sand, her hands still bound before her. Daefyd stood quietly by her shoulder. She made no sound, and Daefyd showed no interest in his suddenly new surroundings. He merely stood, his gaze still fixated upon Bane.

Horbad couldn't hide his shock. His head snapped right and left as he looked around in frantic startlement. But his confusion lasted only a moment. The astonishment on his face vanished, and he turned back to face me across the small glass circle.

"Very clever," he said at last.

I smiled, but there was no humor in the expression. "You named me the Tyr's get," I said. "Truly, I am his get and his heir. He taught me this magic."

"But will it overcome this?" He raised his hand. But no wisp of black mist spun out from his fingertips. I laughed harshly.

"You have no use of your sorcery here, Horbad." I gestured to the raging fury of the storm above our heads. "It's all up there. It won't help you."

A flash of lightning flared in the sky. In the livid blue-white light, his face was pale and set. His lips moved, but his reply was lost in the reverberating crack of the thunder.

"This is just you and me," I said to him. "Man to man. No magic. Just us."

He reached out and put a hand to the hilt of the black sword, his knuckles white on the hilt. Effort twisted his mouth into an ugly line as he dragged it out of the glass. "I have this," he said.

I held up my bound hands. "You'd cut down a helpless man?" I asked. "Not very sporting of you. No gentleman would approve."

His lips drew back over his teeth. "My dear man," he said smoothly. "What makes you think I'm a gentleman?"

Even as he surged forward, drawing the black sword back for the killing blow, I dodged to one side and dragged the ropes around my wrist along the keenly sharpened edge of my father's sword. The ropes parted as if they were made of nothing more than spider silk. I seized Bane's hilt. Lightning flashed again, and the runes along the blade blazed incandescent white, bright enough to sear the eyes. They shimmered, then formed themselves into words. COURAGE DIES WITH HONOR. My sword. My heritage. The hilt fitted into my hands naturally and perfectly. I held it in an awkward, two-handed grip, my hands still clumsy because of being bound so long.

But even as my hands closed about the hilt, a strange burst of elation and triumph and joy flooded through me. But not mine. Bane's elation and triumph. Bane's joy.

The bonding was almost instant. Bane resonated in my hands. Softly at first, then faster and faster until it felt alive. Even over the cacophony of the thunder, I heard its clear, fierce voice singing in the air around me like the note of the pipes calling the yrSkai to battle. The blade shimmered, then glowed as if it took into itself the wildfire bursting out of the sky.

The musical note increased in pitch and volume, wild and keen, sharp, distinct, and crystalline around me, transmitting itself along the blade, through the hilt into my blood, my flesh, my sinews, until every nerve was alive to the music, thrumming in harmony with it. The flash and flare of the blade brightened, moving swiftly through red to orange, then to yellow until it was incandescent white, burning with a radiance to rival the sky's wildfire, too painful to look at directly. The whole spectrum of the rainbow swirled and spun in wild patterns around me, edging the bleak, flat landscape with flashing patterns of coruscating color. The joyous chord rang wildly in the air. I had the distinct impression of something awakening and stretching after a long sleep. For twenty years, it had lain at the bottom of a river, and now it had been called upon to fight for Skai.

"Do you think that's going to save you?" Horbad asked.

"It certainly will help," I said, still breathless with the impact of the bonding.

"We'll see," he said in amusement. "Even a Rune Blade can't compensate for age and weariness."

"I am not so old as all that," I said. "We shall see how you fare against a Rune Blade."

I stepped to my left, took a quick, experimental swing at his legs to test the balance of my sword and his alertness. Bane moved like a live thing in my hand, the balance perfect, even with the awkwardness of my unaccustomed hands on its hilt. Horbad parried the blow, and our blades met with a quick, whispering slither. He disengaged and stepped back, breathing hard. I had made him work to avoid my blow.

We circled each other warily, looking for an opening. Beneath my feet, the clouded glass crunched and popped, splintering to powder under my weight. I watched him, trying to pick out small details of stance and pose that would tell me what sort of swordsman he was. He balanced easily on the balls of his feet, his sword held before him in both hands. Dark eyes narrowed to slits, he studied me as carefully as I studied him. He was certainly as accomplished with a sword as I. Perhaps even more. And he had not the disadvantage of trying to become accustomed to a radically changed body.

But I held Bane, my father's sword. A Rune Blade of Skai. My own magic couldn't help me in this bleak, storm-wracked landscape, but mayhaps Bane's own intrinsic magic could.

Darkness spilled from the tip of the black sword as Horbad moved it in small, wary circles. Then, with no warning, he lunged at me. He came in fast, his sword a flashing ring of black iron around him. Awkwardly, I brought Bane up to parry the blow, and the shock of collision shivered all the way up my arms to my spine.

For a moment we stood, chest to chest, the blades of our swords slithering together. His breath was hot against my cheek.

"I'll have that sword from you," he said, his voice strained with effort. "And I'll have your magic, too."

"I think not," I said. "Not this time."

He ducked and spun away, disengaging quickly and expertly. I staggered with the sudden release of resistance, stumbled sideways a step or two, then caught my balance and turned to meet him again, swinging Bane at his belly. His sword sprayed darkness around him, like ink dropped in water, as he sprang back and away.

He leapt toward me, his sword making a wide, sweeping arc toward my head. I blocked it, then cut again at his belly. He parried the blow deftly, then jumped back out of reach. Each time our blades met with the strident bell sound of steel meeting tempered steel, a blinding explosion of brilliant sparks from Bane and blackness like soot in flame from his sword billowed through the air around us.

I flexed my wrists. Bane felt light in my hands, eager as a leashed hound for the hunt. Horbad feinted to his right, came at me with a slicing cut from the left. I swung Bane down, blocked the black blade with a ringing clang, then carved a blow at his legs. He leapt back, brought his blade up to parry mine.

Again, we circled. He attacked, and I lunged forward to meet him. Back and forth across the clouded glass circle, we danced to the ringing music of blade meeting blade. Both of us blind to everything but the swing and slice of the other sword. My breath rasped in my throat; his face was pale and sweating.

Warily, we watched each other, each of us alert for the opening, the slip in wariness that might allow a killing blow.

My sword flared with light under the boiling fury of the sky. His sucked in the light, spit out darkness and cold. Light and shadow. Day and night. Flashing and flaring, and I was lost in the intricacies of the deadly dance.

Then I slipped. My foot came down wrong in the splintered glass beneath us, and I went to one knee, then landed heavily on my hip. I rolled desperately to avoid the hacking chop he brought down overhanded toward my head. I didn't move fast enough. He missed my head, but the tip of his sword sliced cleanly through my shirt, through the skin of my chest, scraped against a rib. Not a mortal blow, but a telling one. Bright pain lanced through my body, cold as the grave but burning as molten metal. The breath left my body in a gasping rush, and, behind me, I heard Lowra cry out a warning.

I looked up in time to see Horbad step back to get another clear blow at me. Desperately, I eeled around and raised Bane to meet the descending black blade, swinging my arms with every ounce of strength I had left.

Lightning burst around us in an eruption of brilliant frenzy as blade met blade with an explosion louder than the furious thunder of the storm. The force of the blow tore Bane's hilt from my hands, sent the sword tumbling and spinning through the air to land with the crunch of broken glass well beyond my reach.

But the explosion shattered Horbad's sword. The obsidian blade burst to flinders, splintering like the glass beneath us. Spots of blood appeared on Horbad's arm and throat as tiny shards of the blade buried themselves in his flesh. The sword itself vanished in a violent burst of darkness that nearly smothered both of us.

He cried out in fear and shock. But he recovered faster than I and dived for Bane where it lay in the powdered glass. I lunged desperately, reaching for Bane, but I was far too late.

He scooped it up, spun to face me. His face twisted with effort as he raised the sword.

But Bane was a Rune Blade. It wouldn't fight in the hand of a man not born to wield it. Even as Horbad raised the sword, it twisted viciously in his hand, the blade turning downward, slicing toward his legs. Its song became a howling whine, charged with anger and outrage. Horbad cried out again and thrust the sword away from him.

I thought he would drop it. But he spun around, leaping sideways at the same time. His quick sidestep brought him to Daefyd's side, and he thrust Bane into Daefyd's hands. For a moment, Daefyd merely stood holding the sword before him like a banner pole, entranced by the flaring brightness of the blade, his face lit with wonder from within as the incandescence of the blade lit it from without. The note of the sword changed from a screaming whine to a neutral, speculative hum. Daefyd was not born to wield Bane, but he was born to be King of Celi, and hold a Rune Blade, and Bane obviously sensed this. The sword settled into his hands, balanced and ready—waiting.

Horbad fell back, panting, and drew his dagger from his belt. He staggered to his feet and stumbled toward where I lay, bleeding and breathless. Before I could roll away, he was upon me, stabbing downward at my chest with the dagger. I managed to get my hands around his wrist and twisted away. The dagger sank into my upper arm. His lips drawn back over his teeth in a wolfish grin of effort, Horbad yanked the dagger back and raised it again.

I saw the movement out of the corner of my eye. Lowra had come to her knees and launched herself straight at Horbad, holding a shard of his sword in her hands like a dagger. Horbad twisted around and swung his left hand. His fist caught her below the breasts, knocking her away. She dropped the obsidian shard and curled herself into an ago-nized huddle on the brittle glass.

"Kill her," Horbad screamed at Daefyd. "Kill the wo-man!"

Daefyd didn't hesitate. He stepped forward and lifted the sword, turning toward her. No expression moved in his face as he drew back the sword and began to swing it down.

"No, Daefyd," she cried. She raised her bound wrists in a futile attempt to block the blow he aimed at her.

Even as Horbad threw himself at me again, I reached out frantically along the bond between Bane and myself. Somewhere inside Daefyd was the small knot of resistance that had allowed him to retain the secret of his birth, to keep that knowledge from Horbad. Somewhere in that hollow, echoing shell there was still a kernel of the man who was born to be King of Celi, the man who was Lowra's brother.

Then Horbad was upon me again, the dagger in his hand reaching for my throat. I twisted frantically, hopelessly. The dagger buried itself harmlessly in the ground beside my ear. Horbad snarled in fury and tugged with frenzied rage at the dagger.

Lightning exploded around us, and the ground beneath us shivered. But even above the blast of the thunder, I heard Bane's furious shriek. Lowra screamed. Using the last of my strength in one desperate burst, I threw my arms up. But I could not thrust Horbad away from me. He yanked the dag-ger out of the ground, reared back on his knees, and raised the weapon in both hands. Behind him, Daefyd swung the sword in a smooth, practiced motion, the blade arcing grace-fully through the scorched air straight at Lowra's throat. Frantically, Lowra tried to scrabble out of the way.

"Daefyd," I shouted. "You can't kill her. That's Lowra. That's your sister!"

•   •   •

The clouds above us seethed purple and black, like bruises against the sky. A bolt of lightning lanced down out of the turbulent cloud and exploded against the seared and withered ground. The raw fear that tore at my heart was no less primitive than the storm itself.

The sword in Daefyd's hands sliced glittering through the air, and Lowra could not scramble away in time.

"Daefyd," I shouted once more over the pounding fury of the storm. "No! You can't kill her!"

Desperately, I reached out again along the bond with the sword, deep into the vast, echoing emptiness where Daefyd's spirit should have been. But there was nothing there. Nothing . . .

Then I felt something loosen—break—give way. Some tightly clenched knot let go. Daefyd's eyes narrowed, the line of his mouth lengthened, and anger twisted the lines of his face. He flexed his wrists very slightly. Not much, but it was enough to send the sword whirling a handbreadth above Lowra's head. Smoothly, with the practiced grace of a born swordsman, he took two quick steps and turned his body. In one continuous motion, the sword came to the top of its arc and changed directions. Now, Horbad's throat was its target.

Horbad screamed in fury as he saw where the new trajectory of the blade would take it. The dagger still held in both hands, he lurched forward, plunging the dagger upward into Daefyd's belly. Overbalanced, he nearly fell. On hands and knees, he scrabbled away from me, tried to get to his feet. Daefyd staggered, but the force and momentum of his swing carried him around. He took a quick sideways step and let the blade carry through. It caught Horbad just as he came to one knee and one foot, bit sharply into the small of his back, slamming deep into the spine, slicing through bone and flesh and muscle. Horbad's eyes opened wide in shock and surprise. He fell forward onto his face, twitching, horrid little gobbling sounds coming from his throat. It took him only seconds to die.

His blood sorcery died with him. Between one heartbeat and the next, the storm simply stopped. With nothing to oppose it, my web of sunlight and fire magic shattered like the powdered glass beneath us. It snapped us back with a jolt, back to the little farmhouse, back into the midst of Horbad's troop of Somber Riders.

The troop leader shouted in surprise and fear as we materialized before him. Horbad's body lay at his feet, bleeding dark blood into the hard-packed earth of the floor. For a moment, shock held the Somber Rider motionless, unable to move.

A thin, black mist rose from Horbad's body, wavering in the air above him as if it searched for something. The blood magic stench was suddenly stronger in the farmhouse. For a moment longer, the black mist hovered in the air, then dissipated with a rushing hiss.

The shaft of sunlight still poured through the unglazed window like warm honey. I seized it, wove another net. I was weary and hurt, but the Somber Riders were shocked nearly speechless. It was almost too easy to fling the webbing like a hunter stalking a flock of wild geese, trapping all of them. The fine, glowing webbing held them as tightly as steel bands could.

Daefyd went to his knees nearly on top of me, holding himself erect only by thrusting Bane's point into the floor and clinging to the hilt. Lowra crawled across the beaten-earth floor, used Bane's blade as I had done to slice through the ropes on her wrists. She caught Daefyd as he lost his grip on the hilt of the sword and collapsed. She slipped her arm beneath his shoulders and cradled him close to her chest.

"Daefyd," she whispered. "Oh, Daefyd."

I crawled on hands and knees to them. Even as I reached

out and put my hand to the wound, I felt the cold, yawning emptiness of a mortal wound. But the spark that was Daefyd was there, guttering and faint, but present for all that. The echoing void was gone, filled with the patterns that made a man.

Slowly, painfully, he lifted a hand and let one finger trace the line of her cheek to her jaw. He tried to smile, then his hand fell onto his chest, and the light left his eyes. I felt his spirit leave his body, painlessly at the end, and in peace.

I helped Lowra to her feet, and together we lifted Daefyd to carry him out of the farmhouse, out into the sunshine. We left the Somber Riders as they were. The woven sunlight webbing would dissipate when the sun was gone for the day. It gave us time enough to be well on our way.

I picked Bane up from the floor and glanced quickly at the runes. They wouldn't sort themselves into words for me. I could not read them. I wasn't sure whether I was saddened or relieved. Bane was no longer my sword.

As we walked out into the fresh morning air, I felt it. Hakkar's spell was no longer as strong, as pervasive. The portion of his power that had come from his bond with Horbad was gone. And with the loss, his grip on Skai — on Celi — was less secure. More tenuous.

Daefyd had struck the first blow for freedom.

Epilogue

So we brought Daefyd home to his mother. Sheryn had already spent most of her tears for him. As she prepared him for burial, her face was bleak and infinitely sad, but her eyes were dry. Lowra and I stood vigil for him in the small Dance of stones behind the shrine, a Tyran custom, not a Tyadda one, but a courtesy he deserved. I placed Bane on the small altar in the center of the Dance, and sometime during the night, the blade flared with brilliant, incandescent white light. I thought I saw the figures of his people in the dazzling glare as they came for him. Tiegan, his father. Tiernyn, King of all Celi, his grandfather. Donaugh the Enchanter, his uncle. And Keylan, son of Red Kian, with his bheancoran Letessa. And even Kian himself came to take Daefyd home. In moments, they were gone, and the blade was once again only a length of polished steel.

In the morning, we buried what was left of Daefyd and raised a tall cairn over him. There were so many hoops placed on the cairn to honor him, the stones all but vanished beneath the greenery. It was a fitting tribute for the uncrowned King of Celi.

After the burial ceremony, Lowra and I walked back to the village with Sheryn. Davigan was in the great room of the house Sheryn shared with Drywn when we came in. He sat near the hearth, a frown of intense concentration on his face as he blew softly into a set of small reed pipes. A faint, breathy melody whispered around the room, slow and simple but pleasing. He looked up as we entered and gave us a brilliant smile.

"Hello," he said. "See my flutes?"

"They're very pretty," Sheryn said. She went to him and bent to kiss his forehead. "Why don't you go into the kitchen and see if Lena needs some help with the midday meal?"

He scrambled to his feet, looking for all the world like an overgrown, ungainly toddler. "All right," he said, and gave her another bright smile.

I watched him go. It was painful to see him like that. "He's no better off than Mikal," I murmured.

Sheryn turned to me. "Not right now, no," she said.

I hadn't meant to speak aloud. "I'm sorry," I said. "It's just that it looks so hopeless. He has to be King now that Daefyd's gone."

Sheryn walked over to the hearth and put her hand on an elaborate tapestry wall hanging next to the stone fireplace. "See this?" she said.

I nodded. It was beautifully done, depicting a forest and mountain scene. Adriel of the Waters stood on a rocky promontory tilting her enchanted ewer to create the River Eidon. The carefully stitched water pouring over the lip of the ewer looked as if one could put one's fingers into it and draw them back wet, and if one listened carefully, one could almost hear the wind whispering in the beautifully crafted leaves on the trees.

"It's lovely," I said.

"Yes." She raised a finger and traced the line of Adriel's gown. "It is lovely, isn't it? It was done one stitch at a time, Gareth. Hundreds and thousands of stitches, but each one placed precisely and carefully one stitch at a time." She turned to face me. "And that's how we'll help Davigan put himself back together again. One small piece at a time. We could have done it with Mikal, but he's far better off not remembering what happened to him after Francia kidnapped him and took him away from Celi. That's not the case with Davigan."

I looked at the tapestry. "It must have taken nearly a life-time to complete," I said.

"Over twenty years," she said. "But it was worth it."

"Will it take that long to bring Davigan back?"

"It might." She stroked the tapestry again. "But we have no other choice. The process can't be hurried. And as for his being King . . ." She shrugged delicately. "We can't make him into something he doesn't want to be. We'll have to wait and see how he decides."

"He's your son, Sheryn," Lowra said quietly. "And he's Prince Tiegan's son. His decision will be the best one for everyone."

"We'll find some way to keep you informed in Skerry," Sheryn said.

"Thank you," I said.

"Never fear, Gareth," Sheryn said softly. "Your king will be ready when Celi is ready. The Maedun will be repulsed from this island."

"Yes," I agreed. "Yes, they will."

The voyage back to Skerry was a relatively easy one. Lowra and I sailed the small boat, keeping the shoreline just barely in sight. Once we saw a company of Somber Riders on land, but no pursuing ship came after us. Three days later, we sailed into Skerryharbor and secured the boat to the stone jetty. Fyld was there to meet us as I stepped ashore with Lowra by my side and Bane wrapped in a length of leather slung over my shoulder.

For a moment, Fyld didn't know me. I saw the neutral welcome on his face change to startled recognition, then to consternation, then to wonder. He schooled his expression quickly back to neutrality, and stepped forward to greet me.

"You've not had an easy time since you left us," he said quietly.

"No," I said.

"What happened?"

"Magic burned us," I said simply. "It's a long story, and surely time for the telling later. I've come home. Tell me quickly, Fyld. Does my father still live?"

He smiled. "Aye," he replied. "He does."

I could not hide my relief. I had not realized my shoulders and back were so stiff until I felt the tension flow out of them. I smiled. "I've brought back everything I said I would." I put my arm around Lowra's shoulders and drew her forward. "This is Lowra, who is my bheancoran and will be my wife. Lowra, please greet Fyld ap Huw, the man who raised me."

Fyld raised her hand briefly to his lips. "My lady Lowra," he said by way of greeting. "Are you, then, the Healer?"

Lowra smiled. "No, Fyld. Gareth is."

Fyld couldn't hide his surprise. "You, my lord?" he asked, startled. "You're the Healer."

"Aye," I said. "And more, Fyld. Much more. But that tale is for later." I put my hand to the leather-wrapped bundle slung over my shoulder. "I have Bane here. I want to give him back to my father."

"*Bane?*" he said. "You've found *Bane*?"

"I have. My father will want it as quickly as possible, I think. How is he?"

"Weak and thin," he said. "He's holding on through sheer strength of will, I think. Meaghean's potions and salves have done much for him. But he needs a Healer."

"Then let's bring him one now, shall we?"

Fyld escorted us up the hill to Skerry Keep, and came behind us up the staircase to the second level. I remembered the way. Meaghean opened the door to my father's chambers as we approached. She stood back to let us enter and gestured toward the door of the bedchamber.

I hesitated for a moment before opening the door. Lowra

took my hand and squeezed it gently. I smiled down at her, then entered my father's room. He lay on the bed, eyes closed, looking no better than the last time I had seen him, but no worse.

As I crossed the room to the bed, he opened his eyes. For a moment, he stared at me, uncomprehendingly, as if unable to believe what he saw. Then the sun rose between us, as it had in the dreamscape, and joy lit his eyes. He reached out a thin and fragile hand to me.

I placed Bane on the coverlet beside him where he could see the silver filigree along the hilt. "I've brought Bane home to you, Father."

He pushed the sword away impatiently and held out his hand again to me. "I thought I'd lost you, Gareth," he said quietly.

I knelt by the side of the bed, and he put one hand to my head. "And I've brought myself back, Father," I said.

He reached out with his other hand, and I took it into mine. It felt fragile as bird bones. "Did you dream true, as I did?" he asked hesitantly.

"I did," I said. "Yes, Father. We dreamed true."

He closed his eyes, relief spreading across his thin face. "Yes," he said. "We have much to catch up on, you and I."

"We do," I agreed. "Many years, I think."

His hand trembled on my hair. "But time enough," he said.

"Yes, Father. Time enough."